Martin Stephen is High Master of St Paul's Boys' School in London and author of fifteen titles on English literature and military history. The first two Henry Gresham novels, *The Desperate Remedy* and *The Conscience of the King*, are also available from Time Warner Books.

Praise for the Henry Gresham series

'Considerable effort has gone into the mucky detail of early 17th-century London, and the tale is moved on at high speed by Gresham's well-timed revelations. Stephen has a good feel for the momentary decisions that can help to shape the course of history – as well, of course, as the cowardice, vainglory and greed' *The Times*

'. . . a refreshingly different approach . . . dastardly political and religious manoeuvrings . . . all add up to a terific book, the first of a long series, we must hope' Charles Mitchell, *The Spectator*

'Breathtaking plotting and delightful characterization in a Jacobean tale of murder and political intrigue – a pyrotechnic, explosive rocket of a book' Jenni Murray

'Intrigue, high-life and low-life are brilliantly interwoven in a thriller which has a compelling vividness and pungency. The historical details are utterly convincing; one can see and smell Jacobean London and hear its inhabitants speaking. I do hope Henry Gresham has a long life' Lawrence James

'A rollicking tale of passion, treachery and derring-do – and the history is impeccable' John Clare, of the *Daily Telegraph*

THE

GALLEONS'
GRAVE

Henry Gresham and
The Spanish Armada

Martin Stephen

TIME WARNER
BOOKS

TIME WARNER BOOKS

First published in Great Britain in February 2005 by Time Warner Books
This paperback edition published in July 2005 by Time Warner Books

A CIP catalogue record for this book
is available from the British Library.

ISBN 0 7515 3701 2

Pr

ACKNOWLEDGEMENTS

I owe a huge debt to the historians of the Spanish Armada, and in particular to Colin Martin and Geoffrey Parker's *The Spanish Armada*, Roger Whiting's *The Enterprise of England*, Angus Konstam's *The Armada Campaign 1588*, Bryce Walker's *The Armada* and John Cummins's biography *Francis Drake*. Yet time after time I have found myself coming back to Garrett Mattingly's *The Defeat of the Spanish Armada*. I make no apologies for following, in the main, Mattingly's account of events. I apologise if I have imitated his brilliant style as well as his command of history.

Henry Gresham has a number of parents: Jenny Stephen; The Royal Exchange Theatre, Manchester; Sonia Land, my agent; Ursula Mackenzie, my publisher; Tara Lawrence, Joanne Coen, my editors, and Sarah Rustin, my copy-editor. Midwives at the birth have been all three of my sons, Neill, Simon and Henry, whose advice on the novels has sometimes been as beneficially caustic as it has been helpful; the historians Lawrence James and Graham Seel; the actor, director and author Philip Franks; and the Cambridge University Library, the Bodleian Library, Oxford, and the John Rylands Library of the University of Manchester. David's bookshop in Cambridge has been invaluable. My thanks to Handan and Erdogan for providing such a stunning environment in which to write.

Most of all, my thanks go to those who bought the first and second Henry Gresham novels, thereby making the third and fourth possible.

Martin Stephen
Chevalier Island, Turkey
August, 2003

For Don Alonso Perez de Guzman el Bueno,
7th Duke of Medina Sidonia.
And the soldiers and crew of the galleon *San Martin*

PROLOGUE

March 24th, 1587

Death comes from such random throws of the dice.

Thin streaks of grey light signalled dawn bleached across the black, flat Cambridge landscape. The horses sensed their owner's fear, were restive in the yard, hoofs clattering the cobbles, snorting so that the mist of their breath in the cold air joined with that of the panting men charged with their care. The lanterns swung wildly, the gloom still deep enough for them to cast flickering shadows on the walls, highlighting in passing the sheen of sweat on the faces and arms of the ostlers. You could smell the sweat, the strangely warm tang of horseflesh on the cold morning air, and the stink of the dung the Spaniard's horse had dropped.

If the Spaniard had chosen to leave Cambridge as night fell, when he first heard his news, he might have lived. As it was, he gambled that he had time enough, time for a decent supper, time for a few hours' sleep in a clean bed. He made the sensible decision, and it killed him, used up the time he had on earth. After all, few men rode out at dark. The finest horse can see no better at night than a man, and the appalling mud tracks that passed for English roads were quite capable of drowning a man and his horse in the potholes that seemed to penetrate the centre of the earth. Better to make the break at dawn, and hope for clear skies in this interminably damp country. A man determined to find his destiny did not skulk out like a traitor emerging from a dungeon, eyes closed shut from the danger of light. A man – and a Spanish man above all – rode out with his eyes all-seeing. In command. In charge.

The two Spanish servants he had brought with him on his mission to England had succumbed to one of the fevers this Fen-blasted town of Cambridge seemed to breed like a peasant woman in Seville bred children. Their English replacements were shifty, reluctant in their duties. What Englishman could blame them when Spain seemed set on destroying England? In fact, only one of the Spaniard's English recruits was with him that morning, a burly man past middle-age but with a quiet authority that made him the only one capable of calming the baggage horses. What was his name? The Spaniard found it difficult to remember the names of those of common birth, and was increasingly irritated by the English habit of treating servants as if they were real people. It was as if they were ashamed of rank. Nevertheless, the Spaniard smiled patronisingly at the man, thanked him for his calm in loading and quieting the horses (when in Rome, or Cambridge . . .), and dug his spurs unnecessarily into the side of his own fine mount. He had given gold to the inn, more than enough to settle his debts. Pray to God he might never see this miasmic hole Cambridge again. He was away at last. Away to Spain. Away to tell his masters the truth of the fools they had been made to become.

The Spaniard's spirits rose as he felt the thrumming of the horses' hoofs beneath him. Even this early the smoke from the morning fires lay heavy on the ground, stinging the nostrils. His horse flung up mud from the unpaved streets, as if anxious to clear the stench of the town too. Soon they were clear of the poor houses and the stone and brick arrogance of the Colleges. He had chosen to escape through Grantchester meadows. Even he had felt his heart touched here, where the lush grass backed on to the wide, flat river, an image of pastoral bliss. And if one let one's eyes rise, there was the soaring vision of King's College Chapel.

It was the lack of noise that caused him to slow down. Suddenly the Spaniard realised his servant was no longer with him. The man, and the baggage horses he controlled, had veered off for some reason. He was on his own, pounding through the meadows. Then he heard other hoofs, a single horse racing towards him. He turned, lashing his horse with his whip, and the fiery pain of pure fear shot across his chest as he saw who it was pursuing him. The servant had reined in the baggage horses and was waiting quietly by a little copse of trees. From out of those trees two men had erupted, one a burly man on a squat but powerful horse, the other a slighter figure, superbly mounted on a grey. The grey was leaping ahead. The Spaniard knew who its rider was, guessed in an instant and far too late that the English servant had been in the pay of this young man all along, had warned his master of the Spaniard's departure.

Real fear then clawed at the Spaniard's belly, yet he was no coward. He yanked his horse round by brute force, drew the sword at his side and ran at the young man on the grey, sword extended like a lance. If he had hoped to surprise his adversary, he miscalculated. In a second his opponent had extended his sword, and the two men rode at each like medieval knights at the joust. The Spaniard fixed his eyes on the Englishman's heart, determined to plunge his sword into it. Seconds before they met, he made the mistake of looking up into the young man's eyes. They were cold, hard, and his sword seemed to be pointing directly between the Spaniard's eyes.

He had him! The Spaniard exulted, feeling his blade heading inexorably towards his enemy's heart. Yet at the very last possible second, the young man swayed his body aside with an impossible athleticism and sank his own sword into the Spaniard's neck.

The shock of contact should have ripped the sword out of the Englishman's hand, yet somehow he held on to it. His sword cut through the sinew and muscle of the Spaniard's neck until it met cold air, half decapitating the foreigner whose eyes opened wide in surprise. He toppled forward slowly on the still-galloping horse, ludicrously, comically, arm still outstretched holding his sword.

3

Then, as if time had been slowed down, the sword dropped from the nerveless hand, and the Spaniard slumped over the side of the horse, foot caught in the stirrup. His body and half-severed head bounced on the hard earth until his horse felt the drag on its side and reluctantly came to a halt.

It was pleasantly cool in the meadows of Grantchester, the sky a hard blue. The spring breeze fluttered over the grass, the smell overpowering as the sun gently warmed the earth with the early morning heat. The river burbled cheerfully nearby, neither the angry flood torrent of winter nor the sludgy, torrid stream of high summer. The birds were singing their hearts out at having survived the winter, the beauty of the sound hiding the reality that their song was a savage defence of their territory. It was Henry Gresham's birthday, and he, the rider of the grey, had just killed a man.

The body lay in the grass, distorted in death, mouth agape in a silent scream. The man's complexion was swarthy, and from behind the torn doublet a set of hidden rosary beads could be seen. He was only a Spanish spy, of course. Was that meant to make it better?

Gresham was handsome and something in his stance said that he knew it. He was tall, thin-hipped and broad-shouldered, a shock of black hair over a striking and chiselled face, sweat-stained. And now he was a murderer, standing over his victim like a statue carved out of marble.

Mannion, an oak-tree of a man, perhaps five years older, stood silently by Gresham's side as his young master threw up a poisonous yellow bile, obscenely splashing the rich green grass. Mannion waited patiently. Finally, when there was nothing left in the stomach, he spoke. 'Stones, and some rope.'

Gresham looked up.

'You can't take the body home,' Mannion said flatly, 'and you can't leave him here. There's stones on the bank. There's rope in my saddlebag.'

Gresham stared blankly at his servant. It was always like this, Mannion knew, for the first four or five men you killed. The

4

excitement that drove away all conscience and feeling, the blood-lust of combat all gave way to sickness, and the numb nausea.

'We need to sink him,' said Mannion patiently. 'In the river. It's deep here. You get the stones. I'll get the rope.'

Gresham was numbed, unusually obedient. Only half seeing, he moved to the bank to collect stones.

There should be tears, thought Mannion. It was a terrible thing to take a life. It would be better if his master cried. Yet crying was the one thing Henry Gresham never did.

CHAPTER 1

March, 1587
The Queen's Court, London

They had ridden the first part of the journey as if the Devil was on their tail, for no other reason than Gresham's love of speed and danger. He had fresh horses waiting every twenty miles, at the various staging posts between Cambridge and London.

'It was easier in the meadows,' Gresham had muttered when the messenger delivered the summons to attend the Queen's Court. It was a week since he had killed his man. 'At least there I knew who the enemy was.'

The hard riding had driven some of the devils out of Gresham, yet he was still looking glum as he and Mannion rode companionably side by side, some four or five miles before London.

'There's thousands who'd die for a summons from the Queen to attend her at Court,' said Mannion, who hated Cambridge. 'There's no pleasing some people.'

'There's more men who've died through obeying the summons,' said Gresham glumly. 'I go to Court, amid all the fawning and the sycophancy, and it's like I'm walking through a forest I don't know, at night, and maybe there's an enemy behind every tree. Yet I don't know and I can't see, and the first I'll know is when a knife or an arrow lands in my back.'

'Bit like Cambridge, then,' said Mannion.

At the best of times the Court of Queen Elizabeth was a vicious, competitive and back-biting arena. It was increasingly decadent, a shifting maelstrom of new broken loyalties and bitter feuding laid on top of the long-standing clashes. The loyalty was lessening and the hatred increasing by the second as the news of a possible Spanish invasion became more and more threatening. It was clear that the Queen was past child-bearing age, even had she begun to find a husband she could tolerate. Who would be the next King of England? Or even, God help the country, its next Queen? The old order was soon to die. There were factions fighting for power within the Court, factions outside of it. To talk of who would succeed the Queen was to risk an ear lopped off or worse, yet those who formed the Court talked of little else. And recently there had been something else. Something personal against Gresham, an animosity, people turning away as he walked near. Or was it just an overactive imagination?

'That's part of why you go,' said Mannion. 'You like the smell of danger. And you like the sense of power. And the girls,' he added finally.

'I could do without the attention of the oldest girl of the lot,' said Gresham. As the Queen visibly aged her desire to surround herself with well-formed young men increased. To his great alarm, Gresham had found himself one of her new menagerie.

They smelled and saw London long before they entered it. The sea coal that Londoners were addicted to had a deeper, heavier smell than the woodsmoke of Cambridge and seemed to leave an oily, cloying after-taste. Then there was the rotting stench of waste from hundreds of thousands of living creatures, man and beast, their only common denominator ownership of bowels and a bladder dominated by the need to empty themselves. The great city was built on filth, not just the manure of its living creatures but the mangled bones of beef and fish and chicken, the filthy water from washing and cooking. The river took as much as it could, of course, and it had its own smell: dank, rotten yet strangely sweet. And for all of that, in the middle of London, a sudden change of wind could replace the stench of massed humanity with the clear and sweet breath of countryside from the fields of Highbury and Islington, from where the milk was brought in every morning. At night the blazing lights of torches, of lanterns and of candles challenged the darkness with a frail gesture of protest from humanity. In daylight, it was the pall of smoke hanging over the city that first drew attention, with the silver ribbon of the Thames seeming to stand out in stark clarity, however obscured the sky. And then the noise, the deafening, crucifying noise! All the world had something to sell in London and was bellowing the news to anyone who cared to listen and to all those who did not. The traffic in the streets was like a river in torrent suddenly forced into a narrow gorge, men, women, boys, oxen, sheep, horses, clumsy farm carts and lumbering carriages moving, fighting, squabbling, all at full volume.

Coming from Cambridge, Gresham and Mannion had to enter by Eastgate and cross all of London to reach The House, the palatial and neglected mansion on the Strand that Gresham had inherited from his father. It would have been easier to leave the horses by the Tower, and get one of The House's boats to row them upstream. Yet Gresham felt the need to let London and its madness soak back into his spirit, remind him of the days when, as a child, he was penniless and free to wander these wild, narrow streets as he wished, remind him of the days when friendless and alone he had learned to rate survival as the only virtue, and learned how to survive.

He waited now in the Library, his favourite room in The House, dressed in all his finery for Court. Mannion sat with him. The high, mullioned windows looked out directly on the Thames, seemingly more crowded every visit he made. Would Spanish sails fill the view next time he came to London, thought Gresham, their cannons smashing to splinters the ludicrously expensive glass in the windows of his library? There was no hint of impending destruction in the soft, dark glow of the lovingly polished panelling, the even

9

softer gleam of the leather bindings on the books. Suddenly a commotion in the yard broke the peace, the clattering of hoofs, the sound of a loud, jovial man's voice. The Honourable George Willoughby, soon to become Lord Willoughby when his increasingly aged father died, was incapable of going anywhere incognito.

George Willoughby was the ugliest man on earth. A face that looked as if it had been slammed into a stone wall at a formative time in babyhood was further pock-marked by the deep, dark craters of smallpox. A mistake by the midwife had given George a slant to his face, the left side of his mouth pulled down in a permanent grimace, the lid on his left eye – a dark, muddy-brown eye – forever doomed to droop half-closed. He was also a big, burly man prone to knock over anything in his path.

'You're such an ugly bastard!' said Gresham, smiling affectionately at the only friend other than Mannion he had on earth.

A small table with a pewter mug on it went flying as George entered the Library.

'Oh, damn! So sorry!' said George. A lifetime of knocking things over had neither accustomed him to it, nor diminished the pain his clumsiness caused him. Only two things were certain about George. He would barge into everything, and be torn apart by remorse when he did so. Then a smile lit the crags and valleys of his face. 'Wrong again, Mr Fellow of Granville College.' His gaze, impossibly frank and honest, met Gresham's. 'At least on one count. I'm ugly. *You're* the bastard!'

They advanced and hugged each other, Gresham's eyes dancing with fire and life. There were only two men alive who could call Gresham a bastard. And only one other who could call George Willoughby ugly.

'Ignore the servant,' said Gresham. 'He's getting ideas above his station again.'

George released Gresham, rather like a vast bear releasing its mate, and turned to Mannion. 'Been telling his Lordship the truth again, have you? Warned you about that,' said George, wagging a finger at Mannion. With both men in the room it seemed somehow

10

shrunk, dominated by their bulk. 'I've known him even longer than you. I've told you often enough. *Flatter him!* Men with great fortunes can't take the truth. Particularly young men who think with their hips!'

George stuck out a vast paw, and Mannion grasped it in return. He looked approvingly at George. A person's appearance had never bothered Mannion. He judged a man by his heart. And George Willoughby's heart was as big as they came.

'There'll be flattery enough this evening,' said Gresham, as the three of them settled down to a bottle of rather fine Spanish wine brought cobwebbed from the cellars of The House. If there was anything odd about two gentlemen and a servant sharing a bottle, none of the three seemed to notice it.

'But of course!' said George. 'The Queen will be told she dances divinely and that she's the only paragon of human beauty, and several sonnets in her favour will be written on the spot. Despite the fact that she's self-evidently an old cow with a complexion like a distempered wall.'

'You'll be telling Her Majesty that tonight, will you?' said Gresham in a tone of innocence. 'Just imagine how you'd feel if she served up your head on a pewter salver and not a gold one . . .'

'My head's safer on my shoulders than yours is, Henry,' said George. There was a sudden sharpness in his tone that made Gresham look up. 'I tell you, you're playing with fire. There'll be no flattery of you tonight. Only jealousy. Hatred, even. Are you wise to stay as one of Walsingham's men? These are dangerous times.'

Walsingham was Elizabeth's spy master. By now elderly and riven by serious illness, Walsingham had funded from his own income the greatest and the most malevolent network of informers in Europe. He had recruited Gresham as a spy in his first year at Cambridge, when Gresham was still an impoverished student. When Gresham's wholly unexpected inheritance turned his life from penury to fabulous wealth, he had stayed with Walsingham. Danger and risk were a drug to which young Henry Gresham had become addicted.

'Life's dangerous,' commented Gresham idly.

11

For all his foolish exterior, George Willoughby had a sharp brain. It was also one strangely acclimatised to the world of the Court. Just as Gresham only really felt at home in Cambridge and its tiny battles, who was in favour and who was out of favour, who was a rising star and whose star had fallen were meat and drink to George. It was odd that a man so simple could take so much pleasure in charting the shifting sands of the Court.

'But rarely as dangerous as this. And doubly so since we decided to execute Mary Queen of Scots.'

Gresham said nothing.

Mary Queen of Scots. A Queen in her own right twice over – of France and of Scotland. With sufficient English royal blood in her veins to make her not only the obvious successor to Queen Elizabeth, but her present rival for the throne. She had fled to England when Scotland had rebelled against her, and found herself imprisoned for her pains by her cousin Elizabeth, yet remained the centre of continual plotting. And now she was dead, at last. Executed farcically at Fotheringay Castle in February. One Queen murdered on the order of another. A Catholic Queen murdered on the order of the bastard Protestant Elizabeth. The executioner had botched his job. Only at the third attempt had he severed the woman's head from her body. Mary had worn a wig to her execution. When the executioner bent down to grab hold of her mangled head to show it to the audience he had been left with the false hair in his hand, while the obscene, bald coconut of the Queen's head bounced and rolled off the staging. And Henry Gresham would regret to the end of his days the part he had played in that death.

'Apart from your personal involvement,' continued George, emptying half the remainder of the bottle into the delicate Venetian glass cradled in his vast hand, 'there's many who say executing Mary Queen of Scots was a disastrous move. Politically speaking, that is.'

'Walsingham was very firmly of the other opinion. He believed having a Catholic queen with a legitimate claim to the throne was to invite the overthrow of Elizabeth, "to nurture a canker in our breast",' said Gresham. 'I think I'm quoting him direct.'

'Quote him all you like,' said George, 'but remember, fewer and fewer people are listening to him now.' George stood up, endlessly restive, as if the ideas in his head could not be contained while his body was sitting. 'You've never understood the Court,' he said to Gresham, like a father admonishing a child. 'And what's been certain for so long is dying, uncertain. The Queen is *old*, Henry, for all that saying so is instant death for a courtier! Burghley is old . . .'

An outsider would have been surprised to see Gresham rise and the two young men make a formal, deep bow to each other. It was their ritual whenever they mentioned Lord Burghley, Chief Secretary to the Queen. Of worthy rather than noble stock, Burghley had the exaggerated respect for protocol and formality that came with *nouveau* status.

'Laugh on,' said Mannion to the pair of them. 'But just remember the man you're laughing at's the most powerful man in England.'

'Is? Or was?' said George. 'Rumour has it he's losing his wits. Let's face it, the old guard are dying. Walsingham's seriously ill, doubled up by pain sometimes. The Queen has no heir, there's no clear succession . . . is it any wonder the Court's in turmoil? We've enough threats from within without adding more from outside!'

'Adding?' asked Gresham, interested despite himself.

'By executing a Catholic Queen! There's real panic in the Court,' answered George. 'It's odds on executing Mary will tip Spain over the edge.'

King Philip of Spain had once reigned in England as husband to Queen Mary in her disastrous time as Queen. That, and the tortuous Tudor lineage, gave Spain several claims on the English throne. More important to Philip, who had countries enough to rule, was the standing outrage of a Protestant England defying the one rule of Roman Catholicism.

George roared with laughter at a remembered joke. The plaster just about remained attached to the brickwork. 'The Bishops are shitting themselves! Apparently one of them fainted when someone burned some meat on the fire. Said it reminded him of the smell of human flesh burning!'

'Rumour has it that half the Bishops have started to learn Spanish,' said Gresham, grinning.

'Most of 'em can't speak bloody English!' growled Mannion. Clergy and Spaniards were his two least favourite breeds.

'What are the serious minds at Court saying about the succession?' asked Gresham. George would know the latest word if anyone did. Elizabeth had resolutely refused to marry. The nearest thing to an heir was probably James VI of Scotland, son of the executed Mary Queen of Scots.

'Very divided. Some say Spain. Some say the King of Scots. Others want the Queen to marry an English nobleman, even now, someone younger than herself so we get a King.'

'Wonderful!' exclaimed Gresham. 'What a choice! Our next monarch is either Spanish, which means the country torn apart by religious war, or the King of our oldest and bitterest enemy – oh, and someone whose mother we've just had executed! – which means civil war. Or it's Leicester, Essex or even Walter Raleigh, any one of whom would guarantee the other two and every other noble family at Court launching immediate civil and religious war!'

The Earl of Leicester was the Queen's old favourite, increasingly being put in the shade by the young and extremely handsome Robert Devereux, Earl of Essex. Sir Walter Raleigh was a permanent joker in the pack.

'Never mind the danger the country's in,' said George. 'Think about the danger *you're* in.'

''E's right,' said Mannion. 'I know bugger all about the politics, but even I can see they're mad jealous of you. Jealous of your money. Jealous of your looks. Jealous of how you do with women. Jealous o' the Queen taking notice of you. And you haven' exactly been . . . discreet with some o' those girls you've serviced, 'ave you?'

A slight grin crossed Gresham's face, infuriating the two other men. He had never hurt a woman in his life. But he had had an awful lot of mutual pleasure with them. 'What the eye doesn't see, the heart can't grieve for . . .' he said.

'Mebbe not,' said Mannion, 'but there's three or four Lordships with young wives who're putting one and one together and seein' you in bed with their women!'

It was George's turn now. 'It's known that you've meddled on Walsingham's behalf. Not the details, of course, or you'd be dead in a side alley. Walsingham's old, dying. His star's on the wane. No one knows what'll happen when his empire collapses with his death. But for too many at Court you're a young upstart who's been too involved in every shady activity of the past few years. And now you've caught the fancy of the Queen. God knows what you might be whispering to her. On all counts, you're a nuisance. And a nuisance with no friends except me and this man mountain here, God help us.'

'So what's your advice?' asked Gresham, swilling a residue of wine around in the bottom of his goblet. 'Thanks for telling me all the dangers. Now tell me a way to get out of them!'

'Kill yourself!' said George. 'At least then you can make it quick and clean and get there before they do!' he added cheerfully. A beaming grin lit up his face, followed by another great, booming laugh. One of the things about George was that at a certain level of stress his brain cut out, and he retreated from serious matters to the solace of the bottle and friendship. 'Except you'll think of a way, one I couldn't have dreamt of, and I'll stand back in wonder at your achievement! You see, I'm really good at working out the odds. Funny, really. Most people think I'm a fool, except you. Problem is, when I've worked out the odds, I believe them. You . . . well, you decide to get the better of them. Betting man's nightmare, you are.'

'You know what Walsingham's made me do,' said Gresham. 'You and Mannion. Are you telling me I should have refused him?'

'I don't know,' said George. 'I wish I did. Do I think it's clever to

15

attend secret Masses, on Walsingham's instructions? Of course not! Not in this climate. It's madness! Particularly as I've never been sure how much your affection for the Catholics was an act, or whether it's the reality.'

'I've told you,' said Gresham. 'My first nurse was a Catholic. When I couldn't suck her breasts I sucked her rosary beads. It leaves a mark on a man, you know . . .'

'I could tell you how extraordinarily irritating your flippancy is,' said George, 'but as you do it in order to be extraordinarily irritating it would only add to your pleasure. I'm just telling you to take care. Too many people of power go silent when your name's mentioned. And there's new talk. Can I ask you a question?'

'Of course,' said Gresham.

'Are you taking Spain's money? To be frank, rumour is that you're a Spanish spy. I know you'd never betray England,' said George gamely, 'but I can see you'd get involved with Spain just for the excitement of it. Well? Are you?'

'Am I what? You asked two questions. Whether I was a Spanish spy? Or taking Spanish money?'

'Stop playing games! I'm your oldest friend. I deserve an answer.'

'Well, now,' said Gresham, after a moment's thought. 'The answer is yes to one and no to another. It's more fun to leave you to work out which answer fits which question.'

George roared in exasperation, and within seconds the two men were rolling on the floor like two schoolboys in a fight.

'Well,' said Mannion. 'I'm just a working man.' He was used to conversations between George and Gresham ending in blows. Sometimes they actually hurt each other. 'But I don't doubt if your head goes on the block, mine will too. And I just wish you'd tell My Lord Bloody Black Arts Walsingham to bugger off. Then I'd feel safe.' Having got George in a neck hold, Gresham declared himself the winner.

They went by boat to Whitehall, eight liveried oarsmen making light of the Thames. The landing area was ablaze with torches, their light spearing out like fiery lances onto the rippling, black surface of the water.

'Is this wise?' asked Gresham as they were about to disembark.

'Your being here?' asked George.

'No, you great idiot. This whole event.'

'If you mean is it wise for Her Majesty Queen Elizabeth to host a Grand Reception for a very minor noble from the Netherlands who calls himself Ambassador and doesn't have enough money to put linen and cloth between his arse and the wind . . . probably not. After all, it makes it perfectly clear that we are supporting a rebellion in a country claimed as his own by King Philip of Spain. That same King Philip who, by all accounts, is set to invade England and end its Protestant heresy once and for all . . . No, it's probably not wise. But you have to admit, it does require guts.'

The Protestant Low Countries had been in revolt for years against Catholic Spain, which claimed them as a province. English money and English troops – neither of which were in plentiful supply – had stopped Spain from winning total domination over the Netherlands. Yet Spain had the most powerful army in Europe stationed in the Low Countries, under the command of the undefeatable Duke of Parma, an invincible army that many thought King Philip of Spain would send to invade England once his patience finally ran out. And now Elizabeth was holding a grand reception for an Ambassador from the Protestant part of the Netherlands. Kicking Spain in the crotch, or taunting the bull to charge at you when you had nothing with which to kill it? Was it brinkmanship on the part of the Queen, or stupidity?

Nothing was as it seemed in the Court of Queen Elizabeth. The light from candle, lamp and lantern seemed to laugh at the dark until one realised that significant areas of the Palace were blacked out. The food seemed to offer course after course after course, until one looked and realised that there were really very few examples of each, and that the Chamberlain had relied on announcing a late serving of the food so that guests would have eaten at least something before they left their homes. Choice was great, the quantity of each choice meagre. As for the wines, the servants promised the best but pleaded they had just emptied the bottle. Would the honoured guest accept something a little less impressive as a stop-gap?

Gresham gazed ruefully at the cat's piss in his goblet, having to decide whether or not he wanted to get drunk at all costs, or whether he still had some standards. The Queen had refrained from slobbering all over him, though presumably that treat was reserved for the dancing.

As they moved into the Great Hall for the speeches and the dancing, they were surrounded by a throng of people desperate to be seen and to see who else was there.

'That's the Earl of Leicester who cut you dead, and Essex tried to walk over you as if you were a dog's turd,' said George.

'They're jealous, that's all,' said Gresham, who was not drunk but starting to feel detached in a merry enough sort of way. 'Jealous the Queen'll find out what a lover I am in comparison to them.'

He had just decided that his aim for the evening would be to get historically drunk when he became aware of someone standing by his shoulder.

'Avoid drinking too much this evening,' said a gravelly voice, as if someone had read his thoughts. 'You may find that you need your wits about you.'

Sir Francis Walsingham was an old man now, but the intensity in his dark black eyes had not diminished, nor the sense of raw energy held back within the confines of polite behaviour. Gresham was shocked. Walsingham had no time for frivolities such as this evening, preferring to spend his time in the quiet of his house in Barnes.

'Sir Francis!' Gresham sought to cover his confusion, bowed his head. George had melted away subtly, Mannion withdrawn to where he could see but not hear what was happening. A giggling lady-in-waiting with a young man in hot pursuit thrust between the two men, then saw Walsingham and turned pale, stuttering an apology as she backed away, eyes suddenly downcast. Few men had such a reputation as Walsingham. Few men could inspire such fear.

The Ambassador had entered now, as ragged as George had predicted, and was standing awkwardly with a stupid smile on his face as a lackey gave a formal speech of welcome.

Walsingham speared Gresham with a glare. 'Come,' he said. 'The speeches will drag on for ever. Her Majesty will not appear for another half an hour at the least, when for all our sakes we ought to be here.'

Walsingham motioned to a door. Once through, another door opened into a small room furnished with a blazing fire, candles, and a small table with two chairs. Clearly Walsingham had made plans in advance. He drew his old-fashioned, long, fur-lined cloak round about – how thin the man was looking, thought Gresham – and motioned the young man to sit down.

'I thank you for what you have done. For what you are doing. It is not without danger.'

There was mulled wine on the table, steaming hot, though no sign of the servant who must have placed it there only minutes before. Walsingham took a goblet, claw-like hands stretching round to draw out the warmth.

'The danger I accept, my Lord,' said Gresham. 'What concerns me is how little I know about why I'm asked to do what I'm asked.'

'I have spent my whole life acquiring knowledge, believing it to be the root of all real power,' said Walsingham. 'Now I realise that sometimes ignorance is a great safeguard. Too much knowledge can cloud our judgement, make us think too much. Restrain your youthful impatience to know everything. If indeed any of us can ever know everything.'

Gresham was clearly getting no further. One did not debate with Walsingham. One listened to his reasoning, and either did what he asked or failed to do so. And rather too many of those who refused his instructions were washed up face down in the Thames a couple of days later for any of Walsingham's agents ever to feel secure about their freedom of choice.

'My reason for seeing you tonight is this. We have at last begun to move against our enemies with the death of that damned charlatan.'

Walsingham's voice was calm, but Gresham knew the depth of his hatred for Mary Queen of Scots. Not for Walsingham the fear that her death would provoke Spain to invade England. For him, Mary had been a glaring invitation for every Catholic in England and Europe to rise up against Elizabeth and Protestantism. 'One does not deal with the canker in one's body!' he had once said to Gresham. 'One cuts it out!' Throughout his life he had been an implacable champion for the three things he most believed in: the Protestant faith, England and Queen Elizabeth, in that order.

'However, the Queen suspects my involvement and I am out of favour, as are all who sought the death of Mary.'

Walsingham out of favour? One of the men who had most bolstered Elizabeth's reign?

What passed for a smile crossed Walsingham's lined face. 'It is in the nature of ministers to lose the favour of their monarch at times. It is a show. The Queen fears for her own survival when a fellow Queen is executed, but it will pass. The Queen is a realist above all. Yet temporarily my access to Her Majesty is reduced. Also, I am ill. Her Majesty does not like to be reminded of mortality.' He turned to Gresham, brisk and business-like. 'How much do you understand the politics of the Court?'

'Very little, my Lord, if the truth be known.' It was like being lectured by George, only far more threatening.

'Then take a hurried lesson,' said Walsingham. 'My Lord Burghley has been the dominant presence in the Queen's Court since her accession – and if you were considering stupid flattery, do not embark on it. I know and have accepted from the outset my secondary role. Yet he and I are both old. Our days are limited, mine more than Burghley's. The Earls of Leicester and Essex see themselves as taking over Lord Burghley's role, as perhaps might even that pirate Raleigh.'

'Surely a recipe for civil war?' blurted out Gresham.

'Quite,' said Walsingham. 'Yet Burghley hopes his second son, the cripple, Robert Cecil, will succeed him as the Queen's Chief Minister. The battle between Essex and Cecil is intriguing. Breeding against ability. Extreme physical beauty against a deformed body.'

Why was Walsingham telling him this? And whatever this unfathomable man's unfathomable reasons, Gresham's heart sank. Despite Robert Cecil being older than Gresham, they had crossed swords at Cambridge and at Court. Cecil, Gresham sensed, was not his natural ally, nor even a friend.

'I'm not favoured by Robert Cecil,' he said.

'Cecil believes you were responsible for suggesting the nickname by which the Queen refers to him,' said Walsingham. 'Not a wise move, if it were true.'

A warning? Was this a warning? The Queen referred to Cecil as her pygmy. With a crooked back, short build and warped body, Cecil's smile when the Queen used the term was painful to behold.

'I swear I didn't do so,' said Gresham. It was true, though he might have done if he had thought of it. Yet out of such stupid misunderstandings came the hatreds and feuds that filled the tiny, claustrophobic world of the Court.

'In any event, we are ready to strike a second blow at the Catholics,' said Walsingham. 'Despite my being in disfavour, I have managed to persuade her Majesty to authorise Drake to strike at Lisbon or Cadiz. It is our only hope. We have no army to resist Spain if they land the Duke of Parma and his forces on these shores. Our only strength is our ships, and we must strike at the Spanish vessels *before* they can launch an assault on us.'

Gresham loathed the sea. 'What role do I have in this?' he asked.

'I need eyes and ears abroad. I have booked you passage on Drake's expedition. He will land you ashore on some dark night so you can make your way to Lisbon, give me the information about Philip's fleet that we so desperately need. Yet after the attack, I want you also to report on the fighting qualities of our men and our ships. I need to hear at first-hand how they cope in battle. And how their leaders lead them.'

'It won't be easy to be an Englishman in Portugal, or Spain, at this time,' said Gresham.

'Few things that are easy are worthwhile,' Walsingham replied. 'And it is easier for you than for many. You speak Spanish like a native. And you have acquired Spanish friends. On my behalf, of course.' There was no expression in Walsingham's eyes. Was Walsingham becoming concerned about Gresham's links with Spain? 'Will you . . . accept this errand on my behalf?'

'My Lord.' Gresham bowed his head. Well, well, well. How nice to be treated like a package. Gresham was glad that he was not sensitive. He did not want to go to sea. He thought he was worth more than counting ships in a foreign harbour. It was dangerous, what was being asked of him, but without the glamour or excitement that made the danger palatable. And why the mention of Cecil? 'Yet our earlier conversation? About Robert Cecil . . .?'

'The matter on which you embark is sensitive. Too sensitive for your instructions to be entrusted to a messenger. Expect to be contacted by Robert Cecil in the near future. He will give you my final orders. While my illness persists, he is useful to me. You will forget your childish differences and take him as my representative.'

Robert Cecil was a man clawing his way up the ladder of preferment, helped by his father's great power but also sometimes hindered by the enemies his father had built up over his lifetime. Which side was Walsingham on? Did he see Robert Cecil as the new order, the order George had seen as imminent?

'We must return to await the Queen's entry. And by the way, restrain your vanity. It was not the Queen's lust for your fine legs and the rest of your body that made her summon you here. It was because I asked her to do so. I have that much influence left, it would seem.'

As Walsingham rose a staggering pain seemed to hit him in the gut, and he doubled up. If Gresham had not suddenly been there to support him he would have crashed to the floor. The old man's lips were drawn back in silent agony, his eyes screwed shut, hands clutching at his stomach.

'My Lord . . .!' Gresham was aghast, confused. He had never seen Walsingham express any sign of humanity, never mind physical weakness. 'Sit . . . sit . . .' Gresham sensed that Walsingham needed to be placed back in the chair. He lay there, gasping two or three times as spasms crashed through him. Then it seemed as if the pains were easing. Walsingham opened his eyes.

'Stones. There is nothing that can be done. The pain is acute, but it passes. Its cruelty is that it comes without warning. Go!' he said, eyes only half-open. 'Go now. It is important that the Queen sees you there when she appears to welcome the Ambassador. More important than if I remain here . . .'

As the door closed Walsingham stood up straight, all signs of pain gone. The real pain would come later, he knew. As it was, his knowledge of that pain allowed him to act it out with utter conviction when it was useful and he needed to rid himself of someone. The old man moved to the side of the room. 'We are alone,' he called out. 'You may safely emerge.'

Robert Cecil swung back the arras from behind which he had witnessed Walsingham's conversation with Gresham. A small, slightly hunched figure, he moved awkwardly to a chair, nodded his acknowledgement to Walsingham and received the old man's permission to sit.

'Well, sir,' said Walsingham. 'Did you see what you wished to see?'

'I am grateful to you, Sir Francis,' said Cecil. 'I— '

'I ask no questions, Robert Cecil,' said Walsingham, waving a hand to cut Cecil short. 'And, to be frank, I would not believe your answers. Your father asks me to repay a past favour by my seeing you. I agreed. You asked to be given the chance to view and to meet one of my . . . young men. It does not interfere with my plans for that young man. I agreed. My debt is paid. You have what you wished for. If only all life could be so simple.'

There was silence for a moment.

'I confess to being surprised that you do not wish to know more of my reasons, my Lord,' said Cecil, finally.

'Why?' said Walsingham. 'You will certainly have a reason to give me, but quite frankly, it is as likely to be a lie as it is to be the truth.'

'Sir!' said Cecil, outrage in his surprisingly strong voice, a voice with a rasp in it as of something dragged over gravel, at odds with his slight frame. 'I take offence at the accusation of being a liar!'

Walsingham looked at Cecil, an ironic, humourless smile playing on his lips. 'Then you take offence too easily, and will not last long in the world of the Court! I know what you are,' said Walsingham. In those few words Walsingham had somehow crammed the experience of all his years, the idiocy of human life, its vanities, its foibles and its deceits.

'Sir?' Cecil was confused now.

'You were born into power, have grown up with power and expect power as your right. You drank in power at your mother's breast and at your father's table. And now the source of your power, your father, is failing, as I am failing, because time is the one enemy we cannot defeat, your father with his skills and me with mine.'

'I seek to serve Her Majesty in whatever humble capacity— '

'You are not humble, Master Cecil. And the god you serve is your own position and influence. Don't worry,' said Walsingham, holding up his hand to stop another outburst and speaking now almost in sympathetic tones, 'there is many a man who has given good service to his monarch when actually serving only himself. You are such, I suspect.'

Cecil had recovered now. There was ice in his reply. 'You seem to know a very great deal.'

'I know what you are. That you will twist and turn seeking every advantage, sniff the wind of favour like a beast in the field, scent where danger and advantage are. You are different from myself, from your father even. God knows I have ambition enough. Yet always I have known that I served first my God, second my country and third my Queen. You are the future, I fear. You may do good service to all three, yet the person you really serve is yourself.'

'The Queen might be interested to hear your order of priorities,' sneered Cecil.

24

'She is not ready to hear them from *you*, not yet,' said Walsingham. 'There are many rungs to climb on your ladder of success before you reach that level of confidence with her.'

There was silence between the two men.

'And in answer to the question you do not dare to ask, you will have reasons for getting to know Henry Gresham, reasons that I have no doubt will rebound to your own advantage. I see no obstruction to my plans for that young man in whatever you might wish of him, not yet at least. But you may find that he is a young man who has ideas of his own. So be it. And good day to you, Robert Cecil.'

Obligation. Entrapment. Robert Cecil was the new order, or a possible variant of that new order. Yet Walsingham was ready to die only when God gave the command. In the meantime, let the new order be in his debt, in his vision. He doubted that Cecil planned anything good for Gresham. But who knew how valuable the knowledge of Cecil's plans would be when Walsingham finally acquired it, as acquire it he surely would.

'Just checking you came out alive!' whispered George, who appeared by Gresham's side as soon as he stepped into the Hall. Mannion was there too, playing his usual trick of sticking up against the wall so that people thought him to be a royal servant. 'Well, tell me! What did he want?'

'To have me blown to death in Lisbon or hung from a tree as a spy there!' said Gresham bitterly, then angry at himself for taking his depression out on his friend. Further conversation was denied them. The musicians in the Gallery stirred. The Queen's famous parsimony may have been evident elsewhere in her reception, but not in the dress of her players, resplendent in Tudor green. They stood, and a blare of trumpets rolled out through the rafters and rattled the windows of the ancient building. It was a dramatic opening, but not as dramatic as the appearance of the Virgin Queen herself.

The cynic in Gresham noted that a particularly fine chandelier

25

had been hung at the back of the hall, over a narrow, empty dais cloaked at the side with fine hangings. It seemed to serve no purpose, until the Queen stepped out from a door hidden by one of the hangings, two cherubic page boys flinging the door open and standing aside, bowing to let her pass. Every jewel sewn into her dress, on her fingers and round her neck seemed to blaze into fearsome light, as if a glittering portion of the sun had exploded into the Hall. She was not a particularly tall woman, and her hour-glass figure was threatened by matronly wadding. The worth of the fine black and russet-brown cloth of the dress alone, with its intricate filigree stitching on the huge puffed sleeves, would have fed a small town for a year. And the jewels! Apart from the gem stones, some even placed on the vast halo-like ruff that framed her face, there were vast, sweeping strings of pearls around her neck and crowning her hair.

'That,' whispered Gresham to George, 'is an entrance.'

There was an indrawn gasp of breath as she moved to the front of the dais, and a spontaneous round of applause. It was easy to forget how fragile was her hold on power in the face of her magnificence. She gazed down at her adoring Court and a thin smile of triumph crossed her lips. She extended her hand to the Ambassador, the huge emerald ring on her finger looking like a vast open mouth, the light shooting in and out of its facets. The poor man was quite overwhelmed by events. He could not see the short stairs leading up to the dais, yet could not reach Her Majesty's hand without climbing on to the stage with her. A quick glance from the Queen and a courtier jumped to take the Ambassador's elbow and lead him to the steps. Yet he stumbled as he climbed them. The Queen, her hand still extended, looked down disdainfully at him.

'Fear not, sir!' she exclaimed in a voice strangely deep for a woman, 'this is the hand of friendship I extend to you, not the fist of war.'

A gale of laughter swept the Court, far more than the feeble joke deserved. So it was not her best. Yet the Court knew of old that a rough earthiness could cut into the formality and pretence of Court life at any moment, as the spirit of her father, Henry VIII, possessed her. They might hate her when she was not there, blame her increasingly for not leaving England with a clear heir, but here, in the splendour of her own Court, it was not difficult to see why she had survived so long and so well.

Gresham found himself dancing with the Queen before he realised it. The intricate moves had required his whole attention, and it was not until he felt the stink of the Queen's foul breath behind him that he realised the next round would place him in partnership with her. They swept towards each other, the Queen still excellent in the slower dances. Her face was unnaturally white, the pancake-layer of make-up beginning to loosen like bad plaster as the sweat and exertion of the evening wore on. Her eyes were small, narrow, as they had been on the portraits of her father, Gresham noted. She had favoured the Earl of Essex all evening, to the discomfiture of Leicester. Now she fixed her eye on Gresham, still coping apparently effortlessly with the intricacies of the dance.

'Have you spent all that money yet, Master Gresham?' she asked. She never met him without referring to his wealth, nor let an hour pass without referring to her own poverty. 'Have you spent your inheritance on the things young men spend their money on?'

'I would willingly spend it on gifts for Your Majesty,' said Gresham, a sinking feeling in his stomach. This was not the moment to cannon back into the Earl of Somerset or step on the most powerful set of toes in England, 'were it not for the fact that the greatest fortune on earth could not improve on the beauty that nature and providence gave Her Majesty.'

They moved back in stately movement for a moment, then came together again. The dance required them to walk between the other couples, fifteen or twenty in number, in two separate stages. Gresham was vaguely aware of several glances of hatred directed at him as he escorted the Queen up the line.

'Your words are impressive, young man,' said the Queen, 'and

27

even more so because there is even a slight chance you thought of them yourself.'

Ouch. It never did to underestimate the Queen, whose capacity for flattery was only equalled by her ability to perceive when she was being flattered.

'Have care, young man,' the Queen added, her face expressionless. The dance had brought them face to face for a brief moment. 'There are those who despise you as an upstart in my Court.'

And there are those who despise you, Your Majesty, thought Gresham, as the bastard daughter of the whore Anne Boleyn, who many thought a witch. Nonetheless . . .

'Thank you, Your Majesty,' said Gresham humbly, in the few seconds remaining. 'Yet sometimes upstarts are better survivors than those whose entry into life was made easy for them.'

My God! What had he said! He might as well have told her that bastards should stick together! The Queen's eyes were fathomless, unreadable. They parted with the brief, formal bows the dance demanded, his deep and low, hers conventional, neither so brief as to be rude nor so long as to excite attention.

'Well, that *was* interesting.' George had grabbed a table in a room off the Hall, found from somewhere some scraps of food and a half-decent bottle. No servant could sit at table with their master and so Gresham had sent Mannion off to scour the kitchens, where past experience suggested he would find far better food and drink, and probably ruin a kitchen-maid in the bargain. There were plenty of available women above-stairs, for that matter, but the encounter with the Queen had rather knocked the stuffing out of Gresham.

'What was interesting?' asked Gresham. 'Her breath curdles milk inside the cow at fifty paces, and you never know from one minute to the next if it's an axe or a glove in her hand. I— '

'Not that, fool,' said George. 'Who cares about you? I mean the way the Ambassador was received. Didn't you notice, you great idiot?'

'Notice? Notice what?' said Gresham. Perhaps he would get drunk after all, since remaining sober didn't seem to help.

'The Queen was not there to greet the Ambassador, nor to hear the speech of welcome. All perfectly acceptable in diplomatic terms, of course, but it demotes him immediately two or three places below a Prince or equivalent. No, what it shows is that this evening isn't about the Queen listening to the Ambassador, as I feared. Rather, it's to impress him. It's a show of force – or rather a show of wealth. He's meant to go back to the Netherlands and tell them how much money England has, how brilliant its Court is.'

'But that doesn't make sense,' said Gresham, grappling with the issues. 'All it means is that they'll ask us for more money and more men, when all the Queen can do is say that she hasn't got the income to hold body and soul together.' Spend a bit less on your dresses, lady, thought Gresham.

'Of course it makes sense!' said George, exasperated at his friend's inability to see what was obvious. 'While the Netherlands keep on fighting the Duke of Parma, he's hardly going to want to send half his army over to England, is he? It's leaving him completely exposed. If the Protestants think England can keep pouring money and troops into their cause, they're much more likely to keep fighting and not make a deal with Parma or Spain. Don't you understand *anything* about politics?'

No, thought Gresham, I do not. Or at least not enough. And as the waters get deeper and my involvement greater with every minute, I must learn. Even the most dedicated survivor needs lessons in survival.

CHAPTER 2

March – April, 1587
Granville College, Cambridge

The choir were singing in the Chapel. There were only a hand-ful of them, a symbol of the resurgence in the fortunes of Granville College, but they were good. The beautiful, delicate soaring voices escaped the half-open door and drifted over the College like a flock of swifts.

Things had to be bad if the music failed to move Henry Gresham. A young man who had already been hurt too often by a passion for people, he channelled the fiery avalanche of his emotions into the safe release of music. But today he gazed vacantly out of the latticed window, down to the courtyard. Two rooms to himself was a great luxury indeed in Cambridge. Most Fellows shared their room with students, hiring out truckle beds. Outside, what little peace there ever was in Cambridge was being destroyed by the noise of the men building the new wing, the first sign of the money Gresham was pouring into his old College. Two weeks ago the entire scaffolding had come clattering down, with five men on it. One had broken both legs, another an arm. The students had sawn through the ropes holding the wooden poles in place the night before.

The black mood tore at his mind, the face of the man he had murdered in the meadows returning and swimming up at him.

'Snap out of this!' growled Mannion. He was worried. What was it in Gresham that made him bottle so much up? How many people realised the truth about the laconic, assured and confident young man who strode through Cambridge and London as if he did not have a care in the world? It was simply a mask, an imposition of outer calm over a heaving maelstrom of clashing moods and an almost gross sensitivity. And apparently it was only Mannion who was allowed to see beneath this mask.

'What is there to snap out of it for?' said Gresham, bleakly.

Mannion was annoying. Henry Gresham did not want people to care for him. He had been born a bastard, his mother never named, a startling by-blow from the success story that was the life of the great Sir Thomas Gresham. To everyone's surprise Sir Thomas had acknowledged the child. But it had been a cold, clinical childhood. Then his father had died when Gresham was nine years old. He remembered thinking how lucky he was that he felt no urge to cry. He had seen other children cry at the death of a parent. It was a weakness to cry. Emotional attachments were a weakness. A person was better without that weakness. Stronger.

Yet he had wanted to cry, so much.

The child Henry Gresham, armed only with bed, board and a meagre allowance, had become feral, increasingly wild, left to fend for himself, stalking the great corridors of The House, and the cold streets which no one cared enough to stop him walking. He found his own way to school with no one to notice the huge tear in the doublet a servant had bought for him, nor the bruises from the endless fights with other boys who had somehow found out his bastardy. He had food, a roof over his head and clothes on his back. But he had no love. Nor did he allow himself to wish for it.

First George had come into his life when five boys had cornered Gresham in the school yard. He had knocked two of them out, but a third had got a stone and thrown it, hitting Gresham on the head and near knocking out his left eye. Blinded by blood, dizzy, he had fought on until he had dimly seen the stone-thrower fly through the air. George had decided to intervene, not liking the odds and attracted by the sheer courage and guts of the young boy he had never noticed before. Then Mannion, a mere servant, entered Henry Gresham's life and, by caring for him, became the only other person Henry Gresham cared about.

Gresham had battled to win his degree from Cambridge, serving at table to eke out his meagre allowance, suffering the jibes of the spoiled, wealthy undergraduates. George had offered money. Gresham had proudly rejected it. George was at Oxford, his family so rooted to its university that Gresham doubted they even knew there was a similar institution in Cambridge. The lawyer's visit had come as a complete surprise.

'You are a rich young man, sir,' the dry-as-dust old man had said, looking down his nose at him as if he was something slightly distasteful found in the road, 'a very rich young man indeed.'

It was the vast fortune his father had accumulated in a lifetime of serving the financial needs of Kings and Queens. The fortune he had decided to leave to his bastard son, if and when that son obtained his degree.

Gresham had stood there, in the meagre room he shared with five other impoverished students, the remnants of the boiled mutton on the table. The grate was empty, smelling faintly of soot. He had long ago forgotten to feel the cold. He gazed and gazed at the copy of the will, in his threadbare jerkin and thrice-mended hose. The will that meant he would never have to go cold or hungry again. The will that made him not just the wealthiest student in Cambridge, but made him one of the wealthiest men in the country.

Life had been simple as a child. Survival. The enemy had been everyone. Now life seemed impossibly complex, and his problems were not just in London.

His troubles in College were not simply down to jealousy of his wealth. Though never directly accused, he was seen as having dangerous leanings towards Rome and Roman Catholicism, and his fondness for music in Chapel was widely derided. It did not help that he had been one of the most brilliant undergraduates of his time, as precocious as he had then been poor. He had also been one of the most unruly. His absences 'on the Queen's business' at Walsingham's bequest had bred extra resentment against him. Fellows of the College had banded together to deny him his degree, despite the superior quality of his work. A peremptory message from the Privy Council, one of the few favours Walsingham had ever returned him, had put the University in its place and given Gresham his degree. Even those on his side had reacted badly to being told what to do by the Government. And then his election as a Fellow had added fuel to the fire.

'It's a joke, isn't it?' said Gresham, pacing the small room, floorboards creaking under his feet, energy held back like the stretched gut of a crossbow. 'The first thing we do when we're born is cry. We spend a few years dodging disease, if we're lucky, and then we invent things to care about. Then we're disposed of, we rot and stink to high heaven and it's over. What a lot of noise and tumult. And all about nothing.'

'So much for those bloody church services you drag me to!' said Mannion, whose support of religion was theoretical rather than practical. 'Anyway, you knows my view. We're 'ere to eat, drink and 'ave a bit o' fun.' Mannion was not generally troubled by depression. 'Stands to reason. God wouldn't have given us pleasures if he didn't want us to take them. What I'm not here for is to be ordered around by bloody Spaniards,' he added morosely. Now *that* he could get depressed about. Mannion had a thing about Spaniards. The hatred was at a peak with the wild rumours that a Spanish invasion was imminent.

'Spain, at least, has an identity, a belief in itself,' said Gresham. 'I sometimes wonder if England even knows what it is.'

'You wonder a bloody sight too much,' said Mannion. 'What you need is a lot less *wondering* and a bit more *living*.'

'So I'm meant to stop thinking, am I?' said Gresham caustically.

'Well, you can stop thinking Spain's so bloody marvellous, for starters, because it ain't. Load of heathens who want our women and burn people for pleasure. And if you don't watch out the next time a man comes at you, you'll start to think, instead of just stickin' 'im in the gut.' Mannion sucked at the last remnant of small ale in the pewter tankard by his side. 'Fact is, you're alive. He's dead, that bloody Spaniard in the meadows. You've got the luxury of bein' miserable. He ain't.'

'Come on, old man!' Gresham said, jumping up, 'lift your great stomach! Eager young minds are waiting to be filled at The Golden Lion!'

The mask was back, Mannion noted. He was used to his master's sudden swings of mood. But what damage was being wreaked under that mask?

Fellows made their reputation and their livelihood by the students they attracted to hear them teach. Gresham attracted more than anyone. There were a growing number of 'schools' in Cambridge where these groups could meet, but the local inns still provided a traditional venue for teacher and taught to assemble. They had been forced to find a new inn this year to cope with the growing number wanting to hear Henry Gresham. Perhaps his depression fired him up. He taught brilliantly, emerging outwardly carefree on to the street.

Mannion saw himself as an honorary academic. After all, Gresham's seminars took place in a building dedicated to the consumption of drink and food, and a building which not infrequently placed sex on the menu. For Mannion, it was not like attending a place of learning. It was more like attending a place of worship.

'Isn't Cambridge wonderful?' said Gresham, taking a deep breath of air.

'Bloody Brilliant,' said Mannion, adopting his annoying habit of speaking in capitals. The beer had been good, but now the street was full of the throng of students, of dons, carters, tradesmen and local people. Cambridge was more of a village than a town, Gresham thought, for all the splendour of the Colleges. The recent rain had soaked the thoroughfare and everyone had mud spattered up to their waists. A herd of sheep were being driven through to the market, with an ancient farmer in a smock being helped by a boy too young for the job. The sheep, instead of being tired by their long march, were restive and fickle. They swept this way and that across the road, driving into all classes of people and rubbing the grease of their coats onto fine velvet. Last week a student had run into the middle of just such a herd, bodily picked up a fully-grown animal, and run off with it. Gresham shuddered to think why.

'Bloody Brilliant,' Mannion repeated, as Gresham prepared to set forth, having plotted the least mud-strewn path. 'It's set too low down so its air smells like the bilges of a ship. It gets the plague as regular as other places get dawn and sunset. Oh, and the University hate the town and the town hate the University, with neither of the stupid buggers able to see they both need each other.' He stood, glumly. The wind blew the smell of the river towards him. It was still Cambridge's main road, and its main sewer.

'You're getting old!' Gresham jibed. 'This is where you dare to be wise! This is where the white-hot heat of debate burns up the foul vapours of the air! This is life! Young life!'

'Right,' said Mannion. 'Glad you told me.'

Gresham ignored Mannion and set off, looking not so much like a Fellow of a College as the fine young heir to a noble house, a young colt luxuriating in the use of his long limbs.

They navigated the crowded streets, still tame compared to London's frenetic bustle. Ramshackle, leaning wooden houses threatened to topple over, a stark contrast to the pure stone, brick and soaring lines of the Colleges. No wonder there was so often trouble between the University and the townspeople, thought Gresham. There was an arrogance in these buildings, and in the people who taught and learned within their walls.

'Why do you stick with this lot?' asked Mannion as they pushed their way through the crowds to within sight of Granville. 'Any other College would take you with open arms.'

Why indeed, thought Gresham? It was a thought that bothered

him, with half the Fellowship seething with hatred and envy against him. 'Bloody mindedness,' he said, with startling self-honesty. 'I'm damned if I'll let them force me out of My College.' Did he realise he too was speaking in capital letters? He had been truly educated at Granville College. Few men forget their debt to the place that gives them their real education.

Noon was the main meal of the day. In theory the Fellows sat on the High Table, the students beneath them. In practice the wealthier students had created their own High Table, buying in food often more exotic than that served to the Fellows. These same students paid the poorer ones to wait on them and, if they were feeling very gracious, would even allow these intelligent servingmen the leavings of the meal.

They proceeded into the Hall, dark-panelled and with a roaring fire in the great hearth at the end even at noon, and the air rustled as the students stood, scraping back their crude benches. For once, no one upset a bench and sent it crashing to the ground; the students must either have forgotten to greet the Master in the traditional way, or were too drunk to remember to do so. Gresham took his seat, ignoring the frosty looks directed his way by several of the Fellows. He looked to his neighbour opposite, to be met with a glare of hatred.

Will Smith. Fellow of Granville College. Living witness to Cambridge's increasing dedication to hard-core Puritanism. Thin almost to extinction, smaller than average, a shock of fair curls crowning an extraordinarily high forehead and an intensity that would freeze river water. It was no Godliness that Gresham could recognise that drove Will Smith. It was hatred. Hatred, essentially, of anyone having fun.

The interminable Latin Grace was read out by a student who was as nervous as the rest of his fellows were bored. Someone timed a raucously loud fart precisely in-between the end of Grace and the solemn 'Amen'. The students giggled and shifted, the Fellowship looked stolidly ahead. To more scraping of benches Granville College sat down to eat.

Smith almost drove his thin, sweating face into Gresham's across the table. 'The smell of beer is on your breath!' he accused scornfully.

'Well, it would be, wouldn't it?' Gresham replied mildly, hiding the fact that his good humour was vanishing as quickly as it had returned to him that morning. 'It's what they sell at The Golden Lion. You really don't want to touch the wine. It's— '

'Have you no shame? You desecrate our place of worship with idle music. You drink, you swear, you copulate . . . and you deny the word of God!' The man was using his words like daggers.

'Good heavens!' said Gresham, his voice calm, 'All those at the same time?'

There was a splutter of laughter from up the table. Tom Pleasance was a man whose vast bulk showed a serious commitment to the sins of eating and drinking. Fat Tom was one of Gresham's few allies.

What do you do when half the Fellows of your College hate you? Mannion's answer was simple. There were relatively few things in life, and you did four things with them. You drank them. You ate them. You slept with them. Or you thumped them. On the basis that Will Smith and his kind could not be eaten nor drunk, and that it would be unhealthy to sleep with them, there was only one alternative.

'Keep thumping 'em when they're contrary,' Mannion had announced with finality. 'Eventually, they'll give up. If you hurt 'em enough.'

'What happens if they "thump" me first?' a morose Gresham had asked.

'Then you're a stupid bastard.'

Well, that was that, then.

It was not unusual for rising young stars from the Court to visit Cambridge, nor for falling ones for that matter. Gresham noted the arrival of Robert Cecil in the Hall with little enthusiasm, not least of all because in his heart Gresham did not wish to go to sea. Cecil's arrival could only mean that he carried Walsingham's orders for him. Cecil was a Trinity man, here to look at a donation to some new building. Or at least, that was the public story. His presence had excited considerable interest in the small world of College. His father was the most powerful man in England. It was common knowledge that Lord Burghley was grooming his second son to take over from him as the Queen's Chief Minister, common knowledge that there was serious aristocratic opposition to any such succession. What excitement! It was the intrigue of which College life was made up.

Cecil initially nodded to Gresham politely enough, and then leaned over to him quickly when his neighbour's attention had been diverted by the arrival of new dishes.

'We must meet,' Cecil said. 'Privately, after this. In your rooms. I come on Walsingham's business.' He turned away suddenly to engage in conversation with the Master.

'It's the talk of the town, I tell you, sir!' The speaker was Alan Sidesmith, a senior Fellow and one of Gresham's other friends in College. He had recently returned from London. A man of urbane polish, he hid an acid wit under an unflappable exterior. Whatever this talk was, Cecil's body language was showing he did not wish to hear it.

'They're talking of nothing else except the prophecy. I'm given to understand that the Queen is to issue a proclamation condemning its heresy, so concerned are the powers that be.'

'It is nothing!' Cecil interjected, drawn from his conversation with the Master. The man clearly had ears that could stretch down a whole table, thought Gresham. 'A mere fad, superstitious fancy . . .'

Cecil's obvious reluctance to have the topic aired was like a red flag to a bull for the Fellowship.

'What is it, this prophecy?' asked one, a thin man with a streak of venison gravy down his chin.

'The man was popularly known as "Regiomontanus",' said Sidesmith. 'I believe he was actually called Müller. Johan Müller, of Konigsberg. He died over a hundred years ago.'

'Müller? The mathematician? The one who did the calculations for Columbus and his navigating tables?' It was Adam Balderstone, a drunkard who was one of Gresham's bitterest enemies in College.

Now, it was happening, Gresham could see – that strange alchemy of College life, the coming together despite the vicious rivalries and deep enmities. The Fellows had started to gather round Sidesmith, moving the trestle tables aside to get closer, hunching forward in their interest. Students had left their tables, rich and poor, and were gathering on the edges of the group of men. The College was starting to breathe its magic, drawing these disparate men together, declaring a temporary truce even between those who yesterday could have killed each other.

Something started to sing in Gresham's heart. For all its anger and petty hatreds, its turmoil and parochial tumult, these strange, isolated moments of harmony were the reason why he felt at home only here, why he was pouring out money in the face of envy to revitalise this College. We do not own our lives, he thought. At best we are merely tenants. But sometimes we can buy a stake in the future, a stake in something that will outlive our frantic, short share of life. A young man in an all-male community, he was too young to realise that this same justification was what drove men to have children.

'Yes,' said Sidesmith, 'but the prophecy derives from others as well.'

'Its principles are Biblical as well as mathematical.' It was Balderstone again. His eyes were bright, and one could see something of the excitement that had drawn the students to him in droves when he had first taught at Cambridge. Who would have thought that an obscure prophecy could have aroused him so, thought Gresham. Not for the first time he reminded himself: never think you can completely know any human being. 'Müller and others – Melancthon, Stofler, Postel – argued that all human history is contained in a series of cycles.'

'These . . . cycles, are they Biblical?' It was the Dean of the College.

'Only in part,' Balderstone said. 'They are *authenticated* by the Holy Bible – passages in Revelations, Daniel XII and Isaiah – but their structure is numerical, based on permutations of the numbers seven and ten.'

A *frisson* of fear shuddered through the group. Numerology was accepted as a valid path of knowledge, but smacked to some of witchcraft.

'But what is the importance of all this?' It was the Master, part fascinated, part unsettled by Cecil's obvious displeasure.

Sidesmith glanced at Balderstone, who glanced back and shrugged.

'The prophecy of Regiomontanus is based on the belief that the penultimate cycle of human history closed in 1518 with Luther's defiance of the Pope,' said Sidesmith. There was shuffling in the crowd. Cambridge was fiercely Puritan, a Puritanism that had been made possible by Luther's defiance. Yet Gresham knew there were those in the Hall whose outward observance of Protestant ritual covered weekly attendance at the Mass, conducted in secret by priests whose bowels would be hung out to dry in front of them while their hearts were still beating if they were discovered.

'So are we all to die this year?'

'No,' said Sidesmith. 'Not this year. Next year. One version states that the final cycle is based on ten times seven years.'

'The time of the Babylonian captivity?' asked an excited young voice from the back, showing off.

'Precisely. It states that in 1588 the Seventh Seal will be broken.'

There was silence. From far away came the call of a servant in the kitchen.

'Some say that the anti-Christ will be overthrown in that year. That it will be the final judgement.'

40

For a moment the Hall seemed to darken. A cloud passing over the sun? Coincidence.

'What are the words of the prophecy?' It was another young student eagerly questioning.

Sidesmith did not raise his voice, but the sonorous words seemed to echo and reverberate in the Hall:

> '"Post mille exactos a partu virginis annos
> Et post quingentos rursus ab orbe datos
> Octavagesimus octavus mirabilis annus
> Ingruet et secum tristitia satis trahet.
> Si non hoc anno totus malus occidet orbis,
> Si non in totum terra fretumque ruant,
> Cuncta tamen mundi sursum ibunt atque descrescent
> Imperia et luctus undique grandis erit."'

For the Fellows, the Latin translated instantly in their minds. Gresham saw the confusion on the faces of some of the students, and cut in before they started to babble their ignorance to each other.

> '"A thousand years from the virgin birth
> Five hundred more allowed the globe,
> Then is the wondrous eighty-eighth year
> Bringing with it great woe. If, this year,
> Total catastrophe does not befall, if land
> And sea do not collapse in total ruin, yet
> The whole world will suffer upheavals,
> Empires will dwindle
> From everywhere
> Will be great lamentation."'

This time the silence was longer.

'Nonsense!' It was one of the most enfeebled of the Fellows, taken now to spluttering and declamation as the power of his

41

mind left him. 'Superstitious nonsense, from those with brains in their backsides rather than in their heads. We shall not fight Spain if our soldiers and our sailors start in the belief that they are already dead.'

'Why, sir,' said Fat Tom, who claimed ancestry from Julius Caesar, and also claimed his ancestor's skill in military planning despite never having been within shooting distance of an arquebus, 'I hardly feel we need to bring backsides into the debate. I personally always try to keep them out.'

The students laughed, as Tom had intended. Tom called everybody 'my dear' and spoke in a rather high voice from the top of his nose. He had once been challenged by a student who had called him a sodomite. Tom was a man who never willingly used one word where twenty would do. He had looked down on the boy, who could have been sent down for such an insult, and gave an answer that had immediately entered the folklore of the College. 'Young man,' he had said, 'I had to choose some years ago whether my pleasure was to come from food and drink or from sexual congress. My choice of the former makes the latter impractical, as I have trouble finding a bed to support me alone. At best, therefore, I can only be a sodomite in theory, and as you have shown a total inability to grasp any theory whatsoever, I would suggest that if such accusations are to be made then they should come from someone who does not have his brain up his arse.'

Tom's style and voice were deceptively languid. He spoke as if to the general mass. All knew he was talking to the man whose father was the government. 'If there is fear, it is only because men can see what government is blind to.'

'Your meaning, sir?' asked Cecil mildly. He had not pretended that the statement had been directed at anyone but him, but the neutrality of his response made him seem merely courteous and interested, rather than offended.

'There is confusion in our ranks, sir.' Tom was equally courteous. 'It's known that Spain is gathering ships. We have the greatest opposing army this side of antiquity a short sea journey away in the

42

Netherlands, under Parma, the most powerful general in the world today.'

A mutter of agreement and fear went round the tables. Nowhere was dread of Spain stronger than in Puritan Cambridge. The Duke of Parma and his fierce Spanish soldiers were names used to frighten naughty children.

'There is . . . less confusion than you might conceive,' responded Cecil carefully, leaning forward. 'The Queen is eternally vigilant!'

'Why, so Her Majesty is,' said Fat Tom, 'but to us yokels out here in the country her generals appear less so. Where is the army that will repel the Duke of Parma? And with such soldiers as we have, where is the strategy? Are we to defend the whole coast, every port and harbour and beach, spread such men as we have around so thinly that they will report an invasion but be too weak to fight it off? Or do we concentrate our men at focal points to meet the attacker, risking that they land where we do not expect and march on London unopposed. Both tactics are risky, but it's even more risky to have no tactics at all!'

Tom was on the verge of rudeness, the distinction between that and academic robustness always being blurred. Cecil refused to rise to any bait.

'We have soldiers enough,' he said. God knows where they were, thought Gresham. England had never had a standing army, and the few professional soldiers it could muster were most of them in Flanders, failing to defeat the mighty Duke of Parma. 'But more than that we have our ships, surely? Ships enough to drop King Philip's lumbering galleons to the bottom of the sea, with or without Parma's precious soldiers in them.'

'The sea,' said Fat Tom, warming to his cause even more, 'is vast and even the most "lumbering" of galleons is very small. Our fleet and theirs could pass each other in the night as if both were invisible.'

'And we have Drake . . .' said Cecil with an air of finality. There was a slight tick in his left eye, Gresham noted, an almost invisible flickering of the flesh. Drake. *El Draco*. Feared above all others by the Spaniards. Rumoured to have a magic glass through which he could see the position of every Spanish ship at sea. How else to explain the miraculous way he found the Spanish treasure vessels? A murmur of approval swept over the students. Drake was a talisman, a magic symbol to wave away fear of invasion. 'Drake is a mighty figure indeed. And captaining, of course, one of our new fine ships. Ships that can dip and weave across the waves like a dancer, sailing almost into the wind . . .'

In the face of bitter opposition, Hawkins, The Queen's Admiral, had cut down the huge castles that dominated the bow and stern of warships. Instead he had forced through new vessels with low, lean profiles, eminently more manoeuvrable and capable of sailing almost directly into the wind. The great castles had been for soldiers, so that they could pour down a musket fire on their enemy and then launch themselves down on their foe as they came alongside, grappled and boarded. Yet these vast castles fore and aft, their size almost a symbol of the ego of the ship's captain, caught the wind like a vast sail, made the ships almost unmanoeuvrable unless the wind was directly behind them.

'We have ships that can stand off from an enemy and blow it out of the water. No boarding, no coming alongside.' It was Gresham taking over now. He had no need and no desire to offend Cecil, at least not until he knew what this man's game was. Yet if he was to become involved in the defence of England, it would be as wise to hear the answer from London to some obvious questions. 'But Drake has never commanded an English fleet in battle with another fleet. Even the Queen described him as her pirate,' Gresham said. A flicker of laughter went round the table. 'His only experience is in attacking primarily merchant vessels, or inferior forces, for the purpose of taking their cargo and enriching both the nation and himself. Glorious, certainly. But the Spaniards have fought pitched battles at sea, with several fleets.'

Though I wonder how glorious it really is, thought Gresham, or whether it is simply greed. And piracy.

'Our captains, even if they know how to use our ships and can resist the lure of treasure, are reported to be at each other's throats more often than they fight the enemy,' Gresham continued. It was known that Frobisher had threatened to tear Drake's heart out. 'Each ship in our fleet is a mere individual, operating at the whim of its captain. It's like an army where the officers are at war with each other, and each soldier takes a personal decision which enemy to fight!'

'I think,' said Cecil smoothly, 'that our captains can be trusted to unite in the face of any threat we might face from Spain. And if a young man such as yourself, with no experience of sea-faring, can identify these problems, think you not that those with all the experience in the world of seafaring, and their masters, are aware of them as well and have plans in hand to solve them?'

It was a good, telling point. There was a buzz of support from round the table. People needed to believe in this, Gresham realised. He also realised he had not added to the number of his friends by seeming to challenge the reassurance of Cecil, and the reputation of Drake. The thinnest possible glint in Cecil's eyes suggested that he knew he had scored an emotional victory, if not an intellectual one, with the Fellowship.

The knock on the door came shortly after Gresham returned to his rooms. Mannion had been dismissed and was no doubt now haunting one of the less respectable taverns in Cambridge. Cecil motioned his own servant away, ordering him to shut both the outer and the inner door. It was an unusual slip from a man Gresham suspected weighed every move. Gresham could have pointed out that these were his rooms and it was therefore his decision as to whether the doors were open or shut. He kept his counsel.

'It is kind of you to see me,' said Cecil, inclining his head to Gresham and knowing that Gresham had no option.

'It's an honour,' Gresham replied, inclining likewise and knowing that it was not.

'You argued your case well,' said Cecil. The man had small, gimlet eyes. The cut of the long cloak he had donned, and the doublet under it, obscured the crook in his back, and his hair was arranged so as to cover in part the indentation in the side of his head that his detractors said had been caused when his wet nurse had dropped him on to a stone floor.

Yet I lost it, thought Gresham. However well I argued, it was you who took the balance of the Fellowship with you. What had Walsingham once said to him? 'To admit weakness is sometimes to gain strength'.

'Had we been in formal disputation, I think we both know you would have won,' said Gresham. Formal debates were the meat and drink of Cambridge academic life, central to its academic processes.

'Those who say what the listeners wish to hear frequently defeat those who tell the truth,' replied Cecil, something akin to a dry smile passing his lips.

Well now! Two sets of truth following on one from the other! At this rate we'll be in bed together by midnight and married in the morning, thought Gresham. 'I'm forgetting my manners,' he said aloud. 'Can I tempt you to some wine?'

'How kind,' replied Cecil. The voice was thin, reedy, but with the strength of wire. Gresham got up and poured the wine into a fine Venetian glass. If Cecil noticed how expensive his drinking vessel was he did not show it, merely toying with the stem as if distracted. Gresham decided to say nothing. It was Cecil who broke the silence. 'Unfortunately you are correct. We have no proper army to defend our shores. Drake is unreliable. Our ships are individuals, not a unified fleet such as the Spanish possess, with tactics they have tried out in battle.'

Gresham was able to control his face. Here was an admission indeed – an admission that could be taken to come direct from the Queen's Chief Minister.

'You will condemn me, no doubt,' said Cecil. Was he aware of the shock he had caused? It was difficult to know; the man was a courtier and a politician, bred to hide his feelings, as Gresham had been forced to learn to do. 'Condemn me for seeking to defeat your

46

arguments tonight in front of your Fellowship when I knew them to be correct.' Was there the slightest hint of pleasure that he had been victorious?

'I condemn no one,' said Gresham, 'I leave that to judges and to politicians.'

'It is an instinct for one such as myself to calm fears,' said Cecil. 'Even more so if they are true.'

'I am no sailor,' said Gresham, repeating what he had said to Walsingham. 'What role can I play in these great events?'

'From what little I know, you can act as eyes and ears for our country in Lisbon. And I believe for some while you have acted as an . . . agent, for Walsingham?'

'You must know I have,' answered Gresham simply.

'A spy? Are we allowed to use the word?' In using it Cecil had allowed a degree of venom to creep into his voice.

'If *you* don't, others will. And spies are necessary, after all,' said Gresham. 'As are dogs. And even lice must be necessary, or surely God would not have created them?'

'Very necessary,' said Cecil with the same distaste as one might describe the fellow who cleared out the midden. Both men were resisting an urge to scratch. 'In any event, here are the papers Sir Francis wished you to have. He requested that I urge caution on you. As I am sure you know, such orders as he has chosen to give you will mean your death if they are found on your person in a foreign country. Sir Francis suggests— '

'That I destroy them once they are read. It is an order with which I'm familiar,' said Gresham with a thin smile.

'Indeed,' said Cecil, pleasantly. Why did his pleasantness worry Gresham? 'And I wish you well on the voyage. I understand Sir Francis is hoping for a great victory related to barrel staves.'

'*Barrel staves?*' said Gresham incredulously. A sense of humour was not a feature he associated with Robert Cecil. 'Are we going to acquire large quantities of barrel staves and beat the Spaniards over the head with them? I would have thought pikes and muskets were a more conventional— '

Cecil refused to rise to Gresham's sarcasm. He interrupted Gresham.

'My lord believes we can cripple the Armada through barrel staves as much as through cannon fire. A great Armada of ships requires thousands of tons of food, of wine, of water, of powder – all stored in barrels. Where else can such commodities be stored? Have you tasted beer from a barrel made of unseasoned staves?'

Sour beer! Of course! Water was a dangerous drink, and the brewing process seemed to take the badness out of water. Even Gresham knew what happened on board ship if a barrel was broached and the contents poisoned through unseasoned timber. Such timber also bent and shrank, letting out the contents. Mind you, so few hops were used in brewing the beer for the Queen's ships that the stuff was rumoured to be rotten before it got into the barrels. Cecil continued, as if lecturing a child.

'Because the wood for staves has to season and, because Spain needs far more barrels than are currently available, the order has gone out for suitable wood across Europe. Small boats, mainly, in their hundreds. Heading for Lisbon. Walsingham believes if we can sink or capture enough of these vessels, we will give the Spaniards gut rot for food and poison for their drink. Drake's instructions are to patrol off Lisbon or Cadiz, attack if he can. If not, he should pick up all the coastal trade, sink most of it.'

'While this is fascinating,' said Gresham, 'I'm slightly at a loss to see its relevance.'

'It is very simple,' said Cecil. 'Sir Francis needs not only information on the great ships that Philip is gathering – their cannon, their shot and their powder – but he wishes you to ascertain the state of the lesser shipping, the state of those unglamorous supplies that will underpin Spain's fleet.'

An unglamorous mission then, thought Gresham, seeking to find out unglamorous facts. 'Is there enmity between your father and Walsingham?' he asked Cecil. It was almost a random thought, allied to a desire to unsettle him. Why *did* Gresham dislike him so much?

'Not at all,' replied Cecil. Gresham had chosen the wrong question. Or Cecil was hard to unsettle. 'If there were, it would hardly be likely that I would be running errands for Sir Francis.'

I cannot see why you should run such errands, thought Gresham, and it worries me. More layers of intrigue. Yet as far as Gresham could judge, Cecil had not told him a single lie. Who could hope to disentangle the truth from the lies?

'The usual permissions have been given to the College, I understand,' said Cecil. The 'usual permissions' were letters from the Privy Council requesting that 'no hindrance' be given to one Henry Gresham for absence 'required in the service of Her Majesty'. It would, of course, lead to the usual resentments, as if Gresham did not have enough trouble in College already. And he would need to pay someone to cover his lectures.

Some instinct had drawn Mannion back. He stepped into Gresham's rooms as Cecil brushed past him.

'We're going to sea to fight the Spanish, then spy in Lisbon,' said Gresham.

For a moment a strange expression flickered across the face of the normally phlegmatic Mannion. Then it was gone. 'Fight the Spanish?' he said. 'I thought all you wanted to do was to get into bed with them.'

Gresham sighed, and chose to ignore the sally. He relayed his conversation with Cecil.

'I don't like it, not one bit,' said Mannion. 'That Cecil's on the ladder right enough, and 'e don't mind who 'e treads on to get up it. The way these bastards work at Court, I bet 'e 'asn't given you half the story.'

'There'll be battles at sea that'll decide the fate of England. Maybe set the map of Europe for hundreds of years to come. And I've been offered a ringside seat. What man could turn that down?' asked Gresham. Well, it would make a story for the girls, and there was some excitement in it.

'One with more sense than you,' responded Mannion. 'Well, I'm glad I taught you to swim.' He had indeed done so in Gresham's youth. Gresham's hatred of the sea did not extend to swimming in the cool clear waters of his father's lake, or the upper reaches of the Cam before Cambridge's sewage stained its waters.

'Let's hope we don't have to,' said Gresham, with feeling.

CHAPTER 3

April, 1587
Goa; Plymouth; The Attack on Cadiz

Her childhood in Spain had been idyllic, and she was too young to notice the increasing signs of poverty on their estate. The first blow had come with the news that her feckless father had been forced to take up a posting in God-forsaken Goa, India, and rent out what few lands they had remaining, taking his wife and daughter into a prison of prickly heat and alien people. Fortunes were being made in Goa. His breeding could help gain him a post, but nothing could compensate for his lack of basic ability. She had been deeply disturbed by the need to move, though no misery could equal that of life in Goa itself. Then the second blow had come – the death of her father from some nameless, wasting fever that had used up more of their precious money uselessly in medical fees. She had not realised how much she had loved the vain, ineffectual man until she faced life without him. Then came the third blow, the news from her mother, whom she adored, that she was to rescue the family fortune by marrying the French merchant Jacques Henri, a sweating lard-of-a-man she had met only once in Spain, and who had not even lifted his heavy-lidded eyes to meet her own.

The ship upon which she and her mother were to travel aboard, the great carrack *San Felipe*, was vast, crammed to the hilt with enough produce of the Indies to make a sizeable dent even in the debts of King Philip. Normally the prospect of such a great voyage, with all its dangers, would have excited her, and her natural high spirits would have lifted at the sight of the wonderful bustle on the dockside. But now she hardly cared, hardly cared even if the vessel sank and took her along with it. Death looked attractive compared to life with an old, fat merchant. Her nurse had described what men did to women, and she had gagged and felt sick, even as a strange part of her had felt excitement. It seemed terrifying to have this done to her even by a young, handsome man. To be . . . entered in this way, by an old, fat man astride of her . . . it was *filthy*.

Anna Maria Lucille Rea de Santando showed none of her feelings. She stood by the quayside waiting to board, impossibly aloof and cool, in control. The tantrums were over now. She had decided. Emotion was weakness, a betrayal of the armour needed to protect one's mind. Let the fat merchant labour over her body. He would find it motionless, as cold as ice. And she would fuel her hatred of her husband with her hatred of Spain, where the real betrayal was. Her family had lived and ruled there for generations, and now it had thrown them out without hesitation, punishing her Spanish father for daring to marry an English woman.

Her mother called to her in a low voice. As they turned to mount the ornate gangplank she stumbled, falling down on Anna's arm so hard that for a moment it was as if both women would topple over. Anna looked at her mother. She had tried so hard to hate her too these past few weeks. Her strong face was starting to line now, Anna noticed, the flesh hanging in wrinkles on her neck, always the give-away of age in a woman. Yet there was also a new pallor on her mother's brow, an unhealthy tinge on her normally strong face.

'Are you alright?' Anna asked, almost unwilling to show concern. 'Can I get you some waters?' Anna's English would occasionally slip in to eccentricity, revealing it as her second language.

Her mother said nothing, just nodding. She had not bothered to correct the use of the plural, was still leaning very heavily on her arm. Anna noticed the pressure increasing as they entered the hull that would be their world for weeks ahead. The gloom closed over them. The smell was overwhelming: wood, tar, cordage, stale sweat, a multi-layered taint of spices acting like a fine sauce laid over rotten meat to hide its stench. The sudden move from the bright sunlight into the darkness seemed to her symbolic of her life, Anna thought. From sunshine to darkness. Would the darkness ever end?

'Are you strong enough to support me?' asked her mother, breathless now. Anna smiled up at the person she loved most in the world.

'Me? Of course! I have millions of energies!'

The mistake brought a smile to the tired face of her mother. Anna flushed. She was not willing to appear weak in front of anyone, even her mother. You will need those energies, my dearest girl, her mother thought. You will need them more than ever. And how I wish you could give some of them to me, to fight a battle I know I am losing.

It was the masts that first struck him. Taller than trees, they festooned the sky, scoring it with the dark lines of their rigging. The waterfront at Plymouth was chaotic, the *Elizabeth Bonaventure* an asylum gone mad. Hordes of sweating men were heaving barrels of biscuit, beer and gunpowder off the waiting carts in a haphazard manner and bundling them on board the ships drawn up by the quay. Untidy masses of stores were swinging aboard wildly in nets, threatening to smack indiscriminately into masts and men. To wild shouts one such load, the net bulging under the weight of a pallet of cannonballs, swung against rigging and wrapped itself round the arm-thick ropes tensioning the main mast. A succession of boats were scudding across the waves like so many beetles, taking yet more stores to the other great ships anchored out in the sound. Cordage littered the quayside and a spare foresail that had somehow broken free of its binding ropes was flapping forlornly on the cobbles, like a lobster kicking out the last moments of its life on the

53

fish-seller's stall. Like all waterfronts, it stank of the sea, the rotting smell of fish and seaweed, the tang of salt and the earthy, dark smells of rope, tar and canvas.

'Damn them and their cowardice!' ranted Sir Francis Drake, appearing on the side of his flagship with a voice that could cut through a gale rising above even the clamour on the dockside. 'Who do these scum think they are, deserting their country and their captain in their hour of need! More lackeys in the pay of Spain!'

Drake was a short man, barrel-chested and round-faced, brown bearded, with ruddy cheeks like the babies Devon farmers' wives brought with them to market. He was extraordinarily expensively dressed, the ruff as proud as a peacock's tail, his doublet all of slashed silk in a deep, dark green and ostentatious gold buckles on his fine leather shoes. In total contrast, Drake's Secretary was a thin, lugubrious figure with a balding pate, white face and an expression of very long suffering. His clothing looked as if someone had taken a used sail, dyed it black and turned it into an ill-fitting cloak for human nakedness. His scarecrow figure held a strange dignity. He had a slate in his hand, with a piece of chalk, like a rather tired schoolmaster.

'The sailors have run off,' the Secretary intoned in a voice one might otherwise have expected to find coming from the pulpit at evensong in a tiny, freezing village church, 'because they thought they were going off to rob Spanish treasure ships. Now they hear they're going off to attack the Spaniards in their home ports. This is much more dangerous and far less remunerative. It is— '

'Fuck what it is!' roared Drake, his colour now the highest red and his face looking set to explode. 'Fuck what they are! Fuck what you are! Fuck all cowards and traitors!'

The Secretary showed no sign of wishing to fuck anyone as he stood by his master's side impassively. His eyes were perhaps looking rather more towards Heaven than might be deemed customary, but whatever he was saying was being kept private between him and his God.

*

It had not been a good day for Henry Gresham. Nor a good week. The doubts about this mission had grown and buzzed in his head like flies. Why should he risk his life to tell Walsingham how many barrel staves were being landed in Cadiz? The weather had been foul when they set out from London, and now he was soaked to the skin. His great riding cloak was wet, weighing five times its normal weight, and had the dank stink of damp wool. Uncontrollable shivers passed through him without warning. Yet it was more than his shivering cold that bothered him. A deep dread had settled over Gresham at the prospect of taking to sea. Seafaring was something about which he knew nothing. He hated being an innocent abroad, hated his own ignorance, sensed that his carefully cultivated front of superiority and control would be smashed. He had been made to look the fool often enough as a child. An aching heart and a nagging headache told him that he was on course for neither Lisbon nor Cadiz, but rather on course for humiliation. Or a lonely, wet death beneath the greasy rolling waves of the Atlantic.

Gresham also hated the filth of seafaring. He was obsessive about cleanliness, and his usual daily routine was to stand in the iron bath, scrubbing his skin with the cold water as if it would cleanse him of all sin as well as of dirt. At sea, the fine velvet and silk-covered bodies stank more with each day that passed. No soap would work up a lather in sea water, which left salt stains on any flesh and cloth it touched, as well as something of the stink of the sea. That strange odour, of sharp salt water tainted by an unidentifiable corruption just beneath the surface.

The rank smell and clutter of the quayside did nothing to reassure him. Even Mannion's usual banter had deserted him and he had descended into an unprecedented black mood of his own from the moment they left London. For years Gresham had often prayed for Mannion to shut up. Now he found himself praying that he would speak. And to cap it all, if this ranting maniac before him was indeed Sir Francis Drake, it would not be a good time for Henry Gresham to introduce himself. Drake saved him the bother. Drake caught sight of the young man and his servant on the quayside.

'You need not mention your miserable name. I know it,' said Drake with extreme rudeness. Gresham's hand itched to clutch his sword. 'It was a condition of the voyage that I take you on board. It is not a condition that I otherwise acknowledge your existence.'

Gresham bowed his head respectfully. It seemed the only thing to do. Clearly Drake did not like spies.

'*Are* we loaded? *Are* we prepared for our voyage? *Is* there any meaning in this chaos?' Drake was roaring again.

'If you keep distracting me every other minute with requests for information that I cannot supply, my admittedly feeble attempts to keep track of what is being loaded aboard the *Elizabeth Bonaventure* will die in tatters.' The Secretary placed his slate on a nearby barrel. Clearly, he alone on the waterfront had no fear of Drake. The barrel was almost immediately grabbed by two burly seamen, and the Secretary grabbed his slate back just in time. 'To be frank, Sir Francis,' said the Secretary, 'I do not know if twenty tons of gunpowder has just been taken on board, or twenty tons of dried peas.'

Drake looked at his Secretary, with that same speculative glance. Then he rounded, without warning, on the sailors and workmen filling the slippery quayside. 'To Spain! To death and to glory!'

The men on the waterfront heard his words, stopped their work and started to cheer. The sailors caught the mood. Suddenly the whole quay was a feast of cheering. Drake opened his arms, welcoming the cheers. He turned and set off through yelling crowds, mounting the gangplank. Once aboard the *Bonaventure* he vanished below decks.

'Now that one,' said Mannion glumly, following Drake up the gangplank, 'he's a *real* bastard.'

There was a clatter of hoofs behind them, yells and curses and the noise of a pile of barrels being knocked over. Several sailors and half the women waiting to say farewell to their menfolk had run for their lives as the heavy barrels rolled down the quayside.

'Sorry! Sorry!' a booming voice called out. 'Any damage paid for, of course. Truly sorry!' George Willoughby had arrived, plastered with the rain and looking like a drenched mammoth.

'What in God's name are you doing here?' asked an astounded Gresham, his heart lifting already.

'My father's got contacts with Drake. Helped fund one of his voyages five years ago. I asked him to call in some favours. Plus, no doubt the old man'll have landed the bill for half of Drake's powder! Who cares? It's only money, and it worked.'

'But why?' asked Gresham, grinning at his friend. 'Why *choose* to come?'

'Too much theoretical politics, dear boy!' boomed George. 'The fate of the nation's being decided here.' There was a sense of excitement in his voice, a burning in his eyes. 'Do I want to be one of those who comments on what's happened? Or do I want to be the one who tells the girls of my first-hand acts of derring-do against a horde of Spaniards?'

He had a point, Gresham thought. Every young man with fire in his belly had sought to sail with Drake, the eternal rite of passage where men have to prove their courage. And George Willoughby was no coward.

'Will you shout as loudly at them as you're shouting at me?' asked Gresham, noticing an increasing number of the rabble gathering round for this free show.

'Sorry!' George clamped a hand theatrically over his mouth. Well, thought Gresham, the *Elizabeth Bonaventure* was going to seem a lot smaller with this man's bulk on it, but somehow he sensed the horizons would seem a lot wider.

The twenty English vessels were strung out over a vast expanse of ocean so blue that its glittering surface bit into the eyes, white sails looking like dainty seagulls dipping in and out of the waves. So peaceful, so calm in the mild wind driving them to Cadiz. So deceptive. Each patch of white on the blue of the sea was a heaving, straining, iron-fastened box of wood entombing the men who crawled like so many maggots on their deck and up their masts. Fragile things, for all the serenity they showed from afar, built from tension. The tension of straight wood forced to curve and hug a hull. The tension of the huge pressure of sail pitted against a thin wooden mast and the taut pull of infinitely complex rigging, checking and balancing all to keep that sail full of the ferocious and fickle power of the wind. And those tensions broke easily. The savage, ripping, tearing noise of a sail suddenly shredding itself as a tiny weakness opened up into shreds. The crack as a rope snapped, whipping viciously across the deck and then through the body of any man unlucky enough to stand in its way. The seam between planking forced open as the ship plunged and drove time and time again into a heavy sea, the caulking being driven out in what the sailors called a boat spewing its oakum, burying its prow in the water and only after what seemed like minutes rising up and shaking the water from its bow. Those picturesque dots on the ocean were a fragile challenge to the power of the elements.

Gresham and Mannion were munching their midday meal companionably in the waist of the ship, George alongside. All three were now used to the easy rise and fall of the deck. Gresham was surprised at how he felt. Three or four days of dreadful sickness and intense misery had passed, to be replaced by a life confined, simplified. There was hardly room to move on board the *Elizabeth Bonaventure*, crammed to the hilt as it was with 'gentlemen adventurers' such as George, and the extra crew needed to replace those lost by sickness and combat. Luxury was to find room to stretch out to the full on the deck at night, huddled under one's cloak, the rough timbers cutting in to each toss and turn of the body. Even the longing for his bath in the morning was a dull ache rather than an active stab of pain. He had become accustomed to his own rancid smell and that of those alongside him. Seafaring, he was finding, was largely about fighting the elements. It left him with far less time to fight himself.

On English ships even a commander such as Drake would lend a hand with a rope when the need arose. So Gresham had offered himself for some of the simpler tasks on board. It was strangely soothing. There was a task before him – a rope to be secured just so. Barrels and stores to be moved from here to there as they were emptied and the balance of the ship needed to be kept. And at the end of the task, there was a simple measure of achievement. The line no longer flapped in the wind, the stores were in the right place. He felt inordinately proud when he tied his first knot and it held, and a seaman clapped him on the back. The challenges of this world were clear, success easily measured. Was he in danger of relaxing too much?

Sir George Willoughby had bought most of Drake's wine as well as most of his powder for the voyage, as the price for the carriage of his son, and as a result George had been invited to Drake's cabin to share some of that wine.

'Too many ships in Lisbon,' George had reported back to Gresham excitedly. 'Too many even for Drake to take on board, and strong harbour defences. So it's off to Cadiz. Bursting with ships apparently, and far more weakly defended. We'll have our battle after all!'

Gresham had asked to see Drake. 'Sir Francis,' he had asked with a deference he did not feel, as Drake pored over a chart of Cadiz harbour and ignored him. 'The rumour is that we're leaving Lisbon, yet I need to be put ashore there. Will you grant me a small boat to take me ashore?'

Drake gave him the merest of glances. 'We're already too far away. I doubt a boat would find its way back to me in time. And it's not in my interests for you to be captured at this time, as might well be the case if I granted your demand.'

It had been a request, thought Gresham, not a demand.

'It's essential for this expedition's success that the Spaniards do not know I'm at sea until I've got them by the throat.'

'Sir,' said Gresham, trying and failing to hide his impatience, 'my only reason for being here is to land where I can report on the Spanish fleet.'

'If I have my way you'll land in Cadiz on this vessel,' said Drake flatly, 'and get a very close view indeed of some Spanish vessels. Or will that view be too close for your comfort? Do you wish to be taken ashore before to avoid the battle that might take place there?'

The accusation of cowardice was clear, the insult sufficient for a gentleman to fight and die for. Yet Gresham sensed he was almost being tested.

'I'm not sure, Sir Francis,' said Gresham with a calmness at total odds with his fast-beating heart, 'whether your comment was a challenge to my honour or an insult to my intelligence.' Now came the risk. Yet the blood was hot in Gresham, and would not be resisted. 'As it is,' Gresham continued, 'I propose to reject both propositions, and interpret your words as an insult to *your* intelligence.'

It was a standard rhetorical procedure as taught in the University, the first two comments comprising the defence and the third the attack. Suddenly Gresham realised how silly the intellectual gymnastics of the University seemed here, at sea, in the face of a man who could order his death in an instant. Drake looked at him then, without the angry outburst Gresham had expected and with dark, expressionless eyes.

'I care less than a fart for your interpretation of anything,' Drake said. 'I'll let you ashore in Cadiz, where I have no doubt they will find you and hang you from a tree within hours, if it pleases me to do so. Your masters on shore may control what happens there. At sea, I am in command. Now you may leave.'

Gresham could not think of a *riposte*. He left. A stink of sewage hit him as he left the great cabin. Strange. He was used to no longer smelling the stench of life at sea. Those who wanted to piss and shit were meant to go to the bow of the ship, where there were crude facilities for them to deposit their waste matter hanging over the side. Many did not bother to make the journey, particularly in rough or cold weather or if they woke in the middle of the night. A bucket, or a barrel cut down to half its height, stood at each end of the deck and in the middle of the main deck, slopping over even in decent sea conditions. In time everything gathered in the bilges of the ship where the stone and gravel ballast was stored, the lowest level of all. Just as the piss descended, so its stench ascended after a long voyage, filling the decks with its sulphurous tang, and the rank smell of solid waste.

In the end there was no plan. No order. Drake simply led a mad, frontal assault on the Spaniards. It was pure folly. And it caught Spain completely by surprise.

The sun was shining from a cloudless sky over Cadiz. A decent wind kicked over the surface of the sea, making it seem busy and useful. The heat of midday had passed, and the better folk were emerging in the late afternoon to take the air and to be seen. Down at the waterfront a troop of actors were playing to a large crowd whose hoots, cheers and jeers were faintly audible on the wind. The wine shops were busy servicing the needs of the sailors, but it was too early for them to have become troublesome.

In the town there was music, laughter. 'Look!' said the pretty wife of a Cadiz merchant, 'More ships!' Then she giggled, as if ashamed that a woman should notice such things. The merchant turned his gaze out to sea. Ships, indeed. A line of ships, fourteen or fifteen great ships standing in for the harbour, the spread white sails of galleons with smaller vessels in front and behind, like so many hounds after the hunt. Every day new vessels for the King's great enterprise came to Cadiz, yet no convoy was due to land. The best bet was that it was Juan Martinez de Recalde, one of Spain's bravest admirals, returning to port with his squadron. Well, it was all good for trade, even if the King was taking over a year to pay some of his bills. There was a shout from one of a group of sailors who had been standing by a jetty, waving and shouting at the men of their round little merchant ship to send a boat out to them and save them the cost of a ferry. What was it? The merchant craned his head? Dark? Duke?

Drake. DRAKE!

The sailor had recognised the fine, sheer bow at the front, hardly any stern castle. English ships. Lean ships, sharp like greyhounds in comparison to high-sided Spanish galleons. The word cut through the crowds like a river of acid; people were turning, running, scattering as the terrible word reached their ears.

There were officials of the town shouting orders now. 'To the castle! Take refuge in the fortress!' Some soldiers were bellowing back trying to shout down the officials, turn the crowds round, but it was pointless. A river of humanity fled up to the fortress, screaming, jostling, half blinded by the dust kicked up in their maddened rush. The street that led to the main gate was little more than a passageway, the seething mass of people funnelled into it. Screams, yells. A mother was caught, trampled, her little girl knocked out of her arms, sent bowling along the ground in a pathetic little flurry of lace and linen, howling until the noise cut off, suddenly, ominously. A man was spun round by the pressure of the flesh and bone of bodies forced against him, and cannoned into the rough stone wall, crushing his head. The press was so great that he could not even reach his hands up to grasp his wound. His head was visible, distinctive with the great red gash against the white of his skin. It spun round and round, like a top whipped by a child, as the mob roared their fear, until it dropped below the level of vision, dashed to its death on the rough cobbles.

'Open the gate! Let them in!' screamed the guard.

'Idiots!' the fortress commander screamed back. 'Fools! How can I fight a battle over a carpet of babies, old men and women! How am I to despatch my messenger to call for help when these people are in my way?' he cried in desperation. 'A message must be sent to Don Pedro de Acuna. Get out of the way!'

The fortress commander's actions had at least reduced the number of civilians he had to worry about. When he finally opened the gate, bowing to the inevitable, twenty-five pathetically still bodies lay at odd angles, crumpled flotsam in the street. Don Pedro de Acuna, captain of the galleys, was indeed their only hope. He was to be addressed by the brave messenger that set forth through the throng of desperate townsfolk only by his full title. Would his six galleys, powerful ships with twin banks of oars and able to manoeuvre even in the flattest of calms, which had arrived from Gibralter only a few days earlier, be able to defend the harbour? How much help could the town's soldiers be in covering the Puental, the rock-strewn area of wasteland that divided the outer and inner harbour, the most likely place for the pagans to land?

The English boats swept in to Cadiz harbour with as much confidence and bravado as if they were a squadron of ships under the command of the King of Spain. The galleys, apparently the only warships in Cadiz, came out to meet them, the water sparkling in the sun as it cascaded off the rising and falling oars. The English guns belched iron, and the galleys turned away, oars smashed. Like predators with no natural enemy, the buzzing hordes of English boarded, burned and moved cargo. Waste, thought Gresham, war was about waste. Terrible, dreadful, maniacal waste. They had boarded a fine merchantman, no more than five years out of the dock by the look of her. Men with skills that had taken decades to learn had built her, and in a sane world she would have plied the trade routes of Europe for years, doing no harm to man or beast, and feeding the blood of trade through the arteries of Europe's growing population. Wood and oil, salt and wines, olives and cloth would have filled her ample hold, her needs would have kept a fine captain and his crew in work and their wives and children with their bellies filled and made even more fortunes to rich, fat merchants. And now?

The fire took hold immediately. A wooden ship, kept alive by tar and hemp, was a fire waiting to happen. It was getting dark now, and the bay was filled with the hellish glitter and roar of ships aflame. Everywhere small boats were rowing frantically, transferring cargo and in a few cases taking prize crews from the great English galleons back to the vessels Drake had decided to send home. The shadows flickering on the dark waters looked like demented gods of war dancing to the music of destruction. Few of Drake's men slept. There was too much to do.

'You! You there!' Drake was barking hoarsely at Gresham. It was the first contact they had had since the counsel in Drake's cabin. 'Let's see your mettle. Let's see if you can fight! There's a bridge links Cadiz with the mainland. Take two boats and secure it for me. Earn your keep!'

The inactivity, the waiting to be shot at had cauterised Gresham and George. They both leapt into the waiting boat, the sailors accepting their authority simply because they were dressed as gentlemen. 'Action at last!' breathed George, his craggy features lighting up with excitement. If he had any fear in him it failed to show. Probably there was none, reflected Gresham. His friend was not a complicated creature, and above all not a deceiver, for all he relished trying to understand the deceptions of others.

'Why not a bigger force?' gasped Gresham. 'Isn't the bridge the only link with the mainland? It's crucial if he wants to capture Cadiz.'

'He doesn't want to capture Cadiz,' said George excitedly. Even in a relatively large boat his weight was making it slew over to one side. 'What would he do with it if he had it? Send an army he hasn't got to hold it indefinitely against every soldier in Spain? Think, ninny! He wants to raid and burn the ships in the harbour. That's all he wants, the ships and their cargo! If he puts token force on the bridge all it does is disrupt the Spanish communications, make them think twice about sending reinforcements from the mainland until dawn. He only needs until dawn.'

They threw caution to the wind, heading straight for the bridge. As a result of their headstrong, uselessly youthful courage, there was no way they could hide when their nemeses appeared from behind a sand bank. The galleys leaped out at them from the flickering gloom, heading straight for them like an arrow. They had been hiding in the shallows, waiting for just such an assault. Mannion clutched Gresham's arm. Alarming. This was a display of emotion, a revelation of feeling. Even a sense of panic. Mannion never panicked. Mannion was a rock.

'Master!' That word. Mannion hardly ever called him that. After all, Mannion was his father. His brother. His friend. He turned to him, pushing down the new feeling of seasickness that the motion of the small boat caused him, intending to tell him to stop fawning. Mannion's expression stopped him dead.

'Master!' Mannion repeated. 'We're dead meat. D'ye hear me? Dead meat. Those galleys . . .' he motioned to the shadows bearing down on them, 'they ain't got ship-killing guns. They've got man-killing guns! They'll carve us dead. *Get us out of here!*'

Gresham had never heard that pleading tone from Mannion before. But he suddenly saw that the galleys were even nearer than Mannion had thought. George was gaping, open-mouthed at them, realising even before Gresham that to all intents and purposes they were dead. As if on cue, the leading galley opened fire on the English boats. A gout of angry red and orange flame shot out from the bow. The twenty-five-pounder hit lucky. Appalled Gresham saw the second boat dissolve in a welter of timber, blood, flesh and bone, all fragmented into nothingness by the massive impact of the iron ball. Cries, screams from the water.

'Out of here!' barked Gresham, and the tiller swung round and the oars bit desperately into the water. A fighting madness seemed to overcome Gresham, a dizzy excitement at the prospect of death. 'We're dead!' he said to his astonished crew, and saw the oars fumble, fall out of time. 'We're dead by all accounts, because a feeble little boat like ours can't match the oars of that beast!' He motioned backwards with his head to the second galley, which he could hear and feel bearing down on them. 'Or to be more exact,' he propounded, holding himself upright in the bow of the boat as if he was delivering a lecture to his Cambridge students, 'we're dead unless we can row like devils and fuck these Spanish bastards back to Hell!'

There was a cheer from the men, and the boat leaped forward as if it had been struck by lightning. They could smell the galley now, that same raw stench of human defecation that he had caught on the wind earlier. How did those on these ships survive this stench? Or did they simply become inured to it? Gresham turned. It was possible for an intelligent man to admire Spain. It was difficult for him to do at this particular moment. The second galley had pulled round, was heading away from them, chasing two pinnaces who had come too close. The first galley was bearing down on them, like

65

an evil, dark gull, its wings the outspread oars lifting and falling to the rhythm of the drumbeat that Gresham could now hear on the night air. Their relatively small longboat had started faster, being the more nimble. Yet the galley was picking up speed all the time. Would they fire again? Of course they would. Gresham remembered how long it had taken the men aboard the *Elizabeth Bonaventure* to reload their cannon. An equivalent time for the Spaniards? The galleys were crack vessels, front-line ships. What had Mannion said? The bow guns were on brass rails, easily slung back for reloading. So knock seconds off the time for the English crew. His brain was computing loose mathematics at a frantic pace, figures of timing that started from conjecture and vague memory and whose ending could be complete fantasy. From somewhere in his brain came a count-down, a vision of the Spanish seamen heaving their gun back, flushed with pride and excitement at a direct hit on the first boat, and with their first shot! Scour the barrel. Sponge out the gun. Ram the powder charge down the barrel. Pack it tight. Choose the ball, the one that looked most round and perfectly formed – a bad gunner might force the ball through the iron circles he was issued with to test its calibre, a good one would simply judge with his eye – ram it down the barrel, forcing it snug against the powder charge. Prime the pan with loose powder now, or wait 'til the gun was run forward? Wait, of course, in case hurling the gun forward on its brass rails dislodged the fragile powder base in the priming pan. Settle the gun. Aim it, yanking out the iron pins crudely positioned under the brass barrel, lowering the muzzle so that it bore down on the insolent longboat full of men with the impudence to think that they could capture and sack Cadiz. Then, wait for the roll of the ship to bring the gun to bear, guess the exact timing of that roll, allow for the time it takes to apply the burning fuse to the priming powder the time it takes for the powder to ignite and send its flaring message into the barrel of the cannon and its major powder charge . . .

Now, his brain said. At this very moment the Spanish gunner would be applying the slow match to the priming powder in his great cannon. Gresham lunged for the tiller and yanked it round to starboard. The oarsmen on that side found their blades digging deeper into the water, throwing them off balance. It helped the boat slew round even faster. A second later, the burning flare of the cannon was followed by the bellow of its rabid rage. The ball skipped into the water no more than three feet from their side, three feet from where they would have been if Gresham had not instinctively hurled his craft round when he did. A great spout of water drenched the boat, soaking the men. They cheered! The idiots cheered, as if escaping death by seconds was a matter for celebration!

Gresham was counting down the loading process in his mind again. He was too far from shore to beach the boat and run. He could jink to left or right, of course, but his tighter turning circle would bring him inside the range of the Spaniards and their massed ranks of marksmen. He felt a tap on his arm. 'There!' said one of the crew. 'Captain! There!' Captain? Where had Gresham earned his commission, he thought? *Ninety*. Ninety seconds before the gun fired again. Why hadn't they opened fire with the other two bow guns? Because the target was so derisory? Because they were concentrating the best gunners on the main weapon? *Eighty-five*. The crewman was pointing to a line of water rippling in the reflected light from the burning ships in the harbour. Rippling? That must mean the water dragging over shallow ground. Too shallow for their boat? Too shallow for the pursuing galley? Would the galley's helmsman see the shoal from the height of his post, the slight ripples so much clearer the lower down and closer the watcher was? *Seventy-five*.

Life was a gamble. Death was a gamble. Gresham half closed his eyes, took a deep breath. *Sixty*. He commandeered the boat again, this time hurling it round to run over the shallows. If they grounded they were all dead. Would the galley follow them? Perhaps it would just stand off, try to get close enough to rake them with musket fire or send two, three of its own boats to board their own. *Fifty-five*. A musket ball smashed into the side of their boat, sending fine splinters into the nearest crew. Gresham stumbled, regained his balance and touched his shoulder briefly. The crew cursed, but left the tiny spears of wood sticking from their flesh, keeping rowing, rowing, rowing. Lucky shot, Gresham registered. They were fifty or sixty feet out of range still. A musketeer or two risking a double charge of powder? *Forty-five*.

The galley was turning to follow them! The graceful beat and slap of the oars in the water could now be heard clearly, the sheer beauty of the lithe creature pursuing them at total odds with its threat of death. *Twenty*. Something in Gresham's brain rang a warning, some dark and buried instinct. Now! His brain told him. They were going to fire now!

The sharp crack of the cannon came just as the tiller bit into his hand. He saw the flash before he heard the noise, half turned round to check his dread instinct. He would swear for the rest of his days that he felt the passing of the ball above his head, smelled its hot breath as it brushed over them, landing beyond with a great splash of water. The gunner had fired too much on the up-roll, sent the ball high. And it was off-line too, some eight or nine feet to port. The galley's turn had foxed the gunner.

Something scraped, a noise of wood on gravel. Gresham looked over the side. Little wavelets skittled over the surface of the dark water, yet even in that dark Gresham could sense a difference in the texture of light reflecting back from the waves. The shoal! They were over it! The noise had been an oar suddenly hitting shingle, only a foot or two below the surface. He felt the slightest of drags on the hull, and then their boat shot forward, as an arrow released from a bow. Gresham turned to look at the Spanish ship, bearing down on them, now almost within musket range. As if on cue, pinpricks of light started to show from its side galleys, and the air was full of tiny whistlings and the plop of musket balls falling into water. A man cried out, flung an arm away from the double-manned oar as if the wood had suddenly caught flame. Musket ball, on or near his elbow.

Out in the bay several hulks were still burning fiercely, the fierce yellow and orange of the flames clouded by the thick black smoke.

The rising, falling flickering light revealed ships moving, frantic activity. Ashore, the port commander had ordered barrels of pitch to be set at strategic points, and these were adding to the light and the smoke, some trick of the wind taking the smoke from the burning ships and that from the shore to a point in the middle of the bay, and sending a huge column spiralling up towards the moon, as if all the devils in Hell were cooking a mighty meal with damp wood. Gresham stood at the stern of the boat, not scorning to drop to the deck to avoid the musket fire but simply not realising it as a danger. Head flung back, an expression of total concentration on his face, not a muscle moving without it being ordered to do so, he looked like a dark, young god manning a vessel on the Styx. In the boat, in front of him, fifteen men were flinging themselves at their oars, sweat glistening on their filthy brows, breath hoarse and gasping. The wounded man was writhing in agony in the belly of the boat, clutching his arm, the wet, sticky flow of blood staining his tunic and tingeing the water swilling around in the bottom.

There was a gasp from two or three of the men, staring aft over Gresham's shoulder, and with no order given they stopped rowing, the boat rapidly losing way and starting to bob in the slight waves. They sensed the galley shiver as her keel brushed over the shoal. The captain must have realised the danger only at the last minute, ordered the helm hard over, because she was swinging round even as she struck. It was not a dramatic thing. Rather the graceful length of the galley heeled over as it started to turn, but instead of righting itself once the new course had been set, the heel became more and more extreme, the bow and then the whole hull rising up as it was pushed onto and over the shoal. The oars on her starboard side, so beautiful in the rigid orchestration of their movement, started to flail pathetically in the air as the side rose up too high for them to bite into the water. Soon the great, long timbers began to bang and crash into each other, dropping tiredly to smash against the hull like flopping fish too long out of water. With a grinding, wrenching noise the galley finally came to a halt, slewed round on its side, stranded.

Fourteen men stood up and cheered, three of the sailors hurled their hats up into the air, threatening to roll the boat right over and do the Spaniards' job for them. Gresham nearly lost his footing, stumbled and had to fling a hand out to grab the side. 'Sit down you stupid bastards!' yelled Mannion. He had taken an oar right at the back, placing himself closest to Gresham, 'unless you want to swim home!' The men grinned at him, touched their foreheads mockingly, and sat down. Mannion bellowed at George.

'And sit in the middle of the bloody boat, will you? Unless you want to sink us after the bloody Spaniards couldn't!' George roared with laughter, and moved his body. The boat lost its list. Trumpets sounded from way behind the galley, and even this far away the clattering sound of mounted men could be heard from the bridge. The Spaniards had seen a great ship run itself aground. A sentry had assumed it was one of the great English galleons come to land men and cut off Cadiz from reinforcements.

Gresham looked at the men in the boat. He spoke with a quiet authority that belied his age. And the men listened. How strange that the men did not seem to see his fear, the dread of the ball smashing to his body, and the even worse fear of being maimed and crippled.

They found two whole men alive from the other boat, another one clutching a broken arm and a fourth with a splinter in his gut that was like half a spear and would take a day to kill him, agonisingly. And it could just as easily have been any one of us, Gresham was thinking, had the chief gunner on the galley decided to make their boat his first target. A lottery. The role of a dice. It was bad to place too much value on life, thought Gresham, when its chances were so random.

Hands reached down from the deck of *Elizabeth Bonaventure* to haul the wounded men aboard. The Boat was deep in the water, Gresham noticed, riding more sluggishly than he had ever seen her, every corner crammed with looted cargo. There would be even less space to sleep on the decks now. He stepped up, reaching for the ladder but stopped abruptly as he sensed the bulk of Mannion beside him. In the near pitch-black, with the boat heaving and tugging beneath them, Gresham turned to Mannion.

'Did Drake know those galleys were there? Did he even know it was me he was ordering to the bridge? Or was it just another gentleman adventurer he saw in the dark?'

Mannion shrugged. 'Who knows what Drake knows? They say he uses magic to know where enemy ships are.'

'If he knew those galleys were there, then I think he just tried to murder me.'

'But it won't help his case with Burghley if you pop your clogs, will it?' Mannion replied.

There was a cry from above, a tired, impatient seaman wanting the boat for yet another journey, wanting it empty before he and his men climbed down on board.

'What better way to cover a death than that? Hot-headed young man desperate to prove himself, charges off into the dark not knowing two Spanish galleys are waiting for him. Fortunes of war. Perfect.'

'But if that were true, it means Drake was willing to kill fifteen, thirty of his own men as well.'

'Yes,' said Gresham, 'it does, doesn't it? If it were true . . .'

'It's just doesn't make sense!' said George. He was standing on the deck, leaning over with his hand out to help Gresham aboard. 'Be honest. You may have been sent to spy on Drake, but so what? You're a fly, a pin-prick in his scheme of things! Let's be blunt, you're not important enough for Drake to risk offending anyone important in London.'

'Or I'm so unimportant as for it not to matter,' said Gresham, drowning in the confusions of his life.

There was another yell from topside, and the three men clambered up, George leading Gresham. Their limbs were tired now, dragging, aching with delayed shock. Mannion always insisted Gresham went first, reckoning he would at least have a chance to grab his young charge if he slipped and fell.

Drake may have used magic to find Spanish ships. He seemed to need no magic to find Gresham. If he was surprised to see the return, his exhausted, drawn face did not show it. 'AND WHY ARE YOU HERE AND NOT ON MY BRIDGE?' he roared. 'I sent you to guard a bridge, not to run home with your tail between your legs at the sight of a few miserable Spaniards!'

It was a gross accusation of cowardice. Gresham stared calmly at him, the only light the dull flicker of a lantern with the creaking rigging acting as a night chorus. He reached up to his left shoulder, where there was a ragged tear in the Jack of Plate. Gresham fumbled in the tear, enlarging it slightly, and drew out a flattened lump of lead. Mannion had seen him stagger as the galleon had been at its closest to them, but thought it merely a response to the boat dipping into a wave. Gresham's eyes did not leave Drake's. He tossed the fragment of spent musket ball towards Drake, who made no movement to catch it. It fell softly against Drake's doublet, rattled to the deck and rolled away. Gresham was angry now, as angry as he had ever been.

'I'm willing to prove my bravery, Sir Francis,' he said calmly, eyes still locked with Drake's. And for once he felt calm, not having to hide the tremors of his heart, the uncertainties of his mind. 'Prove it in the accepted fashion, if so be your will, and on this deck. But I'm not prepared to be a fool. Eleven of your men are dead, one more likely to be so within days. Only a fool would take a longboat of men armed with swords and muskets against a fully-armed galley. But if you wish me to do so, I'll step back into that boat, with my servant here, and row down the throat of the galley that's still patrolling out there. It won't get you your bridge. Thirty men in small boats will never get you that. But it will get you a death, if that's what you want. And it will give me my honour.'

Sometimes death would be a release, thought Gresham. Secretly did he yearn for its simplicity, a curtain brought down on a life he no longer felt he could control?

There was a stunned hush from the men, a blur of movement. Suddenly Drake had a pistol in his hand and was pointing it directly between Gresham's eyes. His thumb reached up, and without the barrel wavering an inch Drake cocked the gun. Gresham felt rather than saw Mannion stir beside him, knew that Mannion was about to reach for one of the two throwing knives he kept inside his sleeve. He gave a quick flick of his head. Mannion stepped half a pace back. Drake saw the nod, flickered a glance to Mannion and then back to Gresham.

'When I want to kill you,' said Drake, 'I will.'

He fired the pistol. He must have swung it inches aside just as he fired. Gresham felt nothing, saw only the orange flame, smelled the powder. I'm alive, he thought, stunned. Alive. I can still feel. The bullet passed harmlessly into the black void that lay beyond the *Bonaventure*. Drake roared with laughter and tucked the pistol back into his belt.

'The Spaniards couldn't kill you, Henry Gresham, in three tries. I could have killed you in one. And by the way, you're right,' he said conversationally to Gresham. 'I should have sent two or three of the pinnaces, not two longboats with no artillery. It was a mistake. A mistake men have died for. I will pray for them. It was also a mistake I recognised almost as soon as it was made. That's why the second galley turned away, to chase off the two pinnaces I sent as reinforcement,' he said solemnly. 'And you,' he said, talking to Gresham but turning to his crew, 'you'd better be advised to pray that I don't decide to kill you. You see, I'm far better at it than the Spaniards!'

A gust of laughter came from his men as Drake retreated into his cabin.

'Jesus!' swore Mannion, hand only now retreating from the hilt of his knife. 'Where did they get that one from?' 'Not from Jesus, I think,' said Gresham, tiny shudders of exhaustion starting to pass through his taut body. All he wanted now was to sleep. And not to dream at all.

'Interesting,' said George. He had found a strip of dried meat from somewhere, and was munching it. 'My father's money probably paid for the powder in that gun he just fired at you.'

*

How strange it was that Spain demanded two things of its leading nobles, other than faith in the true God, thought the Duke of Medina Sidonia. The first was to know how to service and run an estate, to be a glorified farmer whose responsibility was with the people who grew the crops as well as with the crops themselves. The second was to be a soldier, to know how to kill those very same men and women, to destroy rather than to make anything grow. Well, the Duke's beloved orange groves were in no danger of destruction, and the men tending them looked well enough. He enjoyed it here more than anywhere else. In the great house he could never be alone. Here in the peace of the groves the men had work to do, and knew enough of their master's habits to carry on about their business, seeming to ignore him and speak only when spoken to, allowing him his only moments of relaxation from the inexorable duties his rank and his household forced upon him.

Was it true? Or had the previous day's messenger simply left too early, and therefore merely reported a rumour before the real truth had emerged? What was certain was that the Queen of Scots was dead, a fact that Sidonia guessed would change the whole political perspective of Spain. King Philip of Spain, locked away in the rocky isolation of the Escorial Palace, working eight, nine, ten hours a day at his interminable papers, pained by gout – what would he do now? Would this insult to a Catholic Queen in a land Philip had once reigned over tip Philip's hand over to war? Sidonia would be loyal to his monarch. To be otherwise was unthinkable. Yet here in the quiet of his groves, on the land his family had owned for generation after generation, he sometimes allowed himself to think the unthinkable: To go to war over Mary would be farcical. A woman who had claimed Catholicism as others claim a warm cloak on a cold night, she had first chosen to marry a syphilitic idiot who most of Europe thought she murdered, and then capped it by marriage to a rampaging drunkard of a Scots warlord. And Mary was a product of the French royal line, Spain's greatest enemy and threat! Was Spain to go to war for a changeling whore who had once styled herself Queen of France?

74

Sidonia was no genius. Patience was as important a quality for a Spanish nobleman as brains, yet his mind was no slouch, and faster, he feared, than the slow brain of his King. Here in the quiet of the groves it was clear to him that King Philip was out of touch in his isolation and that it was not always wise to assume that God was totally on one's side. There had to be something humanity could not understand about God, had there not, or else God would be too close to humans? Sidonia would be happier if his King listened less to God and more to the advice of the men in touch with the real Spain. Surely God sometimes chose to speak to his anointed through his ministers and nobles, as God had chosen to speak to his people through the prophets? If war had to be fought at all, better to fight it in the name of the English attacks on Spanish shipping. Something deep in Sidonia's soul rebelled against the possibility of war at sea. An army could be delayed by a storm. A fleet could be destroyed, with neither man nor beast having control over the elements. In the game of chance that was war, why add the wholly unpredictable elements of wind, sea and storm into the equation?

The news – or was it rumour – that concerned Sidonia now was about the one man who seemed to make the sea work for Spain. The Marquis of Santa Cruz was not just Spain's High Admiral, he was the most successful Admiral of all time. It was his galleys that had crushed the Turks at the Battle of Lepanto, saving Europe for Christianity and turning back the tide of Islam that seemed hellbent on placing mosques in Barcelona and Madrid. The irascible, cruel old man had been ill for some while, that was widely known. Now the messenger reported that he was in his death throes. Sidonia came to the edge of one of the groves, and let his gaze rest on the rolling landscape before him. How much more secure was dry land than the rolling fortunes of the sea. Yet he feared King Philip would launch his Armada against England with his High Admiral no longer at its head. Could it be done? Well, anything could be done given enough time, money and the support of God. But without Santa Cruz it would be an infinitely more perilous venture. For once, the gentle scent of the fruit, sharp yet invigorating, failed to cleanse his soul. He left the groves a deeply troubled man.

The messenger from Cadiz reached him in the middle of the night. The harbour was under attack from an overwhelming force of English ships, almost certainly led by Drake himself. He was awake almost immediately, before the servant who brought the message was through the door and halfway across the room. He struggled to sit up from under the rich silk sheets, calling for his Secretary in a calm voice. There was no point in hurrying the dressing process. He could dictate orders just as quickly while a host of men swarmed round him, offering him the pot to piss in, the fine linen shirt and the sheer hose, the value of which would have kept one of his peasants in bread for a year. How many to help him dress? Ten, maybe fifteen, not to mention the maids bobbing and curtseying just outside the door. Great men had to appear to be great, he reminded himself as he had done all his life.

Andalusia was a military province for Spain. The troops, albeit mostly local militia, were there precisely to repel raids from corsairs, and he had hopes of getting three hundred cavalry and nearer three thousand troops ready to march and ride within hours. The problem was assembling them from their various garrisons. Would it be best to make his home at San Lucar the rendezvous? Or get them to join him on the road? Or send them straight to Cadiz? Speed, he decided, speed was the primacy. The troops could march for their lives, straight for Cadiz. He would not make it before midday; many of them would be there by dawn. What matter if he was not there to command them? A half-smile flickered across his face as he struggled into the snug-fitting doublet. They were probably better off being commanded by the Captain of the fortress in Cadiz, the Duke thought, than by a farmer whose family owed more than nine hundred thousand ducats. Any more delay and Drake could have landed men, sacked the town and his sailors impregnated enough women to bring up a whole new city of heathen bastards.

76

He pushed back the urge to grab a drink and some meat and run for his horse. Instead he allowed himself to be sat in the ornate dining room while varieties of cold meat from last night's supper were paraded before him. He picked at them, allowing himself a maximum of twenty minutes for the charade to go on, before elegantly wiping imaginary grease off his moustache and beard, and rising. The footmen stood back and bowed deeply. The retinue was small, only thirty mounted men as guards and fifteen servants, but it would have to do. The mounted soldiers who normally provided his escort were the best riders, and the best mounted. It would have been madness not to send them to the outposts and garrisons to direct the troops and the militia to Cadiz.

He did not give a backward glance to the orange groves he so loved. He simply nodded to his family, hastily assembled to bid him farewell. To show too much emotion would be to show weakness, reducing the distance between himself and the ordinary men and women over whom he ruled. He pushed out of his mind the urge to turn to lock eyes with his wife. They said he was henpecked, married to a Portuguese harridan. How little they knew. Nevertheless, once out of sight, he dug his golden spurs into the side of his horse, feeling it rear up and surge forward like the fine beast it was. Not even the great Duke was safe from the wrath of King Philip if he arrived to find Cadiz a smouldering ruin. Involuntarily, he looked to the skyline, damning himself immediately for a fool, knowing the distance was much too far to see any smoke, unless Drake had set the whole world alight.

CHAPTER 4

May – June 18th, 1587
The Netherlands; The Capture of the
San Felipe

Alessandro Farnese, Duke of Parma and Governor of the Netherlands, read the letter from his kinsman Philip II of Spain with total concentration. His aides waited silently by his side. He was a handsome figure. He had been called from sitting for his portrait. As a result he was extravagantly dressed, with no bonnet or cap but a vast, fashionable ruff angled forward so that its back was halfway up the back of his head. The doublet was picked out with gold lace inlays, the puffed sleeves of a different colour. Yet despite all the finery it was his face that commanded attention: angular, the nose straight, the fine head of close-cropped dark hair, the beard and moustache perfect of their kind. It was the eyes that drew one to him: dark, yet with a mysterious depth to them, the eyes of a man who had seen and felt too much. Strange, newcomers thought. Here was a man, a grandson of King Charles V of Spain, a nephew of King Philip II, born not so much with a golden spoon in his mouth as born with the world at his feet. To add to his birth came striking good looks, a high intelligence and the body of a fine, wild animal. Why did his eyes speak of such sadness? The head of the House of Farnese commanded respect in Europe, not

78

just in Italy. Yet from the start the Duke of Parma had chosen the military life. At twenty-six years of age he had been an aide-de-camp at the Battle of Lepanto. Many young men had died in that epic battle. Those who had survived had an honour no man could ever take away from them and no man equal. Was it not at Lepanto that the infidel hordes had been stopped in their tracks, a victory won not for man but for God?

And then at the ridiculous age of thirty-eight years he had been placed in command of the King of Spain's Army of Flanders, that most troubled of provinces where the local Dutch were not only fighting Spain, their temporal master, but fighting God with their Protestant heresy. He had recaptured most of Flanders by his wits, his unconventional tactics and by his capacity to command the fierce loyalty of his soldiers. They had said Antwerp was a general's grave, crowed in advance at the humiliation the young Duke of Parma would meet there. They had swallowed their words when Antwerp had fallen. If Drake was a god of evil to many Spaniards, a man whose success could only have been achieved by the sale of his soul to the Dark Lord, then Parma was the equivalent to the English.

He finished reading the letter, carefully folding it and handing it back to his secretary. 'We are to invade England,' he announced to his men. They looked at each other, questions on their brows. 'The King will send a great Armada, is assembling it even now. It will occupy the English fleet while we sail over the Channel to England.' His tone was flat, giving nothing away. He had thirty thousand men under his command, the finest army in Europe, in the world. No one doubted that if they could be landed in England they would cut through its heart like a crossbow bolt through paper. There was silence. Finally, one of his aides found the courage to speak. He had served the Duke from the days of Lepanto, was the most trusted of all. He often acted as spokesman for the others.

'We have no deep water port,' he said. 'The Dutch have shallow-draft vessels that can patrol the coast, vessels that can come inshore in a manner that no great Portuguese galleon can.' It was no secret that the recent conquest of Portugal meant that the core of any Spanish navy would be the fine seagoing vessels of Portugal. Spanish galleys were designed for the calm waters of the Mediterranean. Portugal's empire, now subsumed to Spain, had been built on ocean-going galleons, some said the strongest and most durable in the world.

Silence. Parma gazed at the man, but said nothing.

'Those Dutch fly-boats could blast our shallow barges out of the water before we came within sight of a Spanish armada,' the aide continued.

'And we would never take Antwerp,' Parma said, after another long pause. Yet they had taken Antwerp. The implication was clear. They did the impossible.

'How?' It was a senior officer, another man Parma had total trust in. He had been stranded with him for hours behind enemy lines – Parma shared the dangers and rigours of his men. He was as often in the front line with his men as he was found at base. It was one reason why they loved him so much.

'How did we take Antwerp?' Parma replied. 'I thought you knew. Actually, I thought you planned most of it.' There was laughter round the table, an easing of the tension.

'Not Antwerp, my Lord,' said the man with a smile and a deferential bow of his head, acknowledging the joke. 'How to get our soldiers over to England and past the Dutch?'

'There are canals, old and new,' said Parma dreamily. He had shown a savage capacity to cut new canals through the flat lands of the Netherlands in days, getting his men where no one had expected them to be. 'There are empty boats to be sent to the coast, drawing off the damned Dutch in the face of their real enemy. There are embarkations at night-time when not even the Dutch can see what is happening, if it happens fast enough.' He stood up, unexpectedly. His men bowed their heads. 'But most of all, we have an army. What say we take Sluys? Ostend? All of Flanders? Even Walcheren?'

The men stiffened, drawing themselves unwittingly to attention.

Their General was suggesting a smashing, final blow to end the war, that endless haemorrhage of Spanish money and blood in the Netherlands. Parma held out his hand to his Secretary, clicking his finger to demand the letter from the King of Spain back. Parma did not open it again. He held it between his thumb and forefinger, away from his body.

'I will have time to think over these matters. I will not be visiting Parma. The King has suggested my duties lie here.'

So permission had been refused for the Duke to visit the Dukedom he had only inherited that year! He had formally requested leave of absence. Leave of absence in the winter, when campaigning was impossible and the opposing armies settled in to quarters.

It had been refused. But evidently he was too valuable in the Netherlands, Philip too concerned perhaps that if he left there for his ancestral homeland, changed the mist-clinging, cold and damp Netherlands for the hot beauty of Parma, he might never return. The men gathered round the Duke gave a collective sigh. They, the privileged inner cabinet, knew more than any their General's yearning to see his homeland. He had not even been educated there, sent instead to be brought up and educated in Spain.

'Well,' said Parma, 'We have one country still to conquer, here in Flanders. Now let us set about conquering another.'

Gresham could not sleep. They had been becalmed in Cadiz just as Drake was preparing to leave. Miraculously, Drake's luck had held. The two vast cannon hauled on to the beach by the Spaniards had missed the English fleet with virtually every shot, and no Spanish vessels had arrived to block them in the harbour. The Spanish troops marshalled in good order in the town, had no way of reaching the English ships. The Spaniards had tried to send fireships down on the English fleet at night, but the absence of wind meant that they had been easily hauled aside by small boats. Drake strode the quarterdeck, appearing to be in high spirits despite the perilous nature of his position. His Secretary, lugubrious as ever, was trying to run through figures of captured goods. Drake was clearly bored.

The Secretary sighed and looked out over the bay to ten or fifteen flaring points, burning or burned-out Spanish fireships.

'Well, my Lord,' he said, 'at least the Spanish seem to be doing your job for you.'

Drake stopped his pacing, looked down at his Secretary, and then went to the front rail.

'Look you there, boys!' he shouted at the top of his voice. Most of the crew had gathered in the cool of the night on the open deck, few were asleep. Drake waved his hand to point at the burning ships. 'The Spaniards are doing our job for us!' There was a great cheer and wave of laughter from the men. In no time a boat was being launched to check if any of the fireships still posed a danger. Or was the real reason to take the joke around the fleet, Gresham wondered?

It was stalemate, until a fine wind blew up in the morning and sent Drake out to sea a significantly richer man than when he had first sailed into Cadiz harbour.

'Well,' George said, surveying the wreck of the harbour, 'that won't help King Philip invade!'

'Will it stop it?' asked Gresham.

'No,' said George, thinking for a moment. 'Not if the King of Spain keeps his nerve. But it will delay it. For months.'

George was snoring loudly now, his arm thrown part over Gresham, giving him pins and needles. He gently removed George's arm, sat up. It was Mannion, shaking him.

'We're on the move. Thank God I can't smell Spaniards any more.'

'They can't smell worse than you,' Gresham yawned. 'Why do you hate Spain so much?' he said, more to pass the time while his brain reconnected with his aching body than for any real interest in the answer. 'I know I ought to hate it. I'm English. But I can't believe total ill of a country that builds such beautiful buildings. And there's an appalling beauty in the Mass; just listen to Byrd's music. And they saved Europe from the Turks at Lepanto. It's not a country without honour. Why do you hate it so?'

82

'I don't hate Spain as much as I hate that bloody Don Alvaro de Bazan, 1st Marquis of Santa Cruz,' said Mannion. He spoke the name of Spain's High Admiral of the Seas perfectly, with what seemed to Gresham to be an excellent Spanish accent. There was a tone of venom in his servant's voice Gresham had never heard before.

'Why so much hatred of a man you've never even met?' asked Gresham his curiosity aroused now.

'Well, there you're wrong. I have met him, see.' Mannion was refusing eye contact, watching the sway of the rigging.

'Tell,' said Gresham, simply, sitting down with his back to the rail, knees clasped in his arms, boat cloak wrapped round him to ward off the chill of dawn. He knew if he pushed Mannion the man would retreat. Mannion did what he wanted, not what he was told. It was why he respected him and valued his friendship so much.

'Well,' said Mannion, after what was clearly for him some troubled thought, 'suppose there's no 'arm in your knowing. Particularly if it stops you sellin' out to Spain, not as you'll listen to anything I say, o' course. 'Cept for one thing. This stays between me and you, right? No blabbing of it to one of those fine girls you take to bed with you. No blabbing when you're in drink at College. If they ever let us back, that is.' Mannion looked at the prone figure of George, reassuring himself that he was truly asleep.

Who would I tell your secrets to, thought Gresham? I have no one else I trust, except this other lump of a man asleep by my side. Would I break your confidence, you, the oldest, the best and the only friend I have? 'No blabbing,' he said simply. Mannion looked at him, nodded, and sat down beside him. All the action was up in the bow or at the stern, the waist of the vessel for once surprisingly deserted.

'You see, I were a ship's boy. Never known who me parents were. All I know was that the man who brought me up – a cobbler, he was, and a bloody bad one judging by the number of customers who came back to complain – told me that I were a bastard, and a charge on his good nature. That was in between thumpin' me, o'

83

course. Thumping me was about the only fun 'e had. So as soon as I was big enough, and I always were big, he packed me off, sold me to a captain sailing out of Deptford.'

Ship's boys performed a variety of lowly jobs on board ships. If they survived they picked up enough knowledge to get a decent berth as a swabber, the lowest rating. From there was the path to becoming a seaman proper. It was a rough, dangerous way to learn a trade, and there were dark whispers in every port of sailors turning to the boys for sexual satisfaction, of boys who objected ending their lives as an anonymous splash overboard in a lonely sea.

''E weren't a bad man, Captain Chicken, though it warn't the best name for a sea-going Captain.' Mannion's accent, never refined, was slipping back, Gresham noticed. Was he talking to Gresham, or talking to himself? 'Anyway, I stuck with 'im five or six years, 'til I were ready to take on a job as real seaman. Surprised, weren't you, when I knew so much about ships?' He turned to Gresham, who nodded, fascinated, gripped by the unfolding human drama. 'I know more than half these buggers 'ere,' said Mannion gesturing dismissively to the crew gathered fore and aft. 'Then the Captain, 'e got a new ship. Off to Cadiz we was, takin' fine cloth from England and bringin' back fine wine.'

'Cadiz?' Gresham sat up, turned to look Mannion in the face. 'Here? This port? Where we are now?'

'The very same,' said Mannion, 'fuckin' awful hole that it is. We'd arrived, taken the cargo off and were waitin' for the wine to be loaded. Some delay or other, don't know why. Crew went ashore – not me, I was waitin' on the Captain and his good wife – and the crew ashore got into a fight with some Spaniards. Next thing we know, fifty soldiers are clamberin' up the side o' the old *Deptford Rose*, and before we can think we're all of us ashore and clapped in a Spanish jail, God help us! They treat their animals better than they treated us!'

Mannion paused. Gresham sensed that the years had rolled back, and that he was, in his mind, actually back there, in the foul, stinking cell they had thrust him into.

84

'Anyroad, once they've roughed us up a bit, me and the crew, and 'ad their fun, we're hauled in front of what they call a court. Sir Francis Fucking Drake 'ad just knocked off a load of Spanish ships, so the English were really popular in Cadiz. And guess who the senior naval officer is, in charge of this Court and running the whole show?'

'The Marquis of Santa Cruz,' whispered Gresham. 'Was it really him?'

'Oh, it was 'im alright. His bloody galleys had come out o' the Med for some reason, were staying in Cadiz – just like those bastard galleys that nearly did for us yesterday. They do it a lot, send the galleys out, just to prove they're sea-going vessels, not just right for the Med. Rarely get further north than Lisbon, tell the truth. They're not sea-going vessels, really, you see. Not North Sea vessels, at any rate.' Mannion paused.

'What happened?' asked Gresham, caught up in the drama of the story.

'We were 'eathen pirates, apparently. Funny, I'd thought we were just God-fearing Englishmen trying to earn an honest living. The 'eathen pirate was Lord Fuckin' Drake, but they hadn't captured 'im. They'd captured us, so we were sentenced in 'is place.'

'Sentenced?'

'Sentenced. In the case of the Captain, to burn as a heretic. We were all mustered to watch it. Includin' his wife, of course. God wants good women to stand by and see their God-fearing 'usband burned to a crisp, apparently. Or at least, that's Spanish religion. After that, those of us with any muscle were sent to the galleys. It's the smell I'll never forget. That burnin' smell. That smell of a human bein' burned.'

'You were a galley slave?' asked Gresham, incredulous. 'But that's . . . awful! It's unbelievable . . .' He was lost for words. Gresham knew that, incredibly, some of those working the oars in Spanish galleys were 'volunteers', forced by poverty and imminent starvation. Yet he also knew how many were common criminals, in effect condemned to death by their service.

'Not as unbelievable as it was for me,' said Mannion. 'Santa Cruz, 'e was eatin' his dinner when he sentenced us. Three types o' wine, I remember. They chain you to a bench,' he said bitterly, 'all the time you're at sea. You sit at the bench, you sleep at the bench, you eat what crap they give you at the bench, you piss and shit at the bench. And once you get chained there, you expect to die at the bench. 'Cept it's not all bad.' He turned, and grinned at Gresham. 'It's a padded bench, y'see. Otherwise you'd have the skin stripped off your arse in half an hour. Food's alright, really. Surprising. They need to keep you fit, you see. And all because of 'is Highness the Marquis of Santa Cruz. I'll never forget it. 'E couldn't give a shit. We was just dirt, flies to be stamped on by 'is fine leather boot! They called it a court but they'd made their minds up long before we was ever dragged before 'em. It were a farce. Men's lives at stake, and it bein' treated halfway between a joke and when a farmer decides to kill an' eat a chicken.'

'So how did you get out?'

'Luck. Pure luck. The bloody Spaniards talk about Lepanto as if it wiped the bloody Turks off the face of the water. Well, it didn't. We were sent – our boat, that is – to sort out some bloody Turkish corsairs, 'cept they sorted us out. Rams. These galleys have bloody great rams on their front, lined with brass. Our captain must 'ave got it wrong. Anyroad, we was rammed. Three benches in front o' me. I can see that brass end shinin' now, straight through the 'ull. Pulped those men. Then, as we were still movin' forward, their ram splintered the hull, like it were paper, crashin' on down to us. Man on the right o' me, caught by the ram, smashed to bits. Man on the left 'o me, bloody great splinter, straight into his gut.'

'And you?' said Gresham.

'Not a mark on me. Ram broke the bench exactly where the ring was sunk to hold the chain. Result? I'm free – 'cept I've got half a ton of loose chain and a ring bolt round me knees, even if it ain't attached to the ship any more. And, of course, the galley's sinking, isn't she? Water flooding through the deck, already at me knees.'

'So what happened?' asked Gresham, like the child he had never been asking for the end of a story from the mother he had never known.

'The water's comin' towards me in waves, gettin' higher all the time. And then, on top of one of them, I see the key to the padlocks round our feet. The overseer kept it in a leather wallet – 'e must have dropped it. I grab it. By this time the water's at waist height when it's at its lowest, but slappin' me in the face when it's high. So I take a deep breath, and I ducks down underneath the water, tries to get the key into the locks.'

'What then?'

'I does one, and then the ship lurches over. I lose the key. I lose the key! I'm cryin', *cryin'* d'you hear, cryin' underwater. An' I just want to breathe, don't care if it's water or air, I just got to open me lungs. And I'm clenching my fist, without thinking. And when I clench it for the last time, there's something in it.'

'The key?' Gresham breathed.

'The key! So I shove it in the second lock, thinkin' I'm dead so what the Hell. And it opens. My legs are free.'

'And then?' Gresham asked.

'Don't know,' said Mannion. 'All I know is that I'm floating on the surface. And breathing. Breathing.'

'*But how did you get home?*' asked Gresham.

'Well, now,' said Mannion, clearly deciding that he'd made enough of a confession, 'that's a different story. Save it for another day. Ended up in England. Your father gave me a job. Gardener!' Mannion barked a short, savage laugh. 'Can't tell you how good that word sounded. Gardener. Feet on God's earth for evermore. Catch me if you can wi' me feet on anything that moves ever again!' He made as if to stand up, then thought better of it, returned to Gresham's side. 'But I'll tell you one thing. When I 'eard we was goin' to Cadiz, I thought Christ! When I 'eard it was with Drake, I thought Christ Almighty! And when I saw those galleys, ain't no words no Christ ever 'eard passed through my brain. I was about to ask you to kill me if it ever looks like we're goin' to be captured by those bastards.'

'Why didn't you?'

'Thought it was daft. Thought we was dead anyway. Thought it was kind of poetic justice, someone like me being blown to bits by a bloody Spanish galley. Didn't like it, though. Never given up on anything before.'

Gresham looked deep into Mannion's eyes. He was beginning to realise what this journey must have cost Mannion in courage.

'Why did you come with me on . . . this?'

''Cos people like me can't choose what 'appens to them. If they're lucky, they can choose who it 'appens with. I chose you. So the rest follows, don't it? Fall in love with Spain, if you like and you're that stupid. Me, I don't choose countries. I choose people.'

It had been chaos when Sidonia arrived at Cadiz, guided as he had feared by the plumes of smoke. Troops were milling around the town, each under their own command. Some were drunk, and it would only be a matter of time before one or more of them went out of control and started to loot or rape. Yet with relief he saw the smoke was coming from ships in the bay, not the town.

'My Lord, what are your orders?'

The militia officer was respectful, but forceful. He knew Sidonia's reputation. A hard taskmaster, but fair. As for Sidonia, he had no training as a General, but the necessary actions seemed obvious to him. He took fifty of the best mounted troops, and rode through the town, grabbing the disorganised men as he found them, sending the drunkards off to the dungeons in the Castle and organising the remainder into detachments of mixed horse and foot. Small enough to be mobile, yet powerful enough to hurt seriously a landing party, he placed the detachments all along the shoreline, defined a command structure. He gave the command to men who he either knew, or simply those officers with natural authority. Next he ordered such few light cannon as the city could muster and placed them in hurriedly constructed batteries along the shoreline. Now let the enemy land by boat! He had Cadiz scoured for powder and shot, placing it in the cellars of the stoutest brick and stone houses, within reach of his shoreline detachments but out of range of the English guns. Messengers were sent to the galleys, apparently his only effective fighting force afloat, and a line of communication set up. There was no escape from the harbour for any Spanish vessel, so a rider was sent to the next fishing village along the coast, with enough gold to send the entire fishing fleet out to sea to search for Recalde's squadron to tell it to return to Cadiz.

By now Sidonia was exhausted, and a film of dust covered him from top to toe. It would never do. A commander had to be seen to be the part, as well as to do it. He turned to a meagre house and waited for its screeching inhabitants to be evicted by his men. They would come to no harm, and afterwards would become the talk of their friends because the great Duke had changed in their hovel. He wrinkled his nose at the stench inside, but allowed himself to be changed and put into new clothing, more resplendent than his riding garb, more slashed and jewelled. Let the people see the King's representative glitter a little in front of them. It would do no harm.

Could he do anything about the outrageous arrogance of the English ships in the harbour? Very little, he suspected. Fireships must be tried to drift down in the English vessels, but with so little wind the English could easily divert them, if their discipline and control held. Sidonia never underestimated Spain's enemies, as did so many other of his aristocratic colleagues. Heathen devils though they were, they were professionals. Yet the fireships would boost the morale of the garrison and the inhabitants, even if they failed.

He paused to take food and wine, rationing himself to half an hour before riding off to inspect the result of his day's arrangements. In a matter of hours chaos had been transformed into order. His face was calm, composed, showing sign neither of the fact that he was not displeased with his efforts, nor of the fierce anger he felt at the English impudence. For the first time he felt the desire to launch a great fleet in revenge.

The call went out for men to man a boat. Drake wished to know if any unseen problems had arisen now that the ships had left Cadiz harbour and were at sea, and subject to the full stress of wind and wave. As they scudded round the fleet, aided by the brisk wind and the tiny sails they carried, they became more and more amazed. The first shot fired from the great culverin the Spaniards had mounted in Cadiz had pierced the hull of the *Golden Lion* and carved off the leg of its master gunner, but after that, and despite the at times frantic cannonades from the shore, not a single ship reported a single hit nor a casualty. Far from being exhausted by hauling the cables to bring broadsides to bear on the lurking galleys, the crews were becoming increasingly jovial and confident, beginning to think themselves invulnerable.

Mannion was giving Gresham a lesson in gunnery as they bounced over the choppy seas to yet another English galleon. 'How can they miss so often?' Gresham had asked.

'Well, it's like this . . .' Mannion was breathing easily, despite his rowing.

'It's 'cos all gunners are stupid bastards! Pissed out o' their minds!' One of the sailors guffawed. There were no private conversations on a small boat.

'Apart from that,' said Mannion, 'powder costs a fortune, so you ain't exactly encouraged to practise. They'll have fired off more shots this morning than they've done all year.'

'Silly buggers still haven't learned much, 'ave they?' said the sailor, clearly setting himself up as the boat's chief entertainer.

'Then there's the ball. Hardly any of 'em's perfect. It's called windage. Gap between the ball and the inside o' the barrel. If it's big, the ball gets less of a push. If the fit's snug, the ball goes further.'

'Windage, is it? I thought 'as 'ow with gunners it were *all* piss and wind!'

'Then there's the powder,' Mannion continued, ignoring the running commentary made on his every word. 'It's all different, burns differently. Even the same batch can change from one day to the next.'

'End result,' said the sailor, 'is no gunner can 'it a piss-pot even if 'is dick's in it at the time!'

There was no real supply of saltpetre in England. Laborious applications of human urine were the only way to remedy nature's deficit. Every gunner in the fleet knew his powder was composed in no small part of piss. It affected their humour.

Anna had never been so bored in her life, nor so terrified. They had brought books on board, of course, even though there was a current debate over whether or not reading was likely to overtax the weaker female brain and bring on the vapours. And most of the books were sermons or edifying texts, though she had ploughed through them once, twice even, rather than face the prospect of nothing at all to engage her brain. She could walk on the quarterdeck at certain times, provided she was well protected from the sun, and feel the eyes of such men as could see her boring into her back. Well, that had been quite exciting initially, and a little thrill of a shiver had gone down her spine when she had realised how much she was the centre of attention. Then she had turned unexpectedly one day, caught sight of raw lust in a man's eyes before he could properly turn away, and she had felt sick. Her father had tried to breed horses in Goa, as much to pass the time as for any profit, but the venture had largely failed. Yet she had been brought to the field once, by accident, when they had also brought the stallion to the mare. She remembered the little foals she had been allowed to caress and give her easy love to. The end product might have been lovable, defenceless, sweet beyond belief. The process that led to it was brutal, sharp and short, a functional exercise in need and power. Would her French merchant take her like that, she thought?

It did not stop her walking the deck. She was too proud for that, and her young body demanded the exercise. Yet it reduced her pleasure in the vista of the great, rolling sea, with its permanent hint of danger, of worlds yet to be discovered and of the total magnificence of nature. She learned the names of the birds that swooped around them even far out at sea, envying their freedom to fly where they wished, their careless abandon as they found a firm

91

footing on a rolling yard arm, looking down their beaks at the dots who manned the decks below them. They had fired a cannon, once. That had been exciting. Truth be told, most of the cannon on board could not be moved, never mind loaded and fired, because cargo was piled in their way. Yet they had kept one or two ports open and hurled a broken barrel into the sea as a target, laboriously putting the ship round so as to allow the cannon to bear. The men had huffed and puffed, put slow match to cannon one, two and then three times. The thing had bellowed its noise, and Anna had seen the tiny splashes either far beyond or far to the side of the bobbing barrel. So much for battle practice.

That left reading and sewing – not practical sewing, but the highly decorative tableaux that ladies were meant to produce – and practising her languages. At least they had a plentiful supply of books with them, in Spanish, English, Italian, Latin and Greek, their bindings only partly ruined by the damp heat of Goa. Her father had believed that girls should be educated and speak different languages.

Her mother, that unfailing mainstay of her life, was clearly ill. At times she sank into a delirium so deep that for all the world she appeared as if she were dead. At other times she could talk, but was so pale that even Anna's impetuous spirit was restrained from asking her things that might increase her suffering. The ship's doctor came and made noises, but he was better suited to hacking off the legs of men who had fallen from the masthead and mangled their limbs beyond redemption.

Anna knew her mother was dying. She knew it deep down, though her mind and body had decided to cope by not letting her admit the fact even to herself. Not yet. Not just yet.

The days had seemed to pass in a blur. From Cadiz to a sun-blasted hole off Cape St Vincent called Sagres, for no obvious reason. Eleven hundred men put on shore and marched under fire for fifteen miles, and turned round again with many injured and many more angry and semi-mutinous. One Captain Borough had written to complain to Drake. Drake had court-martialled him, placed him under lock and key aboard his own ship! Sent a Captain Marchant to take charge of his ship. Then he had gone back and reduced Sagres castle to a smouldering ruin. 'Lisbon!' Drake announced before his weary crews had wiped the powder stains off their faces, or the dust off their feet. Was this the way Drake managed men? By ensuring they had no time to think? He turned to his Secretary, standing glumly by him as ever.

'We have pulled the King of Spain's beard,' said Drake quietly to him. He looked inquisitively at the Secretary, who looked back, shook his head ever so slightly, and mouthed a word. 'Swinged?' hissed Drake incredulously. 'Swinged' was a slang word used for a man having sex. An even more tired expression came over the Secretary's face, and he mouthed the word again. Drake's brow furrowed, then his bushy eyebrows shot up in delight. He turned to the crew, his voice cutting through the rigging now. 'We have *singed* the King of Spain's beard!' he announced, historically.

'Santa Cruz is in there,' said Gresham quietly. Now Drake had anchored off Lisbon, the home port of Spain's greatest admiral. Gresham asked again to be put ashore, to be met by a curt refusal. This time no reason was given.

'He'd better be bloody glad he ain't out here in front of me,' muttered Mannion.

Were they going to attack Lisbon? The men were starting to mutter. The ships were foul now from their time at sea, Lisbon heavily defended, fewer than a thousand men fit and able to march. Then the wind blew from the north, and Drake was up and away, heading back south to Cape St Vincent. Men were falling sick. Drake sent them ashore, organised two vessels to take the worst affected home. His fleet pillaged up and down the coast, destroying hundreds of small coastal vessels, the vessels Cecil had so dearly wanted sunk, the vessels carrying the barrel staves and hoops for the Armada. And Drake gave Cecil a bonus, virtually removing the Spanish tuna fishing fleet from the seas, destroying the hamlets where the fishermen lived and their nets as well as sinking their craft. The fish they caught, when dried, were a staple part of the diet for all seagoing Spanish vessels.

The release of the small, contained and ordered world of the *Elizabeth Bonaventure* was starting to pale. He was desperate to be landed to complete the task Walsingham had asked of him, paltry though it still seemed. He fretted about College, about London, starting to feel himself alienated from the only world he really knew. And he could not control his strange sense of dread, a sixth sense of unidentified danger. Did some of it come from the tall, lugubrious figure of Robert Leng, a supposed courtier to whom Drake had given passage and announced as his biographer? 'At least one man will tell the truth about my voyage!' he had announced. Gresham was learning that Francis Drake saw enemies everywhere, particularly where they probably did not exist.

And then everything changed.

Five days later, Drake took his fleet out to sea, despatched the vessels with the sick and injured on board back to England, and set off due west into the wide ocean. The Secretary made no appearance. The seamen rubbed their hands together with glee. 'That's it! 'E's seen a Spanish ship in his great glass! We're off to find some real treasure at last, lads!' one proclaimed. Two or three of the other crew muttered approving comments, circling lengths of rope carefully round so that when paid out in a hurry they would run smooth and not snag.

'Have you ever *seen* this "great glass"?' asked George, cynically. He had grave doubts that Sir Francis did actually have a magic glass showing him the position of every Spanish ship at sea. 'Course not,' one replied, pityingly. 'Everyone knows it loses its magic if anyone else other than 'im looks into it.'

Well, that was that, thought Gresham. What the hell was he to do? Drake was showing no sign of landing him, and his swimming ability did not run to jumping off the *Elizabeth Bonaventure* and managing the five miles to the Portuguese shore, even if he knew what direction it lay in.

*

'Land-ho, two points off the bow!'

What came next surprised them. 'Land-ho!' the lookout repeated, not in a normal voice but in a tone that had more than enough of a plain squawk in it, 'Two points off the bow . . . AND A FUCKING GREAT PORTUGUESE STRAIGHT IN FRONT OF IT!' There was a clattering of men to the deck and clambering up the lower stages of the rigging, and a bellow from Drake.

'Belay that language, d'ye hear?'

'Aye aye, sir. Sorry, sir.' The reply came from on high. Long pause. 'But it is truly, fuckin' big!'

There was a roar of laughter from the crew, part compounded of excitement. Drake chose to stand impassive, saying nothing.

'My God!' said Gresham beginning to think after two months at sea that he had lived all his life in the same position on the main-deck of the *Elizabeth Bonaventure*. 'She's vast! I've never seen anything so big!' Drake's ships were impressive, but the great Portuguese carrack's tonnage was probably equal to three or four of the Queen's galleons. 'Will she fight?' She towered over the English ships, making them look puny, and there was a row of potentially lethal gun ports piercing her side.

'For a bit,' said Mannion, very calm by the guardrail. 'As long as that thing you're so keen on, honour, isn't that what you call it, tells 'em to fight. She's back from the Indies, Goa probably. Packed to the gills with spices.' Mannion retreated into his own private world of sensual satisfaction. 'Pepper, cinnamon, cloves, spices. *Spices!*' He recited the names as if they were those of past lovers, which in a way they were. Mannion had a lifelong capacity to fall in love with delicately-spiced food, as well as with women. Spiced or plain. And to eat meat that was near rotten, if that was all there was. 'Silk, calico, ivory,' he added, with less enthusiasm. 'Plenty o' those. And a fair bit of jewellery. Not to mention some gold and silver – not as much as you'd get from a treasure galleon from Panama, mind, but a tidy bit all the same.'

'And women?' asked George wistfully. He had propped his great shaggy head on the guardrail, cupped in his hands like a small child.

'Mebbe,' said Mannion. 'Passengers, few servants. God help 'em! The captain'll fire a few cannon at us,' said Mannion. 'Aimed to miss, o' course, in case he gets Drake too angry. Then he'll haul down his flag, honour preserved. There'll be a lot of sick aboard. Long haul home from Goa. Few passengers. Decks piled high with cargo, so most o' the gun ports won't open, even if they wanted 'em to. Not used to pirates, these boats. Used to an easy ride 'ome.'

They looked at the vessel that they later learned was named the *San Felipe*. Drake ordered four cannon fired. Strange, thought Gresham. They were bow-on to the *San Felipe*, so the four guns they fired discharged harmlessly into the empty sea on either side of them. Three cannon replied almost immediately from the *San Felipe*. If they had been aimed, it did not show. All three splashed harmlessly into the sea, several hundreds of yards from damaging any of the English fleet rapidly closing round the vessel.

Drake responded by hauling the *Elizabeth Bonaventure* round so that her full broadside could have smashed the *San Felipe*'s hull into splinters. He waited courteously until the great carrack had passed by the very last cannon, and then ordered the ship to fire. The sea behind her was torn to shreds, but failed to sink. The *San Felipe* was left miraculously unharmed. In return, she fired a cannon into the only bit of remaining sea free from an English vessel, now that Drake's squadron was gathering in on her. A short while after, her flag fluttered down to her deck.

'Easy as that?' said Gresham to Mannion, flushed as was every other member of Drake's crew with their painless success.

'Easy as that,' responded Mannion, 'if you've got the luck of the Devil. Drake doesn't want her damaged, and 'er captain knows 'e can't win.' Privately Mannion was beginning to wonder whether Drake was God's vengeance or the Devil's revenge.

Drake snapped his fingers at George. 'You! This is your father's return on his investment. Come in the boat. Now.'

'May I beg leave to bring my friend?' It was a stupid, foolhardy gesture. Yet Drake hardly seemed to pause, waved a hand in aquiescence. Mannion was left behind, fuming.

As they boarded the *San Felipe*, a single, sad trumpeter had been mustered to mark the arrival of *El Draco*. He managed, in his abject fear, to blow a passing imitation of a cow's very loud fart. Nothing and no man could stand against Drake, could it? Drake was man enough to recognise the intention of the trumpet salute, rather than to judge it on its actual quality. He approached the Captain of the *San Felipe*, bowed to him and spoke a few words in broken Spanish. The Captain replied in equally broken English.

'Did you give your permission for your men to rape me? Or are they allowed to do what they will with innocent passengers anyway?' The voice was young, female, the English accented but perfectly clear. The tone was ice cold, controlled. She was tall and overwhelmingly beautiful, and was holding, with delicate, long-fingered hands, a shred of her dress to her shoulder where an attempt had been made to tear it off. An English seaman, one of the advance guard, was standing beside her, panting, eyes swivelling from the girl to Drake. Or one eye at least. The other was bleeding from what looked like a heavy blow.

The simple, erotic power of this creature hit Henry Gresham as if it had been a kick to his stomach. Gresham hated beautiful girls. He loved their bodies, hated the power that love gave them over him. They knew the power they exercised over men, and used it ruthlessly. As a result, and revelling in their power, they became proud, ruthless and arrogant in equal measure.

'So? Will you rape me now? Or later?'

For the first, the last and the only time in his life Sir Francis Drake was stunned for words. 'Take that man and put him in chains!' he shouted eventually, pointing to the seaman.

'You have taken this ship by farce . . . by *force*,' she said, correcting herself and going red, which made her look even more beautiful, as the sailors started to laugh. Right first time, thought Gresham. It had been a farce. 'And these cowards of Spanish sailors here . . .' there was a venomous hatred in her voice. In fact,

Gresham guessed, there was a lot of hatred in this girl. For whom and for what? What was her history, he wondered?

Drake was clearly out of his depth. Gresham's decision to move forward took less than a second. He knew how to handle beautiful women. 'Your ladyship,' Gresham said, bowing deeply to her, 'there cannot be a man in this English fleet of heroes who would not see the conquering of you as worth more than the conquering of any Spanish fleet that had ever set sail!'

The Englishmen cheered. It broke the ice, the ludicrous over-statement of the courtier here on this crowded, stinking deck. The girl stiffened at this new threat, held her chin even higher. It made her look even more beautiful.

'Yet we English are gentlemen, gentlemen above all.' Gresham turned to the sailors from the *Elizabeth Bonaventure* who had clambered aboard with him. They roared in his support. They liked him, didn't they? The toff who'd beaten off the galley? The one who didn't mind taking a rope with them? And anyway, this was turning out to be far more fun than usual. He'd have that Spanish bitch, they knew. Good luck to 'im! They cheered again.

'My commander is the legendary Sir Francis Drake, scourge of the seas!' Had he overdone that bit, thought Gresham? The roar from the sailors encouraged him. 'You have nothing to fear from him, nor from his men.' Another roar from those same men, every single one of them with a voracious lust for this girl. She had had everything to fear from these men. You took whatever was on board a captured ship, didn't you? 'I merely implore you to treat Sir Francis with the same respect with which he will undoubtedly treat you.' Gresham retired, still bowing, behind the figure of Drake.

Drake turned to him, scowling. He spoke in a low tone, vicious, hissing. 'If I can manage fucking Cadiz harbour I can manage a fucking Spanish whore without your help!' he said caustically, though he could not hide a slight sense of relief. And, evidently, the girl was no whore, but rather a gentlewoman.

The girl stood her ground. After all, she had nowhere else to go. Gresham would not expect Drake to realise that he had saved his day. Beautiful girls were a threat. They forced a man to love them for more than their bodies and the blessed relief of sex. They gave physical supremacy to the man, and in exchange demanded mental slavery.

'Madam,' Drake said solemnly, bowing as low to Anna as Gresham had done, and perhaps even a patch lower. He learned very quickly, this pirate. Or perhaps he had known it all along and just not bothered to use it. 'You are now on board an *English* ship.'

More cheers from the crew. They were already working out how much the *San Felipe* would be worth. Over a hundred thousand pounds, surely?

'We English respect our women,' Drake continued grandly. 'We are not savages, to violate them in conquest.'

Oh no? thought Gresham thinking back to what he had heard of some of Drake's earlier voyages. Ah, well, it sounds good, he thought.

'You are free to retire to your cabin while I discuss details of surrender with your captain here. As for your safety, I give you my word. There will be an armed guard at your door.' It was a grand gesture, and grandly Drake offered her his ringed hand to kiss.

What followed was so different, so startling that Gresham never forgot it. The girl was defenceless, captured goods, yet she had stood up to the man most feared on the oceans of the world and secured her virginity, if indeed it had not already been claimed by some lucky man on a clandestine meeting. Now all she needed to do was to retire gracefully. Instead she drew herself to her full height. Five foot eight? Five foot nine? It wasn't really a great height at all. No taller than Sir Francis Drake himself. For a brief moment on the deck of the *San Felipe* it could have been seven foot.

'I do not kiss the hand of my conqueror!' she said. There was a hiss of indrawn breath from the English boarders, and from the Spanish crew. 'I offer the obedience to no man.' It was said simply, in her faltering English, yet with great authority. 'I accept your promise of safe conduct,' she announced, 'for myself and for all the other innocent womens on board this vessel.' The Spanish crew grinned. There were a surprising number of 'womens' aboard the *San Felipe*. Very few of them could accurately be described as innocent. 'You have care of all the poor souls on board the *San Felipe*, women, girls, crew. And officers.' She directed a withering gaze towards the Captain of the ship.

If she'd been in charge, thought Gresham, they'd have sunk before they dared surrender. What was it with beautiful women, he wondered? Why did they think they owned the world?

'Yet you do not own us!' she announced finally, gathering up her long skirts and heading for her cabin. She actually headed for the wrong door, and had she gone through it would have fallen to the bottom of the hold. It was an English seaman who, rather apologetically, directed her to the right one.

Drake's excitement at his booty was far more potent than any concerns over a damned woman. He demanded a tour of the vessel. Before leaving with the Captain and four armed sailors, he turned to the other men on the deck.

'There's money here to buy you any woman in Devon!'

Sir Francis Walsingham gagged as the pain hit him, the stones in his kidney cutting into his flesh at its most basic level, making him cry out and clutch the table edge. He knew what the pain was, knew where it would end. The Spanish, his spies told him, now put it about that he was suffering from a 'terrible corruption of the testicles'. Well, there had been pain and trouble enough for the products of his loins, but nothing like this from his testicles.

It passed, as all pain passed, as life itself passed, and Walsingham settled back into the hard wood of his chair. He looked again at the stained sheet of paper in his hand. His agent had rammed it into the hand of one of the sick sailors Drake had sent home, though the only sickness this particular man had was the illness of wanting to take Walsingham's money. The report made interesting reading. So Drake had done damage in Cadiz and hit the coastal shipping. So much the better! Yet he had steadfastly refused to land young

Gresham. Why disobey such a request? Walsingham was still powerful, and for Drake to refuse to send Gresham ashore meant that the order to keep him on board, if indeed it had ever been issued and was not simply some madness of Drake's, had to come from someone with higher authority. Who was higher than Walsingham? Who was important enough to risk offending Walsingham? The Queen, of course. Perhaps Leicester, or even Essex. Burghley, certainly. And if Burghley, then his son Robert Cecil.

Just as worrying as not knowing who the order came from, he did not know *why*. Knowledge to Walsingham was as blood to other men, the stuff of life. Someone was thwarting his orders to one of his agents. As of now, finding out who it was and why they were doing it was his top priority.

CHAPTER 5

June, 1587
Flanders; the Azores; the Escorial

They were hardened soldiers, the usual mixture of nationalities, the usual blaspheming, hard-drinking whoring sons of the Devil. Yet they fought like the Devil too, as they had proved in campaign after campaign. They hardly paid attention to the man in their midst, caked with mud, swearing too as he stumbled waist-high through the water. All were holding their firearms high above their heads, though in the pouring rain God knew what was happening to the powder. Then the man's foot sank into even deeper, invisible mud, and he seemed set to fall forward.

'Careful, my Lord.' A soldier leaped forward and caught the man's arm, halting his fall.

'Thank you,' said the Duke of Parma. 'Whose bloody idea was this?'

A ripple of laughter went round the soaked and exhausted men.

'I think you'll find it was yours, my Lord,' the soldier grinned.

They struggled up out of the channel, a boiling inferno of water at high tide, only just fordable at low tide. Cadzand. What a God-forsaken spit of land. Sand with not a building nor even a tree in sight, yet crucial for guarding the channel that gave access to Sluys, crucial for capturing the port of Sluys itself.

He had rather it had been Ostend, Parma thought, if he was to find a deep-water port for the fleet his King was insisting on sending. But Ostend was too well defended, the English troops he had brushed against the best he or his men had ever fought. Good! If they were in Ostend they could not fight him in England, where he knew there were no soldiers of any standing. Sluys it had to be. No deep-water port, for sure, but at the heart of the system of canals and waterways that would allow him the only battle plan that he believed might work.

He had the army here in Flanders, a mere forty miles off the English coast. Once in England his men would cut through the English like a hot knife through butter. Yokels, militia armed with pitchforks were all the English could muster against him. Spain could and would send the ships, now that her conquest of Portugal had given her a proper, ocean-going Navy. But what about the damned Dutch fleet under the thrice cursed Justin of Nassau? It was that fleet that haunted the dreams of the Duke of Parma. Using their shallow-bottomed yet heavily armed fly-boats, they could bottle up his men, pounding them in their fragile barges as they came out from the canals and before they reached the open sea. The great Armada of his master's dreams could only wait off shore in deep water, and witness the tragedy, unable to sail into the shoals where the Dutch had mastery. If only he could capture a deep-water port. Allow Philip's Armada to sail in, embark his troops and blast the English navy out of their way in the Channel. Yet he had no time!

No. It was cunning that would bring him victory, the same cunning that had won him all his victories, made men talk about the Duke of Parma's army in the same breath as the all-conquering Roman legions. If he held Sluys he held power over a spider's web of canals and waterways. It was clear in his mind. He would send out barges to the north, allow them to be seen, draw the damned Dutch off. Then he would flood the southern canals at night with his men, when the darkness would confuse the Dutch sailors, if they were there and if they were mad enough to sail at night. Shielded lanterns would guide his invasion barges, invisible from the seaward side, and guide them out and over the shoals before the Dutch would see or know what was happening. If the Dutch followed the barges out to sea the guns of the huge galleons would blast them to pieces before they could blink. And if enough ships were sent by Spain, then they could stand as an impenetrable barrier between the frail barges and the English fleet. But first he had to capture Sluys.

He climbed over the sand to what amounted to Cadzand's highest point. Where were the barges bringing his supplies and the heavy guns he needed to set up over the channel? The Duke of Parma sighed. War was never certain. They had known the barges could be, were likely to be, delayed by enemy interference. They faced a cold few hours while they waited, praying their enemy would not mount an assault from the seaward side, knowing if they did with wet powder and priming all they had to resist with was cold steel, praying the barges would get through. Meanwhile, trenches had to be dug, the emplacements formed for the big guns.

The soldier proffered something to his commander. It was a lump of biscuit, soaked through and with the pattern of the man's fingers embedded in its surface where he had clutched the sodden mass. Damn! Why did he always forget to order his servants to pack food when he went out to battle? You would think they'd have learned by now. Yet he was hungry, surprisingly hungry. He looked up at the man, nodded, and grasped the biscuit, cramming it into his mouth. It tasted good.

True to his word, Drake mounted an armed guard outside the door to Anna's cabin. 'Is it to keep us out? Or to keep 'er in?' joked the sailor to his mates as he took up position.

George had been sent off to reconnoitre the cabins at the stern. Since no one had told Gresham not to join him he followed. Their instructions were clear, given to them by Captain Fenner while Drake entertained the captain of the *San Felipe* in what had once been the man's own cabin.

'Anything of value in those cabins, I want it detailed, written down here, immediately.' He tossed a scrap of paper to Gresham, turned to give him the pen and ink, looked at him and thought better of it. He handed them instead to George. 'I *don't* want things going walking the minute the prize crew get on board, you understand. And I don't want anything walking in either of your pockets, either!'

They had opened the door to find the woman in bed, and drawn back instinctively, embarrassed. So much for conquering heroes, thought Gresham, ruefully. In the heat of battle, the red-blood excitement, such a woman might have been raped or simply had her skull smashed in. Now it was all over, decorum had returned, and manners too.

'Come in! Please come in!' The voice was faint, but the accent perfectly English. Exchanging a glance, Gresham and then Mannion pushed through the cabin door.

They knew she was the girl's mother immediately. The lustrous fair hair, now rather lank and thin in the older woman but clearly once a matter of great glory; the high cheekbones, the full lips, the beautiful blue of the eyes. God had starved the rest of the world when he handed out the good looks to this pair. Yet the older woman was clearly ill. The face was pale beyond the demands of beauty, drawn and with fine lines of pain etched on to it. The voice was faint, the spirit of the woman obviously ebbing and flowing as alternate tides of weakness and of pain flushed through her body.

'Tell me . . . tell me what has happened, please. My servant ran away when the first gun was fired . . .' The woman was too weak to raise her head from the pillow. She was bathed in sweat now, not the healthy glistening that covered a man's brow in hot weather or after intense work, but rather something that seemed to have boiled up within her and tainted the surface of her smooth, beautiful skin.

'The ship has been captured, madam,' said Gresham, with a low bow. He felt confused. He had always been as uncertain with mature women as he was certain with the younger ones. If he had known a mother it might have been different. 'By Sir Francis Drake and a squadron of his ships. The battle, such as it was, is over.'

'My daughter! Have you seen my daughter? Is she safe?' A frantic energy crept into the woman's voice, and she struggled to raise herself.

'Calm yourself, Madam, please,' said Gresham, feeling out of his depth. 'If your daughter is that extraordinary . . . young girl, who stood up in front of our Captain, then yes, she is more than safe.' Why are men so weak in the face of women, he thought? 'In fact she's done more to defeat the English navy than anyone else today,' George added, clearly concerned by the woman's state and wanting to reassure her.

'That will be my daughter,' she said, catching the irony, hearing the good humour in the powerful voice and choosing to ignore the youthful irony. There had been no screams, no wild shrieks, no yells of men. She knew what happened after battle. All women did, and prepared themselves each in their own way. But it appeared that at least some semblance of humanity was present in this capture. Surprised, she felt a coolness at her brow. The other man, the brute of a servant, had looked around the cabin, seen the flannel and bucket of water on the deck, dipped it and with extraordinary gentleness had lain it across her brow, stepping back to make it clear that he intended no offence. The tears came then, flowing rivulets down her cheeks. The act of simple kindness had broken through her defences as no act of violence would ever have done.

The tears embarrassed the younger man, she could see. He could not decide whether to stay and comfort her, or respect her grief and leave. She decided to save him his pains. A gentleman, clearly, she noted, from his appearance. Even the seagoing clothes he wore were clearly of the highest quality. She felt herself yearning for the son she had never had. Would he have been like this young man, perfectly formed, the glint of intelligence in his eyes? And something else. A darkness. A sense of something hidden, something . . . She decided to sit up, preparing herself for the ripping, tearing pain that she knew would cut across her stomach as she did so. It took her a few moments to compose herself, hold up her hand as both the servant and the gentleman moved towards her, seeing her pain.

'Thank you, thank you,' she said breathlessly, but with pride. One always had pride, she thought. Sometimes it was all one had. 'To save your questions, I am English. A daughter of the Rea family.'

Recognition dawned in Gresham's eyes. The Rea's were an ancient lineage, original supporters of King Henry VII, and richly rewarded for that support. Then the bad seed had struck, and much of their land was lost in Mary's reign. They were, it was said, the only Catholic family to have failed to make good under Queen Mary. Then they had tried to strike riches in Ireland, but lost most of what little they had left. The male heirs were elderly now, the occasional one hanging round the fringe of Court in threadbare clothes that had been fashionable fifteen years earlier.

'When our fortunes turned, I married a Spaniard. A noble Spaniard.'

A handsome and kind man, for all his lack of even basic financial skills, his family were nearly as impoverished as the Rea's, and they had married against all advice. Now he was dead, dead of a fever in Goa, a sad end for a man destined for far greater things.

Her strength was failing again, she could feel it. 'Please . . . please find my servant and send her back here. But more important . . .' How could she take such a risk with this young Englishman, who for all she knew could be the son of a pirate and a philanderer himself? She looked into his strong eyes, and made up her mind. 'I am dying.' It was said flatly, with no melodrama.

There are all sorts of courage, thought Gresham. This woman, whoever she claims to be, has strong store of at least one of them. He began to understand where the daughter came from, imagining a headstrong, proud Spaniard joining his blood with the lady dying in front of him.

'My daughter has no one. It is essential that she reach Europe to marry her fiancé. Here . . . here . . .' she fumbled in a small case lined with pearls that lay on the bed. Opening it, she produced a small piece of paper, a name and address written on it. 'This is his name. Please keep it,' she said to Gresham. 'I may fall asleep, into a coma, at any time. It would be folly on my part to think I could guard this against a thief.' I must meet this Drake. I must talk to him! I must persuade him to protect and deliver my Anna, she thought in her desperation.

The effort had exhausted her. With a last despairing look she sank back on the stained pillows. Her eyes closed. Her lips could be seen moving, silently framing the word 'Anna'. Gresham sent Mannion to ferret out the servant she had spoken of, standing guard until the mulatto girl, frightened out of her wits, was ushered in by Mannion for all the world like a vast cow-herd driving a frightened heifer back into the field.

They completed the remainder of their search. Most of the other cabins were empty of people, crammed high with extra cargo of spices and, in one room, case upon case of ivory. Trade goods paid better than people on the Indies route, it would appear. Their manifest complete, they returned to the upper deck. Drake appeared a short while later, slapping the Spanish captain on the back and laughing uproariously with him. The Spanish captain climbed over the side with his officers, into the boat that would take him to the island. Any of the seamen who offered to change allegiance would be allowed to stay on board. Illness was starting to take its toll on board the English ships, and seamen were valuable commodities. The passengers would be put ashore to await the next Spanish ship. It would not be a long wait. Many ships from the south headed for the Azores, to catch the westerlies that blew so helpfully towards Europe and the mainland.

Drake was in great good humour, Gresham could see. Now seemed as good a time as any to approach him. George needed little prompting. 'My Lord,' he said, bowing to Drake. 'May I ask to intercede on behalf of a passenger on board this vessel?' Which of Sir Francis Drake's numerous personalities was running the man's head today? Before Drake could answer, George briefly explained their find below decks. 'The lady is English, and her daughter, I presume, half-English. I think the daughter is the girl who bombarded us earlier today. The mother is clearly a gentlewoman.'

'Is the woman able to come on deck?' asked Drake. Well, at least he had not simply thrown George overboard. In fact, he was striking a pose, chest puffed out, one foot firmly in front of the other. He had donned his best doublet for the handover, richly bejewelled with fantastically slashed sleeves.

George looked at Gresham and Mannion. Both recalled the sweating woman and the closeness, the stink of the ship all around them. It was probably healthier for the mother to be here in the sunshine and fresh air of the Azores. But they also remembered the jolt of pain that had visibly gone through her as she tried to sit up, her sense of a mind held together only by determination.

'Sadly, my Lord,' said George, 'we fear it could kill her. We suspect she has only a thin hold on life as it is.'

A cloud of emotion flickered over Drake's face, but he was too pumped up by his own triumph to allow his mood to evaporate. And well he might be. It cost around fourteen shillings a month to feed and pay a seaman on board the *Elizabeth Bonaventure*. You could hire the ship for twenty-eight pounds a month, pay and feed its whole crew for less than a hundred and seventy-five pounds a month. You could build a new version of her for two thousand six hundred pounds. And the value of *San Felipe* and her cargo? 'One hundred and ten thousand pounds,' Captain Fenner had whispered to Drake when the first inventory was complete. 'Perhaps even as high as one hundred and twenty, even forty thousand pounds . . . and that does not include the value of the vessel itself!' No wonder Drake was happy.

The strangely assorted party went down to the cabin: Drake, Fenner, Drake's Secretary, sniffing disapprovingly, George, Gresham, and Mannion of course, who had the capacity to become indivisible from Gresham.

'Sir Francis. Thank you for your graciousness in coming to see me.'

There was active dislike in Drake's expression as he gazed at Gresham, for the first time. And something else? A nervousness, almost? As for the mother, she was conserving her strength, Gresham saw, not even trying to rise, saving her sparse energy.'

'Madam,' said Drake, bowing low, 'I am truly sorry to hear of your indisposition. As I believe you know, your daughter and yourself have my guarantee as to your safety.'

'I am grateful to you, Sir Francis. Might I request that my daughter be present here with us now?' Anna had been in constant attendance on her mother. The faint smell of her carefully-hoarded perfume still in the cabin suggested she had only left as the footfalls of the male visiting party had been heard on the deck.

Drake nodded, and Captain Fenner called out to the guard at the cabin door to request the presence of the girl. There was an awkward silence, broken only when a few minutes later Anna appeared. Her eyes were downcast this time, Gresham saw, her curtsey deep and formal.

'Sir,' was all she said, in a low voice. A stool was brought, and she sat decorously, eyes still downcast, by the bed-head and her mother.

'Sir Francis.' The mother had swallowed several times before speaking. Would she last the course, thought Gresham? 'Though I have married one of your enemies, I am as English as any person here.'

'Madam,' said Drake, 'I do not doubt— '

'*Please!*' Her tone was so desperate that it defused the rudeness of her interruption. More than words could ever do, it said I am dying, I feel my consciousness slipping away from me at any moment and I must have leave to say what I need to say without interruption. All present sensed that this woman was shortening her life with the effort of making this final plea.

'My husband is dead. I will shortly be so too.' There was a sob from the corner where the girl sat, her head down. Then a snap of pride thrilled through her. There were no more noises, no snuffling. 'My husband's family and my own are impoverished. If they accept my daughter at all, it would be at little less than the status of a servant. My daughter has only one champion left in the world. Her fiancé, a Frenchman at present travelling.'

A fat pig travelling through Europe for trade! thought Anna to herself, the rush of hatred and anger for a brief moment overwhelming her grief.

'I have no power, no wealth, no great ships at my disposal. I have only the request of a poor woman, an *English* woman, that I be allowed to name a guardian for my only child, a protector who like a champion of old will guard, protect and keep her, and deliver her to her fiancé.'

There was an appalling dignity in the simplicity of the woman's words. Drake stuck his chest out even more.

'Madam, I am happy to accept the charge which you— '

'In which case . . .' For a moment the woman's voice was strong, riddled with authority, and those in the cabin saw what she had once been. 'I nominate as guardian of my daughter the man I believe is known as Henry Gresham.'

George! Surely if it was anyone it should have been George, Gresham thought! It was a mistake! It had to be a mistake!

The silence in the cabin was as painful as a kick in the stomach. It was madness, all there could see it. How long before the young man with the blood in him did what all young men do, succumbed to the demands of his flesh? How long before the wild spirit of the girl succumbed to the man, as God had dictated all women should do from the time of Eve? Madness! What man wanted used goods? What use would her fiancé be when he realised his virgin bride had been deflowered, and that any child might not be of his blood line?

Gresham had spent years learning to control the reaction of his body – the sweat on the brow, the pulsing in the neck, the flickering gaze, the hand pulling at the beard, stroking the side of the nose or the chin. The give-away reactions that told an enemy the workings of one's mind. But totally out of his control, he felt the red flush rising from his neck, suffusing his whole face. Then he looked at the mother's face. All her breeding was in it. All her beauty. And also the lines of pain, drawn so finely round her eyes these past few months. And the neck beginning to sag, that sagging that soon would turn the proud swell of her breasts into drooping dugs. Yet on that face was the slightest of smiles. A smile for Henry Gresham, he knew. For him alone. For a fleeting moment Gresham wished that he had had a mother, such as her.

'Do you accept this charge?' she asked, her voice a tiny one now, as though receding from life.

The girl had looked up. Her face showed only hatred and anger. He made the mistake of returning her gaze. Those eyes! Huge, dark pools, the colour of fine amethyst, fathomless, endlessly mysterious . . . He tried to shake himself out of this spell, praying to God he had made no gesture visible to the outside world. I would rather be facing a Spanish galley at night with little more than a longboat and luck beside me, he thought. He drew a deep breath. Let them see that. He no longer cared.

'Madam,' he bowed towards her, 'I'm no fit person for such a charge. I'm young, I'm foolish, I've yet to learn to cope with my own life, never mind be responsible for someone else's life.' Her smile was unwavering. Was she in some sort of trance, or did she know in her heart what was coming? 'Yet you, clearly, you are a fit person for such a charge. You have experience. You are wise. You prepare to leave your own life with a dignity that no man can but envy.'

A ripple went round the room from the assembled men. They lived close enough to death to know how much that proximity cost in courage.

'If you trust in me to perform this . . . duty, then perhaps I may grow in stature and prove worthy of your trust in time enough to honour it. With a heavy heart, then, my answer is yes.'

'Thank you,' said the woman, simply. Then she turned her gaze, wavering now as if she was having difficulty in focussing her eyes, to Drake. 'This is the wish of a dying woman, Sir Francis. If you are a gentleman, then you will honour it.'

A shrewd blow, all things considered. Drake was, above all, not a gentleman. He was a commoner whose daring and luck had brought him enough wealth to make him look as if he were a gentleman. Those who had the status through birth to call themselves gentlemen hated him for his jumped-up success, sought continually to humiliate him. A true gentleman might have rejected the woman's charge. One who was forever having to justify his claim to be a gentleman could not refuse it. For a brief moment Sir Francis Drake stood before a dying woman as himself. The ferocious ambition, the paranoia, the trappings of wealth, the endless complexities, hypocrisies and charades of command, the acting and the playing of roles, all suddenly dropped off.

'I will honour it,' he said, simply.

There was a crash at the door, and Robert Leng, gentleman adventurer and self-professed historian of Sir Francis Drake's triumphant expedition to Cadiz, broke into the cabin. Perhaps it was fortunate that all eyes went to Leng's flushed countenance, because at that precise moment, the compact with Gresham and Drake having been sealed with their eyes, Anna's mother allowed herself to die. The true dignity of death is to die alone. After all, we are born alone for the most part, and we are never more alone than when we die. Yet she was not truly alone. The only eyes that had not swivelled round to Leng as he crashed in were those of her daughter. When the curtain of death closed over her eyes, the last thing they saw was the startling, tear-stained blue orbs of her daughter.

'Sir!' Leng was clearly confused by the sight before him. 'I am . . . most . . . most sorry to interrupt . . . I had no idea . . . Yet I beg to inform you, I have news of treason. Darkest treason.'

Well, he had their attention now. And no one except the daughter had marked the passing from this earth of the mother.

'Treason, sir,' he said, warming to his part now, 'directed and engineered by the bastard Henry Gresham!'

Something dark, dull and leaden settled into Gresham's mind. He had never liked Leng, who had managed to ignore him throughout the voyage, while managing to emanate at the same time a distant sense of scorn. Yet this was not about dislike. As Gresham

113

looked at Leng's sweating, pock-marked face, a cruel certainty formed in the cold, analytical part of his mind that he could not control but only read.

'These were found in Gresham's belongings. A rosary. A prayer book for the Roman Catholic faith.' Leng paused. He was clearly saving the best for last. 'And a letter from the Court of King Philip of Spain, authorising Henry Gresham as His Catholic Majesty's agent, and advising all to give him loyalty and support!'

Theatrically, he waved the letter in the air. Drake took it, with a leaden brow. Unseen by all present the girl closed her mother's eyes, whose face in death was still smiling, calm now. Drake glanced at the letter, directing a single glance at Gresham. He dropped it on the table. Leng picked it up. He was really enjoying this, thought Gresham. He paused, triumphant. Then he saw the dead woman in the bed.

'Dear God!' he muttered, and sat down on the deck.

The others looked towards the bed, their hearts aghast. The girl had placed her head on her mother's breast, and was sobbing, silently. There was no drama this time. Indeed, it was clear that for the girl the audience did not exist. There is no more powerful grief than private grief. The men present felt shamed, as if they had defiled the primal act of a child's sorrow for the death of its parent. Drake moved first towards the girl.

'We will bury her,' he said, a kindness in his tone that none present had ever seen or heard before, 'even according to your rituals. Roman Catholic rituals. For all that I could be hung on my return for recognising such rituals exist. Not at sea, either, so the fish can chew her flesh and bones. Not so she drifts where the tide drives. She wasn't one of our strange breed of sailor. We'll bury her on land, on San Miguel, where she can always be known and recorded, and where her children and her grandchildren can visit her grave. In God's good earth, on God's good ground.'

How can a man with so much cruelty in him be so kind, thought Gresham?

'Take the body to the Captain's cabin. Lay her out there,' said

Drake. Laying out bodies was not a skill in short supply among Drake's fleet. 'Follow her,' he said gently to the girl, 'so that you may see that all things are seemly.'

The sailors brought a rough dignity to their job, the body of the woman wrapped in the sheets in which she had lain. The girl followed, still in her private world of grief. The men remained in the cabin.

'I understood you were a spy for England. It seems you are a spy for Spain,' said Drake.

'Will you believe me if I say I've never seen that letter before, nor the rosary and prayer book?' said Gresham. 'I think not. Yet it's the truth.'

'It was found in his belongings, I swear, my Lord!' said Leng.

Drake snorted, moved away. Gresham spoke.

'If Sir Francis Drake of the *Elizabeth Bonaventure* will not hear me, yet will the Captain of the *Judith* listen to his past?'

Drake stopped in his tracks. Gresham bore on. He knew it was his last chance.

'As a young man you captained the *Judith*. A tiny vessel, but yours. You sailed into a Spanish harbour needing rest and succour, with the other ships with whom you had sailed. There was no war between Spain and England, you were simply sailors, cast upon the same waters, facing the same dangers, fearing the same death. You asked for help, were given help, given safe conduct.'

Drake had not moved.

'Then the Spanish decided to take the English vessels, capture them and imprison or burn their crew. You were the bottom of the pile, the smallest vessel, the most insignificant prize. So you slipped out from under their treachery, fought your way home against all odds. You were betrayed.'

Now came the real gamble.

'And you were called a coward, for leaving your fellow sailors.'

Suddenly the air in the cabin froze. All eyes turned to Drake.

'So am I the smallest vessel, the least valuable, the disposable commodity, and so have I been betrayed, by whom I know not. So

115

have I been called a coward, despite my reaction under fire, as you were called a coward, in the face of your courage. Will you believe me, as captain of the *Judith* and the man who brought her home? Or will you believe that there are men trying to deceive you, seeking to use you, to make you my executioner?'

The analytical part of Gresham's mind kept working, thinking, detached from that part of a young man's brain telling him that he was shortly to die. He had to inflame Drake's paranoia, the belief this man had of a world set permanently to betray him. But what a situation for Drake. He had just given his word to allow Gresham to act as guardian to the girl, and it would be far easier for a real gentleman to break his word; far harder for someone desperate to be a gentleman to break it. The *nouveaux* were always the most willing to believe the old lies. Yet here, clearly was treachery, the likelihood that Gresham had lied to him. It was not the letter that would make Drake want to kill Gresham, he thought. It was the fact that Drake had been taken in by a lie, fooled by a young upstart.

'Ask yourself this, Sir Francis,' continued Gresham. 'Any fool can plant any item they want in the baggage aboard this vessel. Our belongings are strewn about the deck, open to the elements. Do I seem to you fool enough to carry a letter that condemns me, a letter so easily found? What man leaves his death warrant openly on board the deck of a ship?'

They could hear the lapping of the water against the hull as Gresham paused.

'You've not landed me on enemy shore,' he said. It was his final play, he knew. 'Yet you were instructed to do so. Has whoever countermanded Walsingham's orders also demanded my death? Doesn't a man deserve to know who it is that kills him? And how certain are you that this same person will not turn and do to you what you have been commanded to do to me?'

'No one commands me, Henry Gresham,' said Drake. 'They may suggest, if they choose. And no one has commanded me to kill you. I hold the power of life and death aboard my ships. I delegate it and give it up to no man.'

116

Yet to be found with such a letter is as good as killing me, thought Gresham. Did you know that I was to be killed? Or were your orders simply to keep me on board? And who gave you the instructions not to land me ashore?

Drake reached his decision with surprising speed. It was clear that he did not like Gresham. Gresham's only hope was that he disliked those who were seeking to pull the strings on board his flagship just as much.

'How good is your knowledge of history?' Drake asked. Gresham was learning, eventually, to cope with the wild swings and tangents of a dialogue with Drake. But was he going to let him live, or die?

'As bad as any College Fellow's,' answered Gresham, struggling to stay outwardly calm.

'You will know that in Anglo-Saxon times justice was rough and ready. Yet effective, for all its crudeness. You are aware of trial by ordeal?'

Good God! Gresham was aware. It was the system whereby a man had to grasp a red hot bar and walk with it a number of paces. If the wound healed clean, he was deemed innocent. If it festered, guilty. Was Drake going to brand him?

'The theory is that man decides the action,' Drake continued, 'God decides the outcome. So I will place you in God's hands. One of my pinnaces has sprung some of her seams. She has been patched up on the island, but one of the many decisions of command facing me was to decide whether to destroy her, or risk trying to take her home. I had decided to destroy her.' Drake looked to his second in command. 'Captain Fenner. You will ready the *Daisy* for the voyage back to England. Starting tomorrow. Provision her as best you can. And choose me a crew for her. Start with that mutinous dog from *Dreadnought*, the one we had decided to hang. I think her present Captain will do very well.' He stood up. 'You will go to the *Daisy*, now. I will send men to pick up whatever belongings you have on board the *Bonaventure*. If you make it home, God will have declared you innocent. As He will have declared you guilty if you do not.'

117

'The girl?' Gresham asked.

'I said I would honour the mother's wishes. They were that her daughter be protected. She will be. And that you were her guardian. I am happy for that to be the case. It is merely that for a few weeks you will be aboard the *Daisy*, while I act in your place here on the *San Felipe*. You will be reunited in England, God willing.'

If I return, thought Gresham. He felt a wild stirring in his heart. A leaking ship, a mutinous crew – Drake was clearly taking the opportunity to scour his decks of all human filth – and a perilous journey home. Well, it was a chance. A real chance. Better than choking to death, swinging from a yard arm.

Yet Drake had not finished. He turned to Robert Leng.

'Have you finished your account?' asked Drake.

'I have just this moment finished my account of your glorious capture of the *San Felipe*,' said Leng. 'The full copy is with your Secretary.' He looked sideways at Gresham, nervous, half expecting Gresham to leap at him.

'Then your job is done, is it not?' said Drake. 'You may leave your manuscript with me. You will be keen to get back home. I have decided to provide you with a fast passage. On board the *Daisy*. You can act as guard to this young man.'

'Sir! This is unjust! I have merely carried out my duty . . .'

The knife moved so fast through the air that it seemed just a shimmering flicker of silver metal. It bit deep into the bulkhead, quivering, half an inch from Leng's ear.

'I smell treachery!' said Drake bitterly. 'My own vanity. It was my own vanity, the need to have this voyage recorded that overlaid my sense of smell. But now I smell it in my nostrils. So shall it be between you and my young friend here. Guilty? Innocent? Let God decide. And the *Daisy*.'

With that Drake let out a roar of laughter, continuing it as he left the cabin and mounted the quarterdeck. Leng had time to grab the letter before half running to catch Drake up.

They could have spent all day comforting a stricken George, to no avail. He pleaded to be allowed to come with them. After one look at the *Daisy*, Gresham flatly refused. Their last sight of the *Elizabeth Bonaventure* was the mournful half-moon of George's face, watching them as they bobbed away and out of sight. Would Gresham ever see that cheerful face again? They had managed only a few snatched moments of conversation.

'I'm sure someone asked or ordered Drake to keep me on board, not to land me ashore. No skin off Drake's nose, if the price was right. He could always give some tissue of lies to Walsingham to explain why. I think what surprised him was when someone quite clearly tried to get him to kill me as well – he hadn't bargained for that.'

'You're lucky Drake felt sorry for you,' said George.

'Sorry? Don't be stupid!' said Gresham. 'Drake isn't giving me this chance because he feels sorry for me. He's giving a reprimand to whoever he takes his orders from, sending a signal that you don't deal with Drake unless you tell him the whole story. If whoever's working with Drake had told him to kill me, and paid the right price, Drake'd have me executed quicker than a blink.'

The *Daisy* was a depressing prospect. Her Captain was a notorious drunkard, and had this last voyage not beckoned he would certainly have been relieved of any command. There were only fifteen crew members now, all minor criminals and one of them suspected of murder, and too small a crew to properly handle and set even the paltry sail area the *Daisy* carried. The pinnaces were often much smaller versions of the great galleons that bobbed over the waves instead of ploughing through them, but with three tiny masts and some popguns on the side. The *Daisy*'s third mast had snapped in the recent storm, and all that remained of it was the stump embedded in the deck. Even though it only carried a small lanteen sail, its absence threw the whole delicate balance of the ship out of true, forcing her bow lower in the water than seemed safe. Gresham knew that the masts on their own could not support the weight of the sail they were required to bear, and that the rigging tensioned

119

them crucially. Was the rigging interdependent, Gresham asked himself? Were the three masts linked together in any significant way? If so, the balance of the other two masts must be out of kilter, subject to unusual strains and stresses . . . He decided there were some aspects of knowledge that were best not pursued.

They found the Captain snoring, drunk in his tiny cabin aft, florid face flat on the table, outflung hand still grasping a pewter mug. A thin dribble of saliva hung from his mouth, staining the crude chart on the table.

'Falmouth,' said Mannion, looking down at it. 'Chart o' the entrance to Falmouth. Bloody load of good in the Azores.'

There were four really quite decent, high-backed chairs in the cabin – loot from some earlier escapade? – and Gresham sat down on one of them, motioning Mannion to sit as well. It was close in the small room, but it was private. The four sailors Drake had set to guard them were happy enough to wait outside. There was only one door into the cabin, and no window big enough to take Gresham, never mind Mannion. Gresham did not think the drunken Captain counted as a listener.

'Well?' he asked Mannion.

'I've 'ad better odds,' said Mannion. 'I've been 'aving a chat with the carpenter. The hull's shot some seams, but they've recaulked 'em. In decent weather they'll hold up long enough, probably. Losing the mast's a bugger; it'll make her sail like a crab. But they're fast these pinnaces. The real problem's rot. Carpenter reckons some of the timbers below the bilge 'ave got rot in 'em. Difficult to say 'ow many.'

Some sailors feared it more than drowning. Rot was inevitable in a wooden ship, giving a natural limit to any vessel's life. The English used gravel as ballast, whilst the Spanish and Portuguese tended to go more for large rocks or even scrap metal. The gravel tended to shift less in bad weather, but it made it impossible to pump water out and increased the incidence of rot, as well as making it more difficult to spot. It tended to affect the central members, well below the water line, and particularly the crucial

120

keel timbers under the bilges. Taking out the ballast to get at these timbers was a filthy, stinking job, and took time as well as energy. On the smaller vessels there came a time when repair was simply not cost-effective, particularly as even a tiny piece of rotten timber could infect any new, sound timber placed by it. The fear of rot came from the stealth with which it tore out the heart of a vessel. Every sailor knew stories of ships that had simply come apart in a storm without warning, crucial and hidden load-bearing timbers with the texture of crumbling clay suddenly giving up the ghost.

'Why have the crew agreed to come?' asked Gresham. 'They must know what the odds are.'

'They didn't exactly agree. They was told. By Drake. The choice was sail with the *Daisy*, or be put ashore.' Putting ashore would in all probability have meant the galleys, or even facing the Inquisition.

'They're either all troublemakers or they ain't made themselves popular with 'is 'Ighness,' said Mannion. 'Apparently half of 'em were set to bugger off with the *Golden Lion*, but bumped into the *Dreadnought* who threatened to blow 'em out of the water unless they turned round and stuck with us. It's a toss-up whether Drake hangs a few of them as an example and sticks the rest in jail, or whether he says good riddance to bad rubbish and packs 'em off home. We come along. Makes it easier to pack every one off 'ome.'

There was a particularly loud snort from the Captain. Something yellow was dribbling from his nose now.

'What about stores?' asked Gresham.

'Good, as far as I can see,' said Mannion. 'Picked up a lot of stuff in Cadiz, didn't they, so they can afford to be generous. Problem is, you never really know what you're going to get until you broach the barrel.' He was to remember that phrase a short while later.

They had gone to the funeral, conducted with dignity and as much ceremony as they could muster, burying some of their own dead a few hundred yards off. Unusual for sailors, whose final resting place was a roll of canvas weighted with lead shot and fathoms of sea water above their heads for eternity. Afterwards, on board the

121

San Felipe, Gresham had talked to the girl. Drake had allowed them a few minutes, though he had not dismissed the guard. She looked thinner than when he had first set eyes on her, but seemed even more beautiful. Her suffering had deepened her cheek bones, given her eyes an even greater intensity and depth. None of that intensity reflected affection. The girl's modest gown was designed to cover rather than accentuate the charms of the wearer, yet she moved like an athlete. Gresham could not banish the image of her naked body from his mind. Damn! This was not what the mother had wanted when she made him pledge his honour.

'I'm sorry that I can't remain with you on *San Felipe* for your voyage home,' he said to her, trying to appear calm. 'I've been banished, in effect, by Sir Francis. But immediately you land in England I'll be there. I propose to house you at my home in London,' the vast Gresham property on the Strand, known simply as The House, stood largely empty, 'where there are some excellent female servants.' Dear Lord! He was sounding like the most pompous type of father. 'I'll also attempt to find a suitable lady to act as your chaperone.' And how the hell did a young man with no family left alive and a scorn for the Court do that, he wondered? He suspected his guardianship would require that he acquire rather too many new skills. God, she was beautiful!

She looked up at him, fire in her eyes. 'Do you know what it is like to be treated as a packages?'

'Pardon?' said Gresham, startled.

'To be packed up, despatched, sent here and sent there. Treated like a packages!'

'It's "package", actually . . .' said Gresham.

'Something with no mind, no will of its own, no desires.' She ignored Gresham. 'Just an object. Well, do you?' Her voice was soft, husky, surprisingly low-pitched, but with a hint of steel in it.

'Er . . . well, no. Actually.'

'It would seem that God has a strange sense of humour.' This conversation was rapidly going away from Gresham. 'He gives His creation the capacity to love, and then rips the people we love out

122

of our lives for his amusement.' There was no sign of excessive moisture in her eyes. 'But at least he has a sense of humour, and he recognises that we care. Men, it appears, simply think women are a packages. I am to be delivered to you. You will deliver me on.' She stood up. 'I hate you!' she said. The quiet control of her voice was more frightening than it would have been had she shouted. 'I hate you and all your kind. You who treat people like objects, who take away their freedom and their right to exist as themselves.'

I think I could very easily hate you, thought Gresham. I really do not need you as a complication in my life at this present time.

'Yeah, well,' said Mannion, picking his hollow tooth, 'you're not alone in that. Most people hate him, actually.'

The girl gave a slight tremor. Was it the comment or perhaps the fact that it was a servant who uttered them? Such freedom was not afforded servants in the best-run Spanish households. Nor, now Gresham came to think of it, in the best English ones either.

'Let's see . . .' Mannion poised for a moment's theatrical thought. 'Drake hates him. His bosses at home hates him. Both of those are trying to kill him, actually. The Spaniards had a good attempt at killing him, so they must hate him. The son of the Queen's Chief Secretary hates him. If you believe everything he says – and I tries to, 'cos I'm a good servant – the Queen, the Earl of Leicester *and* the Earl of Essex could all be trying to get 'im killed. Oh, and I forgot. His College in Cambridge, England, they all hates him as well.'

Mannion gave up excavating his tooth. He had carried on throughout his little speech, causing some problems with comprehensibility.

'And now it turns out you hates him as well. Fancy that, join the club. Funny thing, now as it comes to mind, I've had nothing but trouble since I met him. I hate the bugger too. Shall we all take turns in trying to kill 'im?'

Anna looked from Mannion to Gresham, and back again. Gresham was looking at Mannion with an expression which intimated that he thought Mannion's colliding with a very heavy object would be a good thing.

123

'Why did God give you a mouth to match your belly!' he thundered. 'Why did he put your brain somewhere lower down and facing aft than your belly! I swear . . .'

He turned. The girl had left, silently.

'That could 'ave been better,' said Mannion. 'If you'd left it to me . . .'

'If I leave a girl like that to you I'd be like a shepherd giving the flock over to a lion while he has a rest.'

'Me?' said Mannion incredulously. 'Me a lion? Give over! I'm the donkey. Problem is, sometimes a donkey 'as more common sense than a lion!'

Gresham had become used to the easy motion of the *Elizabeth Bonaventure*. The *Daisy* seemed to fight the water instead of working with it, recoiling when the light waves slapped her thin hull, seeing them as an insult rather than a caress. They left harbour with no fanfares, skulking out at sunset in the hope that the gathering gloom would mean that no one would notice. But even a crew such as this could set sail with a kind westerly directly behind them.

God knew how good a navigator the Captain was, in the rare moments when he was awake that is, but Gresham was gambling on his survival instinct. And if they headed west, they were sure to hit the coast of Europe, he comforted himself. Surely the coast of Europe was too big for even the *Daisy* to miss? Then all they would have to do was coast-hop back to England. Dodging angry Spanish ships, of course, bent on revenge for Cadiz. And supposing the beer and biscuit in their barrels was sound. And hoping the rot did not break the hull open at the first sign of a real sea, or the jerry-rigging collapse the masts. But of all the problems Gresham had anticipated, the one that first arose, barely half a day into their voyage, was one he had not dreamed of.

The *Daisy* had a planked-over waist, unlike many of the pinnaces which left their apology for a gun deck open to the elements. Because it was covered, they put stores there. It was Mannion who heard the tapping. A frail noise, coming from one of the barrels, marked as containing beer. Mannion patrolled the tiny ship as if haunted by the Devil, two throwing knives stuffed openly into his belt, a dagger there as well as a prohibited sword. Not the rapier of gentlemen, more the cutlass of a pirate. Mannion emanated threat, though this did not stop him from calling Gresham to witness the act as he broached the barrel. By then, the tappings had ceased.

So, nearly, had Anna's life. Half an hour more and she would not have been gagging her life up on the deck of the *Daisy*, but communing with her mother. The tiny portion of stores assembled for the *Daisy* had been put on the main deck of the *San Felipe* before they were lugged over to their final destination and left overnight. She had spotted them, seen the barrel of beer left by the chute designed to take sea water from the deck and back into the ocean. Somehow, using the last of the coin her mother had given her, she had persuaded her servant and the sailor she was sleeping with to knock two holes in the barrel so the beer leaked gently over the side and into the sea. Then, with more coin and the last of the wine in her mother's store, she had persuaded them to broach the barrel, replace its cover and nail her into it. Unfortunately, the holes that were sufficient to drain the beer were insufficient to let enough air in. The stench inside the barrel and the heat were beyond belief. For a moment they thought the pathetic, bedraggled, stinking and limp thing they hauled out of the barrel was dead. There was a mutter from the group of sailors as a long, slim leg emerged from under a tattered dress as they lay her body on the deck. Vulnerable. Defenceless. A strange compassion and pity filled Gresham's heart as he watched Mannion cradle the girl's head, turning it to one side to allow her to vomit.

'I will not leave this boat!' she declared firmly as soon as she came to, despite her voice being little more than a harsh croak.

'But this is madness!' said Gresham. 'Madness! We have no room on this sinking hulk for a . . . woman! And what could have prompted you to leave everything behind, your clothes, your jewels, your mother's jewels?'

'The *San Felipe* was a prize of war, was it not? Since when do passengers on a prize of war keep their jewels?'

She had a point, Gresham had to admit. A very small point.

'But I'm sure if you had approached Sir Francis Drake he would have listened to your pleadings . . .'

'I will not be brought back to England in triumph as a prize,' she declared, 'displayed like a Roman Emperor displays his captives.'

So it was pride that this was all about, thought Gresham. 'I must turn the boat around,' he muttered, deeply worried.

'*You will not turn this boat round!*' she hissed at him.

'And why not? You must understand one thing. Your beauty holds no allure for me. There are many beautiful women. Your hiding aboard will infuriate Drake and bring down even more trouble on my head. If you stay you are the only woman on board a ship whose crew think rape no more special than drinking off the contents of a mug. We have no clothes for you, except that ruined article you now wear. Your bodily functions will have to be performed behind locked doors . . .'

She gazed at him with scorn.

'You are my guardian. You will just have to protect me. I repeat, you will not turn this boat round.'

'And what is there to stop me?' he said, finding himself almost shouting at her. He suspected quite a lot of people ended up shouting at this particular young lady. He got control of himself.

'Because if you do I shall throw myself overboard,' she said, simply.

Something like despair clutched at Gresham. Was it a bluff? No, he decided, looking her up and down. She was daft enough to do it. 'But you will be so much more comfortable on board the *San Felipe* . . .'

'I am comfortable here, thank you very much.' She was sitting primly now, hands in her lap, in one of the only two, tiny cabins on the boat. 'I'm sure you've much to do with . . . winching sails or . . . heaving ballasts.' Clearly her grasp of matters nautical was hazy. 'You have my leaves to go and do whatever it is you have to do.'

'It's "leave", not "leaves", and thank you, my ladyship,' said Gresham sarcastically. 'I'm most honoured that your gracious majesty in her infinite wisdom and mercy grants me her permission to do what no one can stop me doing anyway.'

The Ice Queen said nothing. Gresham had clearly been dismissed the presence. In the final count God took the decision for them, as Drake might have said. The steady wind allowed no turning back towards Drake's fleet and the *San Felipe*, and seemed determined to blow them away from it as fast as possible.

'Could be worse,' muttered Mannion.

'How?' said Gresham. 'Just tell me how.' One of the sailors, a huge raspberry birthmark on the side of his face, who had just hurled a coil of rope in Gresham's path, stood there. Gresham looked at him. The smile faded from the sailor's face, and slowly he bent to move the coils.

'Just think, if Drake 'ad gone and got her pregnant. Any child from that pair'd be Anti-Christ.'

They left the captain to sleep in his noisome hole of a cabin, both men standing watch in turn, sleeping on a mattress outside Anna's door.

'This lot'd as soon cut our throats as look at us,' said Mannion. It was not simply that the crew seemed to blame Gresham and Mannion for their exile on to this leaking graveyard. They must have guessed that a man of Gresham's obvious wealth would have at least some gold stitched into his clothing. Robert Leng had clung pathetically to Gresham's side. Let him, thought Gresham. I have questions to ask of you, but later.

The crisis came three days into the voyage. The sky started to take on a hard, metallic sheen on the second day, though the wind stayed steady, and the heat was electric. 'Storm,' said Mannion. 'And she's letting in water faster than we can pump it out.' Two men had been permanently manning the *Daisy*'s battered pump. It was numbing work, but the water level in the bilges was rising and the ship was riding heavily, the bow more happy to drive into the bottom of the waves than to rise up on their crests. Soon they could hear the thump and splash of the water as it surged backwards and forwards, backwards and forwards in the hold.

Then the wind dropped. There was an hour, a fearful hour in which the sailors looked always towards the far horizon, an hour of clammy stillness and heat. They saw the black clouds rolling towards them before they heard their thunder. Within the hour all light was gone, and the sea was a roaring, heaving maelstrom, the *Daisy* plunging down huge walls of water, the careering bow burying itself up to a third of the hull, before dragging itself reluctantly up for the ship to rear stomach-sickeningly high on the crest of the next huge wave. With a snap as of a broken limb, the mains'l split into two halves, and within seconds was mere loose strips of canvas blowing from the yards. The Captain, all alcohol bleached from him by terror, was screaming orders, but the men were refusing to climb the yards, seeing only death aloft. Gresham and Mannion were clinging on for dear life to the guardrail, all pride cast away, kneeling on the deck. Mannion yelled in Gresham's ear.

'He wants them to take in sail! Trying to haul to, ride out the storm with bare yards! 'Cept he's probably wrong!'

The two tops'ls, one on the main and the other on the foremast, were holding, God only knew how, driving the *Daisy* forwards. At times the effect was almost as if the ship was surfing, clinging on the edge of massive waves and driving forward with them. She was almost impossible to hold on the tiller, with three men on it. It gave vicious kicks as the waves slapped and boiled over the stern. Yet now she felt like a lead-filled barrel on the waves, water over the maindeck half the time.

'Pump!' yelled Mannion above the roar of the storm. The two men manning the pump were enfeebled, flapping at the handle. The rest of the crew were cowering under the forecastle. One was screaming a prayer, mouth agape. A great wave passed over the whole bunch, green fury laced with delicate white foam, and when it finally receded there were two fewer men. The one praying was retching, coughing up the bitter salt water from his mouth where he had inhaled it. Gresham and Mannion grabbed the pump handle, and swung themselves into working the antiquated mechanism. They had been soaked through within minutes of the storm's onset. Gresham could feel his skin red-raw where the salt-encrusted fabric was rubbing on his shoulder and elbows, yet where the pain of salt on open flesh should have been there was only a dull, numbing hurt.

They had been driving before the wind for hours when a huge, green boiling sea reared up over the stern and slammed into it. With a wail two men were hurled away from the tiller, crashed into the bulwark and sucked over the side, hands held up beseechingly as if in prayer. The tiller kicked viciously back, flinging the helmsman away from it. What was left of the *Daisy* above the surface started to swing sluggishly round. To be side-on to these gargantuan seas was to be dead, rolled right over and swamped. With a massive leap the helmsman hurled himself back at the wildly flailing tiller, managed somehow to grab and with superhuman strength forced it over. The next vast wave was already towering over them. Slowly, so slowly as to torture every sense, the waterlogged stern swung round. With effortless power, it was as if the tower of water gave the ship the tiniest of little kicks, swooping and streaming under instead of over the stern.

A wave crashed down into the well of the boat. There was a scream from Gresham's side. Robert Leng had been plucked from the deck as if he was weightless, stretched out over the side, his only claim on life one white-knuckled hand clinging with the ferocity of a new-born child to Gresham's upper arm. Gresham looked into the eyes of the man who had betrayed him, wanted to deliver him up to a drum-head court-martial and a hanging. With a shrug of his arm Gresham could have sent him to the bottom of the sea. Instead, with a surging lunge that threatened his own hold on the boat, Gresham reached forward and hauled Leng back on board by the scruff of his neck.

'And would you do the same for me?' he yelled in the teeth of the storm.

But Robert Leng was sobbing, his arms wrapped round the stump of the lanteen mast, clinging to it as if it were his mother, father, wife, brother, sister and child.

The storm stopped without warning. The howl and shriek of the wind through the torn rigging was no longer a constant, but a rising and falling crescendo. Then it lost any rhythm, occasional gusts whipping through the air, snarling at the impudence man had built like an animal circling a beaten foe, unwilling to give up the fight. For hours a huge, rolling sea of mountainous wave after mountainous wave picked the *Daisy* like a sodden cork, flinging her this way and that.

It was a desperate sight that met the salt-scarred eyes of the survivors. The *Daisy* was riding with scarcely two feet of freeboard, the water in the hold nearly up to the level of the hatch. If she had had gun ports cut into her side she would have sunk by now, the water above them and the ports undoubtedly stove in, but her few cannon were placed high on the maindeck, firing through the rail. Three of the guns had smashed through the thin wood, the fourth they had cut free and sent after its companions to lighten the ship. Rigging was streaming from the main and the foremast, and the main mast was swinging ominously.

There were ten of the crew left alive, not including Gresham, Mannion, the gibbering Leng, the man still at the tiller and Anna. The Captain had been swept overboard, as had two crew. Two others lay crumpled, lifeless, on the deck. One had been crushed by a cannon as it careered across the deck, another flung against the bulkhead, the impact smashing his head in as effectively as a blow from a mallet. The survivors were huddled by the forecastle, the position they had taken up for most of the storm.

It was exhaustion that did it. Gresham had gone aft to check that Anna was still alive. She emerged, swinging the wooden door wide open, still somehow composed. Then her eyes opened wide in terror, and Gresham sensed rather than saw a rush of men. He turned, to see that the crew had risen as one, and brought a smashing blow down on Mannion's head with a baulk of timber as he had bent over, struggling to remove the hatch cover. With a sickening

130

thud he collapsed over the half-open hatch, and the men roared their approval, turning like a pack of hyenas on to Gresham.

He did not know what came over him, had no control. It was as if another dark figure stepped up from the deepest recesses of his mind, pushed him to one side and took over his life for the allotted time, the time in which it could and probably should have ended.

Drake had not barred Gresham from claiming his sword from the *Elizabeth Bonaventure*. Stupidly, he had kept the beautiful weapon strapped to his side throughout the storm. Madness of course. Its length threatened to trip him at any time as he was hurled about the tiny deck, and no steel could be a weapon against the ferocious hatred of nature.

The sailors were a vision of Hell. Most had the clothes half-ripped off their backs, most had lost their teeth and the involuntary snarls on their faces revealed gaping black holes. Yet of all things it was the slap, slap of their bare feet on the sodden deck that Gresham remembered most vividly.

The sword flickered once. A backswing to give it momentum, right to left, and then a sweeping curve across the path of the advancing mutineers. He caught the first man in the side of the cheek, and the force of the swinging blow was so great that the metal blade slit through the skin, ran across his tongue and flew out of the other side of his face with a jet-like explosion of blood and particles of flesh. Gresham had cut his face in half, the flap of his lower cheek on both sides hanging down dripping red blood, the man's eyes wide open in shock and horror. There was still force in the blow. The men faltered, stumbled, their primeval instinct seeing the glitter of the blade before their conscious minds registered it. It was not enough for one of them to stop in time. The blade collided with the side of his head, Gresham at full stretch, angling it upwards with a flick of his wrists just before impact. As clean as a surgeon's knife, the man's ear leapt out from the side of his head, flying obscenely through the air like a ball kicked by a child.

The men's eyes swivelled upwards to follow the ludicrous piece of flesh and heard a soft thud as it hit the deck. The man whose face Gresham had opened had been pushed forward by his momentum. As from nowhere, the long, cruel blade of an ornate Italian dagger had appeared in Gresham's other hand. Curling his sword arm, at the end of its swing now, round the back of the man's head he drew him almost lovingly on to the blade, driving it hard under and up through his rib-cage. Blood was streaming from the man's ruined face. His eyes opened wide, a soundless scream in them. In an instant his life flickered out. Gresham stood for a moment, cradling the man as if he were a lover, holding him upright on the blade. Then he flung his sword arm back and savagely withdrew the dagger, at the same time flinging the corpse backwards. Like a wet rag doll it flew through the air, collapsing like a sodden sack of rubbish on to the deck.

The other men fell back. One stumbled over the prostrate form of Mannion, who moaned and stirred. Gresham made two quick paces forward, his sword a lightning bolt pointed at the souls of the mutineers. They fell back, leaving Mannion halfway between them. Suddenly Gresham felt a presence, half turned. The girl was there, clutching the snapped-off half of the pole used for sponging out the cannon. Mannion drew himself groggily to his feet. A line of blood streaked his face, from what was clearly a fearsome gash on his skull. The man must have a skull of iron, thought Gresham. The blow he had been given would have killed any other man.

'Longboat!' he croaked, swaying but staying upright. 'Put the buggers in the longboat. Let 'em row home!'

The longboat was stowed in the middle of the deck though to call it a longboat was a misdirection. It was a stumpy little rowing boat, capable of taking six men at a pinch. What was remarkable was that it appeared to be undamaged, alone of anything on board the *Daisy*. Its lashings had remained firmly secured, and somehow the careering cannons had scraped by instead of into it.

What was Mannion thinking? Was he thinking at all, and had the blow addled his brains? The longboat looked about the only thing on board the *Daisy* that should be floating, that was seaworthy. Wasn't it their only chance? As if reading his mind, Mannion turned to Gresham. Turned his back on his attackers, in an act of supreme arrogance.

'*Do what I says!*' he hissed. '*Just this once, do it without arguing!*'

Gresham looked at Mannion, sword arm still outstretched, looked at the men, huddling back now, courage replaced by stark fear.

'In the boat,' he said, 'and off this ship.'

The men turned to each other, startled. Was this man mad? This was why they had attacked him, to get the longboat, the only chance of survival! The officers and that bloody woman were bound to get it, weren't they? That was how it worked.

Shuffling, they started to free the longboat from its moorings. It should have been hoisted overboard, with a line rigged from the main mast, but that piece of rigging had long gone. Instead, freed of its ropes, the men manhandled the boat to the side and simply tipped it into the water. The surface was so close to the top of the *Daisy*'s hull that the boat hardly splashed as it hit. The one who seemed to be their leader looked enquiringly to where four barrels of water had been lashed to the deck. Two had gone, two were left. God knows if the water inside them had been penetrated by the sea, but the water was fresh enough, loaded off one of the tiny islands by San Miguel. Gresham gave a quick nod. Three men manhandled the barrel into the boat, which sank dangerously under their combined weight, but righted itself again. Without a word, the men pushed off, fumbling for the oars stowed in the bottom of their craft, rowing in an ungainly fashion. Only when long out of sword range did they cry back over the water to them. 'Bastards!' they screamed.

'Why did you give them the boat?' asked Gresham.

' "Are you alright?" might've been a nicer thing to ask me first,' said Mannion, ruefully touching his head where a large hole the size of a salt mine seemed to have been opened up.

'You're talking, so you must be alright. Stupid bloody idiot to get caught out like that anyway. Serves you right. But answer the question! That boat's our only chance of survival.'

'No it ain't,' said Mannion. 'We needed them off here. Ten to three still isn't good odds. And anyway, watch that boat. I should think it'll happen before we lose sight of them.'

'What will happen?'

'You just wait.'

The boat was almost on the horizon when it happened. The mutineers had rigged the tiny sail the boat carried, and suddenly Gresham saw it topple, fall over the side. Men were standing up in the boat, dark silhouettes against the sky. One of them suddenly vanished, as if he had fallen through the deck.

'Rot,' said Mannion, 'the whole boat's riddled with rot. It was one of the first things I checked for. Someone's put a coat of paint over it all, but there's hardly a sound bit of timber in the whole bloody lot. Worst o' the lot round where they seat the mast. Once they put a sail up, they'll tear the heart out of her.'

The men were frantically stumbling and scrambling, arms and legs increasing the speed with which the rotten wood disintegrated. Soon heads were bobbing in the water.

'Don't imagine as any of them can swim,' said Mannion. 'Usually can't, sailors. And they'll panic, of course. Flail out, drive the good bits of timber away instead of grabbing on to them. Couple of them might grab something big enough to keep 'em afloat. Could take, two, three maybe even four days to die, if the weather stays good.'

Across the sea from them men were praying, screaming, not going gently into the good night but fighting for every scrap of life, and losing. Men with thoughts, with feelings, some with wives, all with lovers, men with children, men whose mothers had wept and laughed over them. Bad men, probably, the sweepings of God's earth, but men with the same capacity to feel pain and the same desire to hold on to existence as all of us, life being the only gift they had been given free of charge. Men brought crying into the world, leaving it crying their pain. Until the waters finally closed over their heads. And from the sinking deck of the *Daisy* – how odd that word sounded, redolent of English meadows, the smell of Spring and good solid earth, here on this rolling, oily expanse of grey water where no roots could ever take hold and everything was impermanent, fluid – these little dramas were being played out without sound, the figures in the water mere marionettes, detached, somehow not real.

Except they were real for Mannion.

'Bastards,' said Mannion, with total sincerity. 'Remember not to creep up on me again.'

Gresham had just killed a man, face to face. He was watching six men die. Yet he felt almost light-headed. Nothing mattered any more. It was all Fate. Man decided nothing. It was all decided for him. It felt very different from the time in Grantchester meadows. Was it maturity? Or was he simply becoming even more callous?

They turned away from the pathetic frail figures struggling in the water. Soon they were lost to view as Gresham and the others found a barrel of water, broached it, and drank until the taste of salt was no longer quite so strong in their mouths. The olives and the biscuit they found in other barrels were the best thing they had ever tasted. Was it the food they were tasting, or was it simply the taste of being alive? Anna ate with them. She had said virtually nothing, except to confirm that she had no lasting injuries. The tattered dress no longer concealed the girl's ankles, and Gresham found his eyes drawn unstoppably towards them, a different hunger surprising him now that he had taken the edge off the hunger for food and clean water. Suddenly the feet swirled away, and the girl was back to her cabin. God knew what terrors she had gone through there in the storm. She had seen a man killed in front of her, must have known her fate had Gresham and Mannion been overcome. She had not seen fit to share her fears with them. Perhaps they had had enough of their own.

An overwhelming desire to sleep came over Gresham. He had heard about this, from soldiers who had been in battle. The dreadful tiredness, the total imperative to sleep. The *Daisy* groaned as another wave lifted her water-filled belly up out of the sea. I must not sleep. We must somehow claim back the boat from the elements, must somehow get back to England, Gresham repeated to himself.

'We're sinking.' It was Anna. She had emerged from the cabin. How could a young girl's voice be so commanding? Somehow she had managed to comb her hair. 'I'm pleased to say I know nothing about the sea except that it is wet and unpleasant in ways I had never dreamed of,' she said to Gresham. 'Yet even I can see this boat is settling deeper and deeper into the water, not least of all because there is a foot of waters in my cabin that was not there an hour ago.'

'Water,' mumbled Gresham.

Mannion took over. 'Wooden ships, they're funny. You see, the wood really wants to float. It's what it was designed to do. Seen ships like this stay afloat for days. There's another thing, both bad news and good news. Load of them barrels they gave us when we set off. They're empty. Found that out too, soon after we set off. 'Bout half of them. That's what you can hear now.'

There was a constant bumping and crashing from within the hold as the ship rose and fell uneasily in the swell.

'They're helping us keep afloat, I reckon.'

'Raft,' said Gresham. 'Build a raft.'

They were dead in the water. Miraculously the two tops'ls were still largely intact, but flapping uselessly as the last savage swing of the storm had severed the ropes that hung at their foot, tensioning them and holding the wind. Leng had crept out from whatever corner he had been gibbering in, calmer now, just looking as if someone had held him underwater for half an hour.

'We have to build a raft,' said Gresham. 'Got some water left, got some food not spoilt. Use the empty barrels to build a raft, while the old *Daisy*'s still got some life in her. Rig a sail as a shelter. Keep Anna out of the sun. You can survive for weeks, if you can keep out of the water. That's what kills you, staying in the water.' He was almost raving, feeling his control leaving him.

'Can I ask just one question?' asked Anna.

136

'You just have. Now will you shut up and let us get on with it?'

Why had he rounded on the girl, thought Gresham? Because he was exhausted, because crisis after crisis was piling up in his life, and most of all because he had not asked for her to be there as an extra burden, a burden demanding he think about someone other than himself. He liked being selfish, he had decided. It was safer, simpler, far less complicated. And deep in his soul, he was beginning to think that he would never set foot on land again.

The girl ignored him.

'Why are you going to build a raft?'

Gresham sighed, deeply and long.

'Because this ship is sinking. And because unless we're to sink along with it, we need something on which we can float. Can we carry on now?'

'Certainly,' she said. 'But it would be easier, would it not, to go to wherever we're going on that very big boat that's been in sight for nearly ten minutes now?'

The men turned, their jaws dropping. The *Merchant Royal*, one of the London ships that had separated from Drake's fleet what seemed a lifetime earlier. Scouring the ocean for Drake, blown off course in the same storm that had nearly killed them. The wonderful sight of the ship bore down on them, the two little flapping sails having let her see them before even Anna's sharp young eyes had picked out her bulk on the ocean.

CHAPTER 6

July, 1587
London

'I came as soon as I received your message,' said Robert Cecil.

Well, that was true at least, thought Walsingham. Cecil had come by boat to Barnes from Whitehall, against the tide if the sheen of sweat on his boatmen was anything to go by. The journey would have pained Cecil, Walsingham knew. His warped back made no travel easy, not even by boat. It was intentional, of course. The more pain Cecil underwent before their interview the more Walsingham might catch him off guard.

The room was small, but overlooked the garden at Barnes through a long, latticed window that was disproportionately large. Walsingham had avoided the garish decoration that was suddenly the fashion, and stayed with sombre, dark panelling, while a feeble fire gagged in the grate and gave out no heat.

'How may I be of assistance?' asked Cecil. He was young still, thought Walsingham. In a few years he would shear his last comment of the slight note of ingratiation it now contained, but in his inexperience, he managed to make a straightforward comment ever so slightly patronising.

His family had no breeding. Walsingham was sure that in some way this was Cecil's weak spot. He needed to know for certain.

Insurance. Knowing where this man was vulnerable was important if Walsingham was to be allowed to bow out of power, instead of being kicked out. The vicious battle for power that was taking place at Court was between breeding and ability. Men like Cecil had wits enough for ten, and a supreme sense of politics derived from always having to guard their backs. Their opponents, Essex in particular, had breeding, charm and the easy nonchalance of those bred to power.

'It is possible that I might be of assistance to you,' said Walsingham, with a smile neither of them believed. 'I learned long ago that men of sense acknowledge debt, and ensure that it is always repaid. I am a poor man.' Well, that was true. What money he once had had gone into financing his network of agents. 'Therefore I can give only knowledge, in the hope that one day those to whom I give it might be in a position to return something I need in payment back to me.'

Cecil had to think about that one. Undoubtedly he was thinking that he should beware the Devil bringing gifts. Yet he was a young man, and the curiosity and rashness was there in him, even if it was not vented in wine, women or gambling like most young men. Cecil would take the bait.

'What knowledge is it that you have, and think might be of interest to me?' asked Cecil carefully.

There! He would swallow the bait! 'I can hardly help but be aware of your interest in the young man Henry Gresham,' said Walsingham. Was there a slight colour come into Cecil's face? A slight tightening of the skin round the lips? Only the most suspicious person would have thought so. 'I wonder if you are aware of a most amusing story regarding that young man?'

Cecil shook his head, his leaning forward betraying his interest.

'You know his background?' asked Walsingham.

'I believe so,' said Cecil, on firmer ground now. 'His father was immensely rich, a fortune made largely through moneylending. He apparently conceived a bastard. It was not until quite late in the bastard's life that it was realised his father had left him a vast fortune, having neglected him while he was alive.'

'True, as far as it goes,' said Walsingham. 'But have you ever wondered why such a highly respected man should acknowledge a by-blow at all? A bastard may be a . . . a regrettable fact of life for such a man. Yet we both know the river hides many such secrets. I wonder why Gresham's father took the trouble to acknowledge him? And, moreover, why he chose to make him such a wealthy bastard?'

'I had assumed . . . a sense of duty,' said Cecil. 'And the father died childless, after a boy born in wedlock departed this life, did he not? Perhaps the father felt it preferable that the line continue, even from such flawed seed, rather than it die out . . .'

'It may well be so,' said Walsingham. 'It may well be so indeed. Yet the birth of a bastard was not the only extraordinary thing to happen in the life of Sir Thomas Gresham. You are too young to remember, yet some years ago, he was made guardian to a young lady. A quite extraordinary young lady. The reasons are lost in time. Perhaps they were as simple as a young woman needing a guardian and an old, wealthy man being deemed the most suitable candidate.'

'And the outcome?' asked Cecil, engrossed.

'The young lady in question was a nightmare. Beautiful, independent, possessed of a will entirely of her own. And of very bad judgement. They clashed, violently, from the outset. The servants recollect him complaining that unlike most men he had been made to suffer Hell here on earth by this woman placed in his care, instead of waiting until after his death. In any event, the lady left his household after a period of time.'

'Is that all?' asked Cecil, disappointed.

'In public?' said Walsingham. 'Yes. Except if one listens to the servants, a very different story emerges. A story of a wild young girl deciding to make an old man rather happier than he claims to have been. Of a child born some six months after the lady I have mentioned left Sir Thomas Gresham's house. Born, I might add, in conditions of strictest secrecy. A child later acknowledged by Sir Thomas as his own, and named Henry Gresham. With no mention, now or then, of the mother, her origins, her background or who she was.'

'And are you sure of this?' asked Cecil.

'Yes,' said Walsingham. 'I am.'

'And who was the girl?' asked Cecil.

'Lady Mary Keys,' said Walsingham flatly.

The colour drained from Cecil's face. Interesting, thought Walsingham, very interesting.

'Lady Mary Keys . . . the sister of Lady Jane Grey?' asked Cecil, his voice almost a whisper.

'The same,' said Walsingham. 'Lady Jane Grey, whose blood-claim to the throne of England was sufficient for her to be declared Queen for nine days, placed there by unscrupulous relatives before being removed by Queen Mary and executed for her folly. So you see, the blood of Tudor Kings flowed through Lady Mary Keys, enough of it to make her sister Queen for nine days. In that sense, if in no other, I suspect Henry Gresham's first name was chosen with some care.'

'And why have you told me this, Sir Francis?' asked Cecil, his eyes staring now.

Why, thought Walsingham? Because breeding is the one thing you will never have, and the lack of it frightens you. Because I do not know if you are acting for your father, for yourself, for the Queen, for Leicester, for Essex or for someone whose existence I am not yet aware. All I know is that Henry Gresham features in your plans, and that this news will make you fear him that little more, and in your youth and inexperience that fear might make you reveal just a little more.

'I have told you,' said Walsingham, 'because men of our position should trust each other. Were you to find out from other sources what I have just told you, you might consider that I had been with-holding information from you. You are a rising star. I would wish to have your complete trust.'

'Does Gresham know who his mother is? That he is . . . distantly related to monarchy?'

'That I do not know. Yet it would not surprise me. Henry Gresham is a rather deep young man, who may know more than even I suspect.'

Cecil had emphasised 'distantly related', Walsingham noticed. Good. He suspected that Cecil already resented Gresham's good looks and fine body, as well as the independence his money brought him. Only in intelligence were they a match for each other, Cecil's superiority resting simply on his awareness of Gresham being a bastard. And now Walsingham had taken that away, and as well as unsettling him had perhaps gained an inch more of Cecil's trust.

'Are there others who know the truth about his birth? Others at Court?' asked Cecil.

There! Walsingham had sensed it. The tremor, the flicker of something behind the words. Walsingham sensed that for Cecil much rested on this answer.

'It is possible,' said Walsingham, appearing to think the question over for a few seconds, as if it had never occurred to him before. 'But if you were to ask me to guess, I would say . . . no.'

Cecil visibly relaxed. His parting was as quick as he could make it, only just the right side of civility.

So what did Walsingham now know, he mused as the dust settled after Cecil's departure? Cecil was involved in a plot of some sort or another, and Henry Gresham was probably little more than a pawn in it. Yet for Gresham to play his part it was necessary for those who wielded power in the Court not to know that Gresham had been born not just on the wrong side, but on the wrong side of a very expensive blanket. Well, Walsingham was a long way from an answer, but in the slow, measured and remorseless manner that had served him so well over the years he was gaining a little more information all the time. And Henry Gresham? Walsingham had no doubt that he had lessened Gresham's chances of survival, but Gresham had been a volunteer to join the murky world of espionage. He would sink or swim, as plain luck and merit dictated. Just as Walsingham had had to do when he was a young man.

*

The *Merchant Royal* had mercifully sailed to London, berthing at Deptford. Gresham felt as if the journey from Plymouth to London would have succeeded where a Spanish galley and Drake and his enemies had failed, and killed him at last. He had pleaded with the Captain to be first off. Their arrival on deck would be the talk of every tavern in London the first minute one of the *Merchant*'s sailors made it ashore. He had tried to explain the situation to Anna, felt that he owed her that at least.

'Someone wanted me killed on Drake's ship. I can't be certain of who it is. The minute the ship docks the story will be out in London, and for all I know whoever wants me dead will try again. I can't use my own house in case it's being watched, and George's house in London will be as well watched as my own. We have to smuggle ourselves to an inn, and not even a good one. It has to be one where people don't always want to be recognised . . .'

'What death warrant is out on me?' asked Anna. 'Apart from the social death of having nothing to wear, no servants to care for even my basic needs and no home to go to. Nor any parents to find in this nonexistent home!' Her tone was cold. 'You tell me that my . . . guardian is rich, a person who speaks with the Queen of England.' She gave a sharp laugh. 'Yet he and his ward have to disguise their passage through London as if they were criminals. I believe this is a rich person,' her voice was loaded with scorn, 'a friend of the Queen!' She cursed the hot tears she felt rising up in her eyes, turned her back on both of them quickly before they could see. 'I think you are both criminals, and liars.' Her voice was steady.

Gresham was losing what little patience he had. Mannion looked as if any moment he would take the girl and put her over his knee.

'My being made your guardian and your stupid coming aboard the *Daisy* means that we are now associated, seen as being together. Any enemy of mine will be an enemy of yours!'

'This is a poor country, where honest women cannot safely walk the streets,' she said scornfully.

'It's a country fighting for its existence,' said Gresham, 'and I'm sorry you've been caught up in that fight. Either way, my life is at risk if when we leave this ship I am recognised, or if I am recognised by your presence. We're lucky. We'll land after the sun's gone down. We can shroud you in a cloak . . .'

'There is a simpler way,' said Anna in a matter-of-fact voice.

'There is no simpler way,' said Gresham. Needle shafts of pain were beginning to shoot through his head, and he had never felt more tired, the exhaustion a physical presence pressing down on him. 'I've already— '

'Dress me as a man,' said Anna simply. 'Or as a ship's boy. They have clothes on board, clothes that will fit. What news is there in a ship's boy leaving a ship? Particularly if his hair is crammed under a cap and his face blackened with dirt.'

There was a stunned silence. Gresham and Mannion looked at each other aghast.

'Don't be ridiculous!' exploded Gresham. 'Young girls can't go around in *trousers*, for Heaven's sake!'

'Please stop talking like a father when you are only the age of a son. And a very young son at that,' said Anna, her voice as sharp as a sword being taken out of its sheath. Why were these men so . . . *stupid*. How long did it take them to see the obvious? 'If you really think we're in danger, two seamans and a boy going ashore will attract far less attention than two men and a woman.'

'Seamen. Not seamans.' Gresham looked her over. He guessed her hips were quite boyish, pleasantly rounded for sure but nothing like the vast, child-bearing mountains some women carried. But her breasts . . . even under a loose-fitting linen shirt . . .'

'Now you've inspected the goods at length, do you want to buy?' Anna's voice was acid, stinging, having been insulted by the mental undressing to which her body had been subjected. 'Shop can't stay open all day . . .' It was a phrase her favourite nurse had used. Gresham controlled the flush that threatened to creep into his face. Damn! Had he been that obvious?

'I was thinking . . .' How do you tell a well-brought-up

144

seventeen-year-old female Spanish aristocrat that her breasts were too big? Mannion interrupted.

'It's not as daft as it sounds. She's right, it'll be less dramatic if we're just a lad and two men. And we sure ain't going to get a woman's dress on board this ship. Getting some clothes for a lad'll be a doddle.'

Feeling that he was being ganged-up on, Gresham faltered, losing the battle with the redness in his cheeks. 'But what . . . what about concealing . . . how do we hide . . . you know . . .' He felt like cupping two imaginary breasts to his chest. To Hell with it! 'You know your . . . *female* bits?'

Was there the faintest glimmer of amusement in the girl's eyes at Gresham's discomfiture? Mannion had turned to the tiny window. Why was he silently shaking?

'They can be strapped back, wound with tape, as a long as it's not too long,' she said, as if discussing her breasts with a man was an everyday commonplace. Perhaps it was, thought Gresham, for all he really knew about the girl.

Gresham found himself stirring, against his will, at the prospect of someone taking on that job, and brought himself round by imagining that he was jumping into the cold, clear water of the Cam on a winter's day. Sex was like food. It was an appetite. You didn't let it touch your heart.

Leng had been useless in providing them with information. Gresham and Mannion had bided their time, then cornered him one evening aboard the *Merchant Royal*.

'All I did was look in your belongings! As I was told to do!' he gabbled. His nervousness was not surprising. Mannion was holding a dagger none-too-gently to his throat. 'And make what I found public! I was told if I agreed they could get me passage with Drake – a real chance to make my name.'

'And so have me killed?' asked Gresham, a total lack of emotion in his voice. Something froze in the heated cauldron of Robert Leng's mind at the tone of that voice.

'Well, perhaps not so . . . in reality not so!' Leng's spirit picked up a little as he realised what he was saying. 'Evidently Drake didn't kill you, even when I did what I did. In fact he damned nearly killed me . . .' That wasn't a helpful path to go down, Leng saw immediately.

'The only reason I stayed alive was that no one had instructed Drake to hang me. If they'd squared that with him, he'd have done it to a Spanish spy without a thought. That and the fact the girl touched something in Drake, and he'd given his word. And he spotted you as a mercenary, of course. Someone whose only loyalty is to his own self-interest. You lied to him, you see, which is more than I ever did. You didn't tell him why you were on board, not the real reason. So he left us both to God. So before I send you to Satan,' said Gresham, his voice like a pistol shot, 'tell me! *Who gave you your instructions?*'

'A clerk! A stupid clerk! At Whitehall!' gibbered Leng. 'He gave me a letter guaranteeing a passage on Drake's ship, then a letter giving me . . . instructions. Said it was on the orders of higher authority, for God's sake!'

This was not helpful. He was probably telling the truth. For all Gresham knew, the order to set him up could have come straight from the Queen. Or Burghley. Or Walsingham. Or Cecil. Leicester. Essex. His mind started to reel. He did not know who. He did not know why.

'What are you going to do with me?' asked Leng, panic in his eyes.

'This,' said Gresham, and rammed a stinking piece of cloth in the man's mouth. No point in waking the ship. There was a sudden movement from Mannion, a sharp crack! and Leng's eyes opened wide in fear as he tried to scream.

'It's a clean break,' said Mannion, letting Leng drop to the deck. 'Between the knee and the hip, so it'll hurt more and cost you more to get round on. But if you're sensible and you don't mind waiting, you'll walk just like normal. Quite a long time from now, mind. Time for you to think about what happens when you betray people. Leastways, when you betray people like us.'

Tears were streaming out of Leng's eyes, the enormity of what had been done to him hitting home as the torrents of agonising pain screamed into his brain. His every urge was to wriggle and move, yet each time he did so more unbelievable pain shot through his body.

Gresham looked down at him. There was no emotion in his voice. 'I'm a bad one to betray,' he said quietly. 'Never do it again or it'll be your neck, not your leg.'

Shortly after sunset, Gresham stood on the shore thinking back to the moment over three months ago when he had stood on the Plymouth quayside. Then he had several changes of clothing, chests containing essentials for a sea voyage and barrels with his own private food store, a load that had cost him a small fortune to get taken on board the *Elizabeth Bonaventure*. Now all he had was what he stood in. And Mannion. And, of course, the girl, who was shivering in excitement, disguised in a loose shirt, heavy leather jerkin that was two sizes too big for her and trousers gathered under her knees. Worsted stockings did nothing to hide the shape of her calves, though boys could look good there too. Her luxurious hair was crammed under a working man's cap, and from far enough away she looked for all the world like a lad out for his first night in the big city. It was a cold night for July, the wind driving lances of rain intermittently, shutters banging on the poor houses and warehouses lining the waterfront. He and Mannion looked round, waving the boat off to muffled good wishes from the four crew. They were at an obscure jetty. Stepping back against the wall of the nearest ramshackle, crazily-leaning house and out of the half moonlight, they listened for a full five minutes. All seemed quiet. Carefully, quietly, hugging the side of the streets, they made their way to a hovel a quarter of a mile away in Deptford, used more commonly by smugglers and pickpockets than by gentlemen. In this part of town people averted their eyes from passers-by. Anna did not ask why Gresham and Mannion knew of the inn. At least his knowledge of its normal clientele meant that the landlord let them in. To his surprise, the room was reasonably clean, and there seemed to be no tiny creatures scuttling over the bedding.

Though neither of them said it, the girl was a burden. It should have been Gresham *and* Mannion who went to beard Cecil, but they dare not leave the girl on her own. 'Take care, now,' said Mannion, gruffly, grumpy about having to stay behind. The girl said nothing. At least for all her pride she seemed to recognise that Mannion posed no threat to her virtue. If she still had it, of course.

Gresham used more of the money sewn into his doublet to hail a boat, a lantern swinging from its bow and stern. Up through the dangerous arches of London Bridge, the tide helping them, the river surprisingly full of bobbing lights. There was more shipping moored below the bridge than Gresham had ever seen. England was gathering its forces for the final battle, as Spain had been gathering hers. Yet London's efforts seemed puny by the side of the power they had seen assembled in Lisbon and Cadiz. There were no galleys moored in the Thames, no trained fighting vessels. There were ships aplenty, fine ships, but they were merchant vessels with merchant crews, not warships.

Gresham shivered. Drake may have 'singed the King of Spain's beard,' but beards grew again, and even without his beard his face and body were of immense strength. They would talk about Cadiz as if it was a great victory, yet it might be that all they had done was waken the sleeping giant. And Cadiz had been a raid. Just a raid. For all the noise that would be made, the English had made a quick dash into a weakly defended harbour, with no warships of any significance there to protect it except some galleys, and dashed out again. How would those raiding ships fare when faced with the massed lines of Spanish and Portuguese men o' war?

The city was dangerous at night, men rich enough being led by torch and lantern light, men placed fore and aft. Individuals about their private business slunk in the dark under the leaning houses, burying their heads in their cloaks, seeking the anonymity of the night. Cecil's house was silent, dark. The pounding on the door would have woken the dead, but took longer to wake the servant.

He was an old man with a ludicrous sleeping cap covering his bald head. He peered through the small, square viewing panel set in the door, squinting to outline the figure outside.

'I come with news from Cadiz, straight off a ship of Drake's squadron!'

Was the *Merchant Royal* the first back? Almost certainly not. But there was no chance Drake's main squadron would have returned yet, its speed dictated by the lumbering hulk of the *San Felipe*.

'I have vital news for Robert Cecil! I must report to him on my mission!'

Would it work? Yes! The door was opening. The man had recognised him! It would take some years yet for Henry Gresham to realise just how many people did remember him once they first set eyes on him. He followed the old man along gloomy corridors, the only light that of the lantern. 'Wait here,' the old man grunted. They were in what was little more than a slightly widened corridor, with a poor bench along one wall, inset in a window. The old man vanished, the dancing light of the lantern following him as he stumped along yet another hallway, finally turning a corner. Gresham found himself in a darkness broken only by the feeble glimmer of a single candle in a wall sconce. Heavier footsteps came down the hall, two sets of them. The men were clearly servants, thick-set and expensively dressed in the Cecil livery.

'Come with us,' said the taller of the two men, and turned away. Gresham made no move.

'In the house I own, The House, as it happens, on the Strand here in London,' Gresham stressed, 'I am accustomed to the servants addressing visitors with courtesy.'

The man coloured, seemed uncertain. He was clearly unwilling to recant his rudeness at all – after all, Gresham's dress and his body had been three months at sea – but also unwilling to detain the guest from his master.

'Perhaps the easiest thing would be to send someone with good manners,' said Gresham helpfully.

The man finally muttered something which could have been, 'If you'd care to follow me . . . sir', and Gresham decided to take the olive branch. Judging by the look on the man's face Gresham was likely to find the same branch sticking out of his own back later that evening.

'Do by all means sit down,' said Cecil. The room was lavishly panelled, and to gild the lily expensive French tapestries hung on two walls. They showed mythical beasts pursuing men. One of them had human flesh hanging from its bloodied fangs. Perhaps it was an emblem for the Cecil family.

Cecil's chair was high-backed, with ornately carved arms, one of the few luxuries Gresham had seen in the house. He was in full day dress, the single, fur-lined vestment of an older man rather than the fashionable doublet and hose of the *gallant*. The remains of a meal, simple by the look of it, lay in front of him on an oaken table, polished so that the light of the many candles reflected back from its surface. Cecil gestured, and the two ungainly men made haste to clear the table.

'Will you take some wine?' asked Cecil civilly. If he had felt any shock at Gresham's being alive he had not shown it.

The jug and goblets were of gold. Was Cecil one of those who needed to see his family wealth in order to believe in it? Or was this supposedly solitary dining simply a show to impress?

'What a pleasant surprise to see you so soon on your return. Do tell me about your mission,' said Cecil smoothly, as if asking after the progress of someone's summer vegetables in their kitchen garden. 'I have heard some news, of course. But a first-hand account always has some value.'

Gresham gazed levelly back into Cecil's eyes. There was no response there, no emotion. Just a blankness.

'A major victory was achieved.' Gresham's tone was intense, full of importance. He even leaned forward to make his next statement. 'The Battle of the Barrel Staves was well and truly won by England,' said Gresham. 'We proved ourselves the world's masters in destroying unassembled pieces of barrels. Positively ignoring the many dangers. Splinters, for example, or tripping up over the bits of wood. I'm sure you would have been proud of your sailors. And their commanders.' There was the tiniest tightening round Cecil's eyes. Anger. Not amusement. Gresham leaned back, spoke in his normal tone. 'Oh, and several hundred Spanish fishing families will die this winter as we wiped out their boats, their livelihoods. And the contents of Cadiz harbour were emptied out of Spain's pocket and into those of Sir Francis Drake. And Her Majesty, of course.'

There was silence, for what seemed a very long time.

'That is all you have to report?' said Cecil finally.

'Well,' said Gresham, examining his fingernails, much torn by rope and canvas, 'that's all the important stuff. Oh, and Drake's so-called fleet is like a pack of mad hounds with no training, and he has as much control over them as a bear over the dogs that bait him. Not much else happened, actually. He refused to let me land ashore. It's surprisingly boring being at sea for three months. Oh, and someone planted false letters in my belongings making me out to be a spy for Spain, and arranged to have them discovered,' he said casually, as if the thought had just struck him. 'Or, to put it bluntly, someone tried to kill me. By proxy, of course.'

'Kill you?' There was no tone in Cecil's question.

'Yes. Gives a new meaning to the pen being mightier than the sword, doesn't it? But we . . . spies don't bother much about that sort of thing. All in a day's work, you know. In fact we get quite upset if someone doesn't try to kill us.' Gresham beamed a broad smile at Cecil. 'Can I have some of that wine now?'

'Will you still be flippant in the grave?' asked Cecil. His tone was still measured, easy, conversational.

'Well, I doubt I'll be flippant after it,' Gresham answered. 'But I'm quite keen to know who it is who's trying to send me there.'

The silence stretched to an eternity. Cecil did not move. Even with support from the high back it must hurt him to sit so still, thought Gresham. If that was so, he was hiding his pain as well as he was hiding his feelings.

'I know nothing of these matters,' he said finally.

'Quite so,' said Gresham easily. 'Though I'm forced to point out that whoever is responsible went to extraordinary lengths to cover their tracks, and so is hardly likely to admit to the fact in open conversation.'

'You show your lack of breeding by coming to a gentleman's house and accusing him, without evidence, of murder,' said Cecil carefully.

'You show your lack of judgement by insulting a man in a manner that gives him the right to challenge you to a duel. A duel you would lose,' said Gresham flatly. 'So your comments have handed me either your life, or your honour.' Cecil realised the mistake he had made. No member of the Court would challenge Gresham's right to challenge Cecil after the comment he had made. He would lose his life if he fought Gresham, and lose his honour if he refused to fight. 'Luckily for you,' said Gresham, 'this would probably be a bad time for me to kill the son of the Queen's Chief Secretary. Or dishonour him.' If Cecil was relieved, he did not show it.

Damn! Gresham had to play this so carefully. Cecil was as attractive to him as rotten meat, but he was a prime contender for the new power in the land, could well become the leader of the pack after the death of Walsingham and his father. In the world of politics, it should be almost irrelevant to Gresham if Cecil had indeed tried to kill him. What mattered was that Gresham found out why, and that he was stopped from doing it again. With those two key facts in place, an alliance between the two men was perfectly possible. Half of the Court had tried to harm the other half at one time or another. It was part of the game they played. But still Gresham was no closer to knowing the true identity of his enemy. And if the truth be known he had come to Cecil, of all the suspects, not because he was foremost in Gresham's suspicions but simply because of all the suspects Cecil was the only one he could approach. Burghley, the Queen, Essex and Leicester's servants would provide a far greater barrier than the Cecil's relatively modest household.

The pain finally scored a small victory over Cecil. He shifted, and his lips tightened over his thin mouth.

It was time to get serious. Even if Cecil was his would-be murderer Gresham would not find out tonight. All he could do was plant snares, blocks, so that if he was the culprit he would pause before trying again. Like the poacher, Gresham had to set his traps over a wide ground, wherever the animals might tread. Yet he was now the hunted, not the hunter. 'We live in complex times, Master Cecil,' said Gresham.

'How so?' There was the tiniest hint of a sneer in Cecil's voice.

'You are a man in the midst of making, or breaking, your career. Your main rival for the Queen's favours is the Earl of Essex. Beauty and the Beast, in fact.' Cecil stiffened at that, but said nothing. 'Or more accurately, ancient breeding versus self-made man. You see, for all your father's power and wealth, you have no noble ancestry.'

Why did Cecil bridle at that? Gresham stored away the weakness for possible future use.

'I make no insinuations,' said Gresham, 'against the son of the Queen's Chief Minister. Perish the traitorous thought! Why men have been killed for less . . . not that that was an insinuation, of course. Merely a slip of the tongue. But I do have one more thing to mention, in passing, as it were.'

'And what is that?'

'Your illustrious father is out of favour because he is seen as having expedited the signing and the sending of the death warrant of Mary Queen of Scots. The Queen is claiming her ministers acted without her authority.'

'Gossip,' said Cecil easily. 'Idle Court gossip. If you had attended Court more, you would learn how to treat such tittle-tattle.'

'I'm so glad it's just that,' said Gresham, sounding relieved. 'You're obviously secure in your power and influence. Me? I have someone trying to kill me, someone who doesn't want me to know who they are. So I need a little insurance on my life. And from a number of people, until I identify my real enemies. We're two very different people. I've have no dependants, no family as such, no one to cry for my death.'

'How sad,' said Cecil, with earth-shattering insincerity. 'I suspect that even this early in my career there are many who would cheer up dramatically if I were to die,' said Cecil, with a dry humour that was the nearest he ever got to laughing.

'You miss the point,' said Gresham. 'I'm not interested in who would cry if you died. I am interested in who you would cry for if *they* died. I'm in love with only myself. That's my strength. They tell me you are in love with someone else. That's your weakness. If I determine that you attempted to kill the person I most love – me – I will activate my insurance, and the person you most love will die.'

'You have a window into my soul, do you, Henry Gresham?' asked Cecil mockingly.

'No, but perhaps the beautiful Elizabeth Brooke has one.'

Cecil shot to his feet, and the candles all round the room flickered as if in anger.

'How dare you?' Cecil roared. There was a scurrying at the door, and the two servants appeared, bursting in and halting only when Cecil raised his hand.

Cecil could have tried to kill me then and there, thought Gresham. Outnumbered three to one, disadvantaged by being seated, a quick thrust of a dagger and a lifeless bundle in a weighted sack thrown to join the other bodies in the Thames that night. He could see the thought passing through Cecil's brain. 'You don't know what arrangements I have in place should I not return from this house. It'd be gratifying to kill me. It wouldn't be intelligent,' he warned Cecil.

Cecil motioned the men away with his hand.

He was terrified of women, fearing their scorn of his body. Elizabeth Brooke was the daughter of Lord Cobham and would bring him social respectability as well as a dowry of two thousand pounds. It was also said, extraordinarily, that Elizabeth was both a lovely girl and one who felt some love at least for Cecil. There was no accounting for women.

'As I said, attachments such as this are a weakness of yours. My lack of attachments is my strength. No harm need come to the woman you love. All that's required is that you are proven to have done no harm to me, and attempt no such harm in the future.'

'I do not respond to threats,' said Cecil with acid in his voice. 'And what is most certain, above all other certainties, is that those who threaten me need look first to the threat to their own lives.'

'Wonderful!' said Gresham, suddenly infinitely relaxed. 'Marvellous! You realise what's happened of course?' Cecil did not realise, clearly. He was wrong-footed by the ebullient cheerfulness of Gresham's tone, confused. 'We've acknowledged that we're enemies. At last the slimy protocol of Court has been replaced by some real human feeling. My desire to kill your fiancée if you're the person seeking to kill me. Your desire really to kill me if I make that threat.'

'If my reaction to our relatively brief acquaintance is any guide, there must be many who wish you ill, Henry Gresham,' said Cecil.

'But few who will say it so clearly,' said Gresham with immense cheerfulness. 'How strange, yet how admirable, that from dislike can come honesty. Now we know each other.'

'You will never know me,' said Cecil.

'Nor you me,' said Gresham, 'but we can both know enough to get by.'

'Why did you come here tonight?'

'To see if it was you who tried to have me killed.'

'And have you?'

'Our meeting has prompted interesting thoughts,' said Gresham, smiling, relaxed now. 'And there is something you could do as a gesture of goodwill.'

Cecil shifted uneasily in his seat. Was it physical pain, or mental uncertainty?

'You talk of goodwill after making bizarre threats against me?'

'It was rumoured before I left that there was to be a diplomatic mission to the Duke of Parma, to see if peace could be negotiated between Spain and England. Has it happened?' Gresham asked.

'You are well informed,' said Cecil. It was actually George who had been well informed, but Gresham saw no reason for Cecil to know that. 'No, the mission has not yet taken place. It will not do so for some while.'

'The rumour also had it that you were to be a member of this mission. I need to accompany it. Your influence in allowing that to happen would be helpful.'

'I would have thought Sir Francis Walsingham's influence was sufficient to ensure you your passport? Why not approach him?'

'I may well do so. Yet his influence is not necessarily so massive as to resist an objection from, say, Lord Burghley. That same man who might seek to oppose my presence on this mission in the face of, say, an objection from his son.'

'I repeat, you have just threatened to kill or maim my fiancée,' said Cecil, a vicious anger still in his voice, 'and now you are asking for my help. Do you not recognise a certain . . . irony in your request?'

'I prefer to think of it as pragmatism,' said Gresham. 'You would happily kill me without a moment's thought if I stood in your way. I reciprocate the gesture. The pragmatism comes in because all your climbing of the greasy pole at Court comes to nothing if our country collapses to an invasion and Spain rules in London. My presence on the diplomatic mission might help avert that.'

'And how can I be certain that you work for England, and not Spain? How can I be certain that letter you say was forged was not genuine?'

'You can't. But if I was a spy you would have an excellent chance to catch me out in the close company we would be forced to keep on such an expedition.'

'And what would you do on such a mission? I do not relish one of our members being caught spying when we are in effect in enemy country. I care not if you lose your life, but it would be a sadness if in losing your own life you threatened the lives of the others on the mission.'

'Nothing is certain. Yet I give you my word that what I plan to do will not harm England, nor the members of the diplomatic mission. It is essential that I visit the Duke of Parma's court. To do so openly would be the best cover of all. But there's more.'

'More?' echoed Cecil.

'I also need permission to travel to Lisbon. That permission will have to be openly applied for.' Visits to foreign countries by a gentleman required the issue of a Queen's passport. 'I can obtain such permission, under normal circumstances, either in my own right or through my Lord Walsingham. I would not wish it to be blocked. By anyone with influence at Court, for example.'

'Your . . . relationship with the Queen suggests you might gain most things that you ask for.'

'My relationship with the Queen leaves me with a head on my shoulders simply because alone of those at Court I never ask her for anything. It's not your support I need. It is your word that you will not block my request.'

Cecil looked witheringly at Gresham. 'You understand so little about the world in which I live. My father is entrusting more and more to me, certainly, but my position is by no means secure. The Queen is . . . uncertain of me, though not hostile. The Earl of Essex frantically seeks every advantage he can gain. I have more influence than I do authority.'

Was he asking for Gresham's sympathy? He eased himself back into his chair, though it seemed to increase rather than diminish his pain.

'I will show you my . . . goodwill. There will be no need to trouble Sir Francis. I will not block your proposed trip to Lisbon. You can accompany me on the mission to Flanders simply as a member of my household. You will have the status of a servant on the papers, if your honour can bear it.' He paused. 'Yet I do so not because you threaten those I love. If I believed that lay within your power I would have you stamped on with no more compassion than the filthiest fly under a man's boot. I will do so because I have learned that sometimes a man has to work with scum, and because I believe our country is threatened. And because, despite appearances, you might be useful in averting that threat.'

'I've learned to work with scum as well,' said Gresham, smiling again at Cecil.

The two men nodded briefly to each other before Gresham left. Outside Gresham found a drunken boatman asleep in his ferry, and got himself rowed erratically downstream, flashing past the stone of London Bridge with only inches to spare. It was late now, and even back at the the inn all was silent, with only the occasional howl of a dog disturbing the night. He gave a gentle tap on the door, their signal. Mannion had got a chicken from somewhere, and was picking at the last remaining bits of flesh, a large jug of ale by his side. The girl was asleep, fully clothed. Mannion had placed the coverlet over her, a rough woollen blanket. The thin plaster daubed between the wooden uprights of the wall was flaking off all the time, and a fine layer of white plaster dust had already settled over the girl's hair and the dark covering. It looked like an omen of death. Gresham tried to dismiss it. Mannion spoke in a whisper.

'I 'ad an 'unch. Got a boy to go and see if George Willoughby was 'ome. 'E is. What's more, 'e's sending his carriage round now. Messenger says 'e's convinced no one's watching the house.'

'George? How on earth is it that he's back?'

They found the answer after the bone-crushing ride in the cumbersome carriage kept at the Willoughbys' London house to transport George's elderly parents on their infrequent visits to town. Much as Gresham scorned this as transport for old people, it could convey all three of them out of sight, and if the clattering passage of the vehicle disturbed anyone in the small hours of the morning they made no sign.

The girl seemed dazed when woken up and bundled into a carriage, and just as dazed when they arrived and she was hurried upstairs in the company of a hastily awoken housekeeper and two maids.

'How— ' Gresham began to ask, but George held up a hand and cut him short.

'The stuffing was knocked out of me, seeing you go off in that sieve of a boat. I lost heart for the voyage, to tell you the truth, so

158

when Drake sent a pinnace off to give the good news about the *San Felipe* next day I cadged a ride on it. I suppose I hoped it might catch you up, tell the truth. Drake'd have said yes to anything, he was so fired up with his capture. We had the wind behind us all the way. I got here three days ago.'

'How did *El Draco* respond to the girl going missing?' asked Gresham.

'Hardly noticed, to tell you the truth. Ranted and raved a bit, accused several sailors of rape and murder, then someone suggested she was madly in love with you and had smuggled herself aboard the *Daisy*, and then he went back to counting ducats.'

'Someone?' asked Gresham raising an eyebrow. His friend was an appalling liar, and had gone red as he had spoken.

'Well, me, actually. Guessed she might have gone with you. Didn't want to see a sailor hanged – you could see the one Drake went for loved his mother and wouldn't have harmed a flea, never mind a fly. Anyway, never mind that. Tell me about your journey . . .'

Gresham gave the details, with occasional guffaws, and interruptions from Mannion, and then relayed his conversation with Cecil.

'Interesting,' said George, his great brow furrowed with thought. 'Let's be logical about this. Someone's been trying to kill you. We need to find out who. So let's work through the suspects.'

Gresham stood up, and started pacing the room.

'Obvious first suspect: Cecil.'

'Obviously a suspect,' said George, 'but it's not conclusive. All we know is that he's taken an interest in you. You could be a pawn in a much bigger game. *He* could be a pawn in a much bigger game. No. It's not conclusive.'

'Few things ever are in my world,' said Gresham, 'but let's move on.'

'Walsingham has to be a suspect,' said George. He revelled in this politicking, thought Gresham.

'How so?' said Gresham. The thought had occurred to him, but it seemed less blasphemous coming from someone else's mouth.

'Walsingham was Mary Queen of Scots' enemy as much as Burghley and Cecil. He's out of favour because of the execution. Perhaps he set you up as the villain to get himself off the rack of the Queen's disfavour?'

'It's possible,' said Gresham, 'but I doubt it. He's survived far worse than this, and anyway, I think he's dying. I doubt if killing me to speed up the end of the Queen's displeasure would be a priority in his present frame of mind.'

'There's something you 'aven't thought of,' said Mannion. He had acquired a shoulder of lamb and a tankard from somewhere, but was sufficiently impressed by what he wanted to say to put them down, though only momentarily. 'Walsingham's been setting you up as a spy for Spain, 'asn't 'e? Getting you to go to Mass, letting you give bits of information to them as what we know works for Spain?'

'Has he?' asked George, aghast. 'I didn't know that!'

'You weren't meant to,' said Gresham, looking meaningfully at Mannion. He waved the objection away, with a hand that had magically repossessed the leg of lamb.

''S'no matter,' he said with his mouthful. 'You can trust 'im. I'll lay my life on it.'

'You lay your life where you want. Just leave me to decide where I lay mine!' said Gresham ruefully.

'Well, don't you see?' said Mannion. 'Suppose word got out that you're a spy for Spain? Nothing stays a secret for very long in London! Walsingham could always try and explain that he set you up as a double agent, but at best 'e's goin' to appear a bloody fool – one of his spies working for Spain, sent by Walsingham as a crewman on Drake's bloody expedition to Cadiz no less! At worst they might think old Walsingham was trying to ride two horses at the same time, and set 'imself up with a nice pension if Spain did invade and take over, with one of 'is men on the inside track. Easiest thing is to have you knocked off, safely out at sea, and claim the credit for giving rough justice to a bloody spy. Alright, he loses a good agent, but maybe he saves his own bacon.'

Gresham had stopped pacing now. The first light of dawn was

160

flooding London, sunlight falling through the latticed window lighting half of his face, leaving the other in deepest shadow. Could it be true? Could Walsingham have sacrificed him because one of his men was about to be revealed as working for Spain?

'Next suspect, then,' said Gresham firmly, starting to pace up and down again. He had reached a conclusion himself, but clearly was not going to share it.

'The Queen,' said George flatly.

'The Queen?' Gresham laughed. 'Come off it! I didn't trip her up, I didn't let on that her breath smelled like a latrine pit, and I didn't ask her for money. Why would— '

'You're a very rich man,' said George.

Gresham sighed. He was fed up with people telling him how rich he was. It got boring. 'Yes, I am,' he said tiredly. 'And what's more, I'm even richer than I was when my father died, meaning I haven't run through my inheritance like wild young men are meant to do – and, yes, I do have a business brain in my head despite the business of growing the fortune being even more boring than being told by people like you how rich I am!'

'Who are your relations?' asked George quietly, ignoring the tirade.

'Why . . . there are none,' said Gresham. Something was starting to tighten in his stomach as he began to perceive George's point. George carried on, relentlessly.

'What happens to the estate of very rich men who die with no family, intestate. I bet you haven't even thought about a will . . .'

'Leave it all to me, if yer like,' muttered Mannion. 'God knows, I could use a bit extra . . .'

'. . . and what happens to a vast estate when a man dies *as a traitor!*' George continued.

'The Crown inherits,' said Gresham, turning to sit down. Suddenly he felt very tired. 'The Crown inherits.'

'The Crown is about to face an invasion, and is fighting a draining war in the Netherlands . . . how many ships could your estate buy the Queen? How many soldiers could it equip to fight the all-powerful Duke of Parma?'

'And no one, except a poor fool like you, would mourn the death of the young upstart Henry Gresham,' mused Gresham.

'The Queen's never been under more pressure for money,' insisted George.

'Possible,' said Gresham. 'It's such a terrifying prospect, and for this reason it has more credibility than it should have, as distinct from when it's looked at logically. So I'm going to rank it as a possible. No more.' The Queen was ruthless enough to do what was suggested, that was certain. But was she *desperate* enough?' 'Well, let's see where we stand,' he said. 'I've warned off Cecil. If he is involved he knows I suspect him, so at least he'll be more careful than he might have been. If Burghley's behind this he should get slowed a little by his baby boy; I'm damned sure if Cecil thinks his bride-to-be is in danger he'll have cautionary words with Daddy. Walsingham . . . well, I'd better see Walsingham and scout out the lay of the land. And if it's the Queen . . .'

'And if it's the Queen, we're fucked,' said Mannion morosely.

'Until she gets bored, or thinks of something else,' said Gresham. 'Or does actually get dealt with as you suggested with your usual subtlety, in which case it might take her mind off us.'

'Female spiders let the men do 'em,' said Mannion, 'and then they kill them. I've seen it. In the garden,' he added ominously.

'You are a little sprig of cheerfulness, aren't you?' said Gresham. 'I've got a great idea: shut up.'

Mannion subsided, though words like 'ignorant' and 'can't face truth' passed just on the edge of hearing.

'I think it's time for some sleep,' said George, yawning and rubbing his eyes like a baby. 'And a bath for both of you, if you don't mind my saying so. It's taken me three days to get clean, and both of you are seriously anti-social.'

Gresham could have washed in his friend's house, borrowed some clothes and ridden off to his own house in a semi-decent state. Instead he decided to ride to The House in his salt-stained, ship-wrecked and stinking clothes.

'I can't understand,' said George to Mannion. 'He's normally so . . . fastidious.' George usually complained about this obsession with cleanliness, believing that too much water took away the skin's natural oils and preferring to drench himself with perfume. Yet the change, even if only this once, was so extraordinary as to be alarming.

Mannion grinned, but kept silent. He knew why Gresham wanted to ride through the streets of London as he did. Those filthy clothes, and even the ripe scent of a man who had been at sea for three months were a badge of honour for a young man, a symbol of someone who had taken part and fought in a great adventure. Just for once Henry Gresham was simply behaving like a normal young man. He wanted to show the world that he had been in battle. He let Anna sleep for a couple of hours, then led her, sidesaddle of course, draped in a huge cloak unearthed at George's house that must have been made originally for either a woman carrying triplets or a refugee from a freak show, but which hid adequately for the moment her ship's boy's tunic and breeches.

He gained his admiration. Four of his own servants from The House had brought horses over for him, for Anna and for Mannion. Mannion stationed two of them in front, ostensibly to clear the way through the crowded streets. He also made it clear to the servants that they were free to tell passers-by that here was a hero of Cadiz, returned ahead of the victorious and glorious Sir Francis Drake. Let him enjoy his moment of glory, thought Mannion. He had fought well, shown hardly a flicker of fear despite what he must have felt, and kept his spirits when many a good man would have given in to despair. He deserved to be cheered through the streets, cheered by a populace dreading the sound of Spanish cavalry riding up Cheapside and only too pleased to celebrate an English triumph.

Gresham enjoyed the cheering, but also became embarrassed by it. What was a man to do? Wave like the Queen distributing the largesse of her approval to her loyal subjects? Or ride on through haughtily, ignoring the crowds disdainfully and being very proud? At a loss, instead he let himself draw alongside Anna, with whom he had hardly exchanged a word since disembarking. She was still extraordinarily beautiful; the perfect oval of her face, her dark eyes and full lips, high cheekbones and the glorious mass of blonde hair. Yet there were shadows under her eyes. Was another reason why the crowds were cheering that they were thinking in this superb pair they must be seeing a Prince and a Princess? She held herself proudly on the horse – she had a superb seat, her head held high Gresham noticed – but he had spent enough time with her now to know that she was totally exhausted.

'Are you rested?' he asked, grinning nervously at a passer-by who had yelled 'God bless you sir!', and in so doing making himself look very young indeed.

She said nothing for a moment, though the ground was soft and there was no clattering of hoofs on the unpaved road to drown out her words. 'You realise I am ruined now, twice over? As a wife, I mean.' There was an eternity of tiredness in her voice.

'What do you mean?' said Gresham, shocked. Why were girls so unpredictable?

'Who will believe I retain my virtue after having spent days at sea on a sinking ship with only men around me? Then a night with two men, in a stinking inn where men bring women for . . . business. You think I am blind as to where you took me last night? I am . . . how do you say it . . . ploddy goods? My fiancé will not wish to buy second hand, I think. So, guardian, the value of your package is nil.'

'Shoddy goods . . .' he began to murmur, then realised it sounded as if he was confirming her judgement. Gresham's first reaction was to feel deep offence at the thought that he or Mannion would ever damage a girl's reputation. Dammit, no married or single woman would ever sleep with a man if they thought he would blab on her! It was the basic rule of seduction, wasn't it? His second thought was that there was no one to tell the story, the other men on the *Daisy* being dead. Then, his heart sinking, he remembered Robert Leng, Drake, and all his crew, all of whom would know how Anna had reached England once they heard she was alive. He started to justify himself then.

'As far as I'm concerned,' said Gresham, 'whatever state you're in now is the same state as when I met you. I . . .'

His eye caught the movement of the girl's arm as it swung round incredibly fast to slap his face. The survival instinct cut in, beyond his control, and the girl let out a gasp as a steel-hard hand caught and stopped her swing.

'Do not laugh at me!' she cried at him, eyes sparkling with anger. The pride of her Spanish ancestry rose in her, and the devilment of her Irish. 'I am no whore, even if you try to make me one! How dare to imply that I had lost my virtue! It is not so! *I tell you, it is not so!*'

Here was a seventeen-year-old girl, who had never lived beyond the watchful eye of her loving parents and paid servants, cosseted and protected as all girls of her class were, protected because their virginity was their greatest asset. Suddenly this untutored creature found herself losing her father and then her mother too, left friendless in the company of her country's enemies, hurled by her mother into the hands of a wild young man who she probably hated and whose power over her she found humiliating. Shipwrecked, hauled across half the world with one dress and no servant, with no one to love her, her first night in a foreign country had been spent in an evil-smelling tavern with two men.

Gresham refused to let his heart be moved by her looks. But was she . . . brave? Gresham had never met a girl who was brave. Oh, girls were fun, and quite mysterious, but they were never brave. They never had to be, really, did they? Until it was too late, and the men had lost the battle, and the castle or the house was invaded. And then all their bravery was good for was to make them scream a little less than the others. He relaxed his grip, she fiercely resisting the overwhelming urge to rub her arm where his grip had left it white and burning with returning circulation. There was no sign of tears. He only vaguely understood and refused to listen to what his own brain told him it must be costing her simply to keep control, not to break down, not just now in this extraordinary environment but ever since her mother had died.

165

'Your honour is intact because we know it is so. We would both of us die before allowing anyone to impugn your honour,' he said grandly.

'And what's more,' interrupted Mannion, who Gresham did not recollect asking to speak but who had ridden up beside them, 'we'll kill anyone who says any different.'

'We'll protect you,' said Gresham. 'I have to. I gave your mother my word. That's what the dumb ox means. You're safe with us.'

She looked at Gresham, who suddenly seemed unforgivably innocent.

'I will never be safe again. Ever.' There was a terrible finality in her voice.

Gresham looked at her, matched her despair with his own at not being able to say the right thing, and spurred his horse on.

It seemed to take an age to reach The House. The façade was striking, imposing, magnificent even for London and even for the Strand. Such scurrying, such movements of people, such excitement at the return of the master! The ancient porter, seeing the young man, bowed his sleep-ridden head so low as to bang it against the cobbles. A cry of welcome sprung from the old man's throat, and then he caught sight of the man-mountain and . . . a girl. A very, very beautiful girl. Dressed in a vast cloak. The porter bowed to her, as deep as he had bowed to his master. Then came the hustle and bustle of a great household waking up to its duty, a neglected and forgotten household suddenly being given its purpose back. Henry Gresham, arms akimbo, stood foursquare in the courtyard, bellowing to a flocking horde of servants.

'Now, hear this! I introduce to you the Lady Anna Maria Lucille Rea de Santando!'

It was the first time he had shocked her. Until now, he had not used her name. How had he learned her full name?

'The Lady is my ward, placed by the sacred word of her dying mother in my care and protection, off the Azores, after her fine vessel had been captured in fierce combat by Sir Francis Drake!'

My ward. My care, thought Anna. This was not about her. It was about *him*.

166

'She has survived sea battle, shipwreck and deep family loss! Now who will show her, a stranger on our shores, true English hospitality?'

The flutterings among the assembled servants! The talk in the servants' hall tonight!

Now this was a real challenge to The House. Young Gresham had never quite come to terms with his inheritance of one of London's most desirable mansions. Its cavernous cellars had too many memories of a childhood he would be all too happy to forget, of a person he regretted he had been. Yet The House had never lost its loyalty to him. So how could its formal hierarchy do justice to its young master, and welcome the romantic Spanish princess in a manner that would do him due credit? At this crucial moment, an elderly woman swept forward, hauling her skirt with practised ease above the muck of the courtyard. She had been chief maid to the late wife of Sir Thomas Gresham, retained in service as was the way of great houses long after the said lady had taken her sad parting into the next world, along with the two under maids. And now, the assembly of servants seemed to say with one voice, her time was come again.

'Madam,' she pronounced with kindness to this strangely foreign creature, 'will you care to follow me?' The woman had meant to be more formal, but the sight of the girl had made her realise how young she was, for all her grand name.

Silence fell over the courtyard. They were nearly all there now, albeit stunned by their early awakening and in varying states of dress. The steward, of course, and the manciple. The chief cook and the under cooks, the scullions from the kitchens, the porters, the parlour maids, the men who maintained and crewed the six boats dressed in the livery of The House, the ostlers who looked after the stable that was one of Henry Gresham's few real interests in the place, even the carpenter and the mason who from the outset Sir Thomas Walsingham had retained to carve out and care for his beautiful home. There were over fifty of them there now, the people who kept the complex organism of The House running even

167

in the absence of its master. The truly frightening fact was that to maintain its fifty inhabitants and its huge fabric was but a pinprick in his wealth. And now these inhabitants were looking in the cold light of dawn to a girl dressed in working man's clothes on a dreadful horse. The Lady Maria Anna Lucille Rea de Santando.

It was the kindness that did it. All those defences, put up and so fiercely defended over so many months, crumbled away in the face of a few kind words. A single tear welled up, and hung poised over her extraordinarily long eyelashes. 'I thank you for your kindness,' she said, and curtseyed to them. Even the irritating bird that had sung welcome to the dawn as she had descended had decided to shut up.

One man started to clap slowly, and gradually it took off until a torrent of applause was echoing round the courtyard. Anna dropped exhausted from the horse, the old lady put an arm round her and the line of servants parted, cheering starting now over the applause.

'Isn't it about time you stopped playing the field?' Mannion asked, unexpectedly, of his master. 'That one there, she's got the body and she's got the brains. She'll keep you in order. Give you what you want, on both counts. Why not get something going that'll last for more than a few nights?'

'So I have to apologise to someone all the time?' said Gresham. 'Say sorry because I can't guarantee being there when they want me to be? Sorry because someone claiming to love me has actually just become dependent on me? So dependent that I can't move, breathe or even live? I don't want attachments!' The passion in his voice was almost frightening. 'Don't you understand? I don't want people to depend on me! I want to be free!'

'We're none of us free,' said Mannion. 'It's just that some of us like to pretend we can be.'

Gresham looked into Mannion's eyes, for several long seconds. Then he turned away, and stormed into his living quarters. There were no dramatic gestures from Mannion. He had an attachment, one willingly entered into, though it was not with a woman. And he did not intend to depart from it.

168

The figure that met them several hours later was unrecognisable. Anna swept in, escorted by three women, paused to allow herself to be admired, then curtseyed to her guardian, who bowed a deep and appreciative bow back. Her hair had been brushed back to a lustrous frenzy, worn down as an unmarried girl's hair should be. The dress they had found was a deep black velvet, opened at the front with an intricate linear design picked out with tiny pearls, hugging the upper part of her figure and blossoming out gloriously in an excess of material from its high waist, the flowing sleeves seeming to emphasise rather than hide the fragility of her slender arms. Was it the looks, the perfect face, the promise of the figure beneath the velvet that made her look so hugely edible, wondered Gresham? Or was it the sense of raw energy, an uncontrolled life force that radiated from her?

'I need to talk with you.' His eyes took in the accompanying women.

'You may leave us,' said Anna regally. And then, reverting to the young girl, she flung out her arms to them. 'Thank you!' she said. 'Thank you for helping me!' Several hours of hugging and mutual female support then took place, most of which Gresham tried to ignore by looking out of the window. It was a pity he did not look more closely. It would have revealed a different woman to the one he thought he knew.

'Do you think of yourself as wholly Spanish? Or is there a part of you that is English?' asked Gresham. He spoke bluntly, told himself he did not care.

Anna looked at him as if he had started to burble like a madman.

'I hate Spain. It rejected my father, sent him to exile in filthy Goa and so brought about his death. My mother was taunted as a foreigner from the moment she set foot in Spain. What do I owe Spain? And England? At least Spain gave me warmth and sunshine when I was a child. England gave me nothing, except a mother whose family was rejected by their own country as my father's family was rejected by Spain. I despise them both.'

Gresham was uncertain. He was going to get no more help from her. But he plunged on.

'I need you,' said Gresham. 'I need to go to Lisbon, to spy on Spain. To do certain things that will help my country, England, survive an invasion by Spain. To destroy that invasion.'

She eyed him as a cook might eye a fish to see if the fishmonger was lying about its freshness. 'And how could I stop Spain destroying England?' The irony was so thick it could have been laid on with a trowel.

'Because I could use you as my cover. As your guardian I could claim to be visiting Lisbon to reunite you with your fiancé.'

'You could,' said Anna simply. 'He is based in Lisbon, despite the fact that he is French. And what would be even more convenient for you would be that you could spend a long time finding him. He travels from June, sometimes until as late as December.'

Gresham took in her 'you could' comment. It was not an assent, merely recognition that his journey would be theoretically possible with her as cover. No surprise at his request. No shock even.

'What does he travel so long for, and part of it in the winter months?' asked Gresham.

Anna looked at him levelly.

'He is a stupid merchant. A stupid, fat merchant. He deals in spices. He sails out in June to Goa, where he spends a month, maybe two months, despatching what he ordered last year, agreeing his sordid purchases for the next year. Then he travels back by land, because he buys much wool from the far south, where they do not shear the sheep until October. And carpets. He buys carpets, from the Turks.'

The silence lay thick between them.

'Don't you still have family in Spain?'

'I have family, yes. Some very distant cousins. All my father's estates, they are gone, sold. My cousin has a large family, very many daughters. Another one will not be welcome, particularly if she already has a fiancé. And my English family? What few of them are left cut my mother off completely.'

So the firebrand really was alone. No father, no mother, no family worth the name. In much the same situation, as it happened, as

Henry Gresham. Yet Gresham had wealth, the freedom of a man to plot his own destiny. She, in her own words, was just a package, a woman to be disposed of to the best bidder. A fat French merchant.

'Why do you want to stop this war?' asked Anna.

Why? The question, calmly asked by this ice maiden, shocked him more than anything else she had said or done. Since he was risking his life for the answer, surely he should know it? Yet he found himself having to produce an answer for the first time, fumbling with the unfamiliar words.

'Because . . . because we can all of us find reasons for doing nothing, for giving up. The easiest decision to take is that we're victims. I have to believe I can make a difference. That I can make things better.' He was surprised by the strength of his own passion. 'Otherwise fate makes cowards of us all, and we're little more than dumb beasts in the field who take the life they are given at birth, but can give nothing back to it. My life must be more than mere existence.'

'And?' said Anna. 'You missed something out.'

'What?' said Gresham, startled.

'You are excited by the risk. By the fact that you might be found out, killed. Only when you think you might lose your life do you realise how valuable it is to you.'

'How can you say that? You who knows so little of me?'

'Because my brain works in the same way as yours!' she snapped back at him. For the first time there was raw, jagged emotion in her voice. 'Do you not think a woman fears that she is one of those beasts in the field you so despise, there to breed, with no other justification for her having been given life?'

'But . . . but the greatest fulfilment a woman can have, her bounden duty, is to have children . . .' Gresham replied in amazement.

'It may be so,' said Anna, 'but before that duty can a woman not feel she is properly alive, be inflamed by danger? *Want to make a difference of her own?* She swung away, looked out of the window. She spoke without turning. 'Yes,' she said suddenly. 'I will come with you to Lisbon.'

'Despite your being Spanish, in name at least? Despite the fact that your own country could execute you if we are found out? Despite the fact that you might end the trip . . . conjoined with your fat French merchant?'

She spun round. 'I will not ask why you do what you do, Henry Gresham. In return grant me the favour of not asking me why I do what I do!'

'As you wish,' said Gresham. There was respect in the short bow he gave her. So much the better. Mutual respect would help them do business. But who really knew what went on in a girl's mind? Wasn't it that very mystery that made them so attractive? The mystery that could appear to be present even in the most stupid? 'Do you like horses?' asked Gresham suddenly into the silence, and then wished he had not spoken. He had felt an almost uncontrollable urge to visit the one place in The House where he was fully at ease. Why on earth had he asked her to join him?

'I love horses,' she answered. Yes, thought Gresham, as so many women love horses – until they rear and bolt, or snort too close to a fine dress, or develop sores that need washing and dressing . . .

'Then come with me to the stables of The House,' he said, making it an order rather than a request. It would have been better if he had slept with her, he thought. Then she would have been just like all the others. Perhaps he ought to bed her, to prove to himself that she was. But he had given his word to her mother. In his arrogance and his youthfulness, he did not consider that she might not be willing to bed him.

The stables had always been a different world to Gresham. As a young boy when all else had failed he would come here, sometimes just to nestle in the corner of a stall, saying nothing, feeling the companionship of the animal. That strange smell of horse, part musty, part acrid, yet warm and comforting, the smell of a world without lies and deceit, a world where the boundaries were finite and understood. The scuff of a hoof, the sound of easy breath through nostrils. A horse knew what it was on earth to do.

They entered the stables as a grinning lad bowed and opened a

172

door. The sunlight dappled the stalls, and the smell of fresh straw hit them as the light suddenly faded and became warmly encompassing. There was a wide path between the stalls, raised and built out of the same brick as the walls, almost an avenue. The beasts had just been exercised, the rubbing-down just finished. They were superb animals. The older mares and geldings were put out to a farm near Cambridge, left to end their days peacefully rather than die in distress at the slaughter yards of Deptford. Every animal in the stable, from those who could haul Sir Thomas Gresham's cumbersome carriage if ever it were used again, to the finest hunters, seemed at the peak of their condition.

'I have never seen so many fine horses,' said Anna. Gresham sensed that she was moved, was not being sarcastic.

'The stables at Cambridge are even bigger,' Mannion spoke to her, in a low voice. People never raised their voices in the stables, not so much for fear of frightening the horses but rather out of respect for them in their temple.

'Choose one,' said Gresham, on impulse.

'May I see some of them walk out, please?' she asked. Of course she could. Particularly as it was the first time he had ever heard her use the word 'please'. The ostlers were bored, their master hardly ever there, and were pleased to have something to do. The lady was good to look at, and it would be another story for the servants' hall. As for the horses, it would do them no harm to do a little gentle parading. Would she go simply for looks? Or choose the most placid?

First of all she walked the length of the stalls. She waited by each boarded door for the inquisitive head to pop out and examine this new human. She did not flinch when the massive heads bucked and shook from side to side, nor when one animal let out a whinny of protest at some perceived insult. Firmly, and with no hesitation, she put out a delicate hand to stroke several of the heads, muttering words inaudible to Gresham and Mannion. Then she stepped back.

'Can I truly choose any horse?' she asked.

'Yes,' said Gresham.

'Then may I see the big dappled grey walk out, please?'

Gresham and Mannion looked at each other, and grinned. 'Now that,' said Gresham, 'is a real pick.' The grey was not an obvious choice for a woman, a high seat and a big animal, and it had seemed restless as she approached. Yet it was a glorious creature, a thing of pure beauty, and with a wild look in its rolling eyes. Something unpredictable, a character and a spirit yet an intelligence too.

'Be warned,' said Gresham, who knew every horse in his stable better than he knew himself. 'She can be stubborn, and demands that you talk to her, and while she will let any man or woman sit on her back she will only show her true spirit to the person who masters her. Yet when she is ridden properly, she rides like the wind.'

Walking placidly round the yard, it suddenly stopped, dragged its halter and started to paw the ground.

'Whoa, whoa!' said Gresham gently, walking over and taking the horse from the boy at her head. He dropped the halter to the ground. 'Stand back,' he said quietly.

The grey looked at him for a moment, bobbed her proud head, and then with only the faintest clip-clop of her hoofs turned and walked, with a gentleness at total odds with her bulk, up to Anna. The horse stood by the girl for a few seconds, as if not interested, and then unexpectedly turned its head and nudged her gently under the chin. She turned, at ease, and the horse dropped its great head, nuzzling her again. She stroked it, her own form tiny by comparison.

'Well,' said Mannion, 'that's something as I ain't seen before.'

'Would you like to ride out? There's still light, and time,' asked Gresham.

'What, now!' said the girl, and there was an excitement there, a passion. 'What is the horse called?'

'You may rename her,' said Gresham, 'but I called her Triumph, because I could imagine her hauling a Roman Emperor's chariot as he entered Rome in triumph too.'

The girl looked at the horse, and smiled. Her face changed when

174

she smiled. Another first. 'It is a good name. I will call her Triumph.'

They had found an old riding dress, the maid told him, when they had gone through The House for its female wardrobe, and had just then finished some minor restitching and repair. It was an old dress, they said, but expensive and well preserved. Anna dashed back in to be changed, and in a length of time that made Gresham swear he would never complain again about how long it took a woman to dress, was back in the yard, the cheap, battered sidesaddle she had acquired since arriving in England transferred to the new horse. Gresham stood looking at his ward, clothed in the old dress. The colour had drained from his face.

'I am so pleased we could find a riding dress,' said the elderly maid to Gresham with pride. 'I think it belonged to the Lady Mary, when your late father was her guardian.'

Gresham felt a spasm cut through his body. How annoying. He thought he had cut any link of emotion with his mother. Was this how she had looked as she prepared to ride from The House? An elfin-like shape standing proudly by the bulk of a dappled grey, two things of great beauty united?

Gresham was not fearful for his life, at least not for the present, but it would be inconceivable for form's sake that he and Anna should ride out unescorted. Four men dressed in the dark blue and silver livery of The House accompanied them, one to ride ahead and clear the street, the other three as escort. And Mannion, of course, scorning to wear livery, dressed in a tunic and trousers that made him look either a very well-paid member of the working class or a very badly off member of the middle classes. That was the way he liked it.

Gresham had taken them left out of The House, up along the river to Whitehall rather than into the City. Partly it was through his nervousness at the girl riding an unknown horse through the frenzy and noise of London, partly because the Strand was one of the few paved roads in the city. He need not have bothered. Her seat was superb, and she and Triumph looked to be united in their

175

fluid, easy movement. The horse could be restive, Gresham knew, and, if you could ever ascribe human emotions to animals, seemed to get bored at times. There was no sign of it now. Triumph was concentrating on carrying her new mistress as if she were the only person who mattered in the world. Every person in the prosperous street leading to Westminster and the country's seat of power turned to look at the extraordinary pair, the handsome young man on his superb black mount, the glorious girl controlling effortlessly the great dappled grey. One passer-by started to cheer, as they had on his salt-stained journey earlier, thinking that so dashing a young man must be the Earl of Essex. Then his friend put him right, and he started to cheer anyway. The effect was rather spoilt by Mannion, riding a nag that looked as if it would die of shame before entering Gresham's stables. Yet Mannion knew that it had the heart of a lion, could gallop all day and would not shift aside if a barrel of gunpowder was blown up before it. Mannion liked appearances to be deceptive. But there was nothing they could do to deceive the next person whose attention they attracted. They were about to turn back when there was the rumbling, trundling roar of a great, heavily escorted carriage from behind them.

The Queen was quite capable of gracing a horse, though usually travelled by water in London on one of the great state barges. Today, however, she had chosen the vast, lumbering carriage that must have been a nightmare for the coachman to control in the narrow streets of the capital. They pulled the horses up and drew them to the side, Anna having the sense to realise that someone great was passing by, even if she did not realise that it was the greatest person in the land. Instead of speeding by, spattering them with mud and dust, the coach slowed and then stopped some yards ahead of them. Its escort, in the Tudor colours of green and white, drew up, their horses snorting. They waited, uncertain, and men leaped down from the roof of the carriage. The door was opened, a carpet laid on the road. Queen Elizabeth stepped out on to the street.

Oh no, thought Gresham. Not the Great Bitch Incarnate! His murderess? Please, dear God, preserve me from this!

A ragged cheer went up from the bystanders who had stopped to gawp. Gresham and Anna froze on their horses, then made deep obeisance from the waist, before leaping off their mounts – Gresham bowed low, very low indeed. Anna bowed her head and bobbed down, holding the curtsey at its lowest level. Thank God someone had brought her up to know what to do, thought Gresham.

'Here!' The voice was imperious. When the daughter of Henry VIII wanted something, no one was left in any doubt. 'Cease your bowing and scraping! Come here. And bring those horses with you.'

Gresham had been about to hand the reins to one of his men, but moved forward now, to the edge of the carpet the Queen's men had laid to preserve the hem of her dress. And what a dress. Deep, deep red, bejewelled as if to rival the night sky, and slashed, the ruff extravagant, the sleeves so puffed as to have life of their own. The Queen eyed Henry Gresham up and down appreciatively.

'Young Henry Gresham, unless I am very much mistaken!' she exclaimed.

'Your Majesty,' said Gresham bowing deep again, hat in hand. Alive, he thought. Just in case you wondered, or had wanted me dead.

'Young Henry Gresham who absents himself from my Court, I see,' said the Queen, dangerously. Correction; every word she spoke was potential danger, thought Gresham, including these.

'Your Majesty, I have until yesterday been at sea for several months, with the forces of Sir Francis Drake. Nothing except the urgency of serving Your Majesty overseas would otherwise take from me the pleasure of attending Your Majesty's court.'

'Hmph!' said the Queen, in a most unladylike grunt, 'so I hear that you picked up a prize of your own on your recent sea voyage. Show yourself, girl. Come forward now!' She motioned to two men to take Gresham's and Anna's horses. Eyes lowered, Anna advanced, curtseyed again.

Oh help, thought Gresham, had she been listening? Does this silly girl know who this is? Does she think it's some dowager aunt of mine who's accosted me in the street?

'Well,' said the Queen, 'I could see they would fight over you. Is it true, girl, that your mother died on board ship? That she cast you on the mercies of this young wolf here?'

'Your Majesty,' said Anna, eyes still decorously lowered, 'it is true that my dear mother departed this life at sea. As your all-knowing Majesty will know, I was placed in the guardianship of your subject here.'

'I am sorry for your mother, and for you in your loss,' said the Queen, not unkindly. Anne Boleyn, her mother, had been executed for adultery before she knew her, thought Gresham, and called a whore ever since. It must give her a limited line in sympathy for dead mothers. Of all people on earth she had been dealt a Devil's pack by her breeding. Yet she had survived. Against all the odds. The Queen looked at the beautiful girl and her horse, the striking young man standing beside her. They were an embodiment of good breeding, for all that Gresham was born on the wrong side of the bed. Like their respective horses, they were the summit of their species. The Queen stared at the young bastard in all his glory, and the young girl, the splendour of her beauty shining out despite the riding habit twenty years out of fashion.

'It will end in tears,' she said, but with the slightest of smiles playing on her make-up smeared face, her eyes dancing with fierce intelligence. She looked directly at Anna. 'I of all people know how hard it is to be a woman in a man's world. They would rather own us than obey us, these men. So you, young lady, can I come to your rescue?' Suddenly Gloriana appeared rather tired, and above all old. 'Is this young man terrorising you? Is he haunting you? Would you wish that I make you a ward of Court – though, God knows, I have enough expenses to my charge already!'

Had the Queen looked at Gresham as she spoke?

Anna risked her own tiny smile. 'No, Your Majesty, not terrorising me. He is trying to be very distant,' and here she chanced the

178

smallest of looks up at the Queen and into her eyes, 'as he tries to be very distant from everyone. But he is perfectly proper.'

The Queen laughed out loud, an unashamed belly laugh that would have done a fifteen-stone man in a tavern proud. 'Well,' she roared, 'if you keep them distant you've won your safety! Well, my offer stands.' She was clearly becoming bored, and the wind was starting to blow up the street, the crowds increasing by the minute. 'If you wish me to take you in, find you a good English husband even, you may contact me. And as for you, Henry Gresham . . .' She turned to him. 'Come and see me in my Court! There are enough who would die for such an invitation. Do not be so arrogant as to refuse one from your Queen that others would give their lives for. And one other thing. Lay a finger on that girl and it won't only be your head stuck on a pike on London Bridge!'

And with another roaring laugh, she ascended into her coach. Gresham's shoulders were beginning to sink back in relief as he let out his breath. Then, as she was almost in through its vast door, she turned and motioned to Gresham to come close. His shoulders pulled upwards again. Her teeth were black and Gresham was surprised her breath could not be seen like a putrid brown stain on the air. She leaned close to him.

'Tell me,' said the Queen, 'is it true that Drake said he intended to swinge the King of Spain's beard, and then changed it when that damn fool Secretary of his put him right?'

You never knew with royalty, that was the problem. They could be your best friend one minute, and then have you up for treason for telling a bad joke or being over familiar. And this one could be chatting away knowing full well she had just ordered him killed. Gresham gambled. He leaned forward even closer to Elizabeth, wondering if at that proximity his trimmed beard would catch fire at her breath.

'As a mere subordinate, Majesty,' he said, 'and someone who Sir Francis saw fit to take a shot at . . .' she would have heard that story for certain, 'you would expect me to be the soul of discretion. Yet I can confirm that a certain rather unconventional assault on the King's beard was proposed, somewhat *sotto voce*, before a correction was issued and a rather different threat was made *fortissimo*.' He leaned in even further, almost touching her face. Had he got the mix of deference and the conspiratorial right? 'However, Your Majesty, what is not widely known is that when the first threat was made I was the only person looking away to Cadiz harbour. I swear two additional Spanish vessels sank the minute our commander uttered his unique threat to the King of Spain.'

He had got it right, thank God. An appreciative snort of laughter emerged from the unnaturally red royal lips, wrapped now in a grin of positively malicious enjoyment. Then her face darkened. Gresham's heart sank with it.

'And what does the young man who I hear such things of . . .' Such things, Gresham's mind raced. Talk of good things, or bad things? 'What does he think about the prospect of Sir Francis Drake commanding the only wooden walls that stand between my kingdom and Spain?'

This could not be happening, not in a street with nearly a hundred people watching, pushed out of earshot by the mounted guard. Not happening to a man barely out of nappies, given from nowhere the chance to influence events that he had thought only Cecil would be able to take advantage of. Perhaps he should go to Court more often. At least it would be more comfortable.

'Your Majesty,' he said, his thoughts a bare second ahead of his words. 'I have no concept of defending a kingdom such as Your Majesty must have. In all honesty, most of my life has been concerned with defending myself. Yet your wooden walls are not one line of masonry, but ten, twenty or thirty separate walls, each capable of going its own way.'

'What are you telling me?' The tone had no humour in it now. It was flat, merciless, the voice of her father who had ordered the murder of her mother.'

Well, Gresham thought, it had not been an altogether bad life, and, after all, the only certainty about life was that it would end some time or other.

'I wish to continue serving Your Majesty. My loyalty to you goes without question, as it does with every subject.' One had to put these things in with royalty, Gresham remembered. They tended to remember what had been said with appalling selectivity. And accuracy. 'And my loyalty to Your Majesty is even further secured by the fact that your reign has brought peace to this country. Peace, and an end to bonfires.'

Which was true. Queen Bitch was mercurial, infuriating and unpredictable, not knowing at times whether she was King Henry VIII or Anne Boleyn, and at times trying to be both. Yet ploughman Jack and milkmaid Jill cared little for the goings-on in London. Their life was hard enough, a bad winter killing a third of their village, rain at harvest guaranteeing unfilled bellies for their children and themselves, not to mention the relentless, random tide of plague and illness that haunted every man alive in Elizabeth's England. Yet they were human beings, as human as the Earl of Essex and Robert Cecil. As human as Henry Gresham. Did the peasant in the field not feel pain and loss like other men, were the hot tears absent when wife or child died? With what they had to bear already, what need had they of armies tramping over their fields, driving down their crops, taking their women and burning their pathetic, stinking little huts? What need did their men have of being hauled off to war, a weapon thrust into their ill-trained hands, simple cannon-fodder? She had brought peace to England, and stopped for the most part humans being burned alive because their God differed in meaningless respects from that which their monarch claimed to worship. All of this flickered through his brain in an instant.

'Your Majesty, this young, inexperienced and badly born man would be happy to have Sir Francis Drake fighting for him, and believe himself lucky to have such a man on our side. Yet to fight and to lead are not the same thing.'

The Queen looked at him, waiting for him to say more.

'You would have made a good politician, Henry Gresham,' she said. 'Too many say too much, and too many say nothing at all with many words.' She looked at him, waiting for him to speak, to say too much. It was she who broke the silence. 'Lord Howard of Effingham will command my fleet. Drake will be second in command.' Then, in his silence, she nodded, a neutral gesture, climbed into her carriage, gave one cursory wave at the crowd, and drove off amid rolling cheers and roars.

A little girl was squatting by the roadside, rough shift drawn up over her scraggy knees, peeing into the dust with her thumb firmly stuck in her mouth. Her eyes were wide, transfixed by the sight of the two beautiful ladies and the handsome man.

'Have I just met the Queen of England?' asked Anna, who appeared to be standing upright but was actually leaning against the bulk of Triumph, exhausted. It was a dangerous thing to do with a horse, but Triumph seemed resigned to being used as a leaning post.

'It's amazing how quickly it changes from being a matter of excitement to something to be avoided at almost all costs,' said Gresham. He turned to Mannion. 'Did she try to kill me?'

'You wouldn't know if she had,' said Mannion.

They rode back to The House.

The others, the outsiders, thought that the plottings and the machinations of Sir Francis Walsingham were concerned with the overthrow of monarchs, the sowing of discord and the undermining of states. How wrong they were. He had only ever sought to bolster and confirm one state, the England of Queen Elizabeth. He had chosen her from the outset. The Protestant Queen. How could any thinking man make any different choice? He was aware of his innate homosexuality, aware how men of his kind were prone to worship powerful women as icons. Yet it was not his sexual urges, as much under control as the rest of him, that had driven him, but something altogether more logical. He had seen the vanities, the arrogance, the corruption and the decadence that was Rome and its religion. He had fled to Padua when Queen Mary, in a bungled succession, had tried to impose on Englishmen the Catholicism they had learned to do without. He had shuddered as the news of the burnings reached him, known that the true heir of Henry VIII, and the best man in the country, was Elizabeth. He had thrown his weight behind her from the outset, given his fortune to the support of her monarchy, given her information to counter the troops that the wealth of the Spanish and the French enabled them to have. Well, Elizabeth had reigned for twenty-nine years now, and Walsingham thanked his Protestant God that he had been spared this long, to enter into his final battle for the continued reign of Queen Elizabeth.

Pinpricks, Walsingham thought as he gazed unseeing through the mullioned window, the servant clearing the remnants of his solitary meal at noon. That was all that he had managed so far, pinpricks, important, but in the final count little more than that. He would have to strike harder and deeper, not just at the Armada, but at the whole concept of the Enterprise of England, as his spies told him it had now been christened. But how to do it?

Then there was that damn fool Burghley, as if he did not have enough to worry about. The Queen's long-term ally was increasingly deaf, suffering from gout and losing his edge. What had Burghley said when they had met the Queen? That her vessels should, must be cut down as soon as possible, skeleton crews only, to save money. 'Two thousand, four hundred and thirty-three pounds, eighteen shillings and fourpence!' the old fool had intoned, as if it were some magic catechism instead of the sum the Queen would save by reducing the Navy to half-manning over the winter. 'Two thousand, four hundred and thirty-three pounds, eighteen shillings and fourpence!' he had repeated, saying the figure with all the pride of a midwife holding up the first-born male child. The King of Spain could launch his ships at any time, was fanatic enough to take even the mad risk of sailing in winter. And if he did? If his vessels got through? With even five thousand soldiers he could hold a decent town, even somewhere such as the Isle of Wight, and either advance from there in the Spring or hold it until Parma's troops could be ferried over. There was nothing to stop them, except those ships. If Burghley had his way, would it be the first time that a country had been sold for two thousand four hundred and thirty-three pounds, eighteen shillings and fourpence?

I will die with my mind as sharp as the pains that afflict me, vowed Walsingham. The irony of the situation hit him then, perhaps for the first time. We are all of us ill and dying, he thought, the men playing this great game for the survival of a country, what the religion and the philosophy of the world will be for the next hundred, two hundred or even five hundred years. King Philip of Spain is sixty-six years old, his circulation failing, Walsingham thought, an age which would make him a mythical, almost God-like figure in any English village. The Marquis of Santa Cruz, commander of the fleet, was spitting blood if Walsingham's informants were to be relied upon, though not fast enough. Recalde of Spain was sixty-two, the same age as Santa Cruz. Burghley was a failing sixty-seven, Elizabeth herself fifty-four. Parma, he thought. The Duke of Parma. The youngest of all the players, on the Spanish or the English side. Was it his youth that made Parma the greatest threat to England?

In the final count, it might all depend on his throw of the dice with Parma. Walsingham was well aware that the prize was not just the sovereignty of England, not just his own life, which would soon be forfeit anyway, but his honour, perhaps even his place in history.

CHAPTER 7

September, 1587
London; Lisbon

Has it crossed your mind how dangerous this jaunt you're planning to Lisbon is?' asked George. 'And just how many games do you think you can play at the same time? Agent, double agent, dammit, even triple agent? At times even I don't know what side you're on!'

Gresham chose to respond only to the first part of the question. 'I'm on my own side. And is it more dangerous than being in a rowing boat fired at by cannon from a Spanish galley?'

'About the same, I reckon,' said George. 'In fact, I'm starting to think I'd rather be back on the boat. At least there we knew who the enemy was.'

'There's an invasion coming,' said Gresham almost dreamily. 'I can feel it in my bones. And that invasion, once it touches these shores, could act like a fuse and trigger every sect, every family and every person who's ever lusted after power . . . and all we have between us and chaos are a few ships who've never worked as a fleet . . . wouldn't the real danger be to do nothing?'

They were walking in the Long Gallery of The House, an expanse of polished panelling hung with the very best of Sir Thomas Gresham's paintings and tapestries. It was cool there, despite the long line of windows and the slanting, late-summer sunlight streaming through, creating alternate pools of light and dark along its length. The Queen had demanded a price for licensing Henry Gresham to travel to Lisbon: that he formally present Anna to her at Court. It was unusual for the Queen to be in London in the summer. She preferred to go on progress then, bankrupting her nobles and saving herself a small fortune in the upkeep of the Court. It was the continuing uncertainty surrounding the Armada, which some said was ready to sail despite the damage of Cadiz, that kept the Queen in London. Old fox that she was, she knew perfectly well that if Philip came knocking on her door London was the place for her to be, not out in the sticks being fawned on by an ageing Lord presenting her with endless poems written by someone else praising her eternal beauty.

'I don't know what it is with you,' said George. 'You just can't keep it simple, can you? What do you do with a young man who gets caught up in all this spying business! This double and treble agent stuff! When you should have been doing normal things like chasing girls and drinking yourself stupid!' He paused for a moment. 'Mind, to be fair, you have done those as well. Anyway, my guess is you'll get a knife in your gut the minute we land in Lisbon. From one side or the other.'

There was a crash from a room nearby, a wail and a torrent of rapid English. Gresham flinched, confused. Anna was telling her maid to hurry up, and doing so by hurling a rather fine ceramic pot of pins at the nearest wall. Pots cost money. So did maids, for that matter. He hoped it was only the pot that was broken. In front of him, apart from her obvious excitement in the stables, he had never seen anything except cool control. Had he missed something? Whatever was going on next door was from a very different person to the one he thought he knew.

'Well,' said Gresham, wrenching his mind back to his conversation with George, 'You know the argument. You disguise yourself one of two ways – you hide what you are, or you tell everyone what you are. The girl's fiancé is based in Lisbon. I'm her guardian. It's perfectly reasonable for me to want to fulfil my word to her dying mother. And by getting permission from the Governor General *and* the Queen to make the visit, by doing it in the highest possible profile, they'll think only a madman would make such a noise about a visit when he's actually come to spy.'

'I agree with the madman bit,' said Mannion.

'And I'm coming with you,' said George.

'You!' said Gresham. 'You can't . . .'

'Shut up,' said George. 'Firstly, you can't stop me. I've got my licence from the Queen – and a pretty sum father had to pay for it – and secondly, I'm superb cover for you, second only to the girl. People think I'm just a big buffoon, and they'd think Walsingham had lost his roof timbers and his slates if he was using me as a spy.'

He had a point, Gresham conceded reluctantly, though he was not prepared to concede just yet. He knew his real objection; he was fearful that George would come to harm. Why was it so much easier to contemplate risk for oneself than contemplate it for those one loved? It was another reason for loving no one. They waited for Anna to appear.

Gresham was dressed in a deep, lustrous black doublet, slashed through to reveal the silver silk lining, the black finely embroidered in raised stitching. Some people wore a ruff as if it were a simple irritant; Gresham wore his as if it were simply an extension of his beard. The doublet seemed to emphasise the broad shoulders, the narrow hips, while any young male courtier would have died for the line of his leg and calf in the superb silken hose. Many of the other young men there would have extravagant, high hats, in the full flush of fashion. Gresham's was flatter than the fashion, a thin brim and small top no higher than his head cut from the same material as his doublet. He wore little jewellery; the single diamond on his ring finger, set in a simple setting, alone was worth all the gold and jewels worn by three or four of the wealthiest courtiers. It had been one of the few luxuries his father had allowed himself, and had never left his hand. It reassured the bankers and money lenders with whom he negotiated, he had used to say, to know that he had collateral at his finger tips.

There was another rattle of English from deep within, another crash.

'Should I go and sort it out?' asked Gresham.

'No,' said George, 'leave 'em to fight it out. Women have their own ways of doing these things. You wait. She and that maid'll come out in a minute or two as if they were best friends.'

Minutes later the maid flung a door open as if the Queen had come to The House. In some respects she had. The vision that was Anna stepped forth, and even Mannion wondered where his breath had gone for a fleeting moment. The deep blue of her eyes seemed to be echoed in the equally deep, vivid royal blue of her dress, picked out with so many pearls that at least one ocean must have felt denuded. Her hair had clearly been done by some goddess temporarily on loan from Olympus, the cap not containing but rather complementing it. Her perfect figure was somehow emphasised by the huge sweep of the dress out from her hips, the glorious billows of the sleeves done in some lighter, dancing material that still managed to match the colouring of the whole. God knows how they had got the dress ready in time. It could take a year for a good dressmaker to produce such a work of art, and the cost of a Court dress was staggering. But money talked, a fact Gresham recognised as much as sometimes he felt revolted by it, he who had carefully been deprived of money at a crucial time in his youth, left to fend without it and so learn its value.

'I think your goods have packaged well, is it not so?' asked Anna, making a polite curtsey to Gresham. It was the same cool, infuriating creature, but there was an excitement to her that even her self-control could not hide.

'Did you break all of Mary's limbs, or just selected ones?' asked Gresham cuttingly. She bridled, stifling the movement halfway through and instead drawing herself up to her full height.

'Sometimes you are a stupid man, and this is a surprise for someone who is so rich. Mary is a very good maid and we are friends of best,' replied Anna primly. 'Girls do not talk to each other in the same way as silly men.'

The tone was that of a monarch reprimanding the lowliest of servants. Gresham suddenly realised he was being dismissed as a person of no importance. He found it strangely annoying. It was alright on a deck or where men were in control. Here it was different.

She was passionate, the girl was, Mannion reckoned. It had taken him some while to sense it. Sometimes beautiful women were like alabaster pots, marble, made of a material that somehow you could never warm up. But this one, though it was a real good coating of alabaster, there was fire in her belly alright, though she hid it. She was young enough even not to recognise it for what it was. Virgin? He reckoned so. You could tell. But it was only a matter of time.

They were arguing now, again.

'It's "best of friends",' said Gresham.

'Exactly. That is what I said.'

'No, you said "friends of best".'

'I did not!'

'Why do you always deny things that are the truth?'

'I do not always deny things that are the truth.' Anna paused for thought. George's jaw had still not returned from the floor where it had dropped on first sight of her, and the obviously nonplussed man had tickled her vanity. 'I sometimes do this, but only when it is necessary. And with you it is often necessary, because you are often very pompous and talk to me like an old man, when in fact you are still a boy and hardly older than me.'

'I think I'll take Edmund Spenser's parakeet to Lisbon instead of you. The one he got from the Indies? It's more beautiful than you, and when you want to shut it up you just put a blanket over its cage,' said Gresham. Gresham and Spenser the poet had long been friends.

'Oh yes! So now you want me to climb under your blanket, is that it?'

'I never said . . .'

189

So they had moved from a rather strange formality in their dealings into bickering like an old married couple. Mannion decided to block it out, but was vaguely aware that the pair of them kept it up all the way to the Palace. God help them if this went on all the way Lisbon.

He knew that he had to go and see Walsingham. He both dreaded it and, if he was being honest with himself, felt real fear.

'I hear your . . . ward's admission to the Court went very well,' said Walsingham, no hint of tension in his voice.

'If by that, sir, you mean that she was made several offers of marriage that night, and rather more offers for shorter-lived relationships, then the evening was certainly a success,' said Gresham, who had found himself ignored more and more as Anna had taken the floor *and* the hearts of several young men and not a few old enough to know better.

'My Lord,' said Gresham, who presently felt unable to engage in idle chit-chat, 'I need to know if you ordered my death at sea.' Well, Gresham had never asked a question quite so directly before. The only sign of surprise was a slightly raised eyebrow. Yet even that from Walsingham was the equivalent of a heart attack from another man.

'And why would you think I had done so?'

He had not denied it! Something came near to cracking in Gresham's heart. He could handle any man, even the Queen. Yet of all men, Walsingham was the one who he felt least able to defend himself against. Briefly Gresham explained what had happened, the lethally incriminating evidence planted on him.

Walsingham gazed in silence out of the window for several minutes after Gresham had finished. From far away came shouts of children playing in the Thames, risking their death of cold. It had been a tiresome ride out to Hammersmith and then on to Barnes. Finally he turned to Gresham.

'Welcome to your rite of passage. You are familiar with the phrase? It is when a young man is set a task, or faces one, that defines his move from child to adult.'

190

'I don't understand,' said Gresham, floundering.

'As a child, you could ask a question such as you have asked of me and expect an answer that would either put your fears to rest or give them cause. I suggest that if you analyse your own feelings, you will be responding now as a man. As a man, you will know that were I to deny having issued your death warrant it could just as easily be a lie as the truth. The answer, therefore, serves no meaningful purpose. A few simple words of denial do not mean you can afford to ignore the possibility that I might be seeking your death. You will have to guard against that as a possibility whatever, from now on, if you wish to survive – and you, Henry Gresham, have a finely developed instinct for survival. It is the realisation that there are no easy answers that distinguish a child from a man.'

Gresham knew the truth of what was being said even as Walsingham spoke, knew that he could never again have total trust in this man just as he fought against that realisation.

'As it happens,' said Walsingham, 'I did not arrange for that commission from Spain to be forged or found. It irritates me that someone sought to kill one of my agents. Yet you will be ill-advised to take comfort from my words.'

'Why so, My Lord?' asked Gresham sensing the answer before it came.

'Because I could be lying. Because it would have been simpler for you to identify clearly your enemy, and because you must know that even if this time I did not seek your death I would do so, ruthless, remorselessly and without a pang of conscience if I thought that by your death I would serve the better interests of the Protestant religion, of England and of the Queen. There you have it. I claim not to have sought to kill you. Yet I will do so if sufficient need arises.'

'I thank you for your candour,' said Gresham. Such a ludicrous situation! Could this really be happening? Did people have such conversations? Or had he in fact not woken up that morning? 'And of course, My Lord, I would ruthlessly, remorselessly and without a pang of conscience seek your death were I to truly believe that you

191

'sought mine.' Except you're probably rather better at it than I am, thought Gresham.

'If that is indeed so,' said Walsingham, 'then you have truly become a man.' Something like a thin smile creased one of Walsingham's lips.

'I doubt that I've made the whole of that journey,' said Gresham. 'Yet the journey I wish to make now is to Lisbon. You may remember,' said Gresham, 'certain points you made about Lisbon.' Walsingham remembered everything. 'You believed that there were central weaknesses there for Spain, in the event of a decision to invade England.'

'I still believe so. Though it cannot and never will be the whole answer.'

'And you believed the Duke of Parma and his army in the Netherlands to be the crucial factor.'

'An opinion I have not changed.'

'I had planned to address both issues,' said Gresham simply. 'In my own way.'

'I have been made aware of that,' said Walsingham, 'as I understand you have already discussed a visit to Lisbon and a visit to the Netherlands with Master Robert Cecil.'

Gresham's heart froze. Walsingham and Cecil were in regular conversation! Were both allied against him?

'You will remain aware that you are still working for me,' said Walsingham, ice in his voice. 'We discussed the usefulness of your visiting Lisbon and the Duke of Parma. The situation has not changed. You will indeed make both trips, God willing. But be clear that you will do so on my orders, and under my orders. Is that clear?'

It was clear.

'You might care to include a new issue in your plans. An issue we did not discuss earlier,' Walsingham continued.

'A third issue?' He really must stop sounding like a parrot.

'The Marquis of Santa Cruz is resident in Lisbon.'

'The Spanish High Admiral?'

'The one and only. The victor of Lepanto, and one of the cru-ellest and most savage commanders alive in Europe at the present time. And the best ally we have.'

'The best *ally?*' Gresham was shocked. Was the Spanish High Admiral in Walsingham's pay? 'But Santa Cruz is a brilliant, inspi-rational commander. Santa Cruz is to Spain what Drake is to England – except Santa Cruz knows how to command a fleet.'

'Quite,' said Walsingham. 'Santa Cruz is a brilliant commander. He is an appalling administrator. Ships are piled into Lisbon harbour almost lying on top of each other. Some have a full supply of cannon but no shot. Others are loaded with shot but have no powder. There are vessels with spare cannon, some with no cannon at all. Meanwhile, pay is in arrears for the sailors, and men are dying of illness. Food newly taken on board ships is being eaten first, with the result that the older stock is left to rot. Either the sailors become ill through eating it, or they starve. I repeat, while the ships of King Philip's Armada lie in harbour, Santa Cruz is our best ally.'

'But if and when they leave for sea?' Gresham followed on.

'That would be a different story. King Philip will try to write a battle plan for his fleet. He is prescriptive, fearful of losing control. Santa Cruz will ignore his King's orders if by so doing he can achieve victory.'

'So it would be a good thing if Santa Cruz's health problems became . . . terminal?'

'It would indeed.'

'Surely you've tried to make them so?' said Gresham. 'You must have a horde of spies in Lisbon to know what you know about the state of the Spanish fleet. No man can avoid an assassin for ever.'

'No. But some men are better at it than others.'

'And you would appreciate . . . help in eliminating Santa Cruz, if the opportunity arose.'

'An excellent turn of phrase,' replied Walsingham. 'So will you depart for Lisbon with England's cause at the centre of your heart?' There was a sudden sharpness in Walsingham's tone. Did

Walsingham suspect Gresham's loyalties? 'There are those who think your enthusiasm for the Mass is not feigned. Those who have noted your failure to condemn Spain as a proper Englishman should, your admiration for what you call parts of its culture. Nonsense, of course, but dangerous nonsense, if heard by the wrong people.'

Had one of the wrong people reached the conclusion that he was sympathetic to Spain and thus enlisted Walsingham in having him killed? 'I'll depart for Lisbon with my survival at the centre of my heart. And hope, perhaps, that from that there may be some profit for England. As for Spain, I'm honest enough to see what it does well. That doesn't mean I want it ruling here in England. And my actions so far have shown what I'll sacrifice for England.'

Did Walsingham believe him? It was impossible to know, except Gresham was certain that if Walsingham believed now he was a spy for Spain he would not have left the house alive. Walsingham's final words were ominous.

'Take care, Henry Gresham, that you do not plot the end of your own life, needing no interference from men such as me.'

Well, there was no answer to that.

Gresham regaled George and Mannion with the gist of his conversation with Walsingham. He vaguely wondered about telling Anna, but dismissed it more or less instantly. True, her life might depend on whether or not Gresham's judgement of Walsingham was sound. But these decisions were man's work.

'So do you trust him?' George asked.

'Not completely,' said Gresham. 'It's why I rather wanted to go on these two trips as my own man, and not Walsingham's. It's still conceivable that he set me up to die either in some trade-off with Burghley, Cecil or even the Queen, and he made it clear that I might be spying for Spain. I'm pretty sure he doesn't believe that. What I do think is that if he felt a need to have me killed it's passed, and for the moment he finds me useful.'

'Do spies ever have any certainty?' asked George in exasperation.

'Well, one at least,' said Gresham cheerfully. 'They always know someone wants them dead, even if they don't always know who it is.'

No English ship was foolish enough to sail into Lisbon harbour. Gresham found a ship to take them to St Malo. Even there they found the captains unwilling to sail to Lisbon, for fear of being seized for the Armada. Eventually they came across a tubby little coastal vessel that had never lost sight of land in its long life and whose sole armament consisted of four iron cannons that had probably never been fired since they came out of the foundry forty or fifty years earlier. Gresham doubted it was a ship that the Admiral of the Armada would die for, but even this captain seemed unwilling. In desperation, Gresham asked that if he would not take them for his sake, then would he consider taking them for the girl's sake, in her forlorn search for her French fiancé? He agreed then, grudgingly. He was French, which helped of course.

If Cadiz had been full of ships, Lisbon was, fourfold. If Gresham had been worried about drawing too much attention to himself, he soon realised what a false worry it had been. It was chaos in the harbour, the normal trade of one of Europe's busiest ports piled on top of the vast fleet that Philip was assembling.

'Bloody Hell!' said Mannion. 'You could feed England with what it costs to keep this lot idle here in port!'

They eventually came to rest in a dilapidated grey stone building which had slipped its foundations, leaving a large crack in the wall, and stone window ledges that drooped down to the left like a mouth frowning out of one side. The owner was an elderly Dutch merchant, reduced to letting rooms because of the terrible impact the continuing war in the Netherlands was having on trade.

'Strange, innit?' grunted Mannion, eyeing the meal they had been brought suspiciously. 'I thought as 'ow we'd stand out here, being English. Fact is, I doubt anyone'd notice.'

The port was heaving with every nationality on earth. Walking down the street where their house was situated they had heard Italian, French, Dutch and German spoken as well as Portuguese and Spanish. And English. The speaker was an elderly man, dressed in the simple robe of those aspiring to the priesthood. The Catholic priesthood, of course. Gresham knew of the hundreds of English men who fled to France and trained for the priesthood in Allen's grotesquely named 'School of Martyrs', but he had failed to realise the numbers who came to Portugal to do the same thing. Perhaps, he grinned inwardly, they knew just how deeply Walsingham's spy service had infiltrated the seminaries in France.

'Converting the natives,' Mannion announced. He had been out scouting. 'Most of 'em training here reckon to work as missionaries, either in the New World or in Goa and round there. Bloody sight safer than being sent over to England, I bet.'

'I think a lot of these ships in the harbour are intended to convert the natives. The natives in this case being us, the English.' Gresham gazed bleakly out through the sagging stone window, the shutter thrown wide open to let what breeze there was waft through. If Cadiz had given him an overwhelming sense of the power and wealth of the Spanish Empire, then Lisbon increased the threat to a nightmare.

'Walsingham'll want to see you pretty quick once we get 'ome,' said Mannion, following his gaze. 'You'll 'ave a lot to tell him.'

'If he's still alive when we get back,' said Gresham, his depression deepening. Walsingham was clearly a dying man. 'And I bet his spies have already given him the name, tonnage and condition of every boat in this harbour.'

They presented themselves to the Governor General, out of courtesy and necessity, as it was only by his leave that Gresham had been allowed to enter Lisbon. He was a harassed, grey figure, rumoured to be in permanent conflict with the Marquis of Santa Cruz.

'These are strange times,' he muttered in passable English, 'and it is good to be reminded of matters of the heart,' he paused to smile at Anna, 'when so much other talk is of war. You and your most elegant ward must visit us. We are holding a reception. I will arrange for a card to be issued to you both.' He snapped his fingers at a servant in glorious livery, who bowed and left to attend to the matter. 'I must also apologise,' he added.

'You have been most gracious in permitting us to visit,' said Gresham, 'and I cannot conceive of any need for an apology.'

'No, no, I must,' the old man said. 'I have been intending to find details of this Monsieur . . . Jacques Henri? Is that his name? Yet there has been so much to do here, I fear, so many people, so many orders . . . it has slipped my mind.'

'I am sure it will be no problem. We have an address . . .'

'Better, I think, if you allow me to send you a pair of my servants to guide you there.' The old man saw the expression in Gresham's eyes. 'No, not to keep guard over you as you might think. There is no secret about what is gathering in this harbour, and I would be most surprised to think that your Lord Walsingham was not paying a dozen men here to report back to him on every vessel that enters and leaves.'

It was an uncanny echo of a conversation Gresham had had with Mannion. How much did the Governor General know? Gresham searched the man's face, and looked to George. There was no hint of any ulterior meaning from the Governor General, and a simple shrug from George. Even his refined political sensitivity was on hold here in Lisbon.

'It is simply that the wars in the Netherlands, which many see as only lasting because of the support the English give the rebels, have damaged trade and there is much resentment. Also, *El Draco* destroyed many smaller vessels off this coast earlier in the year, many families are facing poverty now. Shall we say that two of my servants with you when you go out and about might dispel any . . . misunderstandings,' the Governor General replied. 'And of course, you will not be staying long,' he said with a tone of finality.

'As long as it takes to find the fiancé and to ensure that my ward is adequately cared for,' said Gresham, cursing inwardly. He had hoped for at least a week in Lisbon, perhaps even two or three.

The two servants, dressed in the same extravagant livery, turned out to be four, each pair working a twelve-hour shift. They dismissed with courtesy the invitation to reside inside, preferring to sit instead in the small lobby that led in from the street. It was a position from which they could monitor all the comings and goings from the house.

Anna came into Gresham's room unexpectedly, just as he, George and Mannion had laid out on the bed the robes of the trainee priest, the acolyte. The cassocks with their built-in hoods were rough-tailored, coarse. She looked from the clothes to them and reached her own conclusion.

'You are slipping out tonight. In disguise.'

George reddened in the face.

'You know who it is you have to meet. You have thought about this long ago, ordered your clothes. I was, how do you say, a bonus? If I had not agreed you will still have come to Lisbon, perhaps in disguise all the way.'

'Would still have come to Lisbon . . .' said Gresham.

'I do not care about English now! And you will take me with you,' announced Anna. 'You have four robes there. A few pins will hold up the hem of one of them so that it fits me. I have this right. You have been enabled to come here because of me only. I too must be involved. It is only fair.'

'But you can't come,' said George, all his honesty showing through in his face. 'This could be dangerous . . .'

'This isn't fun,' said Gresham angrily, cutting in. 'This is playing with the fate of nations. It isn't a game.' He would make her realise that what was a game to her was life and death to him. He would make her realise.

'No?' said Anna. 'Yet that is exactly how you treat it. A game. A game where the excitement is to lose your life, the prize to value life if you survive. My life is a meaningless game. A marriage with a fat Frenchman. Why should I not play your game? Because the thing between my legs is different?'

The coarseness shocked Gresham. He looked to Mannion and George. To his astonishment, Mannion seemed to be on the girl's side.

'Look,' he said to Gresham, 'we could use her. If she's willing.'

A sudden wave of tiredness came over Gresham, and he motioned to Mannion to carry on. Mannion turned to the girl, took her by the arm and led her into the corner of the room, dust dancing in the slanting beams of diminishing sunlight. They had a whispered conversation, Anna going deep red and then recovering. Chin held high, she nodded. Mannion grinned, and nearly forgot himself, reaching out to pat her bottom in approbation before realising the potential mistake and withdrawing it just in time.

They had travelled with two maids for Anna, including the loyal Mary, and it was harder to get rid of them than it was to avoid the guards. Eventually they were sent off to a separate room, Anna pleading a headache of such intensity that even the noise of the maids sleeping in their truckle beds at the foot of her four-poster would be too terrible to bear. Stripping off down to her shift, she put the gown over her head, clamped her hair rather than pinned it and forced a cap over it, leaving the hood to be a disguise when they left the house. There was a tap on the door. Mannion. He put his finger to his lips, motioned her across the dusty hallway to Gresham's room, ushered her in. Only then did he walk to the end of the hall, click his fingers, and call up the stairs one of their servants brought from England to stand guard outside Anna's door.

'No one goes in, no one comes out. Clear?' The servant nodded.

There was a door set in the panels by the side of the vast stone fireplace, a long-forgotten crest emblazoned over it in stone. Mannion picked its cumbersome, ancient lock in seconds, and it swung open for perhaps only the third or fourth time in ten years. It was a servants' passage, leading down into the kitchens that underpinned the whole mansion, empty at this time of night and stinking of grease and burned meat. All four had put their hoods up now, and they walked carefully past the racks of hanging copper pans, careful in case by knocking one against another they rang out like a peal of bells. The dying embers of the great fire flickered on the metal, caught the three hooded figures first in shadow and then in half-light. A child seeing them would have screamed, thinking hooded Death in four forms was walking the streets of Lisbon that night. A great door led directly from the kitchen to the road outside, for ease of delivery. It was locked with another huge mechanism, and bolted top and bottom. They ignored this, and went instead to a tiny door on the left side of the cavernous room, with its arched ceiling. It too was locked, but its bolts had rusted in. Some attempt had been made to force the metal bar into its receiving half-circle of iron, but the bolt had only engaged very slightly. Easing both bolts back ever so gently, Mannion swung it open when again he picked the primitive lock. He grinned inwardly. The three hours he had spent attempting to seduce the cook and the other women in the kitchen had paid dividends, including the knowledge gained from the lazy walk he had taken out of this very door to piss in the street and making the door appear bolted on his return.

It was lighter in the south at this time of night, Gresham noticed, but the streets were almost deserted, activity seeming to be concentrated in the harbour area. They slunk through the streets, fine stone houses built high but casting even deeper moon-shadow as a result, narrow and with the heat of the day still radiating from their stone and brick façades, in contrast to the cold light of the moon. Gresham and Mannion knew where they were going. A wild sense of excitement filled Anna's heart as she followed Gresham and George, Mannion behind her, excitement tinged with terror at what she had allowed herself to become.

It took them fifteen minutes of walking, their good pace limited by the need to keep in the shadows, their heads bowed and their hands clasped humbly in front of them. Those who wished to officiate at the Mass did not run through streets at midnight. It was suspicious enough that they were out anyway. They started to climb a slight hill, the stone houses giving away to ill-built timber structures, bleached by the sun into premature age. Light was bleeding through the shutters of one, large rambling building, raucous conversation and laughter exploding from it. They ducked into a tiny courtyard, bathed in shadow, and Mannion stripped off his gown, revealing the jerkin and trews of a working man. Anna watched from under the lip of her hood, fascinated. Simple though Mannion's dress was, it was cut in the Lisbon style, a subtle difference from that which a workman in London might have worn, the material thinner, the style more loose and flowing, more generous, to cope with the heat. He ducked into what was clearly a tavern or an inn. A door opened, a shard of light cut through the gloom and suddenly Mannion was back beside them.

'Round the back.'

With a quick look to left and right, they crossed the narrow street, unpaved and little more than a path, through an open side gate and into what had clearly once been a stable yard but which was now weed-strewn and derelict. Evidently guests who stayed the night at this inn came on foot and brought no horses with them.

'For God's sake, George,' said Gresham, 'whatever you do, don't start knocking things over now.'

The tiny room had probably once been a stable, but was rough-plastered now, a small table at each end. By the door were two country stools, three-legged and with the wood hardly smoothed. Two candles were on the furthermost, equally crude table, with a chair behind it, facing the door. Gresham placed the candles carefully together. He took one of the stools and placed it behind the table at the far corner of the room where a chunk of plaster had fallen off some two or three feet up from the earth floor, revealing a patchwork quilt of reeds or straw.

'Sit there,' said Gresham to Anna. He was angry with her for her insistence on coming. He would show her tonight what being a spy meant. She had asked to come, so let her taste the reality of it.

He arranged her hood so that it threw a deep shadow over her face, concealing it. The hoods of the cassocks were unusually deep, she noticed as only a woman would, extending far further forward than was normal. Gresham seated himself in the centre of the table furthermost from the door, the candles half blinding anyone who came in from the night, obscuring the face and figure of the man behind the table. George was seated, as invisible as a man his size could be, by the door.

There was a slight scuffling noise from outside, and Mannion stepped aside from the half open door to allow a bulky figure to duck into the room. He stood there, blinking, trying to acclimatise himself to the half light and the two sinister hooded figures seated behind the far table.

'Sit down,' said Gresham. He was speaking in perfect Italian. Anna knew just enough of the language to follow the conversation. You cannot understand a human unless you understand his language, her father had said. Spanish she had spoken all her life, English she had learned from her mother and French and Italian she had been taught in the schoolroom. What would her father have thought if he had known where his daughter's future lay, here in a stinking room in Lisbon helping an English spy defeat a Spanish fleet?

The man looked shocked. 'You are Italian?' he stuttered. He was not drunk, but had been drinking. The veins on his nose and the bloodshot eyes suggested this had been a lifelong hobby.

'I'm the Englishman you were told to expect,' said Gresham, continuing the effortlessly fluent Italian. He had first learned the language because of an overwhelming desire to read Machiavelli in the original. 'A very unimportant Englishman, an expendable Englishman whose betrayal by you would bring few tears to the eyes of any in Government in England. Indeed, someone chosen because they were expendable. Someone without title or status, yet with access to a great deal of money. A very great deal of money. For the right service.'

The man looked round the small room, nervous, licking his lips. Something flew through the air, a flickering blur of darkness from behind the table. The man swung round, exclaiming, ready to leap out of the door. He found it blocked by Mannion, holding the bottle of wine Gresham had just tossed to him. Grinning, Mannion reached down to the bag at his feet, never taking his eyes off the man, and brought out a simple pewter goblet. He reached down by the side of the man, placed the goblet on the table. Then, grasping the top end of the bottle in one great meaty paw, he placed the neck end in his mouth and yanked down. There was a crack, and the top half of the neck sheared off, smoothly down one side but jagged glass on the side facing the man. Mannion raised the bottle up, almost threatening the man with the jagged glass. He reared back, collided with the wall, struggling to grab the dagger in his belt. Before he could do so, Mannion had, in one seamless movement, plonked the bottle down on the table, reached forward to yank the dagger out of the man's hand and stepped back, plunging the dagger into the cheap soft wood of the table so that it sank in a full inch, and left it quivering slightly there. He motioned the man to sit.

'Bartolome de Somorriva,' said Gresham. 'Italian, chief gunfounder at the Lisbon armouries.'

Bartolome slumped onto a stool, his pulse beating heavily in his thick neck. The skin was stretched over one side of his face. Had it come too close at some stage to one of the great furnaces the gun foundries depended on for their business? He grabbed the goblet, poured wine into it so that it splashed over the side, took a great gulp. Mannion reached over, took the bottle and swigged at it from the sheared glass. He wiped his lips. And held on to the bottle.

'That is my position. And my craft. You know it well.'

'I also know that you've a wife and family in Italy, and two mistresses here in Lisbon, neither of whom is aware of the other.'

Bartolome went pale for a moment, and then shrugged his shoulders.

'What matter if one whore does not know of another?'

'No great matter,' said Gresham, 'unless it becomes known that one Bartolome de Somorriva contracted the pox some three months ago, and has continued making the beast with two backs with his mistresses ever since, despite that knowledge. One of the women is also sleeping with several of the most important men in Lisbon, and has therefore in all probability infected those men as well.'

Bartolome recoiled as if slapped in the face.

'How did you know?' he asked. 'You would not, you could not tell these people . . .'

'I require payment for my silence,' said Gresham in icy tones.

'Payment?' said Bartolome, genuinely confused and totally off balance. 'I am not a rich man. I . . .'

'The payment I require is different,' said Gresham. He had still not pulled back his hood, and the voice came from the black, ill-defined space shrouded by the folds of its cloth. 'Indeed, if you do what we ask, you'll be paid, most generously.' Gresham reached into his gown, drew out a purse and tossed it casually onto the table. It hit with a heavy thump. 'Go on, open it. Count it,' Gresham said.

The gold coins fell onto the table in an avalanche of wealth. One rolled off the edge, and Bartolome scrabbled for it in the dust.

'This is . . . most generous,' he said, looking up, the candlelight catching the sweat on his brow.

'It's a simple down payment,' said Gresham. 'There's five times as much if you do what we ask.'

An expression of knowing evil came into Bartolome's eyes. His assurance was seeping back, and clearly he was starting to feel on home ground. Carefully he fed each coin back into the purse, closed it, placed it somewhere amidst his considerable girth.

'And what is it that you ask of me? I am a simple man. I am a mere maker of guns, a working man.' He held the empty goblet up high, not looking at Mannion, staring at the hooded figure seated in front of him. The silence stretched out. He began to feel foolish, arm outstretched, empty goblet in hand. He turned to look at Mannion, intending to gesture to him to fill his cup. Mannion held his eyes, swirled his tongue round his mouth and very slowly allowed a string of spit to dribble from his mouth into the goblet. Then, carefully, he filled it to the brim with wine, and stepped back.

For a moment it seemed as if he would rise and try to strike Mannion, but it was fleeting. Instead he sat back in his seat, gazing bleakly at Gresham.

'I came here because I was told there was a man who had something I would be interested in. Is that something merely a pack of insults?' He almost succeeded in hiding his fear.

'It's simple,' said Gresham. 'King Philip's great fleet is short of cannon and shot. Far too many of its vessels are armed either with ancient iron guns, or cannon designed to cut a swathe through cohorts of men, not to cut through the thick and seasoned wood of an English galleon. Too many of its ships have a mere five or ten rounds per gun.'

'This I know,' said Bartolome, simply. 'This all Lisbon knows.'

'And you also know that it wasn't until last month that your foundry obtained enough raw materials to start seriously the business of casting new brass cannon, the large cannon the Armada so desperately needs, and the shot to go with them. And that Spain is relying on Lisbon to provide a hundred new, large guns, a hundred and fifty even, and the attendant shot.'

Bartolome spluttered, falling into the caricature he had previously adopted with Santa Cruz's harassed emissaries.

'A hundred cannon! A hundred and fifty! It is nonsense! The God of war himself could not make so many guns in so little time . . .'

'Spare me the drama,' said Gresham calmly. 'There are master gun-makers in France and craftsmen in Scotland who could come here to Lisbon for a price, men of experience and expertise, Catholic men with no love for England. Not only gun-makers, but the underlings, those other men who're so important in seeing that the mix of the metal is correct, that it cools at the right speed, that the bore is true . . . they too are there in Europe and in Scotland. But you've not sought to gain the services of these men.'

'And why should I not do so?' blustered Bartolome. 'I have all sorts of men tormenting me every day to produce more guns. More guns! It is like a litany of hell in my ears! Do you not think I would stop at anything to reduce it?'

'Yes,' said Gresham, 'for two reasons. Firstly, every master gun-maker brought here to Lisbon means less profit for you, who wish to have a monopoly in this most profitable of ventures. Secondly, you're not actually a very good master-gunner.'

Bartolome bridled, tried to rise to his feet. A pressure akin to an earthquake pressed on his shoulder. It was Mannion. He sat down.

'Your record wherever you have worked is bad. Explosions in the casting, explosions in the test-firing, explosions in the guns you've made when fired in earnest. In Italy they called you the widow-maker. You fled to Lisbon, telling them here that you sought more responsibility, and wished to make guns that would fire God's word as well as shot! Fine words, and fine forged testimonials from men in Italy with long titles but who unfortunately don't exist.'

'This is untrue! I . . .'

'Be silent.' Gresham had not raised his voice. The threat in its quiet tone silenced the Italian. 'My requirements are simple. You'll carry on making bad guns for the Spanish fleet. Instead of a hundred and fifty, you'll make no more than fifty, and they'll prove at sea to be more of a threat to the men who fire them than they are to the enemy they are fired at. And the round shot you manufacture, it'll be flawed. You'll ensure that it's cooled too quickly, unevenly, so that each shot will contain flaws. Flaws that mean when it's fired it'll fragment into splinters as soon as it leaves the barrel, and not smash whole into the hull of a good English ship.'

Anna found that she had been holding her breath, for how long she could not guess. She had been to sea, could imagine the Spanish soldiers and sailors putting the linstock to the priming pan of their great cannon, could hear the screams as cut and fragmented men saw their cumbersome weapon blow up in front of them, see the incomprehension on the faces of the men as round after round seemed to have no effect on the weaving, dancing English ships. What futures, what horrors and what lives were being decided here in this filthy room? What a reckoning there was here. Was it Death who had become her guardian?

'And my reward? My reward for betraying my faith as well as my profession? My reward for facing persecution, for being reviled, perhaps even for being exposed?'

'Gold,' said Gresham flatly. 'Exactly five times what you have there in that purse. Not quite a King's ransom, but perhaps a Duke's at least. A passport for you to a life of ease. And the good burghers of Lisbon not realising that their sudden dose of the pox comes as

206

a present from you, of course, nor your wife hearing the good news. And, of course, the King of Spain not being given the truth about the skills of his master gun-maker in Lisbon. I think you'll do rather well out of it. Better than the soldiers and sailors you'll cause to be cut to ribbons by their own guns.'

They were clearly not an issue for the Italian. 'And what guarantee do I have that you will not betray me when you have used me? You come, Englishman, with a remarkably high profile to Lisbon. Carrying a beautiful girl, so they say in the wine shops, a Spanish Princess. Am I wise to place my life in the hands of a man so much in the public gaze?'

'Meet my ward,' said Gresham, reaching over and flipping back Anna's hood.

She was surprised to be revealed. She had had no warning. Her golden curls fell down as the gold had fallen on the table earlier, and in the face of her beauty it was as if the number of candles in the room had been quadrupled.

Gresham let him look at her for a suitable time. 'She's a whore,' he said flatly. 'A Spanish whore, and a very beautiful one, but a whore for all that. She was servicing the Captain of the *San Felipe* when we captured it. I knew then that she was my passport to Lisbon.'

Gresham let the Italian's eyes devour Anna. She was shivering, her eyes downcast. She had never felt so shocked. It was as if she had been stripped naked and paraded before this evil man, like a slave. In the face of the raw power exercised by Gresham, any words she might call up seemed pathetic trivia.

'And she's yours, when all this is over, if you want her,' said Gresham. 'Another part of your payment.'

'Mine?' said the Italian. 'How can that be? She knows I'm poxed. Soon no girl will sleep with me, unless they too are diseased.'

His face wrinkled in distaste. Not at the thought of a diseased girl lying with him, Gresham knew, but at the thought of the treatments he would have to undergo to see if he could be cured. They were all painful and one, Gresham knew, required the surgical use of an instrument rather like a corkscrew.

'She knows nothing,' said Gresham. 'She speaks only Spanish and a little English. She's mine to dispose of as I please. Do this job for me and she's yours.'

It was probably the gold that did it, Gresham knew, not the offer of the girl, though he wondered. His fear had been that the man would turn them in to the authorities after the first purse, reckoning this to be the lesser of two evils. He had needed a distraction, something to stop Bartolome using his brain. What better way to stop him using his brain than making him think with his groin? The man had a voracious sexual appetite, that they knew. Yet no women, not even the whores, would look at him if it was known he had the pox. He could not keep his pox secret for long. Soon he would either have to be chaste, or spread his thinning seed between the thin legs of the women who were already poxed, a despairing pathetic group in any seaport or city whose closest relations in history were the members of a leper colony. To have his own whore, and one of such beauty, while he tried to fight free of the French malaise, now there was something even money would not buy him. And, if he chose to tell Anna what he had offered, it would bring her in touch with the reality of spying. And it would stop him thinking. The hot hunger for sex would override his brain, stop him from taking the money and betraying Gresham.

'How will . . . how will you get the girl to me?' Bartolome asked.

'We've spies everywhere in Lisbon,' said Gresham. Well, Walsingham did. 'I'll hear how the work in the Foundry goes. In Spring, if those reports are what I wish to hear, I'll return with the remainder of your money. And with the girl. She's clean from disease. I'll ensure she remains so. Until I deliver her to you, that is.'

He left then, confused and elated, frightened yet reassured. Under his management Gresham doubted that the cannon and shot produced from the Lisbon armoury would have been of the highest quality. Now he felt certain of it.

'What were you saying to the Italian?' asked a nonplussed George, who despite all the attempts of his tutors spoke only English.

'How dare you,' said Anna, cutting in. Her voice was cold, the authority of her mother suddenly appearing on the young girl's face. Yet she spoke from despair. He felt shocked. Damn! He had not realised she spoke Italian. 'How dare you! To offer me as a whore to that foul man. Is this the way you treat those placed in your protection?'

'It's the way I treat those who ask to come with me when I'm acting as a spy. The way I treat silly, empty-headed girls who think what I do is simply exciting with an ever-so-slight risk. Just enough to arouse them! The way I treat people who think what I do is about amusement. The way I show them that it's about slime, and dirt, and filth. And about killing people who don't want to die. You had to justify your coming along tonight. That was how you paid for your passage.' The image of the Spaniard in the meadows swam before his eyes. Was this what Henry Gresham was reduced to?

The two young people looked at each other in mutual hatred.

'And will you give me to that diseased man?'

'Of course not! It was a ruse! I won't return here. It was all a lie. A way of diverting his mind. I had to inflame him, stop him realising the stupidity of taking an English bribe.'

'And you were kind enough to tell me of this, before you offered me to him.'

No. He had not been kind enough. Because he had used her, as people had used him, and because he had become accustomed to seeing people as mere bargaining points. And the more he hated himself for doing it, the more he refused to admit that he was wrong, and the more he hated her.

'In this spying,' said Anna, with sarcasm that would have cut through granite, 'is it always so that the women have to stay silent and flutter their eyelashes while the men do all the talking?'

'No,' said Mannion, from somewhere beneath a tangled robe that he was having trouble getting over his head, 'sometimes they have to lie on their backs and flutter their . . .'

'Enough!' said Gresham. 'You forget your place!' he hissed in embarrassment. Mannion's head emerged at long last, grinning.

209

She directed a look of cold superiority towards Mannion, who was too busy laughing at his own joke to notice. Yet his laughter did more to reassure her than anything Henry Gresham had done. Mannion made it clear that it was all a game. A hurtful, ludicrous and even shameful game, but a game nevertheless. But was it a game for Henry Gresham? Or had he allowed it to become his life? At the back of her mind was a nagging question. If his 'mission' had depended on it, would he have given her to this foul man?

'I'm not happy with this,' George mumbled to Gresham, confused and with his sense of decency on high alert. Gresham ignored him.

They doused the candles in silence, waited five minutes for their eyes to acclimatise, listened for the padding sound of feet outside that would tell them of men gathering. Going to the back of the room, Mannion kicked sand and dust aside off the floor to reveal a wooden trapdoor. Lifting it, careful to make no noise, they could just about make out wooden steps leading down into darkness.

'Five steps down, missy,' whispered Mannion, close to her ear. She jumped, startled. Then, her anger still filling her veins, she decided that to show weakness would be to give in to the farce that her life appeared to have become. She stood up, straight. 'Six steps straight ahead,' said Mannion, 'bending low like. By then you'll see the stars.'

They descended, and before she had time to start fearing the rats there was a gentle scuffling and another trapdoor was being lifted up from the inside revealing, as Mannion had promised, the stars. They were in another courtyard, also weeded over, leading from the back of the room they had just been in. Noises still came from the tavern, but less so now, muffled. There was no sign of any welcoming party. Gresham and Anna were just feet apart, yet it could have been miles. The cold tension between them crackled invisibly. George stood between them, frantically trying to understand what was beyond his comprehension.

They were nearly back at the house, in ample time before the servants rose to build the fires in the kitchen, skulking through alleyways, when they heard the sound of footsteps coming up the hill towards them. It was one of the servants of the Governor General, off-duty but still resplendent in his livery and clearly very drunk. He was weaving from side to side, singing gently to himself, a child's lullaby, a bottle clutched in his hand. He did not seem to realise that the bottle was empty, nor care very much, raising it every now and again to his lips and smiling happily at the night sky. Drink makes some men quarrelsome. Others it sends to sleep. It had made this man simply happy, an overwhelming sense of being at peace with the world radiating from him.

The four hooded figures froze into the side of a house, but it was too late. The man ground to a halt, his eyes rolling until they focussed. He giggled.

'Religious men bringing blessings to the taverns!' he chortled. 'Or is it to the ladies of the night?' he giggled, swaying gently. 'Or maybe such men using the taverns *and* the ladies of the night!' he said, chortling and hugely amused at his joke. 'Here!' he said, more loudly, 'bless me! Aren't I of the night? And one of God's children?' He meant to fling himself onto his knees, but instead cannoned into Anna. His outflung arm caught the hood of her cassock. She flung her own hand up just in time and held the hood in place. The man collided with the wall, slid down it with his back, ended squatting on the floor, gawping vacuously up at them. Then his whole body language changed, and he seemed to be trying to sink back into the stone. 'I know who you are,' he said in a small, frightened voice. 'I know who you are.'

They were still hooded, still shadowed by the night, but it was entirely possible for the man to have caught enough of a sight of one or all of their faces. Mannion reached inside his sleeve for the dagger he carried there, but it was too late. Gresham had already folded his arms, and Mannion knew that meant he had a hand on his own dagger.

'I am Death,' said Gresham softly, in Latin, the language of the Mass, and for a moment the man seated drunkenly on the ground was as good as dead, the cold blue light of the killing frenzy settling behind Gresham's eyes, the hand tightening on the hilt of the dagger. The slightest of sobs came from the guard. He had to die. He had said the fatal words, *I know who you are*. There was too much at stake for the life of one man to stand between Gresham and his mission. Then Gresham remembered the man a few minutes ago. A man singing gently to himself, a nursery song, a man happy within himself. Walking to his home, harming no man. He thought of the way death had come to the sailors in Cadiz harbour, the way death would come to the men whose cannons would explode in their faces. Was this to be just another casual death in a back alley, another death that showed how cheap life had become to Gresham?

The man looked up at them stupidly from the floor. 'The Four Horsemen,' he said pathetically. 'The Four Horsemen of the Apocalypse. I knew it was you.'

Gresham's hand released the hilt of his dagger. He tried not to release his breath like an explosion.

'Do you repent of your sins?' he asked the man.

'I repent of my sins,' the man gabbled, pushing himself in fear now back against the wall.'

'Then go in peace. And tell no one.'

He raised himself up from the floor, still almost paralysed with fear, and made the sign of the Cross. The four figures gazed silently at him. Gulping, he turned and ran.

'I thought you were going to kill him,' said Anna, back in the safety of Gresham's room. They had slipped back through the kitchen, the servant dismissed back downstairs before Anna was allowed out of Gresham's room. This was not how she had imagined it to be. The excitement and sense of adventure had been soiled beyond recognition. Somehow she felt dirty, mired, revulsion replacing the excitement she had felt on setting out on her adventure.

'So did I,' said Gresham. Suddenly he wanted this girl more than he had wanted any woman in his life. Wanted to fling her on her back and take her, prove who was master. That was foul! He had never taken any woman against her will in his life! What was working within him, what in this girl was getting through his impregnable defences? 'Tomorrow we must see if your fiancé is in Lisbon. Any longer and we will cause questions to be asked.' He sensed the savagery in his mind and marvelled at the civility of his tone. Had she been hoping he would say more? She gave no sign.

'He will not be there. I *know* he will not be there.' Was she trying to persuade herself? She sounded flat, exhausted, as if drained of all emotion. 'I feel it inside me. It is not yet my time.'

'Where is Mannion?' asked Anna, as they gathered to visit the house of Jacques Henri.

'He's some business to do,' said Gresham. 'It's best you don't know.'

Gresham confided everything in Mannion. At the mention of Santa Cruz something had darkened in his eyes. 'Will you give me leave to work alone for a day or two, perhaps a week, in Lisbon? To settle an old score?' Mannion had asked. He had agreed, as he knew he had to. Yet he missed Mannion, desperately. One night, tossing and turning in his bed, he had allowed the unthinkable to enter his mind. What Mannion was doing would inevitably be extraordinarily dangerous, however he set about it. Could he face life without that hulk of a man by his side? He prayed he might never have to find out.

Anna had continued talking. 'Oh, I agree,' she said. 'Women cannot be trusted with secrets. They need simply to be told what to do. Or sold to men with the pox. Or just used generally, for the convenience of a man.'

It was so close to his actual thoughts that he nearly let the colour flood into his cheeks. 'We're not out of danger. We must hurry to leave, in case the Italian changes his mind, pockets what gold he has and takes more for revealing us. If we're taken in and you're asked about Mannion, you really won't know. There's nothing better than sincerity.'

She pursed her lips, a gesture making it clear that belief was at least suspended if not totally dismissed. George intervened.

'I'm sure he's acting in your best interest,' he said, feebly. She flashed a brief smile at him, as if saying thank you to a big brother, and then turned again to Gresham.

'So you can lie to save a friend. I as a mere woman can do no such thing. That is fine. Now I understand.' She was clearly seething underneath.

Privately, Gresham doubted Jacques Henri was in town. Their arrival had not raised the clamour he had expected in Lisbon, there being enough clamour in that city as it was, but neither had it gone unnoticed. Jacques Henri would surely have heard of their presence by now, and come rushing to them. Either he was absent, or regretting his engagement. Anna had made it clear the matter had been arranged without her consent. Yet how clear was she whether the famous Monsieur Henri was a willing partner, or simply coerced?

The address they had been given turned out to be a vast warehouse with a presentable stone house attached. Yet it was as quiet as a mausoleum. They were quite an entourage, Gresham, Anna, two maids and seven of Gresham's servants, all on hired horses, with the two resplendent guards provided by the Governor General, and an interpreter. Several street urchins had gathered at a safe distance, offering their comments in Portuguese on the whole array, and the usual waifs and strays of any city had gathered to watch – maids out on errands, apprentice boys making a short journey last a long time, the occasional boy risking a thrashing by missing his lessons to be out in the sun. The man who had seen the Three Horsemen of the Apocalypse was not one of the guards. He was on sick leave, Gresham had been told as he had enquired solicitously.

The senior guard had tried to hide his horror at Anna riding with them. Clearly he thought it desperately improper for the girl to rush so to meet her intended. Surely the men should have met first of all, agreed what to do, and only then allowed the girl to enter into the scheme of things? 'Ah!' said Gresham, 'but she's importunate to meet her intended! I can hardly hold her back. I've no heart to stem the passion of her love for this man!' he declaimed, enjoying how annoyed this made Anna. Not that an outsider would have noticed her annoyance. Gresham was becoming adept at reading the tiny flickers on her face.

It soon became clear that the problem would not have to be resolved on that day at least. Furious hammering at the door of the house produced nothing but a wizened old man, his face darkened by the sun and cut through with tiny, deep lines, who eventually emerged through a postern gate carved out of the great door into the warehouse yard. No, the interpreter established, Monsieur Jacques Henri was not in residence, had not been so for some months now. It was not known when he was expected back. The warehouse was empty. The last consignment of goods from Goa had been sold before his departure, the last rolled Turkish carpets sold, the great bales of wool disposed of at less than full price. It was believed that the merchant was seeking new markets, new outlets, new products. He had gone north in June, to the Flat Countries, the interpreter said. Flat Countries? It could only be the Low Countries, the Netherlands.

'Why would the fat merchant go to a war zone?' asked Gresham. 'The whole area's been at war for years. Parts of it are like a desert, so I'm told. What profitable trade could there be there?'

'I hope he has gone there because he has realised that it would be sinful to take me as his wife,' said Anna, 'and because he is too much of a fat coward to shoot himself he hopes that one or both of the armies in the Netherlands will do it for him.'

'Do you say that about all your friends?' asked Gresham.

'He is not my friend,' she replied. 'Any more than you are. He is a fat pig.'

They saw nothing of Mannion for the remainder of that day, or that night, when Gresham, George and Anna attended a glittering reception held by the Governor General. Gresham had half hoped to see the legendary Marquis of Santa Cruz there, but no, he was told, the Marquis had too many pressing demands on him. Nor was Mannion there the next day, when they rode out to see Lisbon and its sights, or the day after when they were permitted to leave the city boundaries and ride out in the glorious countryside surrounding the city. It was on the fourth day that Mannion reappeared, quietly and without fuss, a strange grimness in his manner.

'And where have you been?' asked Anna, her insatiable curiosity finally getting the better of her.

'Presenting a visiting card,' was all that Mannion would say.

CHAPTER 8

October 1587 – May, 1588
Cambridge; London; Lisbon; the Netherlands

It was a tricky job, dragging the cannon out of a ship. Like taking out a tooth. Firstly the barrels had to be taken off the short wooden carriages and properly slung. Each weapon was massively heavy, but unevenly balanced, with more weight at the breech than at the tapered muzzle. The lifting tackle had to be exactly positioned to avoid the gun swaying and splintering the timbers of the vessel. Poorly-tied knots, a frayed rope or a pole not seated firmly on the ground and you risked the whole thing crashing down onto the deck. Never mind the people, in one such incident only last year the gun had gone right through the hull and was resting on the sea bed. It was a miracle they had been able to save the ship.

The sailors looked on glumly as the last of the guns were swung overboard, and laid in their padded nest on the vast carts, then to rumble off to be stored in the great armoury at the Tower of London. The disgruntled manner of the seamen was not because they were being laid off with the ships. That had been part of a sailor's lot in the winter for as long as mankind had been daring to set sail. It was fear. A number of the men looked nervously down the reach of the Thames to the sea, as if they half-expected to see a Spanish galleon bearing down on them, its cannon ready to belch destruction into London. Now that the fleet was being stepped down for winter, what was there to stop the Spanish if they chose to come?

Holding one possible answer was Walsingham, sat in front of the remnants of a frugal meal, gazing out over the River Thames. He had taken a tenancy at Barn Elms ten years earlier, falling in love with the combination of its quiet solitude and the easy access to London from the tiny village of Barnes. He had complained fiercely at the decision to step down the fleet, to no avail. Money! Money! How dare they preach saving to him, the man who had spent out his own fortune to keep England's borders its own! Thank God in his wisdom that Santa Cruz was ill again. Had it been otherwise, he knew what he would have done in Santa Cruz's position when he heard, as he would surely hear, that the English fleet had been put to bed for winter. He would have ignored his King, taken a squadron of fifteen ships up the Channel risking wind and weather, sailed them into Plymouth or even up the Thames and landed five thousand troops. Let England stop Parma then with a hornet's sting already working its poison in its belly! Oh what tactics, daring, or fifty of the best ships could dash out from Lisbon, and do to the English fleet exactly what Drake had done to the Spaniards in Cadiz.

It could still happen. King Philip was sending ever more urgent messages to Santa Cruz, demanding that he sail now, even in the depth of winter. The moment the first agent in Lisbon reported back that yards were being stepped, supplies being loaded for just such a venture, then this half-manning nonsense would cease. Walsingham guessed Her Majesty would move with unseemly haste, her dignity in disarray at the prospect of her old knees bending to King Philip of Spain! Then let us see the sycophantic Burghley rush to support the immediate re-manning of the fleet, the noble Lords of Leicester and Essex suddenly feel the foundations of their vast castles tremble beneath their feet!

Yet it was history repeating itself. For most of Elizabeth's reign her soldiers and the idiot nobles sent to lead them had proved a false saviour, just as even a fully-manned English fleet might do now. It had been espionage that had saved England from the Spanish threat so far, and if England was to be saved now it would be by the same measure.

As he rose from his table, the pain stung at his belly. He doubled up, no one there to see his humiliation. You are already dead, his doctor had said. Only a quack will promise you hope. How soon before his actual death was reported as a certainty?

The Fellowship of Granville College were uncertain as to how they should respond to Henry Gresham on his return for the Michaelmas Term 1587. Guilty? He had taken a prolonged absence, and brought back a beautiful Spanish girl who he had met under impossible circumstances and who had to be his mistress, of course. Fellows were not permitted to marry, and were meant to control the sensual excesses of the students rather than set them an example of it. Innocent? He had fought most heroically for his country at Cadiz. It was now an open secret that the money for the extension to the Old Court had come from him, though God knew who had leaked that bit of information. He had at least had the decency to return for the most important part of the year. The arguments for a positive response seemed, on balance, to outweigh those for a negative response, so acting true to form two thirds of the Fellowship decided to take a wholly negative approach.

'We could all of us,' said Will Smith, who ran a mile if someone mentioned the word sword, never mind threatened to use one against him, 'go gallivanting off to sea if we chose, enjoying ourselves at the expense of our students. If, of course, we needed such spurious glamour to bolster our reputation.' It was generally agreed that it was far braver and heroic to remain at home, manning the domestic fort, so to speak, than to rush off to obscure places like a common soldier or sailor. Fat Tom was having none of this.

'Do tell me, dear boy,' he mouthed excitedly, all of his chins wobbling in unison, 'all about it, preferably in the most gory detail. I imagine these sailors are very rough people indeed, and you must tell me all about them as well. And please, do dwell at unseemly length on the episodes with lashings of blood in them!' The most worrying thing was that he was entirely genuine in his interest, both in the details of the fighting and in the men.

Gresham had sent messengers to the Netherlands, seeking the whereabouts of the untraceable Jacques Henri. So far they had drawn a complete blank. He had at least found a chaperone for Anna. The daughter of his father's housekeeper, a rather stern, puritanical girl with thin lips and a thin face, she had a permanent air of censorious disapproval about her. She held her once-expensive but now rather shabby skirt close about her nervously, as if everyone and everything including the ground upon which she stood might rise up and criticise her at any minute. Or, even worse, try to make love to her. She had presented herself at The House with the story of the death of her employers, and in a stroke of genius the housekeeper, an elderly and flustered woman, had recommended her to Gresham. It was an interesting relationship. The chaperone had no actual authority over her charge, merely the requirement to be there and ensure her virtue was preserved. The authority came from the certainty that the chaperone would try to put off any amorous young man, deny them opportunity and, in the final count, report their misdeeds to her master. 'Bit like when you pour cold water over a dog that's after your favourite bitch?' asked Mannion, who was intrigued by the idea of a chaperone. 'Not . . . quite,' Gresham had replied, giving up on an explanation.

The wild set in London with whom Gresham tended to mix when he was there, the poets, the musicians and those trying their hands at the new fashion of writing for the Playhouse, had taken Anna to their hearts. With a chaperone in place, Gresham was less concerned about whether they took her to their beds, not his. Why should he care? Yet he had felt obliged to find a better base in Cambridge than his two rooms in Granville College. The Merchant's House lay in Trumpington, just outside Cambridge, and had lain vacant for a year or more, the dust thick over its old floors

220

and walls. It was ancient, built round the medieval core of its Great Hall, probably a nobleman's house before passing to the Merchant who had given it its name. And now Henry Gresham flickered briefly in its history, setting up a base where he could summon his ward once every six weeks, the state of the roads allowing, from the fleshpots of London to savour the rural delights of Cambridge and the questions of her master. Her nominal master, at least.

The bonus for Gresham was Excalibur's Pool. He couldn't help but call it that, for if anywhere in England there was a place where a magic sword might rise up out of the mist, it was in the bend of the river where the water had scooped out a deep, dark pool, somehow separated from the moving water, a place where time and motion stood still. You could look into the translucent depths of Excalibur's Pool and see the history of England. He found himself drawn to it more and more, spending the night in the simply furnished great bedroom so that early in the morning he could walk out over the meadow and plunge into its darkness. Buying The Merchant's House created more trouble in the College, of course. It showed unseemly wealth. Residence in College was mandatory for Fellows, the core of communal living on which the whole concept of the College was based.

He had spent Christmas in London. No young man with blood flowing through him would refuse his monarch's order to celebrate the twelve days of Christmas with the richest and most spoilt of the land. The memories blurred into each other. The swirling, flickering light from thousands of candles, the stately procession of the dance with the vibrant bodies, hungry for each other under the strict discipline of the music. Anna, with fire in her eyes, being swept round and round by a courtier whose tongue was hanging out, and who later offered her his whole inheritance for one night spent with her. She had sent him home to his mother. The dreaded moment when a really drunken Gresham had looked up to see that the dance had placed him yet again opposite Her Majesty Queen Elizabeth. He had never danced as well, nor sobered up more quickly.

*

The men, the ships, the very countries involved in this great game of life now stood like dominoes stacked in a line, each one carefully placed over years through the scheming ambition of those with a desperate desire to retain power, or those with a desperate desire to grab it. For years those dominoes stood still, silent, and then came the push. It only needs one of those dominoes to topple, and worlds shiver, history is changed.

The first of the great dominoes to topple and knock the next in line, was the death of Don Alvaro de Bazan, Marquis of Santa Cruz, Captain General for the Ocean Seas, hero of Lepanto, victor of Terceira and endless other conflicts and Commander for the Enterprise of England, on February 9th, 1588. He died, the old man, with no tears from his servants for this abundantly cruel man.

Then the worst day in his life came to the Duke of Medina Sidonia. It had started badly. There was rarely peace for any Spanish grandee, living his life from dawn till dusk in the eyes of his people, the few snatched hours of night with his wife the only time he was not on show. It was his duty, he accepted it both as his responsibility and his birthright, but sometimes he ached for isolation. Having returned from Cadiz he had been sitting in judgement on tenants all day, and one particularly unpleasant case where a man had denied God, his duties as a tenant, and his duties as a husband and father had sickened him. So it was that he had a strange feeling that things were not well, coupled with a great restlessness.

The messengers arrived at his home as he did. King Philip never sent one man where ten would do. The letter hit him like a sword through his heart. Santa Cruz was dead. His King required the Duke of Medina Sidonia to become Commander by Sea for the invasion of England. He clutched the parchment in his hand, frozen, the blood draining from his face. For minutes he said and did nothing. Then, with a slow walk, he called for his Secretary. He had no time to think over his response, merely to feel the awful dread pulling at his heart. It was from his heart finally that he wrote to his King.

My health is not equal to that needed for such a voyage. I know this since the few times that I have been at sea I was sea sick and always caught a fever. My family have debts of over nine hundred thousand ducats. I have no money to spend on the enterprise, nothing to spend even for my King. I have no experience of war, nor of the sea. How is it that I can be suited for such a great command? I know nothing of what Santa Cruz has been doing. I have no intelligence of England. I fear therefore that I will let myself and you, Your Majesty, down most terribly, acting as a blind commander, relying on the advice of those I do not know, unable to distinguish truth from lies, the good advice from the bad . . .

As soon as he had sealed it and sent it he regretted the impetuosity with which he had written. Fretfully his mind told him that his response would make him look like a coward. He feared such an accusation against his honour, far more than he feared death itself. Yet equally potent in his growing sense of despair was the realisation that his letter would fail, of course. Like all limited men, Philip was incapable of changing his mind, not seeing that sometimes to do so was wise, but seeing it rather as him being proven wrong. And the King with God's ear could never be wrong.

He knew why he had been appointed. They were proud men, the sea captains of the Spanish Empire, and men uniquely conscious of their rank. Well, Sidonia was superior to any of them in rank and, more importantly, breeding. He had the status to quell the extra proud spirits of the other commanders. Was all lost? These commanders had won and held an Empire. There was huge skill and knowledge in their ranks. They would give him the military advice he would be so desperately in need of. Yet the challenge! Not the challenge of fighting. He was born to that. It was the challenge of marshalling over one hundred ships and ten thousand troops languishing in Lisbon harbour, every month's delay costing seven hundred thousand ducats.

He wrote again, of course, two days later. Useless though he knew it was, he felt he owed it to himself. And to history, if anyone ever bothered to read his laboured offering. He was more reasoned, this time, questioning the whole wisdom of the Enterprise. The sea was a fickle battleground. A storm could destroy the whole endeavour in an hour. As Sidonia understood it, the Duke of Parma was penned in behind shallows patrolled by the infamous Dutch flyboats, waters no ship the Spanish possessed could travel. It did no good. Don Cristobel de Moura, the most influential of King Philip's secretaries, wrote back immediately.

We did not dare show His Majesty what you have written. God will see that the Armada is victorious.

Well, so he might, the Duke thought as he mounted his horse for the journey to Lisbon. Yet in his experience, God rarely made up for man's inadequacy, and there were very many inadequacies that needed to be dealt with before the Armada could hope to succeed.

On arrival in Lisbon the first thing the Duke of Medina Sidonia saw were great sackloads of paper being carted out of Santa Cruz's administrative headquarters. All the paperwork for the Armada. Invoices, bills of lading, lists of ships, charts, all vital to an invasion. It belonged personally to Santa Cruz, of course. There was no doubt about that. History and tradition dictated it was so. Sidonia called over the most sympathetic and charming of his secretaries, gave him clear instructions. Somehow those papers had to be retained and preserved, at all costs. The Duke was starting to realise that the actual fighting would be the easiest part of this endeavour.

And so the dominoes continued to fall. Cecil called for Gresham. It was their first meeting since the night Gresham had returned from sea.

'The Queen has pushed for negotiations with the Spanish forces in the Netherlands, and the Duke of Parma has agreed,' said Cecil. 'I can tell you now that the death of Santa Cruz has just been reported.'

What a surprise, thought Gresham. Mannion will be gutted.

224

'The death of Santa Cruz will throw the Spanish into confusion. We leave from Dover, for Ostend, immediately, in the hope that we can profit from that confusion. I have been allowed to join the party as an observer, as you expected.' Cecil's chest seemed to swell, 'In fact I have been asked to use my best endeavours to obtain the maximum amount of information on the military preparedness of the Netherlands.'

Gresham could not repress a smile. 'I'm sure your extensive military experience will be a wonderful asset to you in that task,' he said. 'In fact, you'll be acting as a spy. Welcome to the club.'

'A spy?' Cecil sniffed. 'An ambassador with eyes is how I prefer to think of it. Spies are employees, after all, paid for their work.' Cecil realised his mistake as soon as he had spoken, but it was too late.

'Really?' said Gresham, who had less need of money than anyone. 'Fancy that. If I'd realised that someone was meant to pay me I'd have asked for the money . . . After all, you can never have too much, can you?' Which might well have been the motto of the Cecil family, come to think of it. Gresham doubted that the magnificent palaces Lord Burghley had built and was building were afforded from whatever allowance the Queen made to him.

'In any event,' said Cecil, moving rapidly on, 'you have the excuse of seeking your . . . ward's fiancé. I gave you my word that I would facilitate your access to Lisbon and to the Netherlands. You may join my party. You will be listed as an adviser, a status little above a servant. But alone. The woman cannot come with you.'

'I wouldn't wish her to do so,' said Gresham. 'The Netherlands is a war zone. There's no certainty of finding her fiancé, perhaps not even a reasonable chance. What I need to do there doesn't involve her. It does, however, need your expedition, as my cover.'

Cecil's lips turned up in distaste at the word "cover". 'It has cost me in credibility to include you in our party,' said Cecil. Already it was "his" party, though as the mere son of a nobleman he was the least important member of it. 'So perhaps you may feel able to tell me, following our "agreement", what you achieved – if anything – in Lisbon.'

'Something. Perhaps nothing. Not enough. As I said previously, it's better you do not know. Particularly as we're heading into a country ravaged by war where even the best-escorted parties can't be guaranteed safety from brigands.'

Cecil blanched slightly. 'I am sure it will not come to that.'

He returned to The House and Anna. She had had a wonderful time over the twelve days of Christmas, though she would never admit it to Gresham, and was glowing as a result. The glow turned to frost when she saw him. The chaperone looked more miserable by the minute.

Cecil was not his only reason for being in London. Gresham very much wished to attend a party hosted by Edmund Spenser, who seemed about to give birth to his own baby, a lengthy poem called 'The Faerie Queene'. It was the least glamorous of the events Anna and Gresham had been invited to, but Spenser was a true friend, and a true poet, so the event was worth dragging him away from Cambridge. Anna refused to talk to Gresham, but had softened towards George and talked to him with some animation, seemingly with complete trust. At an earlier soiree the Earl of Essex had made a pass at her.

'It was appalling!' she said, clearly not at all appalled. 'He is such a handsome man, a favourite of the Queen and they tell me he is a bolted Earl. Yet he dresses so carelessly!'

'It's belted Earl actually,' said Gresham later, as they walked the Long Gallery of The House, 'and yes, he's deemed to be the most handsome of the lot.' George had left to go home, his face long. His elderly parents were about to arrive in London on one of their increasingly rare visits, and spoil his bachelor life.

Anna looked at him. 'I do not listen in to your conversations. I fail to see why you should listen to mine. It is probably unsafe for me to even be near you. The girls at Court, they say you are dangerous.'

Well, dangerous to one or two of their husbands, perhaps. What was a young man to do if a girl flung herself at you? It would be impolite to refuse. 'Not as dangerous as the Queen will be to you, if she thinks you're stealing the attentions of her latest young man. So what happened?' His curiosity overrode his distaste for this foreign creature.

'The Earl – Robert Devereux is he not? – danced with me for the first time, and then took the second dance and even the third. I know he had ladies for the second and third dances waiting for him. I saw, because they were most upset.' There was no sign that Anna had been upset on their behalf. 'And then, in the third dance, he whispered in my ear!'

Gresham paused, and looked at the girl. Why had she not flung herself at him? There was more control to her than he had given her credit for, Gresham realised. The pan might be boiling, as Mannion had insisted to his laughter, but the owner was managing to keep the lid on tight. Now he thought about it, this must be the first really beautiful girl who had not flung herself at him. Did he mind? Of course not. 'And what did he whisper?'

'What men always whisper,' Anna said simply. 'To go to bed with him.'

'So what did you do?' asked Gresham, despite himself.

'I told him that I was a virgin,' she answered simply. 'And more than that, I was a Catholic virgin. So that I could only go to bed with a man who would guarantee me an Immaculate Conception.'

Despite himself, Gresham burst out laughing. 'And his response?' he found himself asking.

'He burst out laughing, like you. Men are all the same. He said that great though he undoubtedly was he was not yet ready to be the father of Jesus.'

Good on him, thought Gresham, his respect for the Earl of Essex reluctantly increasing. Then the bleakness of his situation forced itself into his mind. Once, as a child, he had seen a flock of pigeons scatter up from the roof of The House, winging up towards the clouds. Then, suddenly, one of the pigeons had crumpled in the air, as if shot. Yet there was no man with a gun nearby, no archer trying the impossible task of killing a bird on the wing. The dead bird, transformed in an instant from a thing of beauty to something inert and lifeless, had plunged like lead to earth, landing with a soggy thump on the roof, dislodging two of the tiles by its impact. The still-warm flesh lay motionless, the tiles skittering down the length of the roof to tumble and smash into pieces on the hard ground below. So it was with Gresham's mood at present, as he remembered the bleak reality of his future, the gaiety of the moment crumpling like a dead bird. 'I must leave,' said Gresham. 'I have to go to Flanders.'

'To find Jacques Henri?' asked Anna.

'That's part of my excuse. If this damned man of yours exists, which I'm beginning to increasingly doubt. But it's not my real reason. And I can't take you with me. It's a war zone there, out of control. It's going to be difficult enough keeping Cecil out of trouble and myself free to do what I need. And you would be at real, serious risk.'

She chanced a very rare smile, to herself more than to him.

'More risk than being stranded at sea on a sinking ship with fifteen pirates?'

Sometimes the best way to deal with a woman was to remain silent.

'You are happy for me to remain here?' she asked. 'Living as I do?' She was asking if he consented to her continuing to spend his money.

'Of course. You're my ward, aren't you?' Gresham liked saying that. It gave him a feeling of power. 'Yet for a short time, in a month or two, I may ask you to stay in a new place. Not for long, I hope.'

A puzzled expression crossed her face. It was time. He had no option. He had to tell this girl his real business. The truth. The truth that only Mannion had known hitherto. The truth that would most likely lead to Henry Gresham being killed in disgrace. As she was a Spaniard, perhaps he should have told her much earlier. Who knows? Secrecy becomes like a second skin, and humans are not like snakes who slough off their skin effortlessly. 'Let me explain,' he said. And then he told her the truth that had been haunting him for so long. The truth that he knew would decide his fate, his life. As he did so, he realised how stupid it must sound to an outsider.

When he had finished, he looked at her face. She was white, aghast. There were tears starting in her wide eyes – of shock? Of horror? Suddenly, surprisingly, he realised what a terrible moment this was. For the first time since he had known her she looked into his eyes, and broke down, the emotion shaking her whole body.

'I'm sure you'll be safer where I'm asking you to go than in the Netherlands,' he added lamely, at a loss as to what he could do. He was to remember his words later on.

All Mannion said when he heard of the conversation was, 'You don't make life easy for them as follow you, do you?'

Her Majesty Queen Elizabeth's Embassy to the Netherlands was one of the most bizarre, mad and, in some strange way, ridiculous events of Gresham's life. Perhaps all diplomacy was this ridiculous. If so, it was a wonder that the world was not permanently at war. Then again, perhaps it was.

Why should the Duke of Parma want peace, wondered Gresham, when he had every chance now of winning a war that had cost him and Spain so dearly? All the cards were in Parma's hands. He had the best army in the world at his disposal. He was winning the war to keep the Netherlands in Spanish hands. He had the biggest fleet in history coming to help him get that army over to England, and he must know how little there was to oppose him if he landed. So England was sending a peace delegation. And was this the team to conclude a peace? Henry Stanley, Earl of Derby, was urbane, intelligent and widely-travelled. But the other two nobles, Cobham and Sir James Croft, were bewildered, the two civil lawyers accompanying them pedantic, and Cecil and Tom Spencer, a relative of Derby's, intelligent enough but wholly inexperienced. This was what England was sending, to oppose an army.

Dover in late February was death by ice. The winter weather was appalling, ships huddling in the harbour as if in fear. For days the wind howled, blowing so hard down the chimney of the inn reluctantly occupied by the peace party that it drove smoke and cinders into the main room, setting furniture ablaze. It was just before the end of the month that they managed passage to Ostend. Gresham thought he was accustomed to rough seas, counted himself a seaman now, but this bucking, crazed animal beneath his feet surprised and frightened him. The bitter cold cut like a blade, flecking their beards with sharp particles of ice just minutes after being on deck. God knows how the sailor's fingers kept enough feeling to work the sails for more than seconds.

Ostend was a city surrounded by war, in a country taken over by war in the way that plague takes over a human body. A whole family lay dead a quarter of a mile outside the walls. The father was on the ground, in a shirt, arm outstretched. It had been gnawed to the bone above the hand, which showed white against the brown mud, half his head eaten away, and great chunks of flesh taken out of his body. His wife and children were similarly mangled, holes where their eyes had once been. 'Wolves,' said their guide, 'and birds, of course. The wolves come right up to the city walls at night now. You'll hear them, well enough.'

Ostend was a town where people walked hunched, where even the deputation from England with all its gold found that there was no food in the hostel. Cecil rose to his feet, issued peremptory orders to his servants. Ludicrously, he returned two hours later with two mangy hunting dogs and two thin fishing nets. 'If there is no food, then we shall find it!' he pronounced proudly. The dogs ran off when the servants took them out, the fishing nets proved to have two vast holes in them, and something in the manner of the servants persuaded Cecil not to ask them to set out on the choppy sea in the small boat that was all they could hire. It was Mannion who went out and returned with three eggs, half a cheese and some mouldy ham. They ate it like village children at a feast.

The delays felt endless, the frustration almost like a physical force pressing down on them. They were in Ostend, but Parma was reportedly in Bruges. Messengers were sent between the two camps, frequently crossing to arrange a meeting. Parma was no longer in Bruges. Where was he? No one knows. 'Inspecting his troops.' How much inspection can an army stand? There was no entertainment in Ostend, not even coal. Her Majesty's Ambassadors sat huddled round a smoking peat fire, praying for real warmth. Cecil's education was expanded even more. The smoke from a peat fire does not sting the eyes. Any more than it warms the body.

Dale, Cecil and Gresham rode to Ghent in the second week of March, their only food an orange apiece. There were brigands riding, lurking in what was left of the woodlands on either side of the road, just out of musket range, lean men on horses, watching, gauging the strength and the commitment of their escort. The eggs they got when they arrived were like a King's feast. They did not compensate for the fact that Parma's emissary had gone, with no one seeming to know where. Finally the ambassadors met with Garnier, Parma's secretary, a small man in his mid-thirties, wearing a heavily furred cloak down to his knees, wearing what could only be called a cassock of blue velvet with gold buttons and a gold chain around his neck. There was more talk, more delay. Then, at long last, they agreed for proper negotiations to start at Bourbourg, near Dunkirk.

'I fear this delay is intentional, that we are simply being stalled while Spain prepares her Armada,' said the Earl of Derby to Gresham. He had fallen into the habit of exchanging words with the young man, to Cecil's evident discomfort.

'It's possible, of course, my Lord,' said Gresham, toying with a rock-hard crust of bread that even his starving stomach was unwilling to take. 'Yet it's one of the Duke of Parma's techniques as a leader to be everywhere and yet nowhere, to move around his command to no obvious plan.'

'What advantage is there in it?' asked Derby, intrigued. He was an intelligent man with a quick brain, and a major supporter of the players.

'They say it's one reason why there's been no assassination attempt against him. That and the loyalty of his troops,' answered Gresham. 'Yet it also means that no commander can be secure against a sudden, ruthless inspection. The first thing he demands is a parade of the men, with the muster roll.' The plague of all European armies were the officers who took money for recruits who had either died, or never existed at all except as a fictional entry on just such a muster roll. It was a foolish officer who played this trick in Parma's army, and one who finished his career at the end of a rope. 'And, my Lord,' said Gresham, 'have we considered if this is the Duke's way of testing *our* sincerity, our strength of purpose?'

'Well, it may be so,' said Derby, 'but I will tell you now that he has tested this man's strength of purpose near to breaking point!' He stood up, ordering one of the very few remaining bottles of wine he had brought with him from England to be opened. A whole dozen bottles had been smashed to pieces in their passage over the Channel.

There had always been an old head on Henry Gresham's young soldier's body, but that night the youthful blood must have been running even more strongly than usual in his veins. Despairing of the conversation in the crude inn where they were staying, with the wind shrieking through the ill-mended windows and rattling the doors, he flung a cloak over his shoulders, threw open the door and took himself off through the night air. The houses were close, crowded in on each other, not dissimilar to London except with no roar of traffic and the ceaseless yelling of tradespeople. Mannion tucked in behind his master, silent. They walked briskly for quarter of an hour, reaching the outskirts of the town. The rain was holding off, though the air was thick with wet and cold, and there was a pleasant tingling in Gresham's body after the exercise. The moon emerged briefly from behind the scudding clouds, revealing the dark shape of the town wall before them. It was as if they had the whole town to themselves, apart from a lame, skulking dog that had shadowed them all the way from the inn.

They were halfway back when the attack came. The men must

have been waiting down a tiny, stinking jennel that led off the main route. It was the mud that saved Gresham, that and the fact that for a few seconds the wind had ceased its howling. There was a slight squelch as the lead attacker drew his foot from out of the slime that coated the streets. It was a tiny noise, but it was enough for Gresham and Mannion to swing round and face the men. The jennel was so narrow that only one man could leap out from it at a time. It was the one weakness in the attackers' plan. Without the sudden drop in the wind's noise the dagger would have been plunged into Gresham's back, the first he knew of it the sharp, sudden agony and the drawing down of the blinds in his eyes. As it was he turned to see his enemy, the hand, with the dagger in it held high, was already descending. The man with a ragged beard and pock-marked face, teeth drawn back in a grin of concentration, a strangely incongruous pink tongue poking out between the mis-shapen teeth. A second figure was close behind, already starting to swing a huge cudgel at Mannion's head.

Some instinct made Gresham lunge forward, not pull back as most men would have done, and tuck his head down. He collided with the man, his head burying itself in the stinking woollen tunic. He was under the blow now, and the man tried to pull his arm back, redirect the dagger into Gresham's heart. With one hand Gresham grabbed the man's arm, while bringing his head up with a savage jerk under the man's chin. Gresham's hat was in the mud now, so bone met bone. The man's jaw snapped shut. There was a gurgling scream, and the arm Gresham was grasping suddenly flopped. His attacker had bitten off his tongue. Gresham flung the man away from him, directly in the path of the third man to emerge from the jennel. They were brave, or starving and made desperate by their hunger. There was another gurgling scream, and the first attacker slumped to the ground. From his stomach the tip of a blade poked through. The third attacker must have held his sword out before him, and Gresham had inadvertently thrown the first man back on to its point, impaling him on his friend. This attacker was a slight figure, dressed in a billowing cloak, close-shaven and with a wide, dark hat that hid his face. He placed a foot on the now dead body of his accomplice, sought to drag his sword out of the body. Then his hat went flying, and a startled expression lit his face, before he toppled forward, hand still clutching the embedded sword. Mannion had killed the second man, taken his vast cudgel and swung it into the back of his head with massive force, crushing bone and brain in an explosion of blood. The two Englishmen stood, panting slightly. Gresham had not even taken his sword out of its scabbard.

'Thieves?' he gasped to Mannion.

Mannion put his foot out, rolled over the body of the third attacker. It was clear he was of a different class, his clothing breathing wealth, his complexion clear. And there was his sword, of course. Mannion bent down, withdrew it from the body with a sickening sucking sound. It was immaculate except where it was now stained with blood, the hilt finely decorated.

'Spanish,' said Mannion, taking in both the sword and the dead man. He used the tip of the sword to part the man's doublet. There was a gleam of gold. With the delicacy of a surgeon, Mannion let the sword blade pull on the precious chain, revealing the top of a crucifix. 'Not thieves,' said Mannion. 'Hungry, desperate local men – look how thin they both are – probably hired by this one here, who chooses to lead from behind, with his sword out and ready in case anything went wrong.'

'Damn!' said Gresham.

'Damn right,' said Mannion. 'This wasn't Walsingham, or Cecil. Or the Queen. You've got up everyone's nose, haven't you? It was Spain as wanted you dead tonight.'

The street was empty, the fight almost silent, apart from two gurgling, blood-stopped screams, the greatest noise the weight of their own breathing. They hauled the three bodies roughly back into the jennel. Gresham tried not to think about the starving dog and what it would do to the bodies.

The others had gone to bed when they returned to the inn, with the exception of Cecil. A cloak clutched round him, he was huddled in front of what little was left of the fire. He glanced suspiciously at Gresham.

'Taking the air?' he asked, the irony thick in his voice. 'You might as well yell a challenge out for someone to kill you, to walk these streets at night! Or did you have someone you needed to see?'

Sometimes the truth was the best weapon. 'Someone did try to kill us, as it happened. Three of them. And one of them a Spaniard, a gentleman by the look of him.'

Cecil blanched, his thin hands giving an involuntary tug at the thick cloak. 'A Spaniard, you say? Are you sure?'

The surprise in Cecil's voice was unmistakable. Gresham doubted even he could counterfeit it.

Mannion was wearing something that looked more like a tarpaulin than a cloak. He drew it aside, and tossed the dead Spaniard's sword onto the rough trestle table that was set back from the fire. Spanish steel was renowned throughout Europe, their swords the best. The intricate working of the hilt was unmistakable. A man's sword was as accurate a guide to his breeding as his clothing, and told the viewer as much about him.

'It's not just his weapon,' said Gresham, flinging off his own cloak and settling by the fire, reaching out his hands to its thin warmth. 'Clothes, appearance. And this.' He tossed a purse onto the table. Cecil looked at it, reached for it, fingered the coins inside. 'Spanish money,' said Gresham.

'But this is in breach of our immunity. No one, no one attacks a member of a diplomatic mission!' Cecil breathed. 'In political terms it is the equivalent of blasphemy.'

'Then we have some unbelievers in our proximity,' said Gresham. He noted Cecil's care for his and Mannion's safety. Or, rather, the complete absence of any such care.

'Do you have an explanation for this attempt?'

No, thought Gresham, I do not. Or at least, not yet. Nor will I find one until you cease your prattling and I am allowed to think. 'Welcome to Walsingham's world,' he said to Cecil. 'There's no diplomatic immunity in our world. The enemy don't wear a certain uniform to tell you they are your enemy. The knife can come as easily from the back as from the front.'

Cecil still seemed deeply offended at the perceived insult to English diplomacy. If Cecil ever came to real power, he would deal with ambassadors and not spies, thought Gresham.

Their problem was that they seemed to be dealing with no one. Finally, when they were reduced to despair, they were allowed their first meeting with Parma himself. Cecil was scornful in his despatch to his father, and the rather more formal one to the Queen. The room was full of poor, battered furniture, hardly better heated than their foul lodging, too small for the assembly gathered there. Gresham thought differently. This was a soldier's meeting. Parma would hardly notice the decorations or the fittings of where he met, he who had destroyed so many towns and cities. Meetings for Parma, Gresham thought, were not about gilded chairs, or precedence. They were business. Or was he clever enough to realise that by holding his meeting in such a poor room he disarmed the diplomats he met, put them off balance?

The ambassadors droned their formalities and Parma's intelligent eyes flicked between them as if measuring their worth. The chair he sat in was ornately carved, but across the back, on the left hand side, there was a blackened, circular indent six inches or more long, as if someone had lain a red-hot poker there and let it eat into the wood.

Within minutes Parma had chosen Derby as the real leader of the party, as well as its designated leader, taking him by the arm, pouring his wine himself. And he paid attention to Cecil as well, the man there simply because of his father's name. But the man tasked by the Queen, as Gresham had found out, to write to her daily on the progress of the negotiations.

Gresham received the merest of passing nods, despite a warm introduction from Derby. An hour? Two hours? They had waited so long for this meeting, yet such conversation as there was seemed trivial, meaningless. Gresham lost track of the time. Finally, the delegation bowed out, their eyes stinging. No peat on this fire, but damp wood, so that their clothes would smell for months of the slightly rancid stink of smoke from wet timber. The tap on the shoulder came as the others were ushered to separate rooms to wash before the dinner Parma had organised.

'You have a labour of love to conclude, I believe?' It was Count d'Aremberg, one of Parma's closest advisers. He was smiling. How typical of his master, the smile said, to consider the hunt for a missing fiancé in the midst of considering the fate of nations. 'The Duke can spare you a few minutes, before the formalities, to discuss your search, and report on your initial findings.'

Gresham was ushered back into the conference room, through an arras and into a small back room with furniture no better than in the main hall. The Duke of Parma, General in Chief of His Most Catholic Majesty's Army in the Netherlands, looked calmly at Henry Gresham. They were alone.

'Are they genuine?' he asked, with no preamble, 'these two wise men and these five or six fools they have sent to negotiate with me?'

'They're genuine, my Lord,' said Gresham, 'in that they truly wish for peace. England is by far the weaker combatant. And they'll remain so while they think there's still hope, though in their hearts they don't believe you'll make peace, or even that you have the power to do so.'

'So,' mused Parma, after a moment's thought, 'at last, here is Henry Gresham. The young bastard who dances with the Queen of England, the man who is one of Walsingham's trusted recruits, the brave adventurer who makes his name fighting for England at Cadiz, the controversial academic, the man of fabulous wealth who survives an attempt by Drake to kill him.' He paused. 'And the man who all this while has been spying for Spain.' He paused again. There was a slight smile on Gresham's face. 'The man who attends Mass once a week, at huge personal risk, not just now, but for years,' Parma went on, 'and whose allegiance to his faith overwhelms his allegiance to what he sees as a corrupt state. The man whose reports

237

are deemed among the most important and secret to reach the Escorial Palace, and some of very few sent in their entirety on to me. The man who admits he has been forced to do things to damage the Spanish cause, such as corrupting the chief armourer in Lisbon, so as to retain his credibility with his English masters and to prove himself to the heretic Walsingham. Spain's great secret. The man – the very young man – they talk of in whispers as Spain's secret weapon. The man whose real name is known only to the King, to a single one of his private Secretaries and, recently, to me.'

Henry Gresham bowed his head in acknowledgement. The sense of relief was almost palpable, the sense of no longer having to deceive. 'And the man who would like passage to Spain,' Gresham stated. 'To end deception, and to join the Armada. I have vital knowledge of Drake, of the English fleet. I must be there to advise the Duke!' He was pleading now. The thought of having come so far and not be there at the climax was unthinkable, obscene.

There was a glint in Parma's eyes. 'You have heard the news that your Walsingham is dead?'

Gresham's expression did not change. 'I had not heard, my Lord,' he replied. 'But it was expected.'

The Duke of Parma looked deep into Gresham's eyes. 'We will talk,' he said. 'And you will tell me everything.'

'I have much to tell you, my Lord,' said Gresham.

Neither men noticed that there was a small gap in the planks beneath their feet, a gap not covered by carpet or a thick layer of rushes. Nor did they notice the briefest flicker, as if someone had been crouched beneath the floor listening, and had moved to their exit.

CHAPTER 9

28th May – 6th August, 1588
The Battle of Portland Bill

'What the hell am I doin',' Mannion asked, 'on a bloody Spanish ship, surrounded by bloody Spaniards and fighting for bloody Spain? I hate fuckin' Spaniards! Unlike you!'

They were standing feet apart on the deck of the *San Salvador*, unbothered by the heaving of the choppy seas. The smell of the Spanish ship – the sweet and sour tang of olives, the acidic tang of cheap wine, distinct from the raw, thinner smack of English beer, the richness of garlic and herb – was unfamiliar, exotic. The ship drove through the water in stately progress, rather than rising and falling upon it. The garish paint on the upperworks and on the vast castles at bow and stern, full even now with fighting men, was an alien world. There was no chance of the Captain of the *San Salvador* lending a hand with a rope, as Drake sometimes did. There was deep segregation on board the Spanish ship, and an even deeper hostility between the sailors and the soldiers.

'You chose to come,' said Gresham, more saddened than he dare admit by his friend's misery. 'You knew it was likely to happen. You knew I had to be here.'

'Are you sure you shifted the money?' Mannion was obsessed that their betrayal of England would leave them penniless.

'I've told you,' said Gresham tiredly, 'the money's safe. You may be servant to a traitor. You won't be servant to a poor traitor.' He turned to face Mannion, more in retaliation than to elicit information. 'And the arrangements for the girl? You're sure they're watertight?'

'More than this bloody ship!' muttered Mannion. 'She knows where she has to be and when. Her passage's booked on the vessel, and it's a good one. She's got money. She knows where to go and who to go to when she gets to Calais.'

He had hated telling her the truth, before they left for Flanders. 'You'll be compromised when I'm revealed as a Spanish spy,' he had said to her.

'But why do people need to know? Why can you not continue in hidings?' Anna had said, looking round almost in desperation at the newly-won world and lifestyle about to be wrenched from her, lost in this world of double and treble betrayal.

'If I'm to do my duty I must get close to Medina Sidonia, be allowed to advise him. After that I'll never be able to hide as a Spanish agent again.'

'First you ask me to betray Spain, then you ask me to betray England! Is this fair?' She was close to tears.

'No,' he had said, 'not fair. Not fair at all. But I have a duty. I gave my word. I want you to survive. That's all.' He could not remember ever having had a heavier heart. In all probability he would never see London again, never dive into Excalibur's pool. The Fellowship of Granville College would gloat over his disgrace. He had made Mannion arrange for Anna to take ship to Calais, booked lodgings, appointed an agent for her before embarking with Cecil to the Netherlands. He had given her enough money to buy a small estate in France, set herself up as an independent person. It would only be a matter of time before someone as beautiful as her found a good husband, he reasoned to himself. They would be panting at her door.

They had left the party in Flanders, saying they were following a lead to the increasingly mythical Jacques Henri. They had boarded the ship for Spain and fought vicious, wintery contrary winds. Gresham had become frantic with worry at the delay forced upon them, and it had taken a second ship to get them into Lisbon in the face of even more foul weather, arriving the day before the Armada sailed.

'This is a bit different,' Mannion had said, on their arrival in Lisbon. Medina Sidonia had worked a miracle. The sense of purpose, of efficiency was in stark contrast to their earlier visit. The greatest fleet the world had ever seen lay out there in the harbour, weighing down the ocean with its power.

The final irony was that it had been almost impossible to get on board one of the Armada's ships. The vessels were ringed by guardboats, to stop desertion. They had finally begged and bribed passage on the only available boat, taking a parcel of fruit and additional wine out to the Captain of the *San Salvador* from his wife, and then bribing their way to a place on her decks. The passport Gresham carried from the Duke of Parma was a potent weapon on board one of the Spanish ships. It had been useless with the illiterate and ignorant guards. So it was they had sailed with the Armada.

If God was smiling on King Philip's Enterprise of England it was at best an ironic gesture. Within hours the fleet was facing weather that would not have disgraced a December storm. Then, when more and more stores were opened the water was found to be nothing more than green slime, and the cheese and dried meat infested with rot whose stench made men gag. Drake's rampaging on the Spanish coast had borne a dividend, but so had a fleet kept too long in harbour. Soon the seas were dotted with discarded, rotting foodstuffs, the trail left by the Armada, such sea birds as were brave enough to venture out feeding frenziedly. Three weeks out of Lisbon several ships had been battered to such an extent that they could not dream of entering a battle, sickness was soaring and the fleet had hardly reached Corunna, still just off Spanish land.

"'E'll 'ave to take us into Corunna,' said Mannion, continuing his uncanny ability to predict the actions of the Spanish. It was inevitable. Sidonia ordered the fleet into Corunna for repairs and to take on new supplies, sending the sick ashore so as not to infect the healthy. As if in final revenge, a savage gale scattered two-thirds of the ships through the length and breadth of the Bay of Biscay.

'Bugger this for a lark!' said Mannion, with religious intensity, gazing longingly at the shore line as they were blasted by the ferocious wind out to sea, every rope and spar complaining, water cascading along the length of the deck, jagged splinters where the top tier of the after-castle had once been.

He was more cheerful when the *San Salvador* finally made it into Corunna and for the first time in weeks he could set foot not only on shore but in a tavern. ''Bout bloody time!' he muttered darkly. 'Thought you wanted to get on the flagship?' he asked Gresham, back against a rock as they looked out at the mass of shipping. A full wineskin was clutched firmly in both hands, like a mother hanging on to its newborn baby.

'I've got to meet Sidonia first,' said Gresham. 'Spanish nobility make the English look like democrats. He's a proud man, and he won't like speaking to an Englishman of no real birth, and I don't imagine he's much time for spies either. Yet I've got to persuade him to let me advise him, use my special knowledge.'

'So what if he doesn't want to come out to play?' asked Mannion, who was starting to let the wine talk for him.

'Then I've risked losing everything I love for nothing,' said Gresham bleakly.

'Spaniards could give you a bit more help in all this,' said Mannion, eyelids starting to droop in the welcome sun. 'After all you're meant to have done for them.'

'I get about as much help from them as I did when I was meant to be working for England,' replied Gresham. 'No one loves a spy.'

Yet meeting Medina Sidonia was easier than expected. Gresham presented the Duke of Parma's warrant to the servants guarding the door of the villa the Duke had taken ashore. A day later the summons came.

The room was cool and dark, the wine excellent, and the Duke courteous. Of medium build, the Duke's compact figure exuded authority, and a sense of calm. Gresham imagined that people would instinctively lower their voices when talking to him. A secretary sat in a corner before a small lectern, ready to record or write as instructed. A sallow, thin-faced man in a cheap doublet waited respectfully at the Duke's side.

'I am His Grace's English translator,' the man said proudly.

'The Duke of Parma writes well of you,' said Sidonia, his voice low. The man had an aura of dignity, in part due to his having come from a long line of men for whom the obedience of others was automatic, no doubt, but also emanating from his personality. 'He states that you have been fighting our cause with courage and guile these three years past, at great risk to yourself. As is confirmed by letters from the Escorial. You have met with the Duke of Parma? Recently?' The Duke was speaking in Spanish, the translator speaking fluently and with almost no accent.

'As recently as March, my Lord,' answered Gresham.

'And his view of matters?'

How strange and worrying for Spain, thought Gresham, that in the tangled hierarchy of King Philip's Spain the Commander of the Armada and the Commander of Philip's army had not corresponded directly, but only indirectly through the person of the King.

'It is as you gathered, my Lord. He has assembled boats and transports in the canals. He has no deep-water port, but expects to be able to slip his troops out from the canals through Dunkirk under cover of darkness and with a feint to the north. There are two key issues. Firstly, the Dutch fly-boats are heavily armed and can navigate the shallowest of waters. Yet they are relatively few in number and the Dutch are disaffected. Also there is a faction among the Dutch that wishes him to invade England, believing the rebels' chance of victory is greater if the Duke is away in England. The Duke believes he can deceive the Dutch, that indeed they may wish to be deceived, particularly if Your Lordship would agree to detach some of your lighter and smaller craft to assist him.'

'That would seem hopeful,' said Sidonia. 'And the second key issue?'

'If you can place yourself between his transports and the English fleet for the crossing, the Duke of Parma believes all that's necessary is for your ships to block the English from his ships, not even to sink or defeat them.'

The Duke paused for thought, drumming his fingers on the arm of his chair. 'And you say that you sailed with Drake to Cadiz?'

Gresham gave a brief summary of his part in the raid. 'No one knows the English fleet, its commanders and its operating procedures better than I,' said Gresham. 'I offer that knowledge to your Lordship, as and when you may care to use it.'

'Should I trust a man who betrays the land of his birth?' asked Sidonia. There was sudden steel in the voice, a sharp snap of authority. This was a man who lived his life by a strict moral as well as religious code, Gresham realised.

'No,' said Gresham, honestly. 'Probably not. Yet I've never done what I do for money, of which I have no need. I've done it in part for my faith, which I've carried as a secret for many years, a secret that could have burned my flesh and ruined me at any time.'

'And why else have you done it? Why else have you served Spain?'

Gresham paused. This man would accept no easy answers. There were no easy answers for Gresham to give. 'Because the land of my birth has never accepted me, the bastard son of a rich man. For years it reviled me as a cast-off. Now it pays me lip service because of my wealth yet reviles me still. The land of my birth is defended by pirates who plead patriotism, led by a Queen who preaches service to England but is incapable of serving any except herself, a woman so selfish as to deny her country an heir and therefore condemn it to civil war on her death. Taking their colour from her, its leaders are men such as Robert Cecil, whose God and morality revolve around his own self-interest. Cecil, the Queen, Walsingham, Burghley . . . these people expect me to die for them. They would never live for me.'

244

'You are very young,' said Sidonia, 'to harbour such bitterness. And when you find in your adopted country of Spain that leaders are not selfless, that the true faith has men observing and sometimes leading its worship who are truly corrupt, then will you become as bitter towards Spain as you are to England?'

'I didn't choose England,' said Gresham. 'It was a choice made for me. I chose Spain.'

There was a long silence, Sidonia's eyes resting on Gresham's, Gresham's startling blue eyes returning the gaze without flinching.

'I may call on your advice,' said Sidonia, 'but not yet. God willing, it will be a week or more before we sight England, and the *San Martin* is grievously overcrowded.'

That was true. Apart from the sailors and soldiers crammed on board, there were the forty men of Sidonia's retinue and the hordes of young Spanish noblemen desperate for glory.

'I may call for you nearer the time of our conflict. Or I may not. Yet there is a tension, a conflict in you I sense but do not understand.'

There was a splutter from Mannion, understanding the Spanish before translation.

'You are impertinent!' said Sidonia, the colour rising in his face.

'I apologise, my Lord,' said Mannion in Spanish. 'I've known him since he was this high.' Mannion held out a hand halfway down his own body. 'He was tense then, and at war with himself. That won't ever change. Asking your pardon for my impertinence.'

'I suspect he is not lucky in life,' said Sidonia, 'but may have been lucky in you. You are dismissed. Both of you.'

'Was that helpful?' hissed Gresham as they left.

'It was bloody true,' said Mannion.

They left Corunna on 21st July and made their first sighting of English soil, the Lizard, eight days later. An aching sense of regret drove through Gresham as he saw England again.

'What d'you think they're discussing?' asked Mannion.

The flagship had hoisted a huge flag bearing the image of the

245

Virgin Mary and a cross, and called the various commanders aboard. Gresham and Mannion had just heard Mass with the rest of the crew of the *San Salvador*. They did not consecrate the Host, of course, in case the rolling of the ship caused the body and blood of Christ to be swept or knocked overboard.

'I know what I would do,' said Gresham, eyes clenched in worry, his whole body showing the tension inside him.

'What?' said Mannion, 'Sign up as a spy for France and Holland, so every country in Europe hates you instead of just half of 'em?'

'No,' said Gresham, hardly listening. 'I'd head straight for Plymouth. With this wind the English fleet is bottled up, can't get out. The advantage the English have is their speed. If Sidonia sailed pell-mell into Plymouth harbour the English couldn't manoeuvre, and he could board and take half the English fleet, maybe more.' Gresham waved a hand around. The huge wooden castles at the bow and stern of the *San Salvador* were there to contain soldiers who could pour down fire on an enemy deck from a great height, grapple and sweep a mass of men down.

'Might lose some ships,' said Mannion. 'Difficult entrance, Plymouth.'

'What would a few ships matter if you sank or boarded half the English fleet?' asked Gresham. What would Sidonia decide?

Gathered in the great cabin of the *San Martin*, Medina Sidonia's commanders were pressing him hard.

'We must detach a portion of our fleet and attack Plymouth! We have the chance to halve the numbers facing us and take this campaign by the throat! It is our golden opportunity!'

Sidonia sat impassively, his mind racing beneath the quiet and dignified face he presented to his senior commanders. Who was he, a land-locked noble, to take decisions on behalf of these men with their infinite knowledge of the sea? *Why had Parma not responded to his increasingly urgent letters?* It was two months since he had received his last communication. The fast pinnaces could take and return messages within days. Soon he would have no option but to halt the Armada, perhaps off the Isle of Wight, until he could ensure that Parma's army was ready and waiting to embark.

It was not the risk that scared him. Warfare was all about risk. It was the fear that a simple change of wind, or finding that Plymouth was better defended than they believed, could mean he had thrown some of his best ships away almost before the campaign had started.

'The entrance to Plymouth is narrow and dangerous,' he said finally. 'We have the strictest orders from the King to sail to meet the Duke's army and not simply to seek a sea battle. Our prime task, our only task, is to rendezvous with the Duke of Parma's army.'

True, except he was already proposing to disobey the King's orders by stopping off the Isle of Wight.

'We will proceed in defensive formation to the Isle of Wight and, if needs be, await communication with the Duke of Parma.' He turned to one of his admirals, who bore the scars of sixty years of fighting, with a half smile. 'If we have to halt our fleet there, then you will have your sea battle. With that possibility in mind, I cannot risk depleting our strength so early on in our campaign.'

The Admiral grunted his agreement, grudgingly recognising the logic. Others were tight-lipped, edgy. Yet they were good men, thought Sidonia, good and brave men who had proved themselves as soldiers and as patriots time and time again. Surely God in whose name they fought would recognise what they were? Surely He would recognise the justice of their cause?

From half a mile away, Gresham's eyes strained to see through the rain squalls that sent needles of spray into his eyes. There! The boats were leaving the *San Martin*. Slowly the bobbing dots crept across the sea, back to their own ships, and slowly the Armada began to adopt a new formation. A half-moon shape, the best fighting ships on each wing, and in the centre guarding the pathetically slow *urcas* and a vanguard of the swiftest and most heavily-armed vessels, ready to race in support of any endangered vessel. A defensive formation! Sidonia had decided not to take the gamble on Plymouth but to keep the Armada together.

'Are you rememberin' Cadiz?' asked Mannion drily. The mad-cap dash into a harbour Drake had hardly scouted, the throwing of caution to the winds, captains huffing and puffing and desperately trying to catch up with their commander. 'Bit different, innit? Maybe the Duke does need your advice after all. Or maybe the Spanish need Drake on their side.'

The captain of the barque *Golden Hinde* did not know whether his excitement at sighting the vast fleet of Spanish ships was greater than his terror at the sheer size of their enemy. Flushed and badly out of breath, he poured out his news to Drake. He had finally tracked him down on the bowling green.

Drake turned away, looking out to sea. From land there was no sight of the Spanish as yet. Shit! Shit! The wind was pinning the English in harbour, the tide pushing them further in. What if the Spanish were even now sending ten or fifteen of their best galleons to crush the English fleet before it could move? Shit! They would have to start warping as many vessels as possible out of harbour, a laborious, back-breaking job of cables and longboats. And a job that took time. Time they didn't have. He turned, ready to give the orders, run down to the quayside to supervise the business himself, praying every minute that the horizon would not darken with Spanish sails.

His Secretary came up beside him, whispered in his ear. 'My Lord, they will act as quickly without your presence.' Even quicker, thought the Secretary privately, without you yelling and bawling at everyone. 'You have the chance to go down in history, to establish the morale of your men, if you show you have time to finish the game *and* beat the Spaniards. Because, in truth, there is nothing you can usefully do.'

Drake's brow darkened. He turned to the gathering crowd of men. 'Warp the ships out of harbour. Pull in every able-bodied man on shore if you have to. As for myself,' he raised the volume of his voice to a near-shout, 'There's time enough to finish the game *and* beat the Spaniards!'

The roar of approval was the first good thing he had heard all day.

'Good God!' said the young English sailor as the mist and driving spray parted for a moment and he saw a sight that took his breath away. A hundred, two hundred sails, spread out across the ocean as if they owned every single drop of water. 'Holy Mary Mother of God!' He crossed himself, the unsure cockiness he had professed to his mates replaced by a sick feeling of fear.

The explosion was the most terrible thing Gresham had ever seen. They had sighted the Lizard through heavy squalls and scudding cloud, the Armada's desperately slow pace set by the unwieldy freighters. Then they saw the English sails, a small squadron to their left, between the Armada and the shore, the main fleet behind them. Damn! The English had the wind-gauge. There was a gasp from a Spanish seaman as an English ship skidded across the waves, appearing to be sailing almost directly into the wind. A tiny English boat was sent to within extreme range, fired a popgun and turned away.

'Bloody stupid officers!' grunted Mannion. 'Makin' heroic gestures and risking good men's lives.'

'What's he doing?' asked Gresham, incredulously. A group of seven or so English ships had approached one wing of the Armada. The Spanish had immediately tried to lay alongside the English ships and grapple, the English intent on ducking and weaving, firing ragged cannonades all the while. A faint popping noise came to them over the waves, the wind whipping the smoke away. It was a skirmish, like wrestlers dancing round each other, trying to get the measure of their opponent before going in for the throw. Yet whoever was in command seemed to have taken his ship directly into the English fleet, allowed himself to become surrounded, cut off, only one other vessel in support.

'I reckon he's doing it on purpose,' said Mannion, sucking at a hollow tooth. 'If the English think they've got 'im, they'll come in close and maybe he can board one. If that happens, the other ships'll have no choice but to try and board him, and he'll get a melee – just what the Spanish want!'

The incessant cannonade the Spanish ship was receiving seemed to be doing remarkably little damage. Once, twice Gresham gasped as it seemed as if she might get close enough to an English ship for its grappling irons to bite, but each time the vessel ducked away. Finally Sidonia took his own great flagship heeling out of line to join the embattled galleon, drawing it back into the main body of the fleet as the English retreated. By late afternoon it was over.

'So who won that one?' asked Gresham, confused. Mannion shrugged.

'It's a draw. The Spanish can't get at the English, but the English can't get near most of the Spanish.' The bulk of the Armada was sailing with no more than fifty metres between each ship. Any English vessel getting in between them would face overwhelming fire and the certainty of being boarded. 'Bit like a hedgehog,' said Mannion. 'Clever way to fight, you've got to grant them. Though you can flip a hedgehog over and I can't see 'ow you'd flip this bloody fleet over.'

They both turned at the sound of the bell calling the crew to prayer. Both men saw the Dutchman grapple with the powder barrel, heaving it down from the stern where it was parked with three others, a gunner going about his job, ignored by the others. They witnessed the quick look round, the slow match smoking gently stuck to the side of the barrel, watched the man duck over the rail and into the water. An officer caught the motion, turned round with his mouth open to yell . . . what? A query? An order? No one would ever know, because in that precise moment Hell came to the after-deck of the Spanish galleon *San Salvador*. There were three separate flashes, half a second between. The first, fiery-orange explosion of the single powder barrel, followed in the flicker of an eyelid by the deep red and yellow of the three other barrels parked on the stern castle and then the brilliant, eyeball-piercing explosion of the powder stored in the deck below. Gresham was looking back, he and Mannion right at the ship's forecastle. The split second warning the sight of the Dutchman had given them forced them instinctively to hurl themselves over the side. As if in slow motion Gresham felt the sinking in the pit of his stomach as they started their plunge into the sea, caught a vast flash of red and yellow even through his tightly-closed lids and then, extraordinarily, felt as if a giant had shoved hugely at his feet and legs, spinning him over and over and over before they hit the sea. His eyes forced open in shock, Gresham felt a savage pain in his eardrums as they were pushed in to implosion, and saw tiny little fountains of white water spring up out of the sea as fragments of debris and men were flung out by the power of the explosion.

For too long the green water passed upwards in front of his eyes. Kicking out and up, he finally surfaced, spluttering. Momentary panic. He could hear nothing. He placed a thumb and forefinger over his nose, swallowed sharply, and with a click he knew he could hear again. Knew because the sound of screaming men was cutting through to his brain. A man was bobbing on the water, one arm clutching ferociously at a baulk of timber, his eyes wide with terror. His other arm had gone at the elbow, and when the water bobbed him up and down only one leg appeared on the surface. Both limbs had been cauterised by the blast, and then sterilised in the salt water. He might even live, thought Gresham. If a man wanted to live with one arm and one leg. Then the stink hit him. Burning wood, of course. But above all a singed smell, like overdone pork on a fire. The smell of burning human flesh.

'There!' said Gresham. 'That boat! The one from the *San Martin*!' The vast Spanish fleet had hove to, boats scuttling over the water in a hurried rescue operation. The *San Salvador* lay dead in the water, her stern shot away, sails mere hanging tatters, smoke rising from her deck and an awful, low keening noise of deeply injured men. Weighed down by their clothes, Gresham and Mannion struggled to one of the boats sent from the flagship. As they struggled closer, a man in the water, burned black by some strange decay, was being pulled on board. The sailor hauling his body was suddenly, violently sick as the burned remnant of the man's arm came away in his hand, the rest of the body flopping back into the water.

'There must be easier ways to get on board the bloody flagship!' said Mannion, spitting sea water out of his mouth as he scorned help and hauled himself over the side of the rescue boat.

When they finally arrived, wet, cold and buffeted, aboard the Duke of Medina Sidonia's flagship, they had nothing except the clothes on their backs and the handful of gold coins sewn into each of their jackets – the number was limited by their weight and the amount they could still swim with if they found themselves in the sea. Gresham rubbed his eyes, succeeding in making them sting even more from the salt water dripping down his forehead. From the deck of the *San Martin* he could see the drifting hulk of the *San Salvador*, but also another great ship in trouble. Something seemed to have snapped off her bowsprit and her mizzenmast had tumbled over. As they watched, the ship's mainmast shivered and fell forward in the driving wind. Someone was asking to note down their names, while a seaman offered them a rough blanket.

From the central position occupied by the flagship Gresham saw a group of English ships form up and follow them at a safe distance. There was shouting on the deck, and what looked like Sidonia's own personal barge was lowered.

'That's two great Spanish ships stumbling in our wake, crammed with God knows what in the way of treasure and booty,' Gresham whispered to Mannion.

'So?' Was Spain already losing this battle, Gresham thought, as he shivered in the cold wind?

'Do you think Drake will see them in his magic glass?'

Later that night Sir Francis Drake extinguished his stern light, stating that he had seen the shadows of ships pass him by, and headed off to capture the *Rosario* and make himself fifty thousand pounds. He had been tasked with following the Armada, his stern lantern the marker on which the whole of the rest of the English fleet was relying. The ships following him saw the light ahead of them in the dark flicker and fade, but then picked up another dimmer light. Thinking it to be Drake, they put on sail to catch up. When dawn broke, they found they had been marking the lantern of the rearmost vessel of the Armada all night, and were alone and in range of the greatest fleet on earth. The three English vessels heeled about, and withdrew to search for the remainder of the English fleet, thrown into disarray by Drake's action.

One of the greatest fleets the world had seen was separated from its enemies by only a few miles, and the fate of nations was being decided by the decisions of the warring commanders. And Gresham was almost terminally bored.

The men passed the time gambling, the dice carried in two locking cups, even though the authorities frowned on it. Mannion had carved dice out of a waste piece of wood, begged (or stolen) an earthenware cup from somewhere, and shown himself capable of mindlessly throwing dice for hours. It bored Gresham and he already owed Mannion ten thousand pounds. In the hierarchy of a Spanish galleon a traitorous English gentleman belonged nowhere. There were no cabins or beds on board for even the Spanish gentlemen, fifty or so who had clamoured to be taken aboard the prestigious flagship and who added to its already vastly overcrowded decks. Gresham was reduced to sitting on whatever bit of spare deck there was whenever he could resist Mannion's gambling fever, composing sonnets in his head. The rhyme scheme and the fourteen-line format was demanding and so took more time. He had forgotten what it was like to sleep without another man's body pressing against him on one or both sides. Or should he simply switch his mind off and be lulled by the routine of the ship? Night was marked by the saying of a simple prayer:

'The Watch is set,
The glass runs yet,
Safe on the seas
If God decrees.'

253

The glass, or sand clock, was turned every half hour. A ship's boy, pathetically young and vulnerable, gave what Gresham had learned was the traditional lilt.

> 'One glass has gone,
> Another's a-filling,
> More sand shall run,
> If God is willing.'

Simple stuff, childish words recited by children, yet far more comforting than the tangled precision of his sonnets. Each watch lasted four hours, the new watch being called again by the boys with their shrill 'Al cuarto, al cuarto, señores marineros!' Yet it was the evening ceremony Gresham found most moving. It silenced even Mannion, as the pair of them, still shivering from their soaking, clutched the thin blankets round their bodies and chewed the last of the rations formally handed out to them a half hour earlier.

First a ship's boy brought the newly-lighted stern lantern on to the darkening deck, breaking out into the evening lilt. The thin, treble voice was feeble against the gusting of the wind, the rattle of intermittent raindrops on the bulging sails, the continual creak of timber and cordage, all the more moving because of its fragility. The words were mundane, given meaning only by the rolling deck and the sense of men drawn together in danger.

> 'Amen, and God give us goodnight,
> May the ship make good passage and have a safe voyage,
> Captain, Sir, Master, and all our company.'

The altar was set with candles and glittering images, the candles needing to be continually relit. The ship's Master called in a stentorian voice, 'Are we all present?' A muted roar of male voices greeted the question, 'God be with us!'. It was bad luck not to answer. The Master chanted a *salve*, strange because by now the light was flickering off his face and making him look more like a demon than Christ's representative, strange because of the deep, rhythmic tone of his voice.

'A *salve* let us say
To speed us on our way,
A *salve* let us sing,
A good voyage may it bring.'

The men chanted the *salve* then the Litany of Our Lady, then the *Credo*, their voices firm. For a few moments the rolling, sonorous familiarity of the words brought the men together, bonded them to the ocean and their common purpose. Then the *Ave*, and the usual evening lilt, sung by everyone, the stern lantern hoisted in its proper place.

It was the faces that Gresham could never forget. The smooth, clear complexion of the ship's boys, the hardened, wrinkled faces of the men, stained by sun and sea, gazing into the flickering lights, each one an island in himself. Hundreds of men and boys, each one holding themselves as the most important person in the world.

The next dawn came revealing a sea virtually clear of English ships. The summons came after he and Mannion had collected their morning rations.

Sidonia's cabin was sumptuously furnished, the table behind which he sat bizarrely inlaid with ivory. The Duke did not ask Gresham to sit. Two of the *San Martin*'s officers stood beside him, glowering, and the choleric Diego Flores. The translator was the same man who had been with the Duke in Corunna.

'The *San Salvador*. What happened?' The tone was neutral, the thin, tired eyes expressionless.

'My servant and I were at the bow. We saw a Dutchman man-handle a barrel of powder, place a slow match into it and dive overboard.'

'Just that? No more? A man blows up his own ship and trusts himself to the mercy of the sea?'

'My Lord,' Gresham moved uneasily, 'there were . . . rumours.'

255

'Rumours?'

'Rumours that a Spanish captain had . . . interfered with the German wife of this same gunner.' In the tiny space of a sailing ship there were no secrets. The whole crew and the soldiers had heard the Dutchman vowing revenge. They had thought it likely to be a knife in the back, if the words were anything more than braggadocio.

'Would these two men take a dispute on land to sea? Destroy a ship, and half its crew?' The Duke was grappling with drives and motivations that were alien to his whole upbringing and culture.

'It was not on land, my Lord,' said Gresham reluctantly. 'The offence took place . . . at sea. The gunner's wife was aboard the *San Salvador*.'

'How can this be?' There was a cold fury in the Duke's voice now. He is a prude, thought Gresham. His innate refinement shrinks at the thought of carnality. 'I ordered all women to be removed from ships in Lisbon. Over thirty were found and put ashore. To have women on board this holy mission would be sacrilege!'

Make or break time, thought Gresham. He would not tell the Commander what every sailor knew, that one of the *urcas* was crammed to the gunnels with women, the wives and camp followers of the sailors and, in the main, the soldiers. That for the thirty or so women disguised as men that his marines had ferreted out on board a variety of ships there were two or three times as many on board by the time the fleet sailed. Sailors were used to months at sea without women. The soldiers were used to taking their women with them. These were not the refined, wilting Court ladies that the Duke knew. Many of them were common-law wives. No priest had ever said words over their union with their man, yet with a stubborn determination that defied both the Duke and his interpretation of God's will they stuck with their man.

'My Lord, for one woman to remain hidden in a hundred and thirty ships is no cause for recrimination. Rather it is a matter of wonder that only she remained.'

The officers of the *San Martin* shuffled uneasily. They understood why he hid the truth from their Duke. They also knew the story of the explosion before he told it to them, Gresham realised. It had been a test – you are a spy, you find out things. So did you find out what blew you overboard and near lost you your life? He had passed the first test. Sidonia motioned Gresham to sit in front of him, on a plain, three-legged stool.

'So, my young English, can you tell me why the sea is bare of English ships this morning, those same ships that pecked in such numbers at our heels yesterday? Is this some strange English strategem a true Spaniard is not meant to understand?'

'We left two great ships in our wake. It's my belief that Sir Francis Drake couldn't resist such a prize. I would guess that he's taken off after one or both of your abandoned vessels, and either many ships have gone with him in hope of plunder, or he's just confused the English fleet.'

One of the younger commanders leaned forward, looked into the eyes of his master for permission to speak. 'You are saying that your countrymen are pirates, more interested in plunder than in defending their land?' This man seemed permanently angry.

'I do not think of them as my countrymen anymore, and yes, that is exactly what they are. Brilliant sailors, brave and tenacious. But at heart, pirates,' Gresham replied.

'Tell me about the Isle of Wight,' said the Duke.

'It's a large, fertile area, and a potential death trap for your fleet.'

One of the other men shuffled, drawing in his breath with a sharp hiss. This was not the way one spoke to the Duke of Medina Sidonia. If the Duke took offence he did not show it.

'Why?' the Duke asked. 'Why is it a death trap?'

Clever, thought Gresham, adding the description to the catalogue of features he was building in his mind of this man. Possibly so clever as to be over-sensitive, and to have retreated behind a wall of courtesy and good manners to protect that sensitivity. Yet with steel, plentiful steel. And lonely. Above all Gresham sensed an immense loneliness, here in this gorgeously furnished cabin with all the trappings of vast wealth.

'It has no strategic significance. As close as it is to the good port of Portsmouth, you could be subject to blockade with relatively little effort. Its anchorages cry out for fireships. The English would bring you to no great battle there. Yet they would whittle away at your fleet piece by piece, waiting for winter and the storms to do their job for them.'

'And you who know so much about the English and England, you who have met the Duke of Parma, can you tell me why he does not answer my letters?'

Now Gresham saw how this man was using him. On board the *San Martin*, the turncoat English spy Gresham had no friends and no allies. And so he could talk to no one, not refine the Duke's words for his own advantage, not play off the confidences for political favour. In talking to Gresham the Duke of Medina Sidonia had a sounding board who could talk to no one else. *Careful!*

'The Duke must know that you're coming, from your own messengers and from the King. The country he rules over is vast, his centres of governance widely separated, the country war-torn and difficult to travel. Wolves gnaw the bodies of women and children as well as their fathers, within sight of the city walls of Ostend. He'll assume automatically that you expect him to mobilise his troops, prepare his invasion barges. He'll only put final plans into progress when you and your fleet are close enough to meet with him, in person.'

'And how do you find the hospitality of the *San Martin*, after your experience on board one of Drake's ships?'

The Duke of Medina Sidonia had some way to go before he matched Sir Francis Drake for sudden changes of topic, but was clearly a contender.

'Strange. Disturbing. Comforting. There are no rituals aboard English ships. If they acknowledge God, it is as a fellow sailor, almost an equal. Yet what I have seen aboard your ships concerns me.'

The other Spaniards stiffened. We take offence, their bodies told Gresham.

'You may speak freely,' said the Duke. He raised a hand, and a two beautiful golden goblets appeared on the table, the deep red of the wine taking on a lustrous tinge from the metal. Mannion would be driven to despair at what he was missing, thought Gresham, as he raised the stunning bouquet of the wine to his lips.

'Your gun carriages are huge, long, tailing back into the body of the ship, cumbersome to handle. You lash the gun to the side of the ship for firing, and need to untie it every time you reload. Your company are united when they hear the divine service, but are three separate groups in action – officers, sailors and soldiers. The soldiers are tasked to load a gun, under the command of a sailor. When it is done, they must return to their battle station and prepare to board an enemy. So the gunner has to call them back after each round is fired. It must take a full fifteen minutes for one of your great guns to reload and fire again.' Unless it was on a galley, set on a rail and chasing a longboat, thought Gresham.

'And your English ships?' asked the Duke. The commanders and the officers of the *San Martin* had been motioned to sit. 'How do they differ?'

'*Their* English ships.' The bitterness in Gresham's voice would etch steel. 'I'm a traitor, if you remember. The cannon are placed on short, four-wheeled carriages. The lashings allow the gun to be run back for reloading, hauled forward for firing. Each gun has a crew of seamen, dedicated to just that gun. They think five minutes to reload and fire a long time.'

The silence must have been seconds, seemed minutes.

'Call for the others,' the Duke ordered. 'Get them aboard.' He turned to Gresham. 'You may leave,' he said. 'Understand me. You are either a very honourable man, or a self-serving traitor of a type who offends me deeply. Events will develop, the weighty matters of which I have charge, and in time I will decide your future and your status.'

'Well,' said Mannion, on the deck, 'we're back where we usually are. Everyone hates us.'

The shock of hearing the truth from Gresham had changed something inside Anna, something she was hardly aware of herself but which at the same time left her knowing that her life had altered for her in a way that could never be reversed. Suddenly the candle-lit masques and the overheated, fetid evenings at Court and nobleman's house seemed frivolous, cheap, the glittering jewels little more than baubles, the conversation that had once been so amusing thin and shallow.

The scrupulous travel arrangements made by Gresham would get her to Dover and thence by ship to Calais well before it was likely that he would be unmasked as a Spanish spy. Operating on the basis that the best hiding place was in the open, Gresham had spread it widely around that he was returning from the Netherlands to Calais, there to meet her and start again the search for her fiancé. She felt a growing disquiet in the days before her departure, as what pathetic few belongings she had were packed into wooden chests, a disquiet over and above the appalling confusion she had been thrown into by the death of her mother and Gresham's strange revelations. Nor was it sadness at leaving London and England, where she had hardly had the time to feel at home. It was as if a beacon of danger had been set alight inside her head where only she could feel it, yet with no hint as to where the danger was coming from. From where were these signals emanating? The servants were smiling in her presence, Gresham's friends assiduous in their escort duties without being more presumptuous than all young men had to be.

The chaperone.

It had to be her.

The sour-faced creature accompanied Anna saying nothing, sitting like a stiff pudding in her presence, never smiling, never talking. Yet once, as the great carriage had rolled out of The House, Anna had seen what seemed like the faintest of nods and thinnest of smiles cross her face as she seemed to see someone out of the window. Craning to see beyond her, Anna had spotted two finely-dressed men in a livery she did not recognise, lounging by the main gate of The House. And they had been there on her return, two different men in the same livery there again on her next outing.

The servants were fond of her, and through them it did not take long to find out the identity of the livery. Burghley. Lord Burghley. The father of Robert Cecil. Her instincts had been honed by Gresham's double-dealing. If she was being spied on by any men associated with Robert Cecil, the news was not good. And was her suspicion about the chaperone correct? The woman had asked leave to be absent for a day, visiting a sick relative in Islington. Feeling both guilty and rather soiled, Anna charmed one of the younger ostlers into following the chaperone, swearing him to secrecy and leaving him heart-stricken with love. When both had left, with a week to go before her intended departure to Dover, she waited until the corridor was silent and slipped into the chaperone's room. It seemed innocent, and she started to ask what on earth she was doing in another woman's room. Then she saw the small writing desk placed by the window, a gap between its lid and the wood it rested on. A quill pen had been stuffed in the desk, but the nib end left sticking out, holding up the lid. The letter, nearly finished, had been interrupted for some reason – perhaps someone else had come into the room and the chaperone had thrust the paper and pen hurriedly in the desk? The contents were clear. In a few lines of spidery handwriting it gave Anna's date of departure from London, the name of the ship she was to pick up in Dover, even its Captain's name. The ostler reported later that evening that he had trailed the woman to Whitehall Palace. Cecil was spying on her, through this dreadful woman, had paid a spy to be as close as any person could be short of sharing her bed.

She shivered, fear temporarily replacing blood in her veins. Giving the details of her departure to Cecil could surely only mean that Cecil intended in some way to stop her. Well, she had learned some things in these tumultuous recent months. She called the chaperone into her room, speaking to her in a tone of supremacy that she knew would annoy her.

'I have decided to bring forward the time of my departure,' she announced. 'I have received notification that the ship must leave earlier.' All lies, of course, but if she managed to annoy the

261

chaperone enough she might not seek to see the evidence. 'My belongings are few. I intend to leave tomorrow, must do so if I am to make the ship in time. Your presence will not be required. I will have an escort of servants, and my two maids.'

The woman's colour rose and her lips became thinner than usual, if that were at all possible. She swept out of the room, treading on the edge of impertinence with the shallowness of her bow. Anna made no arrangements to leave, of course. She merely made sure that, half an hour before the time she had given the chaperone, she stationed herself by a window looking out onto the Strand. There were a dozen men in the Cecil livery, six of them on horseback, joking and chatting with each other opposite the main gate. She called the chaperone, and the steward after telling him to bring three of the porters along.

'You have been spying on me for Robert Cecil,' said Anna flatly. The chaperone started to bridle, expostulate. 'It is a fact,' said Anna. She turned to the steward, a loyal, elderly man who doted on Gresham. 'Master Robert, you do not know me. I will happily tell you why I believe beyond doubt that this woman has been spying on me and on The House for one of your master's greatest enemies.'

'I need no such explanation, ma'am,' said the steward sombrely. 'I need only your word. Your instructions?'

'Her judgement must await your master's return.' If he is ever allowed to return, thought Anna. 'My request is that until that time she is kept secured in a room from which she cannot escape, and allowed no contact either by voice or by paper with the outside world in general and the Cecil family in particular.'

The steward nodded, and the last Anna ever saw of the chaperone was her hunched, furious figure being led through the door surrounded by porters.

The ship to take her to France was marked, known. She was under no illusions that the imprisonment of the chaperone was only a temporary measure. She had to assume there were other spies in The House. The minute she left Dover would be reported, possibly Folkestone as well if they wanted her that much. But why did Cecil want her? What to do? The answer was obvious. She would go now, with a handful of servants, when no one could expect it, and she would not head east to the Channel ports, but south, where there were boats for hire in plenty but no one would expect her to go.

It was a good plan, and she handled it in a manner Gresham would have been proud of. The small party slipped out at dusk, spending the night at an inn a few miles out of London. Two days later, at a tiny port so obscure she could not remember its name, she had enough money to bribe a fisherman to risk the dash to Calais. She wrinkled her nose at the stink of fish, recognising that because no proper lady would choose such a vessel it was her best disguise. Scudding out of the small fishing port, the boat's single cabin her own for the journey, three servants and a maid crammed on the deck, she felt a triumphant lifting of her heart. She had beaten Cecil! She had outsmarted her enemy! And done so with no help from the young man appointed her guardian.

She was not aware of the significance of Monday 1st August, a relative lull in between the Armada's first engagement with the English and the renewed battle. She did not know that the captain she had appointed knew the Spanish fleet was coming up on him but had gambled on slipping ahead of them. She did not see his jaw drop as the leading ships of the Armada came out of the drizzle, and the *pataces* leaped forward after his ungainly smack, desperate to capture fishermen for the intelligence they could bring.

She did hear the running on the deck, and the first cry from the pursuing vessels in Spanish, a peremptory command for the English ship to halt. In what seemed like seconds, stunned Spanish sailors were grinning at the unexpected Spanish beauty from the cabin door. They took her over to the *San Mateo*. Let the captain of that great ship decide what to do with her.

Tuesday 2nd August. The stitching on Gresham's clothing was beginning to break now, his salt-encrusted garments starting to fall

263

apart. For those who washed at all there was only sea water, and Gresham began to dream of cool, clear river water, and hot, steaming tubs where a man could rinse the taste of salt from his mouth once and for all. The ship was becoming foul now, the stench of shit wafting up from the bilges as they ate the half-rotten biscuits, the dried strips of what might have been fish, and ate the olives that seemed little more than a thin layer of dry flesh over the stone.

For the rest of his life, when the Armada was discussed, people would turn to Gresham and ask him to describe the battle. After all, he had sailed on the Armada, held a ringside seat on board the Spanish flagship. 'What was it like?' the men or the women would ask, waiting to be shocked. 'Chaos,' Gresham would answer. 'First boredom. Then confusion. Smoke, and noise, and rolling thunder. And chaos.'

Gresham supposed the basic situation was simple enough, though nothing felt clear in the days before the Armada fought through to Calais. The Spaniards kept to their half-moon formation, the growing number of English ships snapping at their heels. Wherever there was any action, when a Spanish ship fell behind or was threatened, or an English ship seemed to present a chance for the Spaniards to grapple and board it, there the Duke sent the *San Martin*.

''E's a brave bastard, I'll grant him that,' grunted Mannion grudgingly, as the Spanish flagship headed straight for a squadron of English vessels, their firepower dwarfing his.

'He's a leader,' said Gresham simply, 'and though he's not a sailor by nature he knows he has to lead from the front, and lead by example.'

There had been a rising tide of excitement on the deck the first time the *San Martin* had heeled over and headed towards the English. Gresham and Mannion were pushed and buffeted as the soldiers, left with nothing to do for weeks on end, not used to the frozen world of boredom that a sailing ship could be, now sensed that a job for them might be coming. Weapons were being checked, priming secured and slow-match lit from a linstock begged from the gun captains.

'He's got to grapple with the English,' said Gresham. 'It's his only hope of defeating them. Yet they won't let him get near them. They'll stand off and try to blow him to pieces.'

Gresham remembered one moment vividly. The *San Martin* had headed for five, six English ships, straight for them. For a moment it looked as if they would collide with the leading English ship. Suddenly, without warning, operating by some pre-arranged signal, the leading English ship suddenly hauled round to port. The *San Martin* responded to a volley of orders, her sailors cursing as they stumbled over soldiers, and heeled round ponderously to match the turn. The two fleets were broadside to each other now. With a trembling, gaping roar the *San Martin* let go her main broadside, two decks of guns blaring out hatred to the English. The deck heaved beneath their feet and the rigging shuddered, a hot wave passing over their faces with the bitter stench of powder on its breath. A vast, thick cloud of smoke covered the ship, and dimly through it the English ships could be seen, similarly wreathed in smoke with the flashes of yellow piercing the gloom. The English vessels appeared and disappeared, firing as they came to bear on the Spanish. Here and there a stay snapped, and skipping splashes could be seen on the waves as balls went low, but the English fire seemed to be doing remarkably little damage. It was chaos, impossible to grasp the broader picture, the noise terrible but the ships still fighting at arm's length.

'Do you think that Duke of yours knows about the Shambles?' asked Mannion.

'*I* don't know about the Shambles!' said Gresham.

Five minutes later he was clambering up to the high poop deck, dismissing the soldier who tried to stop him imperiously and bowing low before the Duke.

'I am in combat,' said the Duke, hardly bothering to look at Gresham. To him the rate of fire from the Spanish flagship seemed painfully slow, the English firing three or four times as fast. Yet for the vast expenditure of powder and ball extraordinarily little damage seemed to be being done. 'This is the time for those who fight with their hands, not for spies.'

'It may be the time for men who drown at sea, my Lord, unless I can impart my knowledge to you.' Mannion was translating. That got his attention.

'Well?' The Duke clicked a finger, and his own translator took over.

'The large English vessel over there . . .' said Gresham. 'You have sent your galleasses and some other vessels to cut her out. Yet look where she is positioned.' Gresham had to remember to pause for the translator to do his work. 'The ship is carefully placed under the lee of Portland Bill. There is a four mile an hour tidal rip there that will draw all but the strongest vessel on to what is known as the Shambles, a long shallow bank two miles east of the Bill. It is possible that the ship is hoping to lure as many of your vessels as possible on to the shoal.'

The Duke looked at him. He turned to the ship's Pilot, and spoke to him in voluble Spanish. The Pilot was deferential, but also angry and sweating.

''E's saying 'e has no knowledge of what you say, but that of course with the coast so badly mapped it might be true. It's balls. 'E's got his tables, they all 'ave. It's just that 'e didn't think we'd be stopping here, so he hasn't done his homework.'

'I shall send a message to the vessels concerned,' said the Duke, dictating quickly to a secretary. 'I write a warning, but also a question; whether what you say is correct. You will remain here with me.'

The wind was dropping, but it did not seem to bother the tiny patache that skipped across the waves like a dog taken off its leash. The failing wind had caused the galleasses to break out their oars, and in theory the vast vessels were in their element, the oars giving them independent power and manoeuvrability. Yet the great oars, with four men to pull each blade and three to push it back, were vulnerable to cannon fire. One or two blades smashed, destroyed the rhythm of the others, causing the blades to damage each other. As they watched the galleasses seemed to dance in towards the English ship, but then withdraw, as if an invisible fence was keeping them from the final kill. The galleasses hoisted sail, but they were difficult to manoeuvre under sail and even at the distance they held the tidal race could be seen to boil the water under their sterns.

Here and there it seemed as if the high-sided Spanish ships were close enough to board the daintier, leaner English vessels. A great cheer went up from the decks of the *San Martin* as it looked as though one English ship had been stopped, grappled to the side of a Spanish galleon. There was a groan as it was seen as a trick of the light, the English ship pulling away. The English flagship suddenly detached from the engagement.

''E's seen those there in trouble, and 'e's going off to help 'im,' said Mannion, straining to see through the thick fog of gunsmoke, Both he and Gresham were semi-deafened now, having to shout even to be half heard.

A sharp cry came from the masthead, and every head on deck turned. A new English force had appeared from nowhere, and was bearing down on the Spanish transports. The Duke had tucked them away to the east, ahead of the main force.

Was Sidonia brave? Or foolhardy? He gave brisk orders for ships to detach and protect the transports, but the *San Martin* plunged after the English flagship and its followers. Gresham saw the Duke's lips move, half-heard words in Spanish through his deafened eardrums.

'What's he saying?' he bellowed to Mannion, coughing as powder smoke bit into his lungs.

'Dunno,' yelled Mannion, 'but I think it's something like expecting at last to have a real fight!'

The *San Martin* ploughed forward, the great banner that had been consecrated in Lisbon Cathedral streaming from its mast. She had to be recognised as the flagship. The English ships, seeing their sole pursuer, started to turn. The soldiers cheered. Now! Now! Now the two Commanders must grapple and fight like men!

The first English ship suddenly slewed round, presented her broadside to the *San Martin* and let loose. Five or six Spanish guns replied. There was a savage crack and the flagstaff vanished, splintered off, leaving a foot-long stump. Shrieks came from on deck, and three, four men slumped at their posts, the thud of a musket falling on to the deck suddenly audible in one of the strange, momentary silences that take place in battle. Then the English ship sailed on, turning to let the next vessel line up and deliver its broadside.

'That's it!' said Mannion in total exasperation. 'Let the buggers line up and take turns at blowing us to bits! We'll just sit 'ere and be awfully brave . . .'

The Duke's face on the quarterdeck was impassive. The English Commander had refused his challenge for combat, preferring instead to stand off and batter the *San Martin* to pieces.

The Duke had not dismissed Gresham. He stood, exposed, a yard or two away from the man who would be the target of every sharpshooter on board an English vessel, a man who had taken his flagship into combat with five or six of the enemy's best galleons.

He is still challenging the English Commander, Gresham realised. Was it Drake? Hawkins? Frobisher? Challenging him to take advantage of overwhelming odds and lay alongside the *San Martin*, trusting in God and his own men to turn the battle in their favour, to start the grappling melee that was the only way the Spanish could win this hopeless fight.

It was the longest hour in Gresham's life. Feeling like the target in an archery butt, Gresham found his fear vanishing to be replaced by an analytical calm. He saw the soldiers, straining in the tops and on the decks to find a target, firing hopefully as the English refused to come within range. Every now and then a figure would drop from the masts or collapse on the deck, a sudden rag-doll of silent stillness among the running men.

He watched the process of the men working the guns. Take the powder charge brought up from the magazine by the smoke-stained ship's boy, ram it down the barrel. Shove wadding home with the rammer. Roll the ball from the rack on the deck into the barrel, ram it home. Prick the touchhole clean, smear a powder charge from horn of flask over. Train the carriage to the left or right with the great metal lever, raise or lower the barrel by banging the iron quoins underneath it or ripping them out. Roll the carriage forward, secure it against the recoil with the thick, greasy ropes that were sometimes like snakes with a life of their own, rubbing at even the hardened hands of the sailors and soldiers. Then the gunner, with his glowing linstock, the end holding the slow-match forged in the shape of dragon's jaws or even a hand, bringing the flame down on to the touchhole. And then the monstrous anger of the gun . . . it became a ritual, almost soothing. And the whole thing in silence. It was as if the body saw no need for it to receive the smashing roar of the guns, the screams of men, almost rejected them and simply cut out hearing as a sense. The *San Martin*'s sails were shredded now, rigging flailing across the heavens. There was only intermittent noise from the carpenters' mallets. They left the holes in the great after-castle and anything which posed no threat to a central member of the great hull or which was not letting in water. The winds had been light, the ship not heeling heavily, and so hardly a shot had landed below the waterline.

Eventually – an hour? Hour and a half? – a body of Spanish ships finally managed to come up alongside the *San Martin* and take her back to the main body of the fleet. The Duke offered no complaint. The battle was declining now, the noise of carnage being replaced by the familiar noises of the sea. The Duke turned to Gresham.

'They will not fight us,' he said simply, revealing for the briefest of moments in his face a depth of tiredness Gresham had never before believed could happen in a man. And speaking in English! Broken English, to be sure, but readily comprehensible. So he had understood all along . . . 'They seek only to delay us. I cannot fight and I cannot stand, and must drive on to my . . . rendezvous.'

'I am sure the Duke of Parma will await you there,' said Gresham, conscious how weak his riposte sounded.

'It may be so,' said the Duke. 'Yet fifty men will not be alive to see it.' Fifty had died on board the *San Martin* in the day's engagements. The Duke's desire to be at the centre of the fighting, to grapple with the English, meant the brave, tough Portuguese-built ship had been by far the most fiercely engaged of the Spanish ships. The transports and their escort had taken a pounding but the English had been driven off. The Spanish had shown extraordinary discipline throughout the day, keeping their formation despite the ferocity of the cannonade they had been subjected to. The reports coming in suggested remarkably little damage to the Spanish ships.

'You may sleep on the deck here,' said the Duke. It was an honour. The command deck was kept clear, even gentlemen allowed on it were there only through direct command of the Duke. For the first time in weeks Gresham might be able to stretch out on the deck. 'The galleasses and my other vessels confirm your warning. Had we sent more ships they would have been dragged on to the shoals.'

The Duke nodded to Gresham and walked off, presumably to his great cabin. Ten minutes later a fine linen shirt and a boat cloak appeared in the hands of a servant, who mouthed something at Gresham.

'What did he say?' Mannion asked Gresham.

'He said, 'From the Duke. From his own private store of clothing.'

Would Cecil have sent a boat cloak to an underling? There were some commanders men would die for, Gresham reflected, and others they would simply wish to kill.

Wednesday 3rd August. Had Gresham slept at all? It felt as if he had been awake all night. His eyes were glued together, his feet felt like lead and there was an ominous ache in his gut. Was his stomach responding to the near-rotten food which was all they had to chew on?

Gresham supposed that there were men who did not feel fear. He had known from an early age that he was not one of them. For him,

270

true courage lay in defeating fear, not pretending it did not exist. And this morning he felt real fear. Could he bear another day of standing on a deck waiting to feel the crushing weight of cannon or musket ball tear into his flesh, maiming before it killed? It was different when one fought a man. It took far greater courage to stand and be shot at, and he was beginning to fear that it was courage he did not have.

He would have prayed then, for courage, if he had not felt so hypocritical. What God could respect a man who only prayed when he needed something? In any event, the prayer that lay fallow in his heart was answered that day. The English ships seemed unwilling now to close with the Spaniards and loose off shot, staying out of cannon range. Yet clearly they had been little damaged by the fire they had received from the Spaniards. What an irony it would be if the entire stock of cannon balls on the *San Martin* had come newly-foundered from the Lisbon armoury. Perhaps God did have a sense of humour.

'Near out of powder, that'd be my guess,' said Mannion. He had rapidly become Gresham's military interpreter. 'Government's too stingy to give 'em enough, or always used to be, and these towns along the coast, they want to hang on to their powder and shot in case it's them as gets invaded. Problem with the English firing so fast,' he added, 'they use up too much powder and shot.'

Then the wind died. The two fleets lay within sight of each, motionless, useless, the entrance to the Solent and the Isle of Wight creeping up with paralysing slowness as the current moved both fleets at perhaps half a mile an hour.

Thursday 4th August. An English squadron had been placed by the entrance to the Solent, to resist any attempt at a landing. A few puffs of wind off the shore were enough to send it moving down on the northern wing of the tightly-huddled Spanish ships. More firing broke out, and with so little wind the smoke hung ghost-like in the rigging, seeming sometimes to ripple and re-settle as two or three guns fired together.

271

'Oh God,' said Mannion. 'Here we go again.' Was he feeling the same strain? Was even Gresham's rock starting to shake and quiver?

The wind was fitful, playing with them, teasing one minute with its strength and then dying away to nothing. Somehow the *San Martin* was standing opposite a great English ship, the largest in their fleet. For a moment the Spaniards thought they had cut her off. Cheering broke out from the masts, mocking laughter as the English ship broke out her boats and tried to haul herself past the Spanish. A hail of musket fire swept from the Spanish ships, and down below the Gun Captains were hoarse at shrieking to their men to reload. Yet the great cannon spoke with tantalising infrequency, for all that the men's hands were slipping with the sweat that poured off their bodies. Men fell in the boats, but none gave in, and suddenly the English ship let her full panoply of sails fall from her yards and swept ahead of the Spanish ships, whose pursuit in the face of her speed was derisory.

The fighting was now sporadic, across the whole front, an engagement here, an engagement there, the sullen thunder of guns insistent, unrelenting.

'Is it planned?' Gresham yelled to Mannion. They had both acquired an arquebus from a pair of dead soldiers, though they could have been firing into a vacuum for all that they had been able to see amid the smoke. 'Look, we're being pushed past the Solent, past any chance of mooring.'

'Next stop Calais!' grinned Mannion. There was nowhere else for the Armada to rest and anchor past the Solent except Calais, and that was a French port whose outer roads were notorious for currents, shoals and freak storms. 'I reckon it's accident as much as anything else. If there'd been a half decent wind he could have sailed in there and stuck regardless. It's the bloody wind that's done for the Spaniards. For Christ's sake, look 'ow much damage *we* haven't had after half an hour up opposite a bloody great English ship.'

It was extraordinary how much punishment a ship such as the *San Martin* could take. Her main timbers were immensely thick, and the lighter cannon simply failed to penetrate. The upperworks were splintered and smashed, and a cannon had been upturned when an English ball had gone through a gun port, but as a fighting vessel the *San Martin* was still highly effective, despite having stood off and traded fire with a series of great English ships.

"'Ere,' said Mannion, 'Do you want history to repeat itself? Or do we really want these bastards sunk?' Mannion yelled into Gresham's ear, and he went to the side, straining his eyes to look ahead. What Gresham saw made him leap up onto the command deck, bow low before the Duke, who was standing without a cloak, his face revealing nothing. There were tiny, thin lines over it now, Gresham noticed, lines that had not been there before. Between his feet the deck planking was gouged, white splinters sticking up. A musket ball must have missed the Duke by inches. Had he flinched? Or hadn't he even noticed? Had the Duke taken any sleep? Was the slight swaying the motion of the sea, Gresham wondered? Or was it tiredness?

'We're drifting east, my Lord,' said Gresham. 'In front of us is what the English call the Owers, hidden rocks and shoals that can rip the heart out of a boat. The English are shepherding us towards them.'

The Duke went to the side, strained to look ahead. There, to leeward, was a stretch of water of an angry green, its surface troubled with sharp, choppy waves unlike those around it.

Their pilot had been hit in the engagement with the *San Martin*. As Pilot on the flagship he would have been experienced, and have his own *routier*, a collection of compass courses, landmarks for entering various harbours and danger points, compiled from what other mariners had written. Many pilots scorned *routiers*, their scorn a cover for the fact that they could not read. Would the pilot have known about the Owers? Realised their proximity? Would another pilot have spotted the danger? Even if they had communication between ships, it was so slow and primitive that they might never have got warning out.

The Duke nodded, a strangely formal gesture, to Gresham. He

ordered a gun sounded to attract the attention of the fleet, and the *San Martin* pulled round, leading the fleet to the south and away from the danger.

'Do you wish to become our pilot?' he asked Gresham. Was the man making a joke? Could he have even a vestigial sense of humour left after the pounding, the incessant strain? 'After all, this is the second time you have performed this service.'

'My Lord, the knowledge isn't mine. My servant here sailed these waters as a child. Alas, his knowledge ceases with this stretch of the south coast.'

The engagement had virtually ceased now, but boats were flocking to the flagship. Yet there had been no summons from the Duke. Two men were led up on to the deck, bowed low and spoke volubly to the Duke.

'They're out of shot,' Mannion translated to Gresham.

'It needn't be a real problem yet,' thought Gresham out loud. 'Some ships have been heavily engaged, others haven't fired a shot. If they distribute what's left they'll be alright for two or three days. After that . . .'

'Three more days,' said Mannion, 'and this shirt'll be so hard you could fire it at the *Ark Royal* and blow 'er apart.' Gresham had taken the Duke's shirt for himself, telling Mannion that it would be wrong for such a refined piece of clothing to go to a mere peasant. From somewhere Mannion had acquired a rough tunic to replace his salt-hardened one, but it was made out of hard canvas and had rubbed parts of his back raw. He bore the pain, aggravated by salt water, phlegmatically.

There is a survival mode for combatants. Broken sleep, periods of intense boredom enlivened by moments of sheer terror, unhealthy food grabbed whenever possible all become normal. For the lucky ones, the mind learns to concentrate simply on the essentials, cutting or filtering fear, pain and worry. For those less lucky, the trembling hands, the haunted eyes, the endless threshing of the body in sleep told their own story. Such men died in their minds several times every hour, each new dawn leaving them like a leaking ship, sinking inexorably deeper and deeper into the water.

'Funny,' said Mannion as the darkness settled over the *San Martin*, 'I didn't know which way you'd go, you bein' a thinker and such like. Wondered if you'd tip over the edge.'

'The only thing that might make me tip over the edge,' said Gresham, 'is smelling you for longer than I have to.' He turned over, his body used to the hard deck, offering the other half of the cloak for Mannion to climb under. 'It was bad enough in Cadiz. Now it's even worse. And try not to breathe on me until I'm asleep.'

Friday 5th August and Saturday 6th August. Men had been working all night, and already a new sail had been hoisted on the mainmast of the *San Martin*. The divers, thin, shivering creatures with immense reserves of strength, had been over the side, plugging holes beneath the waterline, securing the ship. The ceaseless squeak and heave of the pumps was their litany now. Gresham had been woken in the small hours by Mannion's stentorian snoring. He had walked to the bow to relieve himself, then back down the deck where the sailmakers were at their work, eerily silent. There was a tap on his shoulder. It was one of the Duke's servants, motioning him to follow.

There were four or five officers on the deck with the helmsman, and the Duke was standing directly by the stern, gazing back to where he knew the English fleet was shadowing him. Did he ever sleep?

'You possibly saved this ship today,' said the Duke quietly. He had an extraordinary manner. He rarely raised his voice, yet it carried a massive authority, and even the most surly seaman seemed genuine in the bow he offered the Duke. Would Gresham ever command such respect, he wondered, respect that was offered without it ever seeming to be asked for?

'I am grateful you think so,' said Gresham, 'but not sure it is so.' He was too tired to prevaricate. 'I suspect your watchman at the bow or the masthead would have seen the Owers in time, or another ship read its *routier* properly.'

275

'Your modesty does you credit. I do not trust you, you realise?' The tone was soft.

'No one trusts a spy, my Lord,' said Gresham, 'and you cannot know if all this while I am working out who will win this battle, keeping my options open for a return to England, seeking to give you ill advice the moment I think your cause is lost.'

'And are you?' asked the Duke.

'I believe I'm working neither for England nor for Spain,' said Gresham. 'I believe I'm working for peace.'

'A grand claim,' remarked the Duke. 'And even if it were true, on what grounds do you claim peace as our right? Do we not scream when we are first brought into this world? Does not the plague, unrequited love, the pain of a foul tooth, the sickness at the loss of a wife or a son affect rich and poor alike? Surely God in His wisdom placed us in a world where to live is to suffer pain? And the only measure of a true man is to be willing to risk death for a just cause?'

'I'm sure that's true, my Lord,' said Gresham, 'for those of us with a brain between our ears, for whom starvation is not an issue, those of us who have the luxury of time to think about why we are here on earth. And we reach, perhaps, for the sanctity of Christ, the purity and meaning that His vision offers.'

'You talk of "us",' said the Duke, not outwardly alarmed at his ancient lineage being grouped with that of the bastard son of a London merchant.

'Because as a bastard I was left to wander the streets of London and mix with those who do not have the luxury of time for thought, and because I've spent time on my father's country estates, sometimes even been asked into the filthy hovels of those my father deemed peasants, a sub-human species to be worked and used, but never known.'

The Duke of Medina Sidonia had no problem with recognising that not all humankind were born equal. 'God did not make all his creatures equal in their sight. He made them equal only in the sight of God,' said the Duke with finality. 'It is easy to be sentimental about the poor.'

The thousands of peasants under the Duke's command were not necessarily people, to him, thought Gresham. They were souls. Souls demanded respect, to be treated to a certain code, but not to be treated necessarily as people, as fellow humans. 'It is easy to forget that the poor wish to live as much as we do, that if you prick them they bleed as much as any human. Even easier to use them as pawns in monstrous games of power. I've lied to my Spanish masters. I've told them that I've acted for my faith. It's not true. I do not really care that Queen Elizabeth is a heretic.'

He saw the Duke draw back slightly. Had he revealed too much?

'I care that she has no heir, will have no heir. The Virgin Queen knows that while she is all that stands between England and civil war her advisers will do everything in their power to keep her alive. Elizabeth has opted to preserve herself while she lives, and doesn't care for what happens to her country when she dies.' He paused for a moment. 'I think there'll be civil war when she dies. The contenders for her throne? A clutch of rapacious nobles with a pinch of royal blood and an overweening ambition. The warped King of Scotland, son of the Mary Queen of Scots we executed . . .' He had almost said 'I' instead of 'we'. 'Scotland is, of course, England's oldest enemy. A stupid, vapid woman called Arabella Stuart whose blood gives her a claim and whose brains do not exist. And the King of Spain, our oldest enemy of all.' Gresham turned to look back to where the English ships were gathered in the dark. 'So I chose Spain. I chose Spain because I believe that Spain has the power to conquer those rapacious nobles, to conquer the impoverished King of Scotland, the pathetic Arabella Stuart. That it is so powerful that its success is inevitable. Spain will win. And will it matter to the peasant in the field and the woman striving to fill her children's bellies whether it is a Protestant Queen or a Catholic King who holds the final authority over them? I think not. I think what matters to them is that they are left in peace to scrape a bare living out of the earth, left without soldiers trampling down their crops and sticking their babies on the end of pikes as trophies of war. I decided Spain would win that war. And when I had decided that, the other decision was inevitable. Why go through with the war in the first place? Why not work to achieve the inevitable and cut out the need for war? Why not work to install Spain in England without the ritual of yet more senseless death? That is why I chose Spain, my Lord.' He bowed to the Duke. 'I did not choose my path for religion. I chose my path, I always choose my path, because I thought that in so doing fewer people would die.'

The sound of the water lapping against the hull was gentle, the ringing in Gresham's ears after the day's combat nearly gone.

'You will have no place in the new England,' said the Duke after a while, 'if indeed that conquest ever happens. However well it is exercised, power will be in the hands of those with Spanish blood flowing in their veins. You will be thanked, and forgotten. Sidelined. Is that the word?'

'I think so, my Lord,' said Gresham. 'That it is the word, and that it is what will happen. But I've never valued life much, and I value its honours even less.'

'I have an estate in Andalusia,' said the Duke, dreamily. 'A fine estate, with a grand house and peasants who have worked the land for centuries, and think of me and my family as God if they think of God at all. It is pure Spain, sun-drenched yet harsh, proud, certain of its history. It loses me money, every year, despite its fields bursting with growth, its orange groves so full of the smell of fruit that a man might die drawing it into his lungs. The man I pay to run my estate is corrupt and clever in his corruption.' The Duke of Medina Sidonia sat on the stern rail, the gesture revealing a decade of exhaustion. 'Would you run such an estate for me? In time, there would be access to the Court, introductions. Oh, they would deny you access to the top tiers, of course. Yet you would live in a country at peace, an ancient country, be able to rise in the morning and hold rich earth between your fingers.'

Across the boundaries of race and culture, of age, of warring humanity and a flawed creation, something of elemental, simple humanity had been said.

Why were there tears in Gresham's eyes? Why did his body

continually try to let him down? 'I thank you, my Lord,' Gresham responded, finally. 'With all my heart. But before I allow myself to think of the Heaven of Andalusia I cannot help but wish to deal first with the Hell of the English Channel.'

The Duke laughed, a full, strong laugh that showed Gresham yet another side of this most complex man. 'You are right to correct me, right for youth to stop an old man dreaming impossible dreams.' The Duke stood up from the stern rail, rubbing his ungloved hands to warm them in the chill of the night. 'We cannot beat your English ships, can we?' he asked blankly.

'No, My Lord,' said Gresham bluntly. 'You cannot. They are faster and nimbler before the wind. You can only win if you close with them, and they have the power not to let you do so, however courageously you pursue them. Yet you can meet with the Duke of Parma, and stand between his transports and the English fleet,' said Gresham.

'I hope to God that we may,' said the Duke bitterly, turning away to look astern. 'Yet why has he not responded to my messages?'

One hundred and sixty-seven men killed, two hundred and forty-one wounded, the manifest stated to the Duke the next morning. A mere pinprick in the Armada's strength. Only two vessels lost, neither of them disabled as a result of enemy action. The Spanish ships had survived four assaults, their discipline holding, the damage even to the heavily-engaged *San Martin* quite minimal. So why did Gresham have such an overwhelming sense of defeat?

On the Friday morning the Duke despatched yet another pinnace to Dunkirk, begging Parma to send him heavy shot and some shallow draft vessels to get in close among the English. Begging him most of all to name a rendezvous, a meeting point for the Armada and his army. At five o'clock on the Saturday evening, in a strengthening wind, the Armada sighted Calais. The Pilot hastily brought over from one of the great Portuguese galleons demanded that they anchor in the broad, open roadstead outside the Calais breakwater. If they kept on, the Pilot swore, the currents would carry the Armada through the strait and out into the North Sea, sweeping them away from England. The Armada dropped its anchors, the metal flukes seeking to bite into the shallow holding ground.

The English fleet took station, just out of range, reinforced by another thirty vessels from the Channel, lurking, watching, threatening.

CHAPTER 10

August 7th – August 9th, 1588
The Battle of Gravelines

Was Anna in Calais? Gresham hoped so. The Duke had made it quite clear that neither he nor Mannion could leave the *San Martin*, though the Duke had consented to him sending a messenger to enquire after her safety and whereabouts. 'Was she always part of your plans to cover up your allegiance?' the Duke had asked. 'No, my Lord,' Gresham had answered. 'She was . . . an accident.' Which was one way to describe her, he thought.

'Well,' said Gresham, holding a by now habitual dawn council of war with Mannion, the both of them gazing from the bow towards the distant port of Calais, 'what're the odds now?'

'Difficult,' said Mannion, ''cos it all depends on Parma, don't it? As far as your Duke's concerned this is shit creek and we're moored in it.' Mannion had taken to referring to Medina Sidonia as "your Duke" as Gresham's comments on the man had become increasingly full of admiration for the Spanish Commander's quiet courage and dignity. 'Currents here are terrible, and if you wants my opinion this bloody place 'as got "fireship" written all over it. But if I've got it right,' said Mannion, 'Parma could get loads of boats with his troops down through those canals, with the Dutch able to do sod all about it. Or he could get 'em to Dunkirk and give us pilots to take enough of the smaller ships up into the harbour to protect the transports. Or, best of all, you say Parma's got Antwerp?'

'He's got enough of it to shelter a fleet in the approaches to Antwerp, on the Scheldt,' said Gresham.

'So all it needs is for 'im to send a few pilots over here, and get enough of this lot moored off Antwerp. Nothing I've seen of that lot,' Mannion motioned dismissively out to the English ships, 'is telling me they can stop 'em.'

A cold wind came at dawn, from the south, dragging sharp showers in its trail. If the Armada was flushed out of Calais, it would have to drive north and leave England behind.

Gresham's body shuddered involuntarily, and once again he cursed it for its refusal to obey orders. Something terrible was going to happen here, he knew. A deep instinct in him sensed that somehow in this place and in this time the fate of nations would be decided, the prophecy of Regiomontanus come to pass. Or was it simply the cold, the hunger of a young stomach and the insatiable desire, like a terrible itch always just out of reach, to drink gallons of cold, clear water and let it rinse the salt off his red-raw skin?

The translator had to descend into the gloom to find Gresham. For want of anything to do, he had gone to watch the carpenters plugging the holes in the side of the *San Martin*. To their amusement he had got himself holding a block of wood against a wooden plug, with a huge Spaniard ramming the plug home with savage blows of a mallet.

'Don Rodrigo Tello de Guzman's pinnace will be alongside in minutes,' was the whispered message. It was he who had been sent with messages to Parma a fortnight ago. 'You have met the Duke of Parma more recently than any except Don Rodrigo. The Duke wishes you to hear his report.'

From the moment Don Rodrigo stepped on board they knew something was wrong. He was both excited and flustered, a sweat on his brow, a nervousness in his manner, almost an irritation. Then it happened, only briefly, for a moment. As it had happened once before to Gresham. The world and time froze, yet there was still movement and sound in it. Don Rodrigo was poised, fixed in a clumsy half-bow as he leaned forward, his startled eyes fixed on the fractured and smashed upperworks of the flagship. The Duke stood on the deck where he had seemed to take root since they had sighted England, frozen also in a stiff, formal greeting. The rigging flapped and slapped against the tall masts, the suck and plop of the waves still soothed. The rhythmic blow of the mallet suddenly took on the timbre of a funereal bell, and all the while the soggy clanking and tired hiss of the pumps reached the upper decks. Then the people and their surroundings became synchronised again, and moved in harmony. Don Rodrigo was troubled, his eyes shifting to Gresham, Sidonia's advisers, those on the deck. The news he brought could not be communicated on the open deck. It took an age for the Duke to realise the problem.

'We shall move into my cabin,' he said finally, nodding to Gresham and several of the Spanish commanders to follow him.

There were perhaps ten of them in the great cabin, and Gresham was reminded of the meeting in Drake's cabin off Cadiz. Three times as many could have fitted into the Duke's centre of operations. The stern windows were intact, remarkably, or had been mended, and they let in the brisk but almost wintery light of Calais. Down one side there was a neat hole where an English ball had pierced the hull, two or three feet on a jagged wrench of splintered timber where a heavier ball, at the end of its trajectory, had smashed into the timbers. One or other of the hits had reduced the top of a fine, carved chest to splinters.

'My Lord,' said Don Rodrigo. 'The Duke of Parma sends his warmest greetings. He is delighted that the power and might of Spain has reached thus far, feels that England is already trembling beneath the feet of the true Faith.' Then Rodrigo stumbled, fell silent.

'And?' said the Duke, prompting him gently, 'And our rendezvous?'

The translator seemed to think he had a duty, and was whispering the translation into Gresham's ear.

'The Duke . . . the Duke . . .' Rodrigo was gulping, finding difficulty with his words. 'The Duke states that his troops will be ready for their sortie within six days.'

Spanish noblemen and senior commanders did not hiss or gasp in amazement and horror. Centuries of breeding, centuries that Henry Gresham envied with all his heart, forbade the outward display of such emotion. Instead there was a sudden silence of bodies as well as voices, as the men gathered there became immobile.

Six days? Six days for one hundred and twenty-eight ships to remain moored in a treacherous anchorage, nearly out of powder and shot, an ever-growing hostile fleet snapping at them?

'My Lord . . .' Rodrigo was speaking like a woman in childbirth. The pain was extraordinary, the burden unavoidable. He looked round the room, eyes stopping briefly at Gresham and Mannion, moving on. Apart from their strange presence, the men gathered around their commander were true Spaniards. Most had birth and breeding, and even those who had less of either commodity had experience with which to compensate. 'My Lord,' there was a new strength in his voice, 'when I left Dunkirk a day ago I saw no sign of his troops. The Duke has not been seen at Dunkirk, nor at Nieuport, this many a day. He moves between Antwerp, Ghent and Bruges, with no seeming pattern in his movements.'

Well, thought Gresham, it's good to know other people had the same problem as we did on our visit.

'The vessels I saw in both places were paltry things, few in number, rotten in construction. They had no stores loaded, not even sails or oars.' He paused, not for effect, but because the enormity of what he had seen he had only now allowed to hit him. 'My Lord, *the troops are not ready*! The boats, if they exist, are not ready. It is as if my Lord the Duke of Parma had only today received notice that your vessels were leaving Lisbon.'

'How long?' asked the Duke quietly, gently.

Rodrigo looked around the cabin walls, almost in despair, hating what he knew he had to say. 'For the troops to embark . . . My Lord, it can only be my opinion. I may be wrong. A fortnight. Two weeks. At least. Possibly more. Even if the transports exist, will bear the weight of men. A fortnight to gather the men and load the stores. I say nothing about crossing the shallows, reaching us in the face of the damned Dutch and their fly-boats.'

'Thank you,' said the Duke. 'You have done well.' He smiled at Don Rodrigo, reaching forward for the package that he now knew would contain the fulsome welcome of the Duke of Parma and a meaningless promise to assemble an army. An army that should already have been assembled and waiting. The smile was addressed to all those in the cabin now, understanding, forgiving. 'Leave me now. And you, Rodrigo, report to my steward and claim from him some of my very best wine. And then offer it to my friends and fellow officers here. We shall reassemble in the turning of a glass. Please leave me to consider the Duke of Parma's letter.'

The Duke's eyes paused on Gresham's, commanding him to remain. The Spanish officers and nobles bowed formally, unconcerned about who remained, not realising the figure and his manservant who remained behind. There was a strange glint in their eyes, Gresham realised. These were not fools, these men. They knew. The Duke broke the ornate seal on the letter, as if Gresham was not there. He read quietly, occasionally holding the paper up to the light coming through the stern windows where he found a particular line hard to decipher. Then he turned to Gresham.

'I have waited so long for these words, and now I have them, that is all they are. Words.'

'The words are not . . . helpful?' asked Gresham.

'I need an army, an army of trained men to take over England. I need powder, and shot. And I have . . . words.'

The Duke placed the letter from Parma on the ornate table, and stood up, stiff, clearly in pain. He turned to gaze out of the stern windows, onto the ornately decorated stern walk.

'A fortnight? Perhaps. If I could sail up the Scheldt, sail up even to Dunkirk, present my fleet before that army and shame them into embarkation. Yet with no pilots, and no promise of pilots, my ocean-going fleet can make no such inland journey. I must await the Duke's army here, in a treacherous anchorage off a neutral country. And I know that the army will not come, as I know my fleet's survival in this place will be lucky to last one night.' The Duke's face seemed to have sunk in on itself, his eyes hollows in his face, the tightness of his skin almost a death mask. 'Well, my dreaming young Englishman? Am I right?'

All the horror, all the pathos, all the stupid idiocy of the world seemed to come together in that cabin.

'You are right,' said Gresham, as an extraordinary, unprecedented and burning hot tear welled up in both his eyes. He dare not blink, in case it scalded his cheek. 'You have lost.'

Around him, hundreds of men went about their business: mending, making, living, filling the hours with the tasks that stop us thinking; talking to God, pleading with God or hoping with all their hearts that God heard what their poor brains could never put into words. Trusting in God, and the Duke of Medina Sidonia and perhaps even in the memory of the kiss their wife or sweetheart had given them as they set out, trusting in all of these or maybe even just in luck to see them through. Using the one thing God had given them, the belief in each man we are immortal, that death will not really come to us and the hope that we alone will be saved. Unaware that men and events hugely beyond their power to control or influence had condemned so many of them to a lottery of death.

'You'll be blown out of this harbour by storm, or by the English,' said Gresham inexorably. This time the tears would accept no boundary, betraying him by cascading from his eyes down his face. 'And you will fight, won't you, my Lord?'

The exhausted face of the Duke of Medina Sidonia was incredulous. 'Fight? But of course I will fight!' There was emphasis in his voice, but the tone was kind. Almost paternal. 'For hundreds of years my country has stood between the rule of Christ and the Ottomans. When Rome and then Constantinople fell to the infidel, did we measure the odds? Did we count the numbers against us? No! We fought. And we won. And saved Europe for Christianity.'

'But now you'll lose,' said Gresham.

'Sometimes, young man,' said the Duke, 'men must believe in miracles. And sometimes, those older and wiser men who doubt miracles recognise a truth of human history. Men may have to lose now in order for their children to win later. Men who are willing to die become stronger because they lose all fear. It is the fear of death, not death itself, that weakens us.'

'And your . . . reputation?' Gresham hated himself for asking the question but some Devil within him could not refuse to do so.

'They will blame me for this, of course. My family, my children will suffer. So I come to the ultimate problem for a true man. The problem I have faced many times now in my life. And the problem I am amused to see you are struggling to face for the first time.'

How could this man adopt this lightness of tone when at any moment the most important military mission his country had ever mounted could be smashed apart and he be held responsible? 'What problem is that?' Gresham found himself saying.

'Of course the reputation the world affords me matters greatly. But I learned long ago that for all its importance such a reputation is fickle, perhaps even false. When all else fails, and all seems dark and bleak, it is not the judgement of the world I believe will matter to me when I pass into the vale of death. It is my judgement of myself. Do I believe I did everything in my power to make things right? Did I dirty my actions by cowardice, by self-interest, by vanity, greed, lust or avarice? I would love the world to judge my actions as worthy. Yet when all else is done, the judgement that must matter most to me, the crucial, the most scrupulous, the testing judgement must stand as my own judgement on myself.'

'And what will that judgement be?' asked Gresham, fascinated.

'Ask me when I know if I met my death fighting. We cannot control how we are born. We have some control over how we die.'

Gresham spoke softly,

> *'"Go you gently unto death?*
> *Is what you are so little worth?*
> *We enter screaming into life,*
> *And death hurts more than birth."'*

'What is that?' asked the Duke.

'Childish verse,' said Gresham. He made a massive effort to pull himself together. 'My Lord,' he said, 'I hope you don't die. I hope justice prevails.'

'I am not such a fool as to hope to die,' responded the Duke, an ironic smile on the edge of his lips. 'It is merely that I fear I have little control over it, and even less control over justice. You may leave. It would not be good to have an Englishman here for the conference I must hold now.'

'That's it, then,' said Mannion once back outside. 'Fine mess you've got us into. Tonight there's a spring tide right near its top, and the wind's been freshening all day. If our lads can get enough fireships together, they'll come down on this anchorage like shit off a shovel.'

'The Spanish fireships did nothing at Cadiz,' said Gresham.

'That's 'cos there was no wind to speak of, and hardly any tide. And there was three times as much space as there is 'ere.'

'So what should the Duke do?' asked Gresham.

'Piss off and go 'ome,' said Mannion. 'Like us.'

'But he'll fight,' said Gresham.

'Then 'e's a stupid bastard,' said Mannion, 'who ought to know better. If he wants to do it for his honour, let him. I've given serious thought as to whether I want to do it for mine, and I don't. But I bet you he won't let us piss off and go home. So it's the same old place, isn't it? The one people like me 'ave been in for centuries. *I* have to pop me clogs so *he* can keep his honour.'

They stood watching the small boats scuttle between the ships of the Armada, the deliveries of food from shore to ship which the essentially friendly, one-legged Governor of Calais had allowed.

He had lost the leg in retaking Calais from the English fifty years earlier and felt no love for Queen Elizabeth. The tension was tangible. Every sailor on board could sense the tide and wind, and even now, well before sunset, they were looking out to sea and towards the English. That tension had spread to the soldiers, dispirited now, convinced that they had no role in this campaign except to die. For the first time that morning Gresham had seen spots of rust on three or four breastplates, spots that the soldiers concerned had not ferociously rubbed away at the first sign. Somehow everyone on board *San Martin* was moving more slowly, as if there was a deep ache in their bones and a heavy pack on their back. Gresham had caught one of the gentleman adventurers, a young, fresh-faced lad no more than seventeen years old, standing by the bow, crying. He had turned, horrified, determined to hide his face. Gresham had put out a hand, then dropped it helplessly to his side.

'It's a cruel thing, facing your death, when you're that age,' said Mannion drily. Over these past few weeks his master had taken on an extraordinary strength and inner resilience. Only a few years in age separated the young Englishman and the young Spaniard before them, yet there was a decade between them in experience.

Devil ships. That was the fear of every sailor on board the Armada. Three years earlier the Dutch had sent specially-constructed fireships down the Scheldt to try and lift the Spanish siege of Antwerp. Three tons of explosive had been crammed into brick chambers on board. One had fetched up against a fortified bridge, killed eight hundred men in the explosion and inflicted horrific injuries on thousands of others. Of the bridge nothing remained. Federigo Gambelli was the name of the designer. He was known to be in London, working for the English.

'Your job's done, now, you know that, don't you?' Mannion prompted. 'This 'as gone beyond advice. If our lads . . . sorry, if the *English* do their jobs, this lot's going to be burned to buggery, whether you want it to 'appen or not. You ain't going to influence anything any more. That girl's waiting for you in Calais, more as like, and half the girls in England are waiting for me in London . . .'

'So why not swim ashore?' Gresham finished Mannion's words. 'You go,' he said suddenly. He reached out, grasped Mannion's arm, looked into his eyes. 'This has never been your fight, only mine. You've done enough, lost enough. Go on. Leave me. It's only right.'

'Why ain't you coming?'

'Because . . . because I can't.' Gresham knew how feeble it sounded. 'I respect this man, respect him more than any other I've ever met. They'll damn him for what happened here, yet I've seen him, talked to him. I think he knew where it would all end, knew he would die all along, yet he still did what he was asked to do, still carried on fighting for his cause against all the odds, knowing it was hopeless. It's not just courage, it's true dignity.'

'So?' said Mannion. 'Write him a letter, get all that off your chest. And then jump overboard.'

'I just can't do it,' said Gresham. 'I have to be here at the end. I want to stay with him.'

'Sleep now,' said Mannion. 'I'll get us up when it's dark. Then we'll slip back and get as close to the stern as we can.'

'What?' said Gresham, startled.

'Not going to get much bloody sleep tonight, are we? And odds on a fireship hits the bow first. Though if it's one of those bloody Devil ships it won't make a blind bit of difference.'

'Then you're staying,' said Gresham. This tears-in-his-eyes business had just got to stop, he said to himself, not realising just how deep down into his reserves of mental energy the past months had forced him to dig and how exhausted he was.

"Course I'm bloody staying, aren't I?" said Mannion. 'There's got to be somebody with brains looking after you.'

For all that the lead-up to Calais was largely a confused blur in his memory, Gresham remembered that night and day for the rest of his life, could recreate its every moment with total vividness. As he remembered another day. A bald, decapitated head rolling across a hastily erected scaffold, the comic expression of startlement on the executioner's face as he held not a head but a red wig in his hand. And now, thousands of men gripped by a superb discipline fighting a lost cause to the bitter end, fighting a cause that no man should have asked them to sail on, a cause so profligate of human life as to make a mockery of a kind creation. Fighting with simple courage. Why in the depths of his and this life's idiocy did mankind reveal itself as so brave and wonderful?

The flickering of distant fire came at midnight. The sudden, violent ringing of bells, first from one ship then another, until the whole of Calais roads seemed like a vast Cathedral tower. The pinnaces and longboats the Duke had stationed to guard his fleet leaped forward, grapnels ready. Two of the outermost fireships, yards already outlined in a dull red flame, were caught and hauled aside, but the combination of wind and tide was too much, sending the ships at ferocious speed down on to the Spanish ships. One pinnace was engulfed in flames itself, a longboat smashed to pieces as the flaming monster bore down and through it. Then from the lead ship a roar of cannons shattered the anchorage, a series of massive explosions. Devil ships!

The English would say that the Armada panicked. Yet Gresham saw no panic. A hundred and thirty ships cut their cable, left their anchors rotting in the Calais roadstead, and all evaded the fireships, made it out of harbour. The discipline was superb. Hardly a man spoke on the *San Martin* as the men clambering on the yards dropped the great sails, saw them fill with wind. The soldiers were lining the sides in five minutes of the alarm bell sounding. There was no collision, no crashing of great timbers hurled into each other.

'God help us!' said Mannion at dawn the next morning, in the last period of sanity either men would have for twenty-four hours. It was not an expletive, but rather a genuine plea for help. The *San Martin* had cut her cable, dodged two fireships with relative ease and come round, dropping her spare anchor less than a mile from where she had started. And she was virtually alone in the anchorage.

The *San Juan*, *San Marcos*, *San Felipe* and *San Mateo* were within hailing range. The *San Lorenzo*, flagship of the galleasses, was crawling inshore, her rudder destroyed by fouling on a discarded cable, her mainmast broken. And that was all. The remainder of the Armada was scattered out at sea, heading north before the driving wind.

'Anchors,' said Mannion. 'I'll bet most of 'em ain't carrying spare anchors. Most used two, even three to keep themselves steady here.' There was shifting sand on the bottom, and fierce currents. 'Only one spare anchor left, you 'as to stand out to sea. No point comin' back in here and trying to hold fast in a strong wind with only one anchor.'

A squadron of English ships broke off from the main body, heading inshore after the wounded galleass.

'Ain't nothing 'e can do for 'er,' said Mannion, 'don't care how brave he is.'

Orders were shouted, and the *San Martin* started to pull out of the roadstead.

'He's going to put himself and these few ships between the rest of the Armada and the English,' said Gresham. 'Hope the other ships can get back and reform in the time he buys them. It's madness. We're outnumbered ten, twenty to one. We'll be blown to pieces.'

'Yep,' said Mannion. 'Want to watch it from the deck, or get below and try to hide?'

The leading English ships, twenty of them led by a fine galleon, were on a converging course with the *San Martin* and her four companions. The leading English ship made a minor alteration of course, heading straight towards the *San Martin*.

The artillery captains, one for each side of the gun deck, yelled their orders. The *San Martin* was perilously short of shot and powder. No shot could be wasted. '*Fire only at point-blank range! Hold your fire.*' The musketeers on the deck and the arquebusiers aloft braced themselves against deck and yard, many surreptitiously crossing themselves as the enemy ship boiled towards them, crashing the waves aside from her bow in her headlong rush to destroy.

'This is new,' said Mannion, sucking on the inevitable tooth.

The lead English ship was holding her fire, coming within

292

cannon then musket range, coming on even further, until within pistol range, fifty or a hundred yards. Then her bow guns flared out, and she luffed up to present her broadside to the *San Martin*. The two ships were so close that Gresham felt he could reach out and touch the men on the opposite deck, smell the ship and the fear and tension of its men. And there, on the quarterdeck, strutted the familiar figure, Gresham's nemesis, Sir Francis Drake. Yelling, red-faced at his gunners, forcing them to hold fire until the very last minute by sheer force of will alone. Drake looked round, and for a single brief second their eyes came together.

At this range the explosion of the cannon was felt as a pressure and a hot breath, as well as a gout of black smoke, red and yellow flame. Drake's broadside shattered into the side of the *San Martin*, its impact at such close range unlike any other assault the brave vessel had received. The ship actually shuddered in her tracks. There were howls and screams from below. The shot had cut through the thick timbers of the main hull, sending a savage spray of splinters through the gun decks, upending a great gun before it could be fired, half its men crushed and screaming under the great wooden carriage. A ship's boy was crawling along the deck, leaving a trail of blood behind him on the grimy deck, hand clutched dis-believing to his stomach where the grey sausages of his intestine had been exposed. It would be minutes before the shock wore off and the pain came in its place. As quickly as she had come, Drake swung out of line, revealing another English ship behind her, already swinging at monstrously close range to punch the *San Martin* with all her power.

The *San Martin*'s return fire was sporadic, almost measured. At fifteen minutes to reload a gun, and twenty English ships taking it in turns to draw up and empty their broadsides into her hull, the Duke had ordered several guns to hold their fire, so that there was at least something awaiting the next English vessel as it hauled round and poured iron into the long-suffering hull of the *San Martin*.

Without speaking and with no conscious communication

Gresham and Mannion started to haul such wounded as could be moved to the companionways, where other willing hands took them down to the sweated and agonised hell of the surgeon's deck. There seemed no end to the line of English ships, the crash and roar of the guns, the replies from the *San Martin*, the continual crack and pop of the small arms. There were problems loading the guns, Gresham could see. The soldiers whose job it was to return from their station to reload were unwilling to do so. Feeble, hopeless battle though it was, for the first time they had targets on board the English ships, someone to aim and fire their weapon at. Loading a heavy gun would have done more damage to them, and done more to save their lives, but men in battle are not subject to logic. Soon Gresham and Mannion found themselves serving a gun, obeying the screaming orders amid the stench of blood and warm bronze, the bitter biting tang of powder in the nose and throat.

The tone of the battle changed. The *San Martin* seemed almost dead in the water now, a shadow blotting out the light from the open gun ports on the starboard side. Blood was running out from the scuppers and gun ports. A great English galleon had drawn up almost alongside the flagship, struck his tops'ls and started to try to pound her to pieces from pistol shot range. Other vessels were engaging her port side now, though the whine and crack of shot suggested the English too were reduced to firing lighter broadsides than they might have wished.

Three, four, five hours the monstrous cannonade went on. For a moment, Gresham felt his world go dark, came round to see himself looking up at the grating on the *San Martin*'s deck. He felt his head gingerly. A flying piece of timber had cracked his head open, the wound soaking his hair with blood. Mannion dragged him upright. 'On deck!' he said firmly. 'Get yourself taken to the surgeon and 'e's as likely to amputate your head as put a dressing on it.' They stumbled up the ladder. A bucket miraculously still full of sea water lay on the deck, part of the precautions against fire. Unceremoniously Mannion dumped it over Gresham's head. The sting of the salt water on the open wound cut through the mists in his head.

Strangely, as in a dream, he saw the half-naked figure of a man with a rope round his waist, a waist already rubbed red raw. Men were firing, reloading, dropping all around him, yet the half-naked man seemed oblivious. He and an assistant were tying something round the rope on a loop, what looked like a lead plate and some hemp. The diver tugged at them both, nodded to his assistant, and stood on the rail. Strangely graceful, he poised for a moment, and dived into the cold sea, which was whitening around the *San Martin's* hull. A diver. One of three on board, seeking to plug the holes in the side and hull of the *San Martin* even as they were made. How had he survived the marksmen on the English deck? By accident? Or by some strange form of chivalry to one of few men at sea that day who would take no lives, but might save some?

Extraordinarily, with superb seamanship and magnificent heroism, the great ships of the Armada started to appear round their flagship, drawing the English fire and shepherding her back into what was at first a mere mocking copy of the half-moon formation that had served the ships so well, but which as each hour went by became tighter, stronger.

The *San Martin's* sails were in tatters, her rigging half cut away. Four hundred round shot they counted taken into her hull, yet still she sailed, still she fought, the blood running from the scuppers, men with mangled limbs continuing to serve the guns, to hurl abuse at the enemy. Ten, fifteen English ships gathering like wolves around a single Spanish galleon, as they had gathered round the *San Martin*. Twice the *San Martin* herself dragged herself out to relieve besieged vessels. Her crew looked on horrified as they pulled up alongside the *San Mateo*. How could any man have survived the series of smashing blows she had received? Half her men were dead, her shot lockers empty, her decks a bloody shambles. Standing proudly in the wreck of his ship was her Captain, Diego de Pimental. They offered to evacuate the *San Mateo*. Pimental sent the boats back, asking instead for divers to mend his leaks.

It could not last. Perhaps God had some mercy left in Him. At four o' clock a sudden, sharp savage squall blew itself down on the battlefield, and fighting men looked up to see billowing sails thrashing against the masts, hulls rising and falling in the increasing sea. Was their reward to founder in a storm after all?

For fifteen minutes, perhaps half an hour, the opposing fleets fought the sea and not their own kind. The English ships, seemingly undamaged from their encounters, had either turned head to wind or skidded along the edge of the storm under close sail. The Armada vessels, their sails in tatters and losing more wind than they held, simply plunged on off to the north east, the wind full in their tattered and leaking canvas.

When the storm settled, there was clear water between the Armada, huddled now back together, and the English fleet. Gresham lay beyond exhaustion, his back up against the carriage of the gun he had helped to serve, when the tap on his shoulder came.

'Why have they left us?' the Duke asked. 'Why are they not attacking?' He had spoken without the translator, who had one arm bound to his side with a rough dressing. Gresham looked at Mannion. He shrugged, spoke to the Duke directly. All were too tired to care about the breach of protocol.

'Out of powder, most likely. And the wind's driving you north, away from Parma. Why risk more lives when the wind's doing their job for them?'

The Duke nodded, and turned back to stare out over the stern at the far distant white blobs of English sail. It was a dismissal. He was in a tunic, his frame seeming thin in the cold light. He had given his two boat cloaks to a wounded officer, and a ship's boy with a smashed leg who he had put in his cabin.

They lost three ships over the night, the *San Mateo* and the *San Felipe* hardly able to keep afloat, beached on the Flemish shore, their crews tossed overboard to drown. The final act came with the morning. The wind had strengthened overnight, half the ships nearly unmanageable because of the state of their sails and spars.

They were being driven inexorably north west. Ahead of the Armada lay a patch of clear sea, then a layer of choppy water. Beyond that lay the white foam of waves breaking on a beach. The Flanders sand banks.

The Duke luffed up the flagship, shortened sail, and ordered his remaining anchor to be dropped. It did little good, the soft bottom giving nothing for the anchor to hold on to, the ship still being driven hard by the tide towards the sand banks. They ordered a man into the bows, sounding the depth with the lead-weighted line, tallow stuck in its base so that an experienced pilot might judge where they were by the sand or gravel that stuck to it from the bottom.

The *San Martin* drew five fathoms. In less than that depth of water, she would ground and cease to be a living, moving and fighting ship, but merely a hulk to be used as target practice by the English.

'Seven and a half, by the lead!' came the yell from the bow.

Gresham and Mannion sat against what was left of a bulwark, gazing impassively ahead, bracing themselves.

'Seven, by the lead!'

A soldier stationed at the mast head took off his belt, wrapped it round the mast and himself, tightened it, hugging the wood as if it were a lover.

'Seven, by the lead!'

Was there the slightest lift in the shoulders of the Duke.

'Six and a half, by the lead!'

There was a sudden call, and the Duke's priest came up from below, eyes blinking in the light. The Duke knelt before him, quietly asking the man to take his confession. Trembling, the priest reached out his hand. All over the deck of the *San Martin* men were kneeling, heads bowed, some with their hands together, others with them loosely at their side. None spoke out loud, though many had their lips moving in silent prayer, some lifting their faces to the sky.

'Six, by the lead!'

There was a collective shiver through the kneeling men.

Would anyone remember him, when he was dead? Gresham was too tired to be over-bothered by his own demise, but it was a fair question, after all. Mannion would remember, but he would be dead as well. George would remember. Anna? Perhaps, if she did not damn him. And was there no one else to shed a tear for the memory of Henry Gresham? Fat Tom, perhaps, Alan Sidesmith in Cambridge. Inigo Jones, Ben Jonson, Spenser, Donne, some of the wild set in London, if they were sober enough to remember.

Gresham looked up at the vast banner, the banner that had been taken all those months ago from the altar of Lisbon Cathedral, flying out bravely from the main mast of the *San Martin*, the size of a sail. Its tip pointed remorselessly to the sand banks. Then, as if a divine hand had taken it, turned it firmly, it started to blow hard, so hard that the great line of fabric was almost straight. Away from the banks. Out to sea. The ship lurched round, away from the banks, the helmsman instantly sensitive to the sudden, unprecedented change in the wind.

'Six and a half!' The leadsman's voice was almost a shriek, the correct form forgotten.

The Duke's lips were moving now, Gresham saw, his hands clasped together, his eyes screwed tight shut, a line of salt staining his beard and moustache.

'Seven and half, by the lead!' There was an exultant shout from the leadsman now. The whole ship waited.

'Eight and half, by the lead!' Men were climbing to their feet, a cheer starting from the main deck and rolling round and round the ship, men embracing each other, several raising fists to Heaven in triumph.

'Thanks be to God.' The voice was not loud, but it carried to the furthest deck. The Duke was standing now. He looked at his men, the men who had fought and shed so much of their blood, and one by one, they started to kneel again, the men in the mast heads bowing forward as best their precarious positions would allow. Was any prayer ever said as fervently as that led by the Duke's priest that day on board the *San Martin*?

It seemed only minutes later that the summons came. This time the Duke spoke through the translator.

'Word reached me two days ago that one of our vessels captured an English fishing smack weeks ago, interrogated their crew, took the vessel in tow. They found a surprising cargo on board. A girl claiming to be Spanish, on passage to Calais. A girl calling herself Maria Anna Lucille Rea de Santando.'

Gresham felt the shock run through his body.

'They say she claimed to have been pursued out of England, by virtue of her association with an infamous spy. They felt they could not send her back to England, so they sent her to another vessel. To the *San Mateo*.'

Gresham's heart stopped. The *San Mateo*, the most heavily engaged of all the ships, battered to a pulp, sent to sink or beach off the Flanders coast, her crew by now either the victim of the sea or the pillage of the hostile Flemish. The image of Anna being raped on a windswept beach, the men queuing up to enjoy, flickered across Gresham's brain.

'Apparently, they felt she was out of place on board such a ship. Apparently there are woman aboard one of the *urcas*, despite my orders, so they sent her there, to be with the other women.'

Gresham looked at the Duke, voiceless. What was there for him to say?

'I would fight the English again, if I could. Yet the wind will not let me. The most I can do is take what remains of my fleet round the north coast of Scotland, go by Ireland back to Corunna, to fight another day. I can no longer win victory for my King. I can save his fleet.' The Duke paused, looking deep into Gresham's eyes. 'I think more of you than you might imagine. I have decided that you will take a longboat, go to the *urca* and pick up your ward. You may take her back to Calais. I shall not expect to see you return here.'

Gresham started to splutter thanks, but the Duke held up his hand.

'Say nothing. Just go. And perhaps we shall meet again. In Spain. Or, who knows, even in England?'

Gresham bowed low and deep, for such time as those around them wondered if he would ever move.

They plunged towards the lumbering *urcas*, the single sail enough to bring them quickly away from the *San Martin*. Gresham looked back at the battered vessel. A new Henry Gresham had been born on the deck of that ship. How much of a new man he did not realise, yet he did know that in a way he was yet to understand fully he had ceased in any way to be a child. The moment with Walsingham had been a false dawn.

He saw Anna as they brought her up on deck, as he had seen her an age ago. The tattered dress, the wild abundance of hair, the spirit so tough as to seem indestructible, and the ravishing beauty all the more obvious because of the lack of paint and powder, the beauty that needed no augmentation. Yet she too had changed, she too had grown into something more than a child. The smile on her lips replaced any tantrum, complaint or edict she might have issued. It spoke worlds, the smile. Spoke of a world so ludicrous as to be unbelievable unless one lived in it, of a chance so fickle that no man or woman could ever be justified in making plans. Spoke even of acceptance. They needed and used few words. The Duke's commission secured her presence aboard his flimsy boat.

'It seems we are bound to meet at sea,' she said.

'Have you been . . . well treated?' asked Gresham.

'The women here are calmer than the men. And kind. Very kind,' she said, simply. She looked into his eyes. 'I am the only virgin here, of either sex. And the women were determined that there was one prize that would not be lost in this battle.'

A sheet had been placed over the back of the longboat, giving some rudimentary cover. The clouds were scudding low now, over a grey sea. The wind that was pushing the Armada ever northwards, so that it was already almost out of sight, was difficult for Calais even despite the little boat's nimble ability to tack before the wind. It was hard, desperately hard luck. Determined to stick as close inshore as possible, they crawled back down the treacherous coast, too small to be of any use as plunder, too close inshore for the

300

great ships of England to bother with the shoals and treacherous water. Except for one man, of course. One man who had heard of great Spanish ships beached on the shore, seen the great galleass beach itself under the guns of Calais. One man whose anger at missing such chances knew no bounds, and a man, therefore, whose pursuit of the Spaniards came close, close inshore in the hope of seeing yet another great galleon detach itself from the Spanish fleet and fall into his hands and not those of the undeserving Dutch.

Sir Francis Drake.

The *Revenge* bore up on them out of a squall as they were on the outermost leg of their painful tack. For a moment they thought the ship would cut them in two, but at the last minute it hauled round, shortened sail, sending three grappling hooks to cling them to their side. A rough ladder, rope with wooden steps knotted into it, was hurled overboard, instructions yelled to climb. Whistles and roars greeted the sight of Anna.

'Well, well,' said Sir Francis Drake, standing in front of Gresham and Mannion on the quarterdeck of the *Revenge*. 'The man who fled England. Deserted his country. The man I saw but yesterday standing companionably by the side of the Duke of Medina Sidonia on the quarterdeck of his flagship.' He paused. 'And the man who is going to hang for traitor!'

CHAPTER 11

August – September, 1588
London

Would he hang them there and then from the mainyard of the *Revenge*? Mannion and Gresham were bundled down into the stinking hold, its damage minimal in comparison with the wreck that had been the *San Martin*. Drake hardly looked at Anna. To his relief Gresham caught sight of her being ushered into one of the cabins under the quarterdeck, if not with deference then at least with rudimentary respect. Two men bound their hands, flung them on loose planks covering the bilges. It had been a powder room, buried in the heart of the ship. Now it was empty, scraped clean. There was no hook for a lantern in a powder room, no fitting for any flame, and they would not have hung one even had it been otherwise. The feeble light retreated, the door slammed shut, a bar scraped across it. Gresham and Mannion were left in total darkness. The rank stink of the bilges rose around them.

'They say despair's the ultimate sin,' said Gresham. 'Worse than all the others, because if you feel despair you've accepted that God can't forgive you. And if you do that, you're bound to be damned. I don't think I've ever felt despair before. Not really. Not like this.'

'The ultimate sin, is it then?' Mannion's voice came from somewhere in the total darkness.

Gresham had not really expected an answer, sunk as he was in his misery. He had spoken merely to ease his internal pain. 'Yes,' was all he could find to say.

'Well, that's good, isn't it?'

What was Mannion on about? 'Good? How can it be good?'

'Well, if it was gluttony or lechery, I'd be in real trouble, wouldn't I? 'Cos I ain't going to stop both, if we ever get out of this, and it'd be bad news if there was no forgiveness.'

'How can you talk about "after this"? "After this" is us swinging on the end of a rope. And choking slowly if Drake has his way.'

'Well, as my old captain used to say, where there's life there's hope.'

'Your old captain? The one who got burned alive by the Spanish?'

'Well, no one's perfect.'

There were fumbling noises in the dark, the sound of something rasping, a gasp of relief.

'Stupid buggers,' said Mannion. 'Never did search us properly. I allus keeps this little knife strapped on me leg, high up near me crutch. It's a brave man who puts his 'ands there, I can tell you.'

Gresham did not dare to think of the prospect. Soon Mannion's hands were feeling for him, finding his hands, untying the rope.

'At least this way we can piss in the corner and not wet ourselves. Or worse. Helps you keep your dignity, that does. Keep the rope in your hand. Wrap it round when they come. They'll not notice the difference. Half of 'em's knackered after the fight, and the other half looks half dead.'

Gresham found his interest stirring, against all the odds, against any objective valuation of their situation. 'I saw that. Yet the ship's hardly damaged, unlike what they did to the Spaniards.'

'I reckon as that poxed bugger in Lisbon did his bit, then. You know what happens as well as I do when a ball's not been cooled properly, or the mix ain't right. It blows to fragments when it leaves the barrel. But if the hull's in one piece, lot of the men ain't. Ship's fever,' said Mannion firmly. 'That, and I bet they're on short rations. Remember how long this lot'll have been at sea? Queen

Elizabeth, she'd rather have her tits cut off than give a ship more than a month's food and drink. And even if they get that much, you can bet half of it's rotten.'

'As much as the Spanish stores?' Gresham could sense Mannion's grimace as they remembered cask after cask being opened on the *San Martin* to have the men reeling away, gagging and swearing at the stench of its contents. 'Will they starve us? Will we get ship's fever?' asked Gresham, angry at his own fear.

'Precious little food comin' our way, that'd be my guess. Even less water, and sour beer if we're lucky. As for ship's fever, you tell me. 'Cept I reckon as 'ow if we was goin' to get it, we'd 'ave got it by now. A series of slight snaps came from the direction of Mannion's voice. Here, grab this.'

Gresham found two strips of what could only be dried meat thrust into his hands. 'Where did these come from?' he asked, incredulous.

'Always keep three or four strips sewed on the inside of my jacket. Easy, if you drill a hole through each end of the meat first. Eat it now. If they keep us short of water, you won't be able to manage it. Get the goodness in you now, while you can.'

And so the two condemned men sat in the bowels of the *Revenge*, in total darkness, munching companionably the cast iron of the meat, slowly, in order to guard their teeth.

It was Berwick that saved them. Desperately short of supplies, half his men sick and numbers dying by the day, Drake paused in his pursuit and sent boats into the town that had changed more hands than any other in the troubled history of England and Scotland. Their jailers flung back the door, and stood reeling gently before them, clearly half drunk. A loaf that had been fresh two days ago was thrown into the compartment, and a scuffed and wrinkled wineskin, lying on the planking. One of the sailors laughed, then reached into the room, wrinkling his nose, and placed two apples carefully in the gap between two planks.

'There!' he roared. 'On yer knees, if yer wants it! Go on with you! Let's see you grovel!'

Both sailors were reduced to paroxysms of laughter as Gresham and Mannion, hands apparently bound before them, tried to catch the apples in their teeth, scrambling for them on their knees. The sailors were still laughing as they slammed the door shut.

Gresham thought he had lost his sight when finally they were hauled on the deck of the *Revenge*. Blinking frantically, filthy, his beard as ragged as a wild man's from the hills, he could only think of Mannion's words. Dignity. It was all a man had, after all, when God, life and other men had taken everything else away. They were bundled, half carried into a boat, and thrown across a horse.

Gresham arched his back, newly-bound hands and legs meaning he could not stand as he landed badly on the ground. Swearing, cursing, the sailors picked him up, prepared to throw him back on to the horse.

'I fought on the *San Martin*!' he managed to say, through cracked lips. He could vaguely discern the sailors now, clear shapes moving in a blur of browns, grey and blue. 'I stood up like a man as you threw everything you had at me, as did that man.' He motioned with his head, all he could move, at where he thought Mannion might be. 'Does that merit riding through London with my arse as my highest point? Or have we earned the right to ride with our heads held high?'

There was a muttering among the men.

'We made no pleading with you at sea, did we? We fought to the end! Yet I plead with you now. Allow me my dignity, and my man here, as fighting men.'

They were decent men, as most are. They cut the bonds round his ankles, let him ride the mangy horse, kept his hands tied but thrust the reins into his hand, a secure tether leading to the man ahead. And so Gresham's ride began. Every bone in his body crying out for release, wanting nothing more than to slump across the horse, to give up. Somehow he stayed upright, seeing through the pain and agony of his body the sight he had most dreaded. He had ridden through London once before in sea-stained clothing, in triumph. Now he rode through as a prisoner.

When the Normans had conquered England five hundred years earlier they had built two symbols of power in London, the four towers and keep of the Tower of London, and St Paul's Cathedral, its mass sending an unequivocal signal that those in power in London held supremacy over men's souls as well as their bodies. But it was not to St Paul's that Gresham was headed. It was the Tower, whose bulk squatted over the Thames. First the drawbridge leading over the moat, coated with scum and full of noisome lumps that did not bear close examination, to the Lion Tower. Then over the wooden planking, shouted words. A sharp left turn, under the Lion Tower, across the moat again and the second drawbridge. The two round, squat forms of the Middle Tower stood in their way. More shouted instructions, a rattling of chains, and they lurched forward again. Yet another drawbridge, and then the taller, round form of the Byward Tower. Under its rusting portcullis. Into prison, with three vast towers and their gates blocking their route to freedom. To prison? No. Worse than that. Bundled off his horse, into the White Tower itself, down damp, stone stairs, down and seemingly ever down. Flickering torches in rusted iron sconces hung on the walls. A huge, heavy door, black iron hinges set deep into the wall, flung back.

The rack.

They used to show it to prisoners, knowing that even the sight of it would send them into paroxysms, make them willing to sign whatever was needed, welcome the clean simplicity of the axe. Anything except the torture of the rack. It was a simple enough structure, crude planks and timbers making up for what might seem little more than a giant's bed. Except this bed had ropes at either end, ropes connected to wicked cogs and wheels and handles that turned. And how those handles turned. With the man strapped to the ropes, those handles, cogs and wheels could coax a man's body to extremities of pain no person was capable of imagining, drag his muscles and sinews into one long agony that burned and fried the soul of a man as if it were turning on a spit above a roaring flame. No man walked from the rack. He might collapse off it, if he was lucky and the final cog had not been turned, his mind seared and horrified by the impact of pain as much as his ravished body had been, never to walk again and to spend what little remained of his life as a discarded, crumpled heap thrown into a corner. All would choose death rather than the rack. Its final cruelty was to deny men even that solace.

Gresham had no power to resist as he was laid on the rough planks, stained with something foul that could once have vented from a human being. He felt the ropes clutch his wrists and ankles, smelt the corrupt breath of the grinning jailer, saw the arched stone ceiling flicker in the dim light of the torches, felt his grip on consciousness loosening, knew that the first sharp stab of appalling pain would bring him back to this world.

And from out of the gloom of the Tower, a vision came to him. Not of Christ, nor even of the Devil. A vision of a man. The Duke of Medina Sidonia. *When all else fails, and all seems dark and bleak, it is not the judgement of the world I believe will matter to me when I pass into the vale of death. The judgement that must matter most to me, the crucial, the most scrupulous, the testing judgement must stand as my own judgement on myself.* Was Henry Gresham to die here on this foul contraption, venting his own piss and shit as he shrieked what his interrogators wished to hear? Die before his time, die without issue, die as a traitor to England, reviled for ever more, if even he was remembered? *Could a man die with dignity on the rack?*

Suddenly, the world fell into place. He was no longer in a swirling, dream-vision of hell. It was a simple, large stone chamber, with an arched ceiling and soot marks smearing the walls. The walls glistened with moisture, throwing the light of the torches back, except to his right where bricks encompassed the dull red glow of a furnace, fitted out like a blacksmith with bellows. Opposite him were manacles for feet and hands, set deep into the stone. To hang men there, until their very bones and sinews cried out for release.

He heard the shuffling before the voice spoke. Someone was coming from behind the apparatus of the rack, now that he was

307

secure, thrusting himself into Gresham's line of vision. 'Welcome back to England, Henry Gresham,' the voice said. Cecil. Robert Cecil. Looming above him, his pinched face outlined by the ancient stone. A beatific smile on that same sour face. A smile of triumph.

'Robert Cecil,' croaked Gresham. 'What an immense surprise.' Gresham was surprised by his own control. 'As you undoubtedly intend to tear me limb from limb, perhaps you might arrange for some water to be given me? Not to keep me alive, you understand. Merely to let me speak clearly. Just think on it. My screams will be all the more clear when the time comes . . .'

Cecil smiled, a smile of immense cruelty. Not so the jailer. He looked worried, confused even. Men on the rack did not talk about their impending pain in this matter. Particularly young men, with fine, strong bodies, bodies that would never again delight the girls.

The water was the best thing Gresham had ever taken through his lips. He hoped they had not drawn it from the moat, though it hardly mattered. He was dead anyway. Perhaps that was why he heard the noise as of a door opening, a rustle of cloth that was unfamiliar, even a faint smell as of . . . perfume. In his mind, of course. 'There was this small thing between us,' Gresham managed to say in something closer to his normal voice. 'I thought we had agreed to work together.'

'I do not work with traitors,' said Cecil. He was enjoying this. 'The Spanish fleet has been sent with its tail between its legs to weather Scotland and face the rocks of Ireland as best it can. The Armada is defeated. This business is over.' There was a crowing, exultant tone in his voice. 'The Enterprise of England has failed. As all remaining spies for Spain must fail. Preferably in as much pain as possible.'

'You wish to destroy me?' asked Gresham. Had it been Cecil all along?

'You have destroyed yourself. You have no need of my help. You are a declared Spanish spy. You deserted us in Flanders, using the goodwill and influence I had given you to spy for Spain. You told me the truth about you when my spy – yes, I too can employ spies! – overheard your treasonous conversation with Parma, the conversation where he hailed you as Spain's greatest asset in its war against England! You told the truth about yourself when you took ship for Spain. You confirmed it when you sailed with the Armada, were seen conversing with its commander by no less than Drake. You were captured, with your Spanish whore, by mere accident. An act of God, the true God, as was the defeat of the Armada. Now all that remains is to extract the confession from you. A traitor, proven and confessed. Your estate to go to the Crown. How wonderful that the fabled Gresham wealth will go to repay Her Majesty for her grievous expenditure in fighting off Spain.'

Gresham was tied to the rack, and Cecil apparently in command of the jailer. And of everything else.

As if to confirm his power, Cecil motioned to the man standing by the great wheel at the head of the rack. Ropes creaked, and suddenly Gresham's arms, lying loose at his side, were pulled taut, not yet painful, merely at full stretch.

That faint whiff of perfume again. And something rotten, corrupt. Was it angels with bad breath come to take him to his rest? Yet he knew he would have to pass through Hell before he came to Heaven.

'I'm no spy for Spain,' said Gresham, thinking Christ must have felt such as this, stretched, exposed, before the first nail was hammered in. 'And you, you've no fear for Elizabeth Brooke? Your fiancée?'

'I spit on your feeble threat!' said Cecil, ignoring his denial. And he did spit, the globule landing on Gresham's cheek. 'With you dead, your man dead, the name of Gresham a stench on the lips of every decent Englishman, will your henchmen carry out your contract? No! With you dead, they will take their money and laugh at you for thinking it worth their while to offend a man such as myself!'

'A man such as you might be,' said Gresham, surprisingly gently given his condition. His arms were beginning to ache now, the

309

blood supply contorted. 'But are not yet. Anyway, there never was a threat. I have no quarrel with women. I set no men to murder your fiancée.'

'You mean there were no men set to murder or disfigure my . . . future wife?'

'Of course not,' said Gresham. 'Only a man who would consider such a thing himself might believe it in another man. It was a threat to frighten a child. What use is vengeance to me after I'm dead? I'll never savour its taste!'

Cecil had believed it. He had believed that Gresham would kill his fiancée. That much was clear from his rising colour, visible even in the light of torches and from the viewpoint of a man spread-eagled on the rack. 'And so you have nothing left with which to threaten me, Henry Gresham?' Cecil was crowing now, exulting in his victory.

'Only the truth,' said Gresham. 'I was no spy for Spain. I fought for England.'

'And who will believe you?' asked Cecil, actually shaking his head in his own disbelief.

'The Queen of England might believe me,' said Gresham simply. 'That same Queen who entered by the far door, outside my limited range of vision, some minutes ago, and has stood there in silence ever since. Yet I pray to her to be allowed to state my case.' He had known it from the perfume. And the stench of bad breath.

Cecil smiled across his lips, and turned towards the door, arm outflung in a gesture of disbelief. The arm hung for a moment, dropped, became part of a bow that somehow transfigured him into a man on his knees, dropping below Gresham's line of vision.

Why had the Queen come here? She hated the Tower. Loathed it for the memories of her voyage into it through Traitors' Gate, never visited it unless absolutely necessary. And as well as visit it, come to its darkest and most painful chamber? It was inconceivable. And with Walsingham dead, there was no one to tell her of the complex double and triple betrayal he had been engaged in these past three years, three years where under Walsingham's guidance he had worked his way up to becoming Spain's most trusted spy in England. In that position he had fed Spain the information Walsingham wanted Spain to hear, always with enough truth to give it the smack of reality.

The Queen swam into Gresham's view, her pasty white face peering down clinically at Gresham. She stepped back, motioning to Cecil. He rose from his knees, head still inclined towards the Queen.

'Your Majesty!' Cecil made as if to kneel again, confused, perhaps even appalled, his world falling about his ears.

'Get up!' she said, 'and cease your fawning! And you,' she glanced down at Gresham, 'you can stay there. You!' The voice was a snarl, directed at the jailer, its rasp the killing edge of Henry VIII. 'Get your Queen a seat! And do so now.'

A stool appeared as if from nowhere. She sat.

Gresham considered a clever comment that he would bow if his circumstances allowed it, but thought better of it. His limbs were really aching rather seriously now.

'So, my little pygmy, you propose to interrogate a man you tell me is a very great traitor, without my knowledge. Nor, indeed, my consent for torture.' She looked towards the rack and its splayed occupant. In theory and in law, the consent of the monarch was required for torture to be used. 'Yet I am ever generous as Queen. I grant you my permission. Carry on your interrogation. Now.'

Gresham's heart failed him. The Queen had just commanded his torture.

Cecil was ever quick to recover, Gresham noticed. Clearly the presence of the Queen had not been part of his plan, had shocked him to the core, yet already he had adapted, mutated to meet present circumstance.

'You deny you have been a spy for Spain, here in England? A regular attender at illegal and illicit Mass?'

Were his ears still ringing from the drubbing the *San Martin* had received? His eyes still weak from his incarceration in the bowels of the *Revenge*? His wits addled by weeks of poor food and continual stress? What other condemned man had to speak in his defence strapped onto the rack, with no advocate to plead his cause? No matter. This was here and now. The next few words would decide his fate. And how tall he was at burial.

'I deny I've been a spy for Spain. As for an attender at Mass, I've been so for three years, God preserve my soul. An attender in Her Majesty's Service, as instructed and advised by my Lord Walsingham.' That same Lord Walsingham who was now dead, and his only alibi.

Cecil was nearly spitting now. 'Attending Mass in Her Majesty's Service? How can it be?' Cecil raised his hand to order the jailer to tighten the rack.

'Hold.' It was the Queen. The man dropped his hands from the wheel. 'Let him speak before the pain fogs his judgement.'

'In Her Majesty's Service. On the orders of Walsingham. When I was sixteen, seventeen years old. A student. An impoverished student. I was offered money. To seek out a priest, attend his secret Mass. Present myself as a Catholic.'

'And you sold your soul for money?' asked Cecil managing to make his voice sound incredulous.

'No,' said Gresham. The pain in his limbs had ceased to be an ache, was a real, sharp pain. 'I kept my soul and its Protestant heart. I did it because it would allow me to pose as a spy for Spain. And also, I did it for excitement!'

'And not for money, of course!' said Cecil trying to sound scornful. Why was the Queen here? How was it that she was here? The questions were clearly screaming in Cecil's brain, so loud as to interfere with his control.

'Those who have money from birth confuse it with blood,' said Gresham. 'Only those who've known what it is to live without money realise that there are things more important.'

'Such as?' sneered Cecil. It was his first mistake.

'Such as excitement, the thrill of living, when one is young and life seems to offer bleak prospects elsewhere. Such as honour. Such as love of one's country, when one feels no love for any fellow human being. Such as doing what is right.'

'Yet you spied for Spain!' Cecil taunted, playing his trump card.

'I *appeared* to spy for Spain.' Gresham's left arm was shooting agonising barbs of pain into his whole body. Why only the left? Why not the right? Reluctantly, Gresham wrenched his mind back to the main issue. 'They received information from me that seemed to be true. Bits of truth, sanitised so as to do as little damage as possible, passed on to me by Walsingham so that I could pass them on to the Spanish.'

'So you had access to the Court of Spain, did you?' said Cecil, the disbelief in his voice almost visible.

'No,' said Gresham. How long could an arm cry out in protest before it became gangrenous? 'Access only to a courier. A courier in Cambridge who found out the truth about me, that I was no spy but a double agent. A man I had to kill, early the next morning, in the meadows round Grantchester, before he could tell his masters the truth and ruin years of preparation.'

There was another rasping of a door. Strain as he might, Gresham could not force his head back far enough to see who had come into the chamber. There was a ringing in his ears now, blotting out hearing. His throat had dried, his voice becoming hoarser by the word. Something moved in the room, and blessed clear, fresh water was being held to his lips, passing down like an iceberg to his throat and stomach. The jailer stank, Gresham noticed, of rank sweat and stale piss.

'So you say!' snarled Cecil. How had Gresham heard the door open, staked out as he was, and Cecil been oblivious to it? 'Yet you forced your way on to Drake's great expedition to Cadiz. A true spy of Spain!'

The other arm was starting to shriek pain now. There was a strange comfort in the balance. The legs were not feeling too good either. He had to concentrate! He had to beat the pain! 'A spy for Spain only on the evidence of a forged letter and a planted prayer book. A letter forged by you, Robert Cecil,' said Gresham. 'You never knew that Walsingham had set me up as someone who could infiltrate Spain. So you set up your separate path to damn me to

Drake, as a Spanish spy. So that you could dispose of me as a man you disliked, but more importantly so that when I died, conveniently far away at sea, you could deliver my fortune to the Queen, as a traitor and a man with no heir. You arranged my death to buy credit with the Queen, and no doubt with your father as well.' He thought better of mentioning Mary Queen of Scots in front of the Queen. Of course Cecil had wanted to blame Gresham for the delivery of the death warrant, and take some of the blame off the Cecil family. But as Gresham had come perilously close to doing just that it did not seem wise to raise it.

'You are feeble,' scoffed Cecil. Where was the Queen? If Cecil's nervous glances were to go by, at Gresham's feet, below his line of vision. 'Where is your evidence?'

How extraordinary that a man stretched out on the rack could have his interrogator on the defensive. 'Evidence? Well, there is a tiny bit, actually,' said Gresham.

A bar of pain had started now across his midriff, threatening to outweigh his arms and legs in the stridency of its signal of pain.

'You see, Robert Leng kept the letter damning me as a Spanish agent. He would do, wouldn't he? And I . . . acquired it from him.' It had not been difficult to take the letter from a man with a broken leg. 'The extraordinary thing about that letter is that it reads correctly, it's even got a passing imitation of the right seal, but the writing . . . it's in the hand of your chief clerk. You could have given the letter over to my old friend Tom Phelippes to forge, if you'd been prepared to pay his price. But you're a mean man, aren't you? Unwilling to spend where you don't deem it necessary? Drake wouldn't know your clerk's hand. You gambled on forging that letter in house. Used one of your own men because it was cheaper. Gambled on Drake taking your bait. Gambled on that letter never surviving, never being subjected to scrutiny.'

'Your Majesty!' Was there the slightest hint of squeak in Cecil's voice? From the direction of Cecil's bow, Gresham had got it right. The Queen was seated at the end of the rack, beneath his line of vision. 'It is clear this man is a traitor!'

Another rustle, another waft of that perfume and the stink of bad breath. A face like that of the Queen appeared in his vision, swimming in and out of his consciousness.

'Walsingham told me nothing of you,' she said, her voice cold, the eyes unfeeling. 'You had a miraculous escape from the hands of the Spanish galleys, Drake tells me. Escape? Or free passage when they realised they were firing on a spy? You were in Lisbon before the Armada sailed. You were welcomed aboard the Spanish ships that fought my fleet. And you have been consorting with the daughter of a Spanish nobleman. There seems more in favour of Spain in your actions than of England!'

'The girl was an accident,' Gresham said, repeating himself. She would love being called that. It would confirm everything she had ever thought of him. Well, there would be little for her to admire after the rack had done its work. Was there another man alive – albeit barely – who had said the same words to Duke of Medina Sidonia and the Queen of England? At least he would carry that small distinction to his painful grave. 'I went to Lisbon with my credentials as a spy already established, sent ahead of me. I knew I would be allowed to roam free, or nearly so, and the Spanish girl was a simple bonus. Yet at all times I was under Walsingham's orders.'

'And what were those orders?' the Queen barked.

'To suborn the head of the Lisbon armouries. To bribe him to miscast his cannon, to bring his shot too early out of the heat so that his guns would shatter when they were fired, his shot also shatter when it emerged from the barrel.'

'What evidence have you of this?' Cecil was barking now, dangerously close to ignoring the presence of his Queen.

'I left the *San Martin*, flagship of the Armada and of the Duke of Medina Sidonia, a battered hulk with barely a whole plank of timber to its name. I was bundled aboard the *Revenge*, one of the *San Martin*'s main attackers, which in comparison was fresh out of the builder's yard.'

'You claim the credit for this!' exclaimed Cecil.

315

'No,' said Gresham. His heart was beginning to strain against his chest now, hurting as did his arms and legs. Was it too about to burst, before a real ratchet had been tightened on the rack? If this was the pain now, what would it be when the torture started? 'Not all of it. Perhaps not even most of it. The Spanish guns were clumsy, slow to load, their command structures all wrong. Yet I swear as the *San Martin* fired on the English ships coming up in line to fire on her, not once did I see a shot of hers hit the enemy . . . the English ships. Coincidence? Perhaps. But the *San Martin* had shared her load of shot through the Armada, taken on a new load from the Lisbon armouries.' Gresham stopped, looked up, said nothing. The jailer brought the water again. This time he was nervous, spilling some on to Gresham's chest. His skin seemed on fire, the water scalding his skin with cold. 'And there was more. In Lisbon.'

'More?' Cecil was scathing. 'More lies.'

'The Marquis of Santa Cruz was a bad administrator, the worst man to keep the Armada fed and maintained over winter. So we . . . Walsingham wanted him there. Yet he could have been a perilous commander, might have done what Medina Sidonia's caution stopped him from doing and attack the English fleet in its base, make a landing in the Solent. So we killed him. We knew his replacement would be more cautious.' Gresham was amazed by how calmly he said the last words.

'You killed the Marquis of Santa Cruz?' Was there, for the first time, the slightest sense of fear in Cecil's voice?

'I didn't kill him. Mannion did. My servant. He'd been sent by Santa Cruz to the galleys as a captured English sailor. He had a reason. More than anyone else. He got into dalliance with one of the Marquis's cooks, became used to visiting her in the kitchens and waited until the Marquis's favourite food was to be served before sprinkling it with an odourless and taste-free poison. We were surprised at how easy it was, though he was an ill man anyway.' The pain was now affecting Gresham's brain, sending sharp lances of red-hot iron into his head, splintering his thoughts like a sharp stone shattering the flat reflections of a pond.

'So you say!' snarled Cecil. 'Yet again there is no evidence, except from a hulk of a man who would say that Satan was his father to save his life. You cannot explain your defection from our mission to Flanders, to the Duke of Parma. You deserted your English compatriots. You broke my trust, the trust I had offered you by allowing you passage with my party.'

The Queen's party, actually, thought Gresham, but Her Majesty could read that nuance as well as he.

'To sail to Spain. To join the Armada. On the flagship. To stand by its commander.'

'I didn't just stand by him,' said Gresham weakly. 'I saved his ships. From the shoals. Warned him, when his own pilots couldn't see what was happening.'

'You saved the ships of the Armada!' said Cecil, incredulous. He was shocked at the prospect, shocked that Gresham would own up to it.

'*Helped* save them,' said Gresham through his pain. 'Why should more men die? More fine ships be sunk? The Armada wasn't the point. It never was.' As he paused for the breath he really did need, he realised how feeble it sounded.

'Wasn't the point?' said Cecil, again in what seemed to be genuine disbelief. Perhaps he was sorry that his victim had gone mad before the rack had done its work. 'If the Armada wasn't the point, what was?'

'The Armada itself, the ships, could only have made a difference if it'd landed its troops, taken the Isle of Wight, gone into Plymouth. Then it might have achieved something. *I had to make sure it didn't stop.* That's why I saved it. If they'd lost half their ships on shoals they'd have had to be defensive, cut their losses, might well have landed, stopped their advance. They only kept on to Calais because they were more or less intact.' Gresham stopped again. His breath was coming in rasping grunts now, and he was having to pause in mid-sentence to fill his lungs. It was as if the potential of the rack was squeezing them to half, a quarter of their capacity. 'The ships weren't important, as long as they didn't land

317

the troops they had on board. The ships were only ever half of what might happen. *It was the army*, Parma's army, that was all that mattered. Without Parma's army, the whole thing was useless. Wouldn't work.' Gresham saw Cecil's throat move, saw him about to speak. Mustering all his strength, he cut in. 'I went to talk to the Duke of Parma,' said Gresham. 'That was all it was about. That was all it was ever about. *To meet with Parma*. To stop him sending his troops to join the Armada.'

'I know you met with Parma. One of my men heard you confess yourself to him as a Spanish spy! Hid under the floor! You were greeted by him as a long-lost friend!'

A wave of exhaustion had appeared on his horizon, rolling on to the beach where some enemy had pegged him out. There were no flowers on a sailor's grave. He would die shouting his pain under the water, unheard even by the fish. When would this farce end? He had done what he had to do. Now it would end in a tearing and wrenching of limbs. Make it now, dear God, let it start now so that it might end the sooner. 'I've told you,' said Gresham, 'Parma thought I was a spy working for Spain.'

'And all this on Walsingham's orders, of course!' said Cecil scornfully.

'Talking to Parma was Walsingham's idea,' said Gresham dreamily, a strange peace starting to settle over him, anaesthetising his limbs. 'That was the whole point of my being set up as a Spanish spy. So I could talk to Parma. I think the Spaniards surrounding Parma must have got wind of what I was being sent to do. They tried to kill me. Just before we met Parma.'

'How can that be? You tell us that the Spanish think you are a spy for them, and then that they tried to kill you?'

'Very few people in Spain knew that I was meant to be a spy on their side. You don't broadcast these things. Other Spaniards, the ones keeping watch on Parma, didn't know. They must have suspected the truth. That I was one of Walsingham's men, smuggled in with a diplomatic mission. To suborn Parma. You see, I didn't obey Walsingham's orders. I was only meant to tell Parma about the fly-boats. But I had an idea. What I said to him was my idea.' He heard himself give a strange giggle.

'More water. Now.' It was the Queen's voice, coming as if from far away. Something splashed in his face. He turned sharply away, found fluid forced into his mouth. He gulped, drank, suddenly grateful for the cool flow down his throat. 'Your idea?' Something had happened in his brain, and he could not tell if it was the Queen's voice or Cecil's.

'The Duke of Parma . . . he was the key, all along. I knew it. *I knew it*.' How many times had he said that? 'If his army didn't move, there was no invasion, no Spanish rule in England. The Armada, everything . . . it was just a joke! A great big joke! A terrible joke, an awful joke, a joke at the cost of human lives . . .' He was crying now, he noticed, writhing under the grip of the ropes. What a waste of fluid tears were. He would need that fluid soon, to cope with the rack tearing his body apart. Or would its absence ease the pain? 'So I had Tom Phelippes forge a seal. Paid him a King's ransom to forge a letter. Unlike you. I pay for proper forgeries. A Queen's ransom . . .' Suddenly it was overwhelmingly important for Gresham to get this right. 'The Queen's seal. And a letter under that seal. A secret letter.' Who was it giggling in the basement of the Tower? Surely it could not be Henry Gresham, who had spent so long gaining control of his body? 'A letter from the Queen offering him the throne of the Netherlands. If he let the Armada pass him by. If he let it swimmy swim swim . . .'

Something slapped hard across his face. Again. There was no doubting the hand this time or the voice. It was the Queen of England. One of the rings on her fingers had cut into his chin.

'*You offered the Duke of Parma the throne of the Netherlands in my name?*' she bellowed.

'Yes,' said Gresham simply. Despite the slap, the world was shifting softly in and out of focus. 'And I did a bit more than that, your Majesty.' He was very proud of himself for remembering the correct mode of address. Very, very very proud. Very, very very . . . 'I offered him your throne, actually. As it happens. The throne of England, in your name. Under your seal . . . If he left the Armada to its own devices. Well, not your seal actually, but your forged seal.' It was so important to get these things right. The room was starting to swing round again.

He was glad he could not see the Queen's face at that particular moment. She would probably be quite cross at the thought of a young nobody offering her throne to a foreign general.

'I thought he might like that. To be King of the Netherlands. It was only English support stopping him from winning for Spain. So if England came in on his side, he'd be bound to win. For himself. Then if he ran the Netherlands, a Catholic running a Protestant country, why not England? Rubbish, of course. Should never have a Catholic on our throne again. Too much trouble. But he wasn't to know that. Seemed a good idea at the time. So I gave him a letter he thought was from the Queen, offering to name him as her successor if he agreed not to invade. Don't worry. I bribed a secretary to steal the letter back and destroy it once Parma had read it. They lose a lot of things on campaign, you know,' he said stupidly.

Gresham turned his head, searching for the Queen. He wanted to see his death sentence in her eyes. Her face appeared from somewhere. From several somewheres. It looked venomous, angry beyond belief. Gresham meant to apologise. But it did not quite come out like that.

'I didn't do it for you, you know,' he said very seriously. 'Well, not exactly. I did it for peace. For the peasants. To stop the burning. I don't believe in war, you see,' he gabbled. 'It kills people. And I want them to live. If they can. Though a lot die anyway, don't they?'

He fell back, his head thumping on the bare wood. It hurt. How strange that he should notice that among all the other pain. The slight noise seemed to echo round the silence of the chamber. A hoarse, gravelly laugh came from the corner. A laugh Gresham knew. The laugh of a dead man.

Walsingham looked half dead, but whatever his body was telling him was clearly denied by a brain that had lost none of its edge. He could only walk with a stick, and a wide-eyed servant boy hovered near him, torn between fear of his master falling and fear for where he was and who also was in the chamber. And, perhaps, fear of what happened in that chamber. Walsingham laughed again. He bowed to the Queen, who nodded back. Cecil he ignored.

'Your own idea! Very good, very good! Your own idea!' Was Walsingham barking or speaking?

'Is it good, Sir Thomas, that a man can forge his Queen's wishes? Offer her crown to another Prince? That an upstart can forge a letter giving away a crown!' asked the Queen, angry, venom in her voice.

'It is undoubtedly better if it is done without her knowledge, Your Majesty,' said the old man. 'As it is better that sometimes you do not know many things that have been done in your name. But most of all, better if it means the Duke of Parma is still in Ghent rather than laying siege to London and Your Majesty's person.'

There was silence after that.

'And remarkable,' said Walsingham, 'if it was done by a stripling who far from being rewarded for it was likely to end up here. He was indeed meant to tell Parma that the number of Dutch fly-boats was far in excess of his estimates. That his invasion barges would be swamped by them. Those were my orders to him.'

'Wouldn't have worked,' mumbled Gresham. 'Man like that, sees overwhelming odds as a challenge. Made him fight even harder. Needed more.' How strange that as well as being ferociously thirsty he also felt extraordinarily sick. 'Please,' said Gresham, 'I'm very sorry, Your Majesty, but I think I am about to be sick. Could you please start the torture now before I disgrace myself?' Dignity. After all, it was all one had.

There was a very long silence.

'Cut him free,' said the Queen.

The jailer was even more nervous, rubbing his hands together, bowing and scraping. 'I'd rather not cut the ropes, Your Majesty, as it means so much work threading new ones through the ratchets, and no little expense to replace all that rope. You see, you can't use them again if . . .'

'Cut that man free *now*,' said the Queen in an icy tone, 'or you will be the first person to test the new ropes through the ratchets.'

A knife appeared from nowhere, and suddenly the stretched figure of Gresham slumped amid a tangle of rope.

The agony of returning circulation was pain enough to send a man mad, as if white hot needles were being pushed through every vein and artery. He rubbed at his arms, could not stand up, did not know if he was allowed to.

Walsingham's voice cut through the thick air of the chamber. 'Your servant told us that you believed I was dead. Apparently the Spanish ambassador responded rather too enthusiastically to a report that I had succumbed to my illnesses, and sent a message to Parma.' Another stool had appeared, and Walsingham was seated on it, like a father by the bedside of his poorly child.

'Has my servant been tortured?' asked Gresham hurriedly.

'I think he had received a few blows before we reached his cell. The man who gave them has a broken leg and a broken arm. A remarkable man, your servant. He said you were the biggest fool in Christendom because I was the only person who knew the truth and the only person who could bail you out, and still you went forward on your mission believing me dead. Yet he stayed with you.'

'He lacks sophistication, and beauty,' said Gresham, smiling slowly for the first time in days. The pain was easing now. It was simply agony, rather than unbearable agony.

'This man sought to offer your throne to a Catholic.' Cecil's voice was higher-pitched than normal, his body seeming even more hunched, drawn in on itself.

'I did so to stop a Catholic ruling over England,' said Gresham simply. She was bound to kill him. Even if only to stop the story getting out.

The Queen hated any talk of death, had banished courtiers for seeming even to hint at it. It was the Queen who spoke next. The tone was harsh, condemnatory.

'Why did you risk your life? Your honour? You had been set up as a spy for Spain. Only one man knew the truth. With him dead, as you thought, you lose your lands, your wealth, the respect of your countrymen, everything a man lives for. Why did you go on?'

'I . . .' Gresham hunted desperately for the words. 'Your Majesty, you have brought peace to this country. There would be no peace in England under a Catholic King. And if I needed further persuasion, I saw the bodies of ordinary people, half-eaten by wolves, outside the walls of Ostend. I met the Duke of Parma, a great man, a great Prince and a great leader, and spending his whole life plotting the death and destruction of fellow men, turning the country he fights for into a desert.' He paused, trying to roll all his half-understood feelings into one tight ball of words. 'Sometimes a person has to take a very great risk, if he is to achieve a very great reward.'

'You took an unpardonable risk in offering my Crown to another, Henry Gresham. An unpardonable risk. A treasonous risk.'

Well, that was that. There was no jury in the bowels of the Tower of London. And no justice. Suddenly the tiredness hit him, his mind started to dissolve, his eyelids pressing as if a ton weight was forcing them to close. From somewhere he heard his own voice. 'So be it, Your Majesty. What's done can't be changed. Yet I acted for what I believed to be the best. I betrayed none of my countrymen. I beg your mercy to grant me a clean death. Give me my dignity, if I can't have my life.'

'Fetch me a sword.' There was a peremptory bark in the Queen's voice. A darkened blade was hurriedly pulled off the wall, a sword of a design that had been fashionable fifty years ago. Yet for all its dullness, the blade was sharp, Gresham saw. Heated until red hot and the flat of the blade placed on human flesh? Forced into men's bodies to tear and gnaw? There was only one reason for a sword in a room such as this.

He felt the blade prick into his neck, tensed himself. A moment of pain, and then blessed relief. Would they bury him here, under the stones of the Tower, he wondered, or bury him in the light and good soil?

The sword lifted, and touched one shoulder. It lifted again, and hung poised. It was heavy, but for all her age the Queen seemed to feel no discomfort with its weight. Why was her face blurring and the image of Henry VIII seeming to impose itself on her face?

'If this sword descends on your other shoulder, you are Sir Henry Gresham. The first to be knighted thus in this desperate place.' For a moment the Queen's hatred of where she stood showed clear, and then it vanished. 'Yet if it bites into your neck, then you are indeed the dead man you have thought you were these many weeks. The choice is yours. Do you give me your word that you will speak of these events to no one while I live, and to no one for the term of your life, howsoever long it might be, regarding your offer of my crown to the Duke of Parma? Do you give me your word that there is no written record of these events? And do you give me your solemn word that if you believe that servant of yours, who clearly knows all of your secrets, is ever likely to tell anyone then he will die at your own hand?'

'Of course,' said Gresham. What need had he to tell others? And Mannion would commit suicide rather than betray his master and his friend.

'And do you give your solemn oath that despite your hatred of my little pygmy here, you will not pursue him in vengeance but rather will work with him for my greater need if and when I so command it?'

That was harder. Far harder. Too hard to justify a life? 'I do so swear.'

The silence stretched into eternity.

'Then you are Sir Henry Gresham.' The sword touched his other shoulder, with intense lightness. 'I will forgive you for not standing. Yet you may kiss my hand.'

He struggled to get himself upright. No one offered to help. All those present could sense the importance of his doing it himself. Gasping, weary beyond belief, he found himself sitting on the edge of the rack, that foul thing of torture. He bent his head, and kissed the cold, white hand of the Queen. She nodded, matter of factly, and turned to Cecil.

'Your time will come, Robert Cecil. You have a usefulness for me, and before you protest your loyalty, I know it. Your loyalty is based on your seeing me as the route to power and influence. His . . .' she gestured to Gresham, swaying gently, 'is based on something different. Together, your hatred binds you to me. I can and will use that unity of opposites. And as I have bound Sir Henry to swear, so do I you. You will cease to pursue this man with your vengeance, and will work with him for my greater need if I so command it. Do you so swear?'

'I swear, Your Majesty.' Cecil knew when to shut up as well, thought Gresham with a strange, sneaking admiration. It sounded as if he was the one who needed the water now.

'Remember,' said the Queen, who had been declared illegitimate on the execution of her mother, looking appraisingly at Gresham, 'there is need in the world for bastards. And as for you, Robert Cecil,' she said, turning finally to him, 'it was not Henry Gresham who first called you my little pygmy. It was your own father.'

She swept out and up the stairs, the men bowing their heads.

Chapter 12

September, 1588
London

Mannion and two servants from The House had come down into the dank chamber, empty now of its high-born visitor and with only the jailer present. The two servants were shivering, with cold or fear, or with both. Mannion was simply tight-lipped, eyes narrowed to slits. He visibly relaxed when he saw Gresham still in one piece. He helped dress Gresham with surprising tenderness, saying little. He made only one sharp movement, when the jailer came close in an apparent offer to help. Mannion's snarl was that of a wolf defending its young. The jailer recoiled against the dripping wall. Minutes earlier he had been willing to turn the wheel that would have torn Gresham apart, and Mannion knew it. Only at the very end, as Gresham was standing, balancing on his legs as if learning how to walk anew, was there any sign of relaxation.

'Well,' said Mannion grimly, 'you could always walk without my help when you were plain Henry Gresham. Now you're Sir Henry Gresham, will you need a servant to help you walk as well?'

'I'd walk on water if it meant getting out of this place,' said Gresham, whose world still tended disconcertingly to swim round him.

The servants waiting for them at The House acted differently. Even more deferential. Scared, frightened at what they had heard – when a master was executed the servants had good reason to fear for their lives – yet proud of their master's knighthood, excited by the wild stories of how it had been earned. They gathered round in the courtyard, whether they had reason to be there or not, as the bedraggled figure of their master more or less fell off his horse, only just managing to stand upright.

Anna was different. Even in his present state he sensed that. Where had the girl gone? This was a woman now, with immense authority. She bowed formally to him, and he to her, as best his body would allow. Then, at last, the three of them were together again.

'When you told me all the truths I could not believe it! So much plot and double plot! And you so sure you would die!'

'It's only luck that 'e didn't, Miss,' said Mannion, 'and 'e would have taken me along with him, of course. Not that that matters, of course. I'm just a servant.'

They were in the library of The House, Gresham's favourite room. At long last he could lick his lips or place his tongue on the back of his hand and taste no salt. He felt clean, scrubbed, rejuvenated. Soon it would be back to Cambridge, the battle with the Fellowship, the back-breaking task of rebuilding Granville College in body and spirit.

'I'm sorry,' Gresham said. 'I find this really difficult.' He had never said that to anyone. He finally dared to look at her. She was still the most beautiful thing he had ever seen. He took a deep breath. 'I'm truly sorry,' he said. 'I've wronged you. You've been . . . great. I hated you because you made my life more complicated and because you forced me to have to think of someone else because your mother swore me to a vow. And because you were beautiful I decided to hate you, because all the beautiful women I know have used their beauty to ensnare and entrap men. Yet you're not like them. And . . .'

I think I may have fallen in love with you. That was what he

327

was about to say. And if it had been said at that moment, who knows that it might not have altered both of their lives? Instead it was interrupted. There was a clatter of horses outside, the sound of men shouting, the great gate being opened. Normal traffic in a great house? Had the Queen changed her mind, and sent her soldiers? Perhaps a collection of poets come to read their latest work to Gresham and to flirt with Anna. Who knew? A servant knocked on the door of what had become a private sanctum, and Gresham called him in. He bent low to whisper something in his ear, clearly not wishing the others to hear. Gresham's face went pale. He whispered something to the servant, sent him out of the room. He stood up from the ornately carved, high-backed oak chair, walked over to Anna who was seated in only slightly less splendour. She looked up at him, excited yet perplexed, sensing something in him.

'Someone that I think you will need to meet has come. He announces himself as Jacques Henri. A French merchant.'

Anna's eyes stayed open wide for a few seconds, then her face seemed to collapse. She stood so hurriedly as to knock the chair back, retreated to the corner of the room, as if seeking to hide in the dark.

'Look,' said Gresham desperately, 'I know you gave your word to your mother. But things change . . . if this thing is too horrible for you, then we must change it . . .' He was stumbling, almost incoherent.

'Did you break your word to Walsingham?' she asked in the smallest of voices.

There was a clatter of boots and stirrups from outside, and another knock on the door.

'Sir Henry, may I present Monsieur Jacques Henri?'

A startlingly handsome young man in his mid-twenties stepped through the door, stepped under it, a giant of a man over six foot tall, with dark brown hair and wide-set eyes of striking honesty. He was dressed for riding, but the mud and dust on his boots and cloak could not hide the expense of his dress, nor the lean muscularity of his walk.

'Sir Henry!' He had not seen Anna, hidden in the shadows, was not expecting her perhaps. 'I am so sorry! Word came to me from Lisbon and then from Flanders, yet each time I was too late . . .' The accent was French, but only very slight. 'I have led you . . . how do you say it . . . a merry dance, and I am devastated.'

He bowed low. Gresham returned the compliment.

'You . . . you are not as we were led to expect,' said Gresham, eyeing the young, muscled body and the overwhelming sense of youthful energy. 'We understood Monsieur Jacques Henri to be . . . rather older,' said Gresham limply. And fatter, he thought to himself.

'Ah!' said the young man horror struck. 'You have not heard? My father died last year. His caravan was taken by brigands, and though they fought bravely and he with them he died of his wounds. The young lady has not heard? We sent messages to Goa immediately, and to Spain.'

'The young lady has not yet heard,' said Gresham. 'The messages to Goa would find her gone, and those to Spain would cause no interest in the uncaring remnants of her family there, I guess.'

'I come to say that the young lady is, of course, absolved of any duties to my family. Our circumstances have changed. My father was a wealthy man, and I have decided the life of a merchant is over for me. I have an estate, in France . . . that will now be my major concern.'

'And you have a wife to share that estate with you?' asked Gresham.

Jacques Henri blushed. It made him look strangely vulnerable.

'My life has been one of travel, with my father,' he said rather lamely, and with some evident sadness. 'It has allowed me little time for matters of the heart, to my regret.'

Gresham turned to look into the corner. Anna was standing there, gazing levelly at Jacques Henri.

'May I introduce . . .' Gresham started.

Anna advanced into the room like dawn. Up rose the sun, and up

329

rose Anna. She had not taken her eyes off Jacques Henri since he had entered the library. He turned slightly, started to bow and then stopped the bow ludicrously, a few inches down, his mouth open. The two young things looked at each other for a very, very long time.

'I am sure, Monsieur Henri . . .' he started to say. Then he said it again, much louder.

'I AM SURE, MONSIEUR HENRI . . .' The young man jolted as if a shock had gone through him, remembered himself, finished the bow without taking his eyes off Anna, and then turned red-faced to Gresham.

'I am sure that my ward here will wish to hear all the details of the sad loss of your father, for whom I know she felt great affection. Perhaps if I sent refreshments to the Long Gallery you might spare the time to regale her with the necessary details. But first, perhaps I might be allowed a few words with my ward?'

Jacques Henri nodded, unable to speak. He backed out of the room, as if leaving royalty, and collided with the door. As they finally shut the door on his retreating frame, he was still looking at Anna. There was a long silence. It was broken by Mannion.

'Well, I feel a real urge. To be somewhere else.' He looked glumly at the young couple, and left.

'He is a real baby, Jacques Henri, is he not?' said Anna, the slightest of smiles on her lips. 'You saw how he could not take his eyes off me, and backed into the door.'

'I'm not a baby,' said Henry Gresham. Then things went out of control.

They were in each other's arms before either realised that they had moved. They held each other as if there was no tomorrow, their lips meeting in a hungry exchange. They both felt the rising tide of excitement, the sweeping urge to throw away all caution, to give in. In some way that neither understood, Jacques Henri's arrival had broken the flood gate, released the tidal wave of emotions and physical attraction that had been building up for so long now. Now. It had to be now. They had both waited too long. There was no chaperone there, merely two young bodies.

And they both pulled back from the embrace.

'I'm sorry,' Gresham said, 'I . . .'

'I'm sorry,' Anna said, 'I . . .'

Then they laughed, the two young voices together, a peal of laughter. Gresham bowed to Anna, stepping back but not releasing her arms.

'I think I fell in love with you the first moment I saw you,' she said. 'On the deck of the ship, when I thought I was being so brave. And you stood up, among all those other men, and you were so young and so handsome and you took control . . .'

'Control!' said Gresham, years of care falling from him, 'You were the one in control. You were fighting. Against all the odds. You dominated Drake and the whole English fleet! And while I thought I hated you for being so much in control and so beautiful, all the time I was falling in love with you.'

They kissed each other then, slowly, lingeringly.

He wanted her more than he had ever wanted any girl. The bedraggled figure emerging half dead from a barrel, the girl who had fought Drake, fought him, met a Queen. Good God! She had even sailed with the Armada!

'I put myself in that barrel, for you, you know,' she said, disengaging after what seemed a wonderfully long time. She was so beautiful, her hair in disarray now, stirred by his hands. 'I wanted to be with you. Silly. Stupid.'

'Don't ever say wanting to be with me was stupid!' Gresham said, and pulled her towards him. They kissed again, and he felt the desire within him, the need to die within her. Yet he controlled it, somehow, using all the power over his own body he had taken so long to develop.

'I've been so scared,' he said, 'so scared of committing myself. I'd decided I hated people, could only love a cause. Then I hated it when I found I was loving you . . .'

What triggered it? Who knows? Who cares? It happened then. As it was always going to happen. As perhaps Anna's mother had known. Loss of control? A total, marvellous loss of control. A delirious, wonderful, extended loss of control, a blending of body and mind. Controlling everything always was overrated.

Had they fallen asleep? It was possible. Suddenly she was standing before him, fully dressed, her hair somehow magnificently rearranged. Prim. Proper.

'I love you very much,' she said, smiling at him. Yet why were there tears streaming down her face? Were they tears of happiness? Why that sadness in the smile?

'And I must marry Jacques Henri,' she said. There was a break in her voice, a bleak intensity in her eyes, red-rimmed now, something like an occasional shiver seeming to shake her body.

His world exploded.

'Marry . . . how can you . . . I thought we . . . We've just . . . The best I ever . . .'

'Henry . . . my Henry . . . my very first lover . . .' The tenderness in her voice would have melted the frozen Thames. 'Please don't blame me. Please don't blame me!'

She moved towards him, and gently drew him to her.

He was sobbing! Henry Gresham was sobbing in front of a woman! The total shame! Crying on her shoulder, like a little boy reunited with his mother. Uncontrollably, as if a great wall had suddenly collapsed in on itself, the tears burned his cheeks, threatening to stain her dress.

'How can you . . .,' he spoke through his tears.

'You must listen to me,' she said softly. 'Now will you listen to me?'

Gresham nodded, his mind a lightning flash of discordance. Never commit yourself, his mind screamed at him. Never depend on another human! Never fall in love!

'I love you,' said Anna gently, 'as I believe you love me. And it is not only that I gave my word to my mother that means I must not marry you. It is more than that.'

'What more can there be other than what we feel for each other?' said Gresham bitterly, biting back the tears, too ashamed to wipe them from his cheek.

'I am all that is left of my family now. It dies with me, unless I make it live on.'

'Could we not breed easily enough?' asked Gresham, flinching at his own harshness.

'Children need a father. Henry Gresham could not give up his life of danger, not even for what we have between us. Henry Gresham has to push at the gates of death for him to feel alive. And we both know that one day soon the gates may close on him. And a woman needs her man, just as a child needs its father. I can love you, Henry Gresham. I can make love with you. But I cannot marry you, because you are not ready for marriage. You would chafe in marriage, feel imprisoned. It is not your time. Yet it is my time. Not my time to be a mistress to a man who has many more years of roving before him. My time to grow from being a girl and become a woman. To have children by a good man. A man for whom I will not have to drown, tell lies, be shipwrecked and spend nights in strange taverns. How strange that I shall miss it so much. You see,' she said, and there were tears in her eyes now, 'you have grown me up.'

'You're so sure this man will marry you?' asked Gresham. 'When you have seen each other for minutes, and exchanged no words?'

'I think he would walk out of a third-floor window for me, never mind backwards through a door. Women know these things.' She looked up at him from under her eyelashes, with the slightest hint of an impish grin on her full lips, at odds with the sadness and the tears in her eyes.

So much certainty. So much control. Would Henry Gresham ever have such certainty?

'And you will be content with him?' asked Gresham. He had not given up yet.

'I think he seems to be a good man, a kind man. At least, that is what the servants of the father said the last time we met.'

A terrible suspicion began to form in Gresham's mind.

'Have you . . . did you . . . was this always a possibility in your mind? That you might marry the son?'

'I remember the son, when his fat father came to visit us. I remember him being very handsome, and very kind to me, like a sister. Yet with respect. And so I asked the servants how he behaved to them. The servants always know. People reveal themselves to their servants.'

Good God! Could any man ever understand the way a woman's mind worked?

'It is a good match for me,' said Anna. She was speaking to convince herself. Yet the tears were still gathering and rolling down her cheeks, Gresham noticed. 'He has wealth, and I will make sure it grows and he does not squander it. He is handsome, and I will make sure he does not regret coming to the same bed every night. And I will give him good, strong children, and run his house for him so that he thinks he is doing it all. And he will obey me, without realising it. That is what men want, is it not?'

'Will you allow us to meet again? If a certain Henry Gresham were to come calling in France . . .' whispered Gresham, placing his head close to her ear, feeling the warmth of her, smelling the delicious perfume, feeling her hair stroke his face.

She did not turn away, but stared ahead, not turning to meet him. 'I would remember a hero, the man I chose as my first lover. A man I will always love. And I would refuse him access to my bed, seek to calm my pulse and deny my desire. A good woman does not cheat on her husband, not when he is well formed and virile and gives constancy in return.'

'So why did you sleep with me?' asked Gresham.

'Because all women are allowed one secret. I chose you to be my first lover. I choose Jacques Henri's son to be my second, and last. Only two people will ever know who my first lover was. And neither of them will tell the tale.' She turned and pushed him away gently. 'I am sorry. We were two wild creatures, and I think we needed each other. You are still that wild creature. I cannot be so for any longer. All things have their term.'

A red flush came across Gresham's face. It was as if she'd read his mind.

'Used goods?' she chided him gently. 'How will Jacques Henri know that he married a virgin? Oh, Henry Gresham . . .' it seemed as if he was about to giggle.

'*Sir* Henry Gresham, please,' he said, trying to gain control of the situation.

'Sir Henry,' she said with a decorous little curtsey. 'Men are so naïve. A little blood and a little gasp of pain . . . He will believe what his heart and mind tell him he wants to believe.'

Was it his imagination that recollected her small gasp of pain? Yet with him there had been no acting. He wondered at the vast clash of emotions in his head. A deep, deep sadness, a sense of an aching void that would never be filled. Anger, even, that someone he had chosen could reject him. And, despite it all, despite the void of loneliness that was his life, something of a slight sense of . . . relief.

Relief.

The irresistible force of his passion had collided with his immovable strength of need to be free of attachments, and had subsided. Rest in peace, he thought in a prayer to her dead mother. She has done what you wished. And I do not think I have harmed her in pursuing that wish.

There was a tap on the door, and a gruff call. Gresham flushed and opened it. Had Mannion been standing there all this time? Guarding the door? Closing his ears?

'Young Jacques Henri'll be having his ninth course for lunch unless you get a move on.'

They left Jacques Henri and Anna to make their mark on each other, and strolled to the other end of the Long Gallery.

'She's going to marry that Jacques bloke, ain't she?' said Mannion.

'Well, yes, she is,' said Gresham, hating the sound of the words yet feeling that fleeting sense of relief at the same time.

'Damn it,' said Mannion. 'I'd 'alf 'oped she might have settled you down. 'Cept she's probably right, I suppose. You ain't ready for marriage yet, more's the pity.'

'Why is it a pity?' asked Gresham lightly.

'Because I've got this 'ope that when you does get wed we might not be spending quite so much time being shot at, tortured or threatened.'

'Sorry,' said Gresham, 'but I thought I was the only one about to be tortured.'

'Where the master leads the servant follows,' said Mannion.

Why did he keep getting involved in arguments with Mannion? And losing them. The picture of Anna floated across his mind.

'She's the body of a woman . . .' said Gresham.

'You can say that again,' said Mannion appreciatively.

'. . . but the heart and stomach of a man,' he finished. Rather like Queen Elizabeth, he thought, though they were very different bodies. Maybe he would use the phrase to the Queen as a compliment. He had been summoned to Court that evening.

'Why did you stick with me?' asked Gresham unexpectedly. Everything else in his world was fickle, poisonous or destined never to last. 'You hate Spain. You hated it when I agreed to pretend to be a Spanish spy for Walsingham. You were convinced I'd end up being hung either as a Spanish spy in England or an English spy in Spain, and never see England again. And I made you go to sea, when you'd vowed never to do it. Why did you stick with me?'

Mannion was silent for a few moments. I love you, thought Henry Gresham. I'll never tell you, because it would embarrass us both beyond belief, and God knows for once it's got nothing to do with sex. And it doesn't say anything for my taste, does it? He looked at the great, muscled bulk of the man he had first met in his father's gardens as the lowliest of servants and thought that he didn't really want a place in Heaven if it ranked people on the basis of class or breeding.

'Why?' said Mannion. 'We're all goin' to die, ain't we? I reckon as 'ow with you around at least I won't die bored.' And that was all he proposed to say.

He got rid of Mannion eventually, who was spending far too much time grinning from ear to ear when anyone called him 'Sir

Henry'. It was quiet now in the library, but he did not feel like reading. Soon they would announce the engagement between Jacques Henri and Anna. The couple would stay a day or two, until Anna's belongings were packed, and then she and Mary the maid – Gresham had offered her the girl and Mary had wept at the thought of losing Anna as her mistress – would depart for France, this time, hopefully, without being intercepted by Drake. He felt a tearing ache of loneliness at the prospect. So what? That ache had been there most of his life. It was almost his oldest friend. He would see Anna again, he knew that. The bond was too close, forged in fear and against common enemies, for it to be allowed to die. And when they met he would be scrupulously correct. He had thought he might make her his wife. He would have to be content with making her the sister he had never had. And he would always have his memory.

He stood, in his magnificent house in one of the most brilliant cities in the world, a man with four of the five great blessings of the world. He had almost obscene good health. He had brains. He had wealth beyond the dreams of most men. Above all, he had luck. There were few men who walked whole out of that chamber in the Tower of London. The one, the fifth blessing he did not have, was to be loved by someone, always excluding a hulk of a servant and a woman who had decided that his love could not be her priority for life. You can buy sex. You cannot buy love. And he stood here, in his splendour and the magnificence of being a young man whose ship had come home. He was here, with his feet on dry land.

Yet in his mind, he was with a man on the quaking waters of the sea. He could not banish from his mind the figure of a proud, lonely man, standing on the stern of a torn and battered ship that had hurled itself so often at an enemy determined not to be caught. A man who might die off the rocky shore of Ireland, who would be reviled by his peers and by history if by some miracle he survived. A man of honour, and a man of courage, in his own way the bravest man Gresham had ever known. It is easy to win. It takes more courage to face defeat and keep fighting, he thought to himself. No man could control his reputation. When the time came for the Duke of Medina Sidonia to die, Gresham hoped with all his heart that he would feel he had done so with his dignity intact.

There was an immense noise in the courtyard, the sound of a booming voice. George had come to offer his congratulations.

HISTORICAL NOTES

When we look back in time and we know the outcome of events, we give certainty to things that in their time were wholly uncertain. We know that the Spanish Armada failed, yet it remains one of the great historical conundrums of all time. Why in 1588 did the most powerful fleet in western waters fail to meet up with the most powerful army in the world and sweep England, as we know it now, off the face of history? I hope I have not falsified any of the known and historically-proven events of that time. Henry Gresham, Mannion, George and Anna are fictional, though based on a composite of contemporary people. All other major characters existed in history, including the corrupt armourer in Lisbon. Robert Cecil, 1st Earl of Salisbury went on to achieve great power. I hope I have not falsified the historical record in his case, though the portrayal of his character if not his body owes rather too much to someone I have met.

The Armada and its commanders resolved to return to Calais and unite with the Duke of Parma, but the wind never allowed them this option. Instead, they drove round the north of Scotland, seeking to return to Corunna by skirting the west coast of Ireland and at least preserve most of the King of Spain's fleet for another day. The battered ships were hit by savage storms. Some modern opinion believes that the charts held by the Spanish, and their knowledge of currents, meant that they sailed far closer to Irish shores than was safe. Many ships were smashed to pieces on the rocks of Ireland and, in some cases, Scotland. One Armada vessel moored in Tobermory Bay was blown to pieces by a spy sent by Walsingham. Sixty-five ships made it back to Spain, including the flagship *San Martin*, and at least forty-five were lost, mostly to shipwreck, including twenty-seven of the largest and most prominent vessels. Of the thirty thousand men who sailed with the Armada, twenty thousand lost their lives. One estimate is that one thousand, five hundred died in battle, six thousand in shipwrecks, one thousand were killed 'judicially or unlawfully' when shipwrecked and the remainder died through diseases such as typhus, scurvy, influenza or simply of malnutrition. Of the huge number of sick men aboard the returning Armada ships, an official reported that 'If they are brought ashore the hospital would be so overcrowded that infection would spread, and if they are left to sleep in the stench and wretchedness of the ships, the fit are bound to fall ill. It is impossible to attend to so many.'

Ironically, the situation was not so different with the English ships. Sent out to sea without adequate stores of food and water, conditions on board those which followed the Armada as far north as Scotland were desperate. There were stories that seamen on board some ships had to drink their own urine to survive. Perhaps no more than one hundred English seamen died in combat with the Armada. Then an epidemic of what may have been food poisoning broke out, with some ships losing half their complement. Conditions were so appalling and Government help so tardy that Lord Howard was forced to use his own money to support many of the starving and diseased sailors.

Don Alonso Perez de Guzman el Bueno, 7th Duke of Medina Sidonia (1550–1619) was never blamed by his King for the failure of the Armada, though this lead was not followed by most of contemporaries and, until recently, by history. Confined to his cabin by chronic dysentery and other illness for much of the return journey to Spain, he retired to his estates and his beloved orange groves to die in his bed thirty-one years after the Armada sailed, at the age of sixty-nine.

Alessandro Farnese, Duke of Parma (1545–1592) did everything in his power to dissuade his master King Philip of Spain from launching the Armada. He was so incensed by accusations of cowardice following its failure that he issued a public challenge and waited in the Grand Place of Dunkirk for a whole day with his rapier ready to face any accuser. No one turned up. Unable to bring the war in the Netherlands to a successful conclusion, and his reputation with Philip damaged, he died four years after the Armada having been wounded in combat.

King Philip II of Spain attempted to send a second Armada against England in both 1596 and 1597. Both attempts were defeated by bad weather. There were no further attempts following his death in 1598, ten years after the first Armada set sail.

Sir Francis Drake (c.1540–1596) had his finest hour with the Armada campaign. After 1588 his star waned, and he was involved in a number of disastrous expeditions. He died of dysentery on the final one, at Porto Bello, in 1596, and was buried at sea.

Sir Francis Walsingham (1532–1590) died in poverty two years after the defeat of the Armada, his poverty the result of having spent his fortune on creating one of the most effective espionage systems in the history of the world. Scorning worldly honours, he preferred to fund the Universities of Oxford and Cambridge, as well as his espionage network. He was seriously ill at the time of the Armada.

Robert Cecil, 1st Earl of Salisbury (1563–1612) was the son of Queen Elizabeth's chief minister, Lord Burghley. He rose to become a pivotal figure in English politics under Queen Elizabeth I and also under her successor, James I.

Queen Elizabeth I is as she has been variously described. She died in 1603, after one of the most extraordinary reigns in English history. Following her death, peace with Spain became a priority. It was achieved by her successor, James I, and for several years thereafter a comforting flood of Spanish money in the form of 'pensions' for leading nobles ensured that the old enemy became the newest friend.

Recent years have seen numerous dives on the wrecks of galleons from the Spanish Armada. A significant number of the cannons recovered show signs of having been miscast, and numerous cannon balls show flaws associated either with impure materials or over-hasty work in the foundry.

Other bestselling Time Warner Books titles available by mail:

☐ The Desperate Remedy	Martin Stephen	£6.99
☐ The Conscience of the King	Martin Stephen	£6.99

The prices shown above are correct at time of going to press. However, the publishers reserve the right to increase prices on covers from those previously advertised without further notice.

TIME WARNER
BOOKS

TIME WARNER BOOKS
PO Box 121, Kettering, Northants NN14 4ZQ
Tel: 01832 737525, Fax: 01832 733076
Email: aspenhouse@FSBDial.co.uk

POST AND PACKING:
Payments can be made as follows: cheque, postal order (payable to Time Warner Books), credit card or Switch Card. Do not send cash or currency.

All UK Orders	**FREE OF CHARGE**
EC & Overseas	25% of order value

Name (BLOCK LETTERS) . . . .

Address . . . .

. . . .

Post/zip code: . . . .

☐ Please keep me in touch with future Time Warner publications

☐ I enclose my remittance £ . . . .

☐ I wish to pay by Visa/Access/Mastercard/Eurocard/Switch Card

Card Expiry Date ☐☐☐☐   Switch Issue No. ☐☐